Mother Love

❧ ❧

A Village of Ballydara Novel, Book Two

Susan Colleen Browne

Whitethorn Press

To Patty —
Thank you for all the
wonderful feedback
for this story! support
With love and gratitude,
Susan

Mother Love

A Village of Ballydara Novel

Copyright ©2013 by Susan Colleen Browne.

ebook ISBN: 978-0-9816077-4-0

print ISBN: 978-0-9816077-5-7

Library of Congress Control Number: 2013948040

This is a work of fiction. Names, characters, places, and incidents are either the product of the author's imagination, or are used fictitiously, and any resemblance to actual persons, living or dead, business establishments, events, or locales is entirely coincidental.

Published by Whitethorn Press

Cover and book design by Kate Weisel, Bellingham, Washington
(weiselcreative.com)

www.susancolleenbrowne.com

For John,
always

Cast of Characters

The Larkins

    Grainne Larkin

    Eileen Larkin, Grainne's mother

    Mary Alice, Grainne's elder sister

    Rory, Grainne's eldest sister

    Ciara, Rory's daughter

    Brendan, Rory's son

    Darren, Rory's ex-husband

Joe Corrigan, the man Grainne is dating

Sinead, an employee of Joe's

The Egans

    Justine Egan, Grainne's best friend

    Helen Egan (aka Mammy Egan), Justine's mother

    Nate Egan, Justine's elder brother

    Aine Egan, Nate's wife

Frank Kenny, the man Justine is dating

The Byrnes

    Rafe Byrne, Justine and Nate Egan's cousin
        and Nate's best friend

    Bernadette Byrne, Helen Egan's sister and Rafe's stepmother

    Jack Byrne, Rafe's grandfather and Bernadette's father-in-law

    Ian Byrne, Rafe's younger brother and Bernadette's stepson

    Lindy, Rafe's fiancée

    Gennifer, Ian's fiancée

    Isabelle, Ian's previous fiancée

The Gallaghers

    Sara Gallagher, Grainne's boss

    Alan Gallagher, Sara's husband

    Geoffrey, Anna, and Ivy, Sara and Alan's children

    Una Gallagher, Alan's mother

A little help with the Irish...

Grainne—pronounced "Grawn-ya"

Aine—pronounced somewhere between "Ahn-ya" and "Own-ya"

Ciara—pronounced "Keira"

Craic—sounds like "crack," which generally means fun, a good time. *Craic* and crack often used interchangeably.

Oul'—Irish colloquialism for "old," like ol' or ole

THE GALLAGHER POST

Gai Lannigan's Girl Talk

Baby Hunger

Lust for a guy is one thing. But lust for babies is a whole different story. And a lot harder to satisfy. The old cliché about biological clocks is just a polite way to describe waking up one morning, realizing you've wasted your youth, and now you can practically feel your eggs shriveling. The viable ones, that is. The duds are probably sashaying merrily round your ovaries, snickering at their rapidly dissolving sisters.

If you've baby hunger but no daddy material on the horizon, you're probably thinking, how can I joke about this? I see your point. Your average baby fanatic is actually a bit of an addict, with a terrible craving for her fix. The trouble is, like other common addictions—say, drink, drugs and gambling—the temptations of babies are everywhere. (Which only increases the baby longing.) Another painful truth is that baby-cravers often gravitate toward careers that provide maximum contact with babies, like pediatricians, or playschool teachers. Unfortunately, jobs like that give baby-lusters minimum contact with what they can't do without: unattached sperm-providers.

You might be one of the lucky ones, though, with several paternal prospects to choose from. But what if you're keener on having a baby than having a man? If word gets out, people will think you're quite heartless, if not altogether mad. Which bothers true baby-lusters not a whit. Your road to motherhood couldn't be simpler: You pick a fellow you know will drop his drawers for you, no questions asked. Unfortunately, any guy who'll sleep with you at the snap of your fingers is a guy who's had it off with every available female who's crossed his path—not the sort you'd want condom-less.

You could always bide your time and wait for the perfect,

baby-making love machine. But who knows how long that could take? So my advice is to go for a nice guy with a presentable gene pool, who won't make a scene when you cool the relationship. After the deed is done, that is. Trouble is, nice men want to do the decent thing...

One

"You don't think Gai *really* wants a baby, do you?" Justine Egan tapped the screen of her mobile, then drained her pint.

"Don't tell me you're reading that blog again." Crunching a shortbread finger in a dim corner of O'Fagan's, I stared enviously at Justine's glass. A pity I'd no head for drink. Today of all days, I'd have liked something to take the edge off. "Aren't you meant to be checking recipes for birthday cake?"

"Not now." Justine thrust her phone across the scratched wood table. "Check out today's *Girl Talk*."

"I came to the pub to relax," I said as she went to the bar for a refill, "not read about angsty girls with too much time on their hands." But to please Justine, my flatmate and best friend, I scanned her favorite blog, helping myself to a third biscuit. As if a self-induced sugar coma might help me forget why I was mainlining the stuff in the first place.

You know how it is—the day your ex-boyfriend gets married, it's like a huge insect squished on the windscreen of your life. It's not like you *care* or anything, it's just that the oul' bugger is blocking your vision.

O'Fagan's wasn't the best place to clear your head either, with strings of Guinness flags hanging listlessly from the ceiling and ancient, smoke-stained paneled walls. And today, the place felt more claustrophobic than usual—a far cry from the flower-bedecked, sun-drenched nuptials I could see in my mind's eye half a world away. Not that I wanted to be shackled to some guy for life, but there's something about people you know tying the knot that gets you pondering your own future. Even if it's a wedding you'd no interest in attending, if they prostrated themselves at your feet and begged you.

"Is that *Girl Talk* you're reading?" Eamonn winked at us from behind the taps. "What's she on about today?"

"Getting pregnant," Justine told him. "With the right guy."

"And before your ovaries wither like raisins," I put in.

"Aw, Grainne." Eamonn shuddered. "Who wants to hear that female stuff?" In a former life, he'd attended seminary, even if he hadn't lasted long.

"Well, you asked." I took another bite of shortbread. "Although," I added under my breath, "there's something to be said for ignorance is bliss."

"Amen to that," said Eamonn. Really, the man had ears like underwater sonar. He resumed his glass polishing and pint-pulling and whatever else a barman does at Dublin's least trendy and most morgue-like pub, on a late spring afternoon. "Sure, I can't see why *The Gallagher Post* publishes such rubbish, though."

"Because it's trendy," Justine retorted. "And every girl I know reads it." She returned to the table with her second pint, and plucked her mobile from my hands. "So, what do you think of the post? The baby bit is rather strange, but when she mentioned the perfect man—"

"No such thing," I said. "That's why most girls end up settling for good enough."

Justine took a sip. "Sure, I'm not looking for the perfect guy."

Maybe you should, I wanted to say, but kept my mouth shut. She'd a here-and-there thing with a tosser who worked close by, currently in the "there" status, as he hadn't rung for a week. Worse, though, was that Justine was secretly hung up on another guy who didn't know she was alive, except as a friend. If that wouldn't doom a girl to misery, I don't know what would.

My own #1 Relationship Rule: a bloke can put me first or not at all. *But if you hadn't been so keen to cut and run,* a little voice answered, *maybe you'd still be with—*

I jumped up from the table, setting my biscuit down. "Enough of this lounging about. Time for some *craic*." Really, hanging around this right mortuary, even if it was our usual meeting place after work, was no way to get out of a funk.

Justine pulled a face. "Count me out—I was thinking of leaving a comment on this post—"

"C'mon, a few throws won't hurt you," I coaxed. Justine had

apparently forgotten why I could use a little distraction—after all, today was my ex's wedding day—despite the fact he was her brother's closest friend. "Up you go."

Heaving a long-suffering sigh, Justine picked up her glass and dragged her feet to the cleared floor in front of the dartboard. "I don't know why you like this eejit game—"

"How else will you get a culturally approved pass to throw lethal weapons?" I asked, pulling darts off the board, and dumping them onto the nearest table.

Justine rolled her eyes. "Or why you'd play with someone as desperate at sport as I am. I'd rather sort out Gai's take on the perfect man."

"Who'd want someone too perfect? He'd probably be a right pain in the arse." I chose a dart, rolled my right wrist to loosen things up, and threw a warm-up. "But if I read it right, she's talking about perfect for fathering a child."

"Oh." Justine looked thoughtful. "Like someone who doesn't go for the booze?"

"That's it," I said. "He should have pristine DNA, not pickled in drink. And he'll be certified STD-free, of course."

"Must you blather about such things?" said Eamonn. He was a great one for shameless eavesdropping. "I'm trying to run a business here."

"That pair's not going anywhere," I told him, glancing at O'Fagan's two other patrons, slumped at the far end of the bar. One male of indeterminate age seemed ready to fall asleep into his pint, while the second, wearing a long black coat like Neo in *The Matrix*, roosted on his bar stool like a giant crow. I turned back to Justine and handed her a dart, since she clearly wasn't going to do it herself. "Ready for a go?"

"What about the guy as a person?" Holding her pint in one hand, Justine absently lobbed the dart—and barely hit the board. "That's got to count for something."

"Well, you'd want to start with a bloke who has a few brains in his head." I slipped over to our table and popped the last of the shortbread into my mouth.

"For decent genes, I suppose," Justine said. "Jaysus, you're over-whelming me with the romance of it."

"There's the genes, sure, but you've got to be interested enough in him make it to bed," I said. "So you'll want someone who's intel-ligent, without lording it all over you, though witty enough so your eyes don't glaze over every time he opens his mouth."

"Sure, a fella hardly needs conversational skills for what you've in mind," Eamonn said to no one in particular.

If you ask me, it seemed only polite to chat up the bloke before the knickers come off. "He should be in decent shape too." I said, and selected another dart. "Not that he'd need washboard abs or anything, but I read somewhere that men with big bellies have low-quality sperm."

"Grainne Larkin!" Eamonn's crew cut seemed to stand on end. "Spare us the gory details, will you?"

"It's not gory at all," I said, and threw. Not bad—middle of an outside pie. "We're talking about the health of future genera-tions." Picking up three more darts, I gave one to Justine. "But let's not forget the guy's face—for reasonably cute offspring, you'd want to stay away from the out-and-out Quasimodos. But no sense in holding out for an Adonis that you'd have to drag away from the mirror to get in bed."

"Well, yeah, but back to Gai—do you think she *really* wants a baby?" Justine wrinkled her freckled nose.

"How should I know?" Just for fun, I threw with my left hand, then grinned triumphantly. "Look at that! An inside pie!"

Justine paid no attention. "She doesn't seem the sort."

I refrained from asking, *What sort is she, then?* I didn't want to encourage Justine's tiny girl crush on some anonymous blogger. "Will you get on with your throw?"

Justine raised her arm, then dropped it without throwing. "Maybe Gai's just nattering on about babies 'cause it's a popular topic. You know, what a lot of girls our age are thinking about." Looking relieved, she flung her dart. It bounced off the board then clattered onto the nearest table. Naturally an empty one, though Eamonn let out a gasp.

Justine giggled, apparently unfazed by her hideous throw, and took a slurp of her pint. "Gai left out the most important thing—all the guy needs is a working rocket."

"Girls!" Eamonn looked scandalized. "That's it, the last straw—"

"Jaysus, Eamonn, if you'd mind your own business you wouldn't be getting your boxers in a twist," I said. Then to Justine, "Right, getting pregnant isn't rocket science. But let's hope our man's aim is better than yours." Taking a deep breath to get centered, I threw— and almost touched the bull! Who says I was in a mood! "One last go?" I asked Justine.

She shook her head. "Are you finally done, with requirements for your donor bloke?"

"Actually, there's one more thing," I said. "The guy should be from out-of-town—or better yet, out of the country altogether." I chose my final dart. "It's a win-win all round. You're spared the meddling in-laws, and the expense of the medical donor process too. Then, once you've hit your bull's-eye—your positive test— you can go your separate ways. And with no embarrassing chance encounters."

Justine appeared lost in thought. "Right, right," she said vaguely.

"Of course we've been talking about a fantasy guy," I pointed out. "If you want a baby right away, it's no time to hold out for Mr. Perfect. Like I said before, he doesn't exist."

Justine's eyes took on a mischievous glint. "Oh, but he does."

I laughed. "In your imagination, maybe."

"No, a real guy. For *you*. Who'd be grand even though you don't want a baby."

I casually rolled the dart between my thumb and forefinger. "Who is it?"

"Smart, great smile, and not too keen on the drink," Justine ticked off, without answering me. "No STDs either—no germ would dare come within five miles of him."

"And where'd you meet this paragon?"

"Oh…around," she said, smiling mysteriously. "He's even taller than you. Some might consider him off the market, but if anyone can talk round a fellow, it's you."

I tightened my hold on the dart. "Will you just get on with it and tell me?"

"And he hasn't a big ego, despite having looks and talent and pots of money *and* every other reason to think he's God's gift to womankind," Justine said, still teasing me. "In fact, he's quite nice."

Really, if by some miracle there was such a thing as the perfect guy, this one sounded close. Then Justine's grin widened. "Okay, I get it, you're having me on," I said crossly. "He's too perfect. He can't be real."

"He's real, all right. And though he's visited Ireland a lot, he lives *far* away. As in…" she paused, *"Seattle."* I forgot to breathe as she giggled again. "You know exactly who I'm talking about, don't you?"

I gulped for air. "You are *so* mad." Feeling my wrist go floppy, I turned and threw.

"The ideal man," Justine pronounced as my dart missed the board entirely and skidded under a table. "My cousin Rafe."

Two

Rafe Byrne was actually Justine's step-cousin, her aunt Bernadette's stepson, and the first man I'd ever taken a fancy to. A violent fancy, I might add. I've often told myself meeting Rafe simply happened to coincide with one of those angst-ridden adolescent episodes that at fifteen, seems to last eons, when the duration was likely closer to a fortnight or so. But the fact remains: I was stuck on him.

God knows, you can hardly trust your taste in men at that age. But at our first meeting, I made two important discoveries. One, that I had power over men, and I liked it. And two, a man could have power over me, which I didn't like at all.

But who was I to resist a Yank, who had amazing American white teeth, a shock of dark hair blacker than mine, and shoulders like a god? *And* who treated me like I was the last word in *femme fatale*-ity?

Since then, I've realized rich, cerebral, athletic guys are *so* not my type. I usually make a beeline for superficial, malleable, middle-class ones—or to be more accurate, I let them make a beeline for me. But back then, Rafe Byrne's dazzle factor had rather blindsided what little sense I possessed.

You might think, Jaysus, you were only fifteen, you've changed a lot since then. But I wonder if I've changed at all where Rafe's concerned...

"Well?" Laughing, Justine followed my hasty retreat from the dartboard. "Is Rafe Byrne your man? Mr. Perfect?"

"Love of God," I hissed, snatching my rucksack off the back of my chair, "Will you keep your voice down?"

"Not Rafe Byrne?" Eamonn dropped the glass he was polishing. "The American who blew the—"

"We're off to catch the Dart," I said breezily. "The biscuits were grand, Eamonn—thanks." I jerked my head at Justine. "We'd better hoof it," I said under my breath, "or we'll run into you-know-who on the train."

"Let's go then." Giving her half-empty glass a regretful look, Justine grabbed her handbag and mobile and trailed me out of O'Fagan's.

Pounding the cobblestones of Temple Bar, I tried to forget I'd just made a spectacular arse of myself—at darts and everything else. "That pint really did go to your head," I told Justine, and managed a credible chuckle as we strode up Crown Alley. "As of today, Rafe's officially taken, remember?"

"I can't believe I forgot this was the big day!" Justine hit her temple with the heel of her hand. "Remember, Mam made the whole family take a vow of silence about the wedding, since she and Nate couldn't go."

Justine's brother and his wife Aine's baby was due in the next few weeks. And Helen Egan, as much as she was dying to attend a super-posh society do, hadn't been about to run off to America and risk missing the birth of her first grandchild.

"And Rafe is so *not* perfect," I couldn't help pointing out. "If he was, he wouldn't be marrying that airhead." Even a pedigreed airhead, with a baccalaureate from Brown or Cornell or somewhere.

"Part of me never thought he'd go through with it," Justine said as we turned onto Fleet Street.

"Come on," I scoffed. "As if the Honorable Rafe would ever leave a girl at the altar."

"Well, not that—I just hoped something would happen to call it off."

"Like your aunt Bernie would ever allow *that*," I said, wishing I'd taken just one more shortbread finger for the road. "Anyway, the man's married *now*."

"Actually, he's still single for..." Justine ticked off the time zones on her fingers. "Another hour or so."

"He's probably getting ready to walk down the aisle, as we speak," I countered. "If that's not taken, don't know what is."

We reached the Tara Street Dart station just as the northbound train approached. As we boarded and dropped into our seats, I was *so* ready to drop the subject of Rafe Byrne altogether. Seeing a big lump in Justine's oversized handbag, I said, "Looks like you did some shopping on your lunch break. Did you find a gift for the baby?"

"I was meaning to show you," she said, and as she burrowed in her bag, I leaned in for a better look. "I happened onto the loveliest..." and she pulled out a shiny-new cookery book, with a drool-inducing strawberry trifle on the cover. *New Irish Puddings for Every Occasion.* "What do you think?"

"I don't think the baby'll be able to use it," I said, shaking my head. "You couldn't track down a pair of booties or something?"

"Well, you've seen the layette Mam's bought Nate and Aine, enough for three babies," Justine said, "so I thought, might as well spend my money more wisely."

She'd a point—if you were into baby yokes, like tiny vests and babygros, Mammy Egan's layette was to die for. "So, another cookery book, though we've acres of them back at the flat."

"But now I'm all set to make something scrumptious for the baby's christening or first birthday." Tap-dancing the book in front of me, Justine opened it to display another gooey confection. "Speaking of birthdays, how about if I make crème brulee for you instead of cake next week?"

"Could I have both?" I asked hopefully. I could use some extra compensation for closing in on another dead-end year.

"If I can sneak out of work early," Justine said, then bit her lip. "And if Mam doesn't hear about it."

I rolled my eyes. If *my* mam made a peep about how I ran my life, I'd set her straight. "And what if she did?"

Closing her cookery book, Justine began her usual litany of how she could never hurt her mam, who'd paid for her business course, and who always said she wouldn't have any daughter of hers end up a bag lady.

"You know Mam wants me to focus on my real job." Justine looked mournful. "With this economy, she's so proud I've been able to hang on to my job this long. Still, if I was made redundant, I could hole up in our flat and cook all day, then maybe look around for a restaurant job. But if Mammy got wind of it she'd frog-march me back home in no time flat."

Since Justine and I had had this conversation about a jillion times before, I knew my only escape was to jolly her out of it. "And where would you be then? On the dole, putting on plain boiled meat and two veg for your mam and dad every night."

"And where would you be without *me*? Living off beans and toast."

"I'm quite keen on beans, actually," I said with relish. "There's no washing up either, if you eat right out of the tin."

"Ha, you and your lazy rebel bit." Justine shook her head. "If you ever seriously hooked up with a guy, he'd want you to cook for him."

"Pardon me," I said, "while I gag—"

"And varnish your nails. Fellows like knowing a girl has gone to a bit of trouble for them."

"And who needs to do that narky, girly stuff to get a man?" As far as I was concerned, if a guy didn't like me in the original package, he could take a flying feck into the River Liffey.

"It's not narky," said Justine. "Most girls will try facials or bikini waxes, or…" She looked forlorn. "Freckle-removal cream."

"I wouldn't," I said loftily.

"Rub it in, will you, that you haven't a freckle on your entire body."

As an unwanted memory surfaced, I felt myself grow warm. "Everyone has at least a few," I said quickly. "But I could see lots of guys fancying you madly, for all the lovely things you'd cook for them."

"You think so?"

"And if you did get a restaurant gig," I told her, "you could easily be the head pastry chef. At the finest place in Dublin."

Justine's face glowed, but it quickly faded. "Mam thinks working in a restaurant would be the death of me. 'You'd work your fingers to the bone,' she always says."

"I suppose all that grease floating in the air would give you spots too," I consoled her. "But your dream's sure to come true some day." I had to believe that. Because if a long shot like hers could, then so could...anyone else's.

Justine's the perfect flatmate, I was thinking as we settled in for the long ride up to our flat in Howth. While I've generally taken the leader position, and she the follower since our schooldays, we've a certain Yin and Yang dynamic that's kept our relationship at an even keel.

Take our wardrobes. We both go for the casual look, but she sports white cotton shirts and loose trousers, orthopedic-ish clogs, with her brown hair pulled back from her face and stuck in a slide. In case it's not obvious, Justine is a professional chef-wannabe. Although my...colleagues don't care about attire, I wear mostly black jeans and tops. For one thing, I like the sophisticated look of black. And it doesn't show stains, if you slop tea on yourself, or go ten rounds with Justine's jam cake. Naturally, our opposite fashion tastes mean we avoid any clothing-borrowing conflicts— but it helps that I have nine inches *and* three stone on her.

We'd complementary mind-sets about keeping house too. Justine's keen on a kitchen floor you could eat off of with no fear of contracting the typhoid, while I've firsthand knowledge that people can eat the narkiest, dust-encrusted stuff under the fridge, and it would do them no harm whatsoever. But she's never given a crap about the bathroom, when one hair in the sink would completely stress me out. So we each cleaned what matters.

Best of all, we were Yin and Yang about food. Both of us were, quite frankly, obsessed, but we'd completely different appetites. As in, "Jack Sprat could eat no fat, and his wife could eat no lean." (One look at us would tell you who was Jack, and who was the wife.) It's a good job I threw our bathroom scales in the bin, since Justine's Yin had never met a recipe she couldn't master, and my Yang could muck up heating fish fingers. So she did the cooking, I did the eating—and was living proof behind the old adage "beware the skinny cook."

Our guy philosophy was the only arena where our Chinese cosmology was clearly out of sync. Justine drove me bonkers sometimes, nursing her hopeless, secret (except to me) love, while settling for the unworthy Frank Kenny, the bloke she was sort of going out with. At least I knew when to give up on a guy.

Not that I was brooding over Rafe, of course. "You know, if you want to break in your new book, you could always do a practice crème brulee."

"I'd love to," Justine said, "but I should probably bone up on casseroles instead. Mam's asked me to cook for Nate while Aine's away, visiting her mam."

"Your mam still likes to think your brother's helpless, at the age of thirty-six?" I felt a spike of envy. Mammy Egan *lived* for her kids.

"She's trying to be supportive," Justine said. "She thinks Nate wasn't quite ready to be a father, that Aine pressured him into it. But, Mam says in Aine's defense, she was hitting her mid-thirties, and time was getting short. Nate would just have to go along with it." A look of dismay crossed her face. "Actually, I wasn't meant to tell anyone that."

"I can keep a secret," I said. "But didn't Aine have trouble getting pregnant?"

"She thought so," said Justine, opening *New Irish Puddings* again. "Whenever she'd get discouraged, Mam would tell her, 'There's no rush—when God made time, he made plenty of it.'"

"But how long did it take?" I pressed.

"Six months." Justine scanned a page of her book. "Hardly 'having trouble.'"

"But that's half a fecking *year*." I could tell Justine wasn't really listening but I went on anyway, "If *Girl Talk* Girl is right, the fertility for a girl Aine's age would've been heading straight downhill. Another year or two, she'd be all but barren."

Justine glanced up as the train stopped at Connolly Station. "Baron of beef! That's brilliant. Nate's very keen on a roast, and he could make sandwiches from it all week. What do you think?"

"I think Nate was relieved when they got a positive test, or else his sex life would have been misery," I said. "All about taking temperatures, shagging on a schedule—" I broke off as a familiar figure plopped onto the seat next to Justine. "Hey, Sinead," I said weakly. *Drat.*

"Who's shagging on a schedule?" Sinead Fallon arranged herself in an artful sprawl.

Sinead was one of those friends you put quotation marks around. You know, "friend." She worked as a barista/waitperson on Talbot Street, and was our inside track on bizarre human behavior— starting with her own. She'd a lone dreadlock sprouting above one ear, and drank more coffee in one day than most sane people did in a week. And she had the worst posture I'd ever seen: torso shaped like a permanent question mark, hips thrust forward, stomach concave, and shoulders hunched in a permanent slouch. She walked like a runway model with a spinal condition.

The strange thing was, Sinead worked at her narky posture, as hard as she did at her job. I once made the mistake of referring to her job as food service. Sinead informed me that "pulling" coffee was an art. There were espresso-making competitions, apparently. "Who's shagging on a schedule?" Sinead repeated.

Justine looked alarmed. *Secret,* she mouthed. "My sister," I said quickly. "The one living in America. She's terribly bossy." Since Mary Alice controlled her husband's every move, I'm sure sex was a part of it.

"So tell us," Sinead said, "what's new with—"

"Grainne's on about one of her theories." Justine shut her book with a snap. Sinead was *not* one of her favorite people. Nor Frank Kenny's, Justine's guy. He worked at the same place Sinead did, and I think he and Justine had bonded over their mutual dislike of her. "There's something sneaky about that Miss One Dread," Justine said once. "Frank thinks so too."

"Oh, totally," I'd agreed. "Slinking about, so you can't see her coming until it's too late." Now, since my dart game kept us from taking an earlier train, we were stuck.

"Theories?" Sinead puckered her mouth in an annoying way, like she was ready to kiss air.

"Thirty-something infertility isn't a theory, it's a fact," I said.

"*I'm* hardly worried—I won't be thirty for *ages*," Sinead said.

"Three years isn't ages," Justine muttered.

Sinead's dreadlock swung toward me. "Aren't you thirty yourself?"

My motto's always been, don't lie unless you've absolutely no choice. "Almost," I said, more glumly than I meant to. "Friday next, actually."

"Then you'll want to settle on a guy, right?" Sinead's gaze sharpened. "I mean, any thirty-ish girl'll want to hop to it—they say thirty is the new forty."

I poked my finger into the armrest, resisting the urge to do the same to her sunken chest. "I think it's the other way round," *you eejit*. Suddenly, it came to me that *settling* didn't necessarily mean you couldn't get what you want. "If you keep your options open," I said, "the right guy will show up."

Justine cast an irritable look at me. "Why are you angsting about turning thirty, and bloody theories, and finding the right man, anyway?" she groused. "I mean, you've got Joe."

Three

Like any career, I mused the next day, professional child-minding has its pros and cons.

The day I got my first nanny situation, I assured Dad I'd built-in job security—like car repairing, or toilet paper manufacturing. You'll never run out of customers.

While I didn't know much about children—and could hardly ask my mam, whose maternal instincts had done a runner long before I showed up—I decided I could learn what I needed on the job. Which unfortunately leads us to the paradox of nannying: you do it because you like kids, but once you start, you can no longer harbor any illusions of what it's like to be a mother.

Still, most nannies dote on their charges—in my case, a trio of tow-headed, blue-eyed angels. But sometimes, like today, the little Gallaghers made me wish I'd a few fantasies left to shatter.

As I simultaneously bathed a squalling eight-month-old Ivy and supervised Anna's still hit-and-miss attempts on the potty, Geoff barged in and threw a fleet of boats into the tub—two of which had recently seen service in the mud puddles outside the kitchen door.

"Geoff!" I scooped Ivy up before the filthy water slick could stick to her, just as our four-year-old cherub plunged both arms into the tub. "I'm making a hurricane!" he crowed, swooshing the now-polluted bathwater.

Trying to maintain my Mary Poppins-ish composure, I slung Ivy, still wailing, onto my hip, and guided him away from the tub. "Geoff, there are toys meant for the garden, and toys meant for the house." I whisked his arms with Ivy's towel. "Which sort are the boats for?"

"The bath," he hollered, then tore out of the room.

Making a mental note not to let him see any more extreme weather reports on telly, I dried the still-bawling Ivy with the clean parts of the towel. "Now it's straight downstairs to fix you the yummiest bottle ever," I told her. I averted my eyes from the brown-tinged tub, floor, and bath toys. I'd have plenty of opportunities to see them up close later, since I'd be spending the kids' naptime cleaning the lot.

"'Dawnya, Dawnya, look!" Anna yelled over Ivy's howling, and stood up. She'd made her wees into the bowl—well, most of it anyway, with twin dribbles trickling down each leg.

"Lovely!" I shouted back. "Mammy will be so proud." As I one-handedly helped Anna pull up her wees-spotted dungarees, greenish goo dripped from her nose onto my sleeve. (Didn't I say black was a good color for me?) "Now, can you say, Grrrr...Grawn-ya?"

"Drrrr...Dawn-ya!" she screeched in triumph. Before I could swipe her nose, she scrambled out of range, and raced after her brother.

Earlier, while Ivy half-heartedly gummed a chunk of apple, then pelted remnants of toast fingers across the room, I dutifully checked my mobile for texts. Sure enough, there was one from Sara Gallagher, my boss:

> Una stayed the evening so Alan and I could go out. :-) But I'm afraid she did her predictable indulgent-granny thing—gave the kids too many sweets, then kept them up late...:-(
>
> So early naps all round. And keep Anna and Geoff away from the biscuit tin.

Great. The price I paid for the occasional afternoon off was Sara's mother-in-law taking over the nanny chores. She'd let the kids mainline sugar—okay, I'm from the do-as-I-say-and-not-as-I-do school of nannying—and stay awake until they were bug-eyed, rendering them completely unmanageable the next day.

As I pretended not to hear Geoff and Anna skirmishing over which DVD they got to jam into the player (permitted while Nanny checked their mammy's texts) another text came in.

> Almost forgot—let me know how Ivy gets on with the new formula.

Texts were Sara's primary means of parent-nanny communication. Which happily meant I'd no need to hang round when Sara came home from work, for a friendly catch-up on what her little darlings had got up to that day. On the other hand, texting seemed cold. Here I am, caring for the fruit of her womb, and all she wants from me is electronic memos relating the minutiae of the day—books read, screen time logged, and all digestive activities, intake and outflow.

But texting is perfect for people like Sara. As the owner and executive editor of *The Gallagher Post*, a weirdly eclectic mix of pop culture, news nobody cares about, and celebrity worship (rather like Sara herself), she's terribly keen on technology. In fact, I understand that round the GallPo office, nobody talks—everyone e-mails or texts. Same goes for her and her husband Alan. And now that she's got three kids, with her passion for efficiency, she's likely restricted their sex life to the online world too.

But maybe I was being too hard on Sara. After all, she was the reason that in little more than a fortnight, I would be experiencing my best holiday ever. Well, almost the best, anyway.

The thought so cheered me I felt almost serene as I retrieved Ivy's toast missiles. Then I texted Sara back, magnanimously leaving out mentioning the biscuit crumbs I'd found in the kids' beds. As the day progressed, though, Granny Una's indulgences became more evident. Anna and Geoff got into a scrum three times before lunch. And Ivy spat her first and only mouthful of the new, improved formula in my face, then screamed through her bath.

Now, Bath Time From Hell concluded, the baby's shrieks had hit the veins-sticking-out-on-forehead level. So I made an executive decision: back to the old formula. We galloped upstairs, Ivy riding my hip as her bottle warmed, to herd Geoff and Anna into their respective bedrooms, just as the microwave and my mobile went off at the same time.

Back downstairs we went, Ivy's cries becoming more urgent. I just hoped Sara wasn't breaking with tradition and actually ringing me. Aiming for unflappable competence—especially crucial with my fabulous summer holiday approaching—I lassoed the bottle, then dug my mobile from my bag.

It wasn't Sara. "Hallo," said Justine brightly.

"What do you want?" I shifted Ivy into the crook of my arm and popped the bottle into her mouth. Blessedly, her cries ceased.

"Still upset about yesterday?"

I squirmed inwardly, thinking of the Sinead episode on the Dart. "If you weren't my best friend, I'd tell you to piss off. How could you mention Joe in front of Sinead?"

Ivy pulled the bottle out of her mouth, like she was curious too.

"Mental lapse," Justine said humbly. I didn't answer. "Temporary insanity, then?"

"That's no excuse," I said. "You can't have forgotten Sinead pushes for a Tell-All about Joe at the slightest provocation." Ivy made a tiny cough, so I readjusted her bottle, and noticed her sleeper needed fastening. "But I can't talk now."

"Bad day?"

"Pandemonium's a nice word for it," I said, settling Ivy more securely. While today's chaos had kept me from dwelling on yesterday's Sinead run-in *and* Rafe Byrne's wedding, somehow I didn't feel that grateful.

"You poor thing." Justine oozed sympathy.

"You have to wonder what the hell Sara and Alan were thinking, to have three kids in four years," I said, trying to snap up Ivy's sleeper with one hand. "Anyway, I've got to run. Geoff and Anna are alone upstairs, and God knows what they've got up to."

"Right." Justine's voice dropped. "But I have to tell you—I just heard my boss is going to hire one of those home chefs for her family. Can you believe it? For two pins, I'd offer *my* services. But then she'd know I never think about my job except when I'm here and sometimes not even then—"

"Hello!" I broke in. "I've really got to ring off. Sara's probably got a nanny cam somewhere, to track unauthorized chatting with mates." I wiped some formula off Ivy's nose with my shirt.

"I'll bet if you got Joe to the altar, he'd let *you* have a personal chef—"

"Why do you keep mentioning Joe?" I said, as Ivy belched. Can't say I blame her. Linking Joe and marriage in the same breath would give anyone wind. "He's *so* not up for discussion."

"You say that, but I'll bet Joe would be your soul mate, if you'd let him."

Joe? Now *I* had to burp. "Too bad there's no such thing as a soul mate."

"Of course there is—it's someone who cares about everything you do, is always there for you, and like, totally adores you, no matter what."

"Okay, I'm wrong." I carefully reinserted the bottle in Ivy's mouth. "That sounds like your mam."

"Maybe she is sort of a soul mate." Justine sounded pleased. "Although when I showed her last week's *Girl Talk* column about mothers, she didn't really get it. She stroked my hair for a minute, but then she said if I grew it out and curled it a little, Frank would be sure to—"

"Justine! I'm definitely ringing—"

"All right, all right," Justine grumbled. "But the other reason I rang—I want to make up for blathering on with Sinead yesterday. How about one of your all-time favorites for supper?"

Ringing off instantly lost priority. "Which one?"

"Garlic fettuccine with baby asparagus—now, am I back in your good books?"

Really, I should've made her pay for the Joe-Sinead faux pas, but it was too late to give her the silent treatment. And I could already taste her butter-drenched pasta. "Like you never left."

As a frantic "Dawnya!" reverberated down the staircase, I stashed my mobile in my pocket, slung Ivy back onto my hip and headed upstairs.

Naptime got delayed when I discovered Anna's dungarees were damper than I thought, then we had to search for her must-have sleep aid, Raggy Blankie. Once she was down, I caught Geoff jumping on his bed with the mud-caked toys he'd fetched from the bathroom while I was minding Ivy. I bribed him to take an hour's "rest," nanny-speak for letting him tear up his room with the door closed, and fantasized about inventing a child-friendly tranquilizer. Then I needed to check in with Sara again.

I set Ivy on the rug for tummy time, then pulled my tatty notebook from my bag, to retrieve the details I'd jotted in earlier. Checking Sara's earlier text, I typed:

1) Anna: wees in potty twice. 2) Ivy: ate ½ apple. 3) Geoff: 20 minutes of physical activity. 4) Ivy: loves new formula.

Real life: 1) Absolutely True. 2) Okay, more like three teeth marks, but Sara insisted on healthful eating. 3) I didn't mention Geoff's activity was jumping on his bed instead of wholesome kiddie exercise. 4) What Sara didn't know wouldn't hurt her.

With my memo duties out of the way, I'd just heaved a sigh of relief when in came another call. Justine again. "We've no parmesan cheese at home, and I've a ton of stuff to finish up here. Can you pop into Tesco and pick some up before you catch the train?"

"Gotcha. See you later." Ivy started wailing again. My nanny-sanity breaking up like a radio signal from the Outer Hebrides, I tucked her back in my arms with a second bottle, and collapsed into Alan's overstuffed recliner.

She latched onto it, then stared up at me expectantly.

I stroked her butter-soft cheek, wondering if babies could read your expression, like dogs. "You've guessed what I'm thinking?" Ivy blinked, and kept suckling. "Joe's a problem."

Joe Corrigan was the sort who looked good on paper: reasonably attractive, a successful businessman, and went easy on the drink. Everyone said I'd be mad not to snap him up.

While no one needed to tell me—especially in the last five years—that there were other fish in the sea, I'd more of a catch-and-release approach to men. Given Joe's stellar qualities, some might consider him a keeper. But I couldn't bring myself to take him seriously.

Joe was the eldest of five brothers, all of whom lived at their dad's house in Dublin. The Corrigans were mad for sport, and gathered en masse in front of the telly for any and all Gaelic Games, football, and rugby broadcasts. Joe's mam had died four years ago, and the house didn't appear to have been cleaned since. So you can imagine the state of the place. I can tolerate some dirt here or there, but the overflowing bins, fridge full of rotting food, and—to put in bluntly—an unspeakable bathroom really put me off.

My dilemma: A long time ago, I'd...encouraged Joe more than I should have, and he proposed marriage. Which of course I turned down, then we avoided each other for years. But the avoidance thing got rather silly after a while. We'd always run into each other, which Dublin people seem to do. After several months, he asked me to dinner, and we started going out—casually, that is. But invariably, the sex thing came up.

I pulled a face, then leaned down to kiss Ivy's forehead. It felt a bit pervy, to think about sex while cuddling an eight-month-old, but I had to talk to *someone*. "How could Justine blab about Joe, in front of God and everyone?" I asked Ivy, still sucking energetically. "He's Sinead's fecking boss!"

Ivy paused for a moment, then commenced suckling again. "Sorry," I said, and smoothed the fuzz on her crown. "But what did she say on the train, with Sinead right there?" Ivy wrinkled her forehead, clearly fascinated. "The nerve of her! She said, 'You have Joe.'"

Yesterday, as the Dart rocked northward, I'd stared at her, aghast. "I do *not* have Joe."

"You do," chimed in Sinead. "His brother Billy came into the cafe last Thursday, and asked Joe when he was going to bring you round again. When Joe didn't answer, Billy said he hoped it was soon, 'cause your bum's as nice as Jennifer Lopez's. Joe almost hit him—and in front of five customers too. He wants you, all right."

"It doesn't mean I want him back," I sputtered. "Or Billy either!" Don't get me wrong—it was all very well to have your bum compared to J-Lo's, but it wasn't like the rest of *me* was built like the rest of *her*.

"Sounds like luuurve to me too, with Joe," Justine said. Odd, since she usually went out of her way to disagree with Sinead. "I heard him say once you'd lovely goldy-brown eyes."

"Joe said that?" Sinead said, incredulous. She peered at my eyes. "They're actually more mustardy. And did you know one of them is half green?"

"I never noticed," I muttered, as Justine continued, "So what's the harm in Joe taking a mad fancy to you?"

"God help us," I said. "Every time I tell him I'm not ready to go to bed with him, he gets this *will you just kick me again* look on his face."

"You're not having it off with him?" Sinead almost, but not quite, sat up straight with the shock of it.

"We're not like, exclusive—"

"You mean it? You're *not* having it off?" Sinead repeated.

"Well…no," I said. Sinead made me feel like I was meant to apologize somehow, for not having sex. I knew she saw Joe as *the* catch-of-the-day, but come on. "Bed's no place to find out if a guy is right for you."

Justine stared out the window, as Sinead poked her finger in her ear. "My hearing must be going—you couldn't have said bed's no place to—"

"Well, it isn't," I said, annoyed. I'd legitimate reasons for avoiding casual sex, but none that Sinead would understand.

"Never say you were the sort who wanted to be a nun when you grew up," Sinead jibed.

"No, I wanted to be a pirate," I said, going along with the joke. "But Dad put his foot down on that career after I'd cut a pair of his Sunday trousers off at the knees."

"Why not have it off with any fellow you fancy?" Sinead sounded skeptical.

"Well…" I thought hard. "There've been studies that show when you have sex with a guy, your hormones surge with 'this is the real thing, he's the one,' bonding messages, when he's likely nothing of the kind."

"Hmm," Sinead said, clearly not a convert. "I could always test the study or whatever with Billy—really, he's not half bad."

Justine turned to exchange a grimace with me. "I think you can feel close to a guy without going to bed," she said.

"Right," I agreed. "I mean, you've never been with—" Oops. Not in front of Sinead. If Rafe Byrne was unavailable, his brother Ian, Justine's Secret Love—the guy she had to be referring to—was truly Mr. Unattainable. At least Rafe, way back when, had definitely had the hots for me.

Justine pretended not to hear my gaffe. Sinead, luckily, was still following her own thread. "Billy's not the looker Joe is, of course, but a decent sort, in his own way. I'm sure he'd be good for a ride."

"If you kept your eyes closed." Justine laughed. Which sounded awfully fake.

"Don't you think he's sort of..." *a dork...* "inexperienced?" I asked.

"He'll sort it out—he's a man, isn't he?" Sinead chortled and slapped her knee.

"Or so the rumors go," Justine said, with that false merriment still in her voice. Unless she'd decided Sinead was her new mate, she had to be playing along with Miss One Dread to distract herself from her terminal case of unrequited love.

I'd glowered at the pair of them as they proceeded to compare the relative shagability of Joe and his brothers, and which of the brothers they'd be most embarrassed to admit they'd had it off with, until Sinead got off the train.

Now, sitting with Ivy a day later, I said aloud, "Since time is of the essence...maybe I should consider giving Joe a real go. What do you think?" I looked down at her.

She'd fallen asleep, milk drool rather adorably trickling down her cheek. I cuddled her closer, then my mobile chirped *again*. I frantically dug into my pocket. "God sakes, Justine, I just got the baby to sl—"

"It's me," said my sister Rory. "You're needed in Ballydara tomorrow. Mam's called a family meeting."

THE GALLAGHER POST

Gai Lannigan's Girl Talk

The Mother Wound

You've grown up, left home, evolved. You have your own life. Then why does your mother still drive you round the bend?

Psychologists say that no matter how hard mothers try to do the right thing by their kids, a child's emotional needs can never be *really* satisfied—the "mother wound" theory. Motherhood's a dodgy business, I'll admit, but when it comes to dealing with female offspring, the experts have barely scratched the surface. Because the potential tumult of a romantic pairing-up has *nothing* on the mother-daughter relationship. If you ask me, when Pat Benetar sang, "Love is a battlefield," she was secretly referring to her mam.

Of course, with the conflicting emotions between you and your mam—love, hate, fear, admiration, attraction, repulsion—isn't feuding inevitable? You want to be the center of her world, but you keep your distance. You long to lay your head in her lap, have her stroke your hair, then cringe from her touch. You yearn for a heart-to-heart about your boyfriend or job, but in the blink of an eye, your mam's the last person you'd share your grocery list with.

And in the end, you're forced to admit it's your ambivalence that keeps you apart. You can't stand her—and wish you did, you can't talk to her—and wish you could, and you make fun of her to all your friends—and wish you didn't. But it's not your fault. You can blame that little girl inside…who not only remembers every unkind word, every time your mam was distant, or let you down, but even now, wishes she paid more attention to you. Wishes she knew—or wanted to know—the real you. Despite everything, all you want is your mother's approval—even if you wouldn't know what to do with it if you had it…

Four

I clutched my mobile. "A family meeting?" I couldn't have been more surprised if Mam had scheduled a striptease in the window of Brown Thomas on Grafton Street. "What are we—the Brady Bunch?"

"Grainne, I'm really not up for your cracks today," said Rory. "Mam'll expect you at two."

You might wonder, why hadn't my mother rung me herself? Well, she was a great one for outsourcing—phone calls...housekeeping... parenting.

"Did you hear me?" Rory asked, edgier than Justine's best chef's knife. "Two sharp!"

What was with Rory? "Wait just one minute." Bad enough, that Mam never rang me. It *really* grated that Rory had got into the habit of only ringing me when *Mam* needed something. "I haven't said I can make it." I mean, I'd the crucial issue of whether to shag Joe weighing on me.

"You'll come if you know what's good for you."

There were times when Rory sounded like our Granny O'Neill, Mam's mother, instead of my eldest sister. Like right now. "And who are you to order me home? I don't have time to be riding the bus all weekend."

"A few hours to and from County Galway is hardly all weekend."

"It's almost an entire day," I countered. "And it so happens I'm busy tomorrow." After sleeping off today's stress, I planned to settle in with Justine's pasta leftovers and a *Downton Abbey* DVD.

"Too bad. You can go round to the pub or whatever another time."

"But I promised," I lied, wondering if Rory's crankiness was from lack of sex. Though after three years of singlehood, you'd think she'd have gotten used to celibacy by now. "I could use some downtime, after the day I've had—"

"You should try motherhood," Rory said implacably. "Eighteen years without a break. And it's not like you come to see your own mother except on holidays, and sometimes not even then."

Well, she had me there. "But Jesus, Rory, we're not the sort of family that has—" I couldn't bring myself to repeat the foreign concept, *family meetings*. "Mam's not losing her marbles, is she?"

"She's perfectly fine, and no thanks to you," said Rory.

"Well, if Mary Alice won't be there, I don't know why I should have to," I joked, hoping to coax Rory out of her tiresome Granny O'Neill imitation. "Unless she's flying in from America."

But no. "Don't be late." Rory rang off before I could muster any more feeble protests.

"I'm fecked," I told Ivy, now fast asleep. My first free moment, I tied up the day's loose ends: noted Ivy's dirty nappy count, tidied the kitchen, then checked e-mail. Bad move. Because I found the group e-mail Justine's mam had sent round about Rafe Byrne's nuptials. Which, courtesy of her sister Bernadette Byrne, Rafe's stepmother, was splashed with his wedding photos.

If only I'd sent the message to Trash before I'd opened it. But once I had, it was like coming onto a train wreck. I couldn't stop staring. Snaps of the glowy bride, the breeze catching her mile-long train, with at least a dozen attendants, all of whom were clones of her: Kate Middleton look alikes, only honey-blond. In the background, a gossamer white tent, the lake sparkling in the background. Her parents, looking as satisfied as if they'd pulled off the coup of the century, posed with an equally smug Bernie Byrne. And Rafe, wearing an unexpectedly serious expression, his windblown hair lending a rakish flavor to the otherwise carefully choreographed scenes.

And now, I'd Mam to contend with? Grinding my teeth, I forced myself to delete the e-mail. Then for good measure, I emptied my Trash folder. After packing up my gear, I escaped as soon as Sara Gallagher banged the front door and tossed her handbag on the kitchen counter. With the wedding photos still taking up all my mental bandwidth, I didn't remember my Tesco errand until *after* I'd boarded the northbound Dart, so there'd be no lovely pasta tonight.

But brooding on the Dart home to Howth, I was sure that no matter how awful today had been, tomorrow would be even worse.

When I was twelve, Father Christmas (aka Dad) had a book-shop epiphany, and gave me *Gone With the Wind*. I began devouring it immediately—he'd actually had to bribe me to come out of my room for Christmas dinner, if you can believe that—until I came to the part about Scarlett O'Hara adoring her mother Ellen.

Bloody unnatural, if you ask me. Even if Ellen was the polar opposite of my mother. See, all my life, Mam and I had rubbed each up the wrong way. And from what I'd observed, most girls who got on with their mams were actually faking it.

So I'd tossed the book into my closet, not to touch it again for six months. When I did, an idle flip through the pages—I think it was Rhett's hot black eyes and Scarlett's heaving bosom...or was it Rhett's heaving eyes and Scarlett's hot bosom?—got me hooked again.

Gone With the Wind turned into my ultimate comfort read. For me, Scarlett O'Hara became a grand inspiration for how a girl can go after what she wants. It was the next best thing to a pudding whenever I needed a pick-me-up—and I read the book at least once a year.

Confession: I'd still skimmed over the Ellen O'Hara bits.

The next afternoon, I stepped off the bus in the middle of Ballydara, looking round as if I'd never seen the place before. But then, maybe I hadn't. I'd always rushed to and from Mam's house with tunnel vision—usually because it was pouring rain, but I'd concentrated only on how fast I could get back home. But today, as the lush green hills surrounding the village caught my eye, their tops shrouded in mist, I felt like I'd just been dropped into another world.

Instead of Dublin's petrol fumes, cacophony of cars and lorries, and crowds of people rushing everywhere, Ballydara's rain-washed air smelled almost sweet, despite the slightest whiff of earthworms and manure. The quiet was broken only by the lowing of cows in the distance and the hum of voices emanating from Hurley's pub. If I was a drinking girl, I'd have popped in for a fortifying pint, but with the mood my sister was in, I'd need my wits about me.

As I started down the narrow, stone-lined road toward Mam's house, not passing another soul on the way, I felt an odd sensation, like…a tiny pull on my heart. *God sakes, you're only hungry,* I told myself quickly. And even if Ballydara was *beyond* the back of beyond, hadn't I been here ten times before, without feeling any pinch at all? Ready to get my visit over with, I stepped up my pace, reminded that there an upside to my trip to Ballydara. Actually two. It was just for the afternoon, until the early evening bus back to Dublin. And doing my duty this weekend meant I'd have a two-month reprieve, until the August bank holiday.

When I walked into Mam's dining room, Rory was setting out Indian takeaway she'd brought from Galway City, while my mother flitted about, splashing Chardonnay into spotless wineglasses. Freshly-lipsticked, she wore a flowy sort of outfit that seemed over the top for lunch at home, but that was Mam for you. She thrived on overkill.

People said Eileen Larkin could've been a film star. If Dad had a pint in him—and if he and Mam were getting on, that is—he'd always say she looked like Grace Kelly, with the bloom of a girl. I privately thought Mam's smooth, unlined skin was rather Dorian Gray-ish. Though to her credit, her complexion owed nothing to cosmetic treatments. Mam vowed she'd no more inject Botox into her skin as lard.

But looks aside, Mam's always been more like an actress in search of an audience—the reason she'd made quite a success as a sort of Vanna White for Dad's furniture store adverts. It was the sure-fire way she could be the center of attention without the rigors of a stage career.

Catching sight of me, Mam waved the bottle. "Well, here she is, our changeling." Some might interpret her greeting as fond, but since when is "changeling" an endearment, I ask you? "Wine with your curry, Grainne?"

I was tempted. I mean, how I'd get through the afternoon without some mind-altering substance was anyone's guess, but I was actually more annoyed than anything. "None for me, thanks." Wine didn't agree with me any more than pints did, a fact that regularly slipped her mind. But then, Mam had a famously selective memory.

As usual, Mam went up on tiptoe to air-kiss to cheek. I bent and aimed one toward her impeccably-highlighted hair. Then I sidled away, back to the buffer zone I generally kept between us. Not that she seemed to notice. She brushed a speck off her immaculate linen tablecloth, then slid gracefully into her chair.

"It's about time," said Rory, passing Mam the fuller glass.

"It's only half-two," I retorted, and dropped into my regular place at the far end—symbolic of my perennial role as Larkin Outsider.

Our looks had a lot to do with my being out of sync. Rory, along with Mary Alice, our middle sister, took after Mam. The three Insiders hardly cleared five-feet-three, with peachy-pink complexions, blue eyes, and varying shades of wavy fair hair, while I've skin inclined to sallowness, and at just under six feet, barefoot, shoulders like a footballer. In fact, the size of me could've won me a spot in the All-Ireland league.

Apparently, I'm the spit image of Dad—a fair looker in his prime, but not so great when you're a girl. Although my Granny O'Neill, a right terror if there ever was one, swore the day I was born the fairies had stolen Mam and Dad's real baby, and left this half-and-half yellow-eyed creature—"cratur," in her country accent—in its place. Which, given the fact that Mam never defended me, I'd believed far longer than I should have. And every time I visit Mam's house, I start thinking there's something to it all over again.

"Eyre Square Centre was a madhouse today," Mam observed as Rory served a modest portion of chicken curry and rice on two plates. While Mam nattered on about her shopping expedition to Galway City, I emptied the cartons onto my own plate, and tucked

in. Food was just what I needed to keep my mind off Day One of
Rafe Byrne's honeymoon, and steer it more in Joe's direction.

Unfortunately, the curry wasn't good enough to distract me
from whatever trumped-up excuse Mam might have for requesting
my presence. Calling a chat with Rory over mediocre takeaway a
"family meeting" was likely Mam's hyperbole, with only the three
of us. Dad had been gone for two years—the reason for the takeaway, since he'd also been the family cook and grocery-shopper.
And since Mary Alice lived in Chicago—with her husband Jim and
a miniature Dachshund so spoiled he'd not one, but three pairs of
doggie rain booties—she got a pass too.

Rory, as usual, had left her two kids at home with a minder.
Mam had white carpet—that's white, not ecru, ivory, or a family-
friendly beige—and Rory's Brendan was still at that snakes/snails/
puppy-dogs' tails stage. Ciara, the elder, was tidier, but not by
much. She liked to assert her age-of-ten independence by snacking
wherever she pleased, invariably leaving a trail of crumbs. Not quite
cause for banishment, but the straw that broke the Larkin back—
that is, Mam had thrown a rather legendary fit—was the blackberry
trifle Ciara had dropped onto the carpet, and the footprints Brenny
had left after he'd pretended it was a purple mud puddle.

As I ate and continued to ponder if I should give Joe a go,
Mam suddenly broke off her monologue. "And how was your week,
Grainne?"

I dropped my fork. Mam, asking after *me*? Flattered, I began,
"A bit mad as usual—the Gallagher kids are growing up fast." But
I didn't bother elaborating as Mam turned back to Rory. "I wasn't
able to make it to the cleaner's today—is there any chance…?"

"No problem, Mam," Rory said. "I got your things—and your
order at the chemist's too." Accustomed to Mam's flea-like attention span, I just thanked God it was Rory who had the misfortune
of living in Galway City, not terribly far from Ballydara, and not
me. With her proximity to Mam, she'd inherited Dad's household
management duties—which were so extensive I'm convinced the
poor man had to give up the ghost to have some rest.

"What's for pudding?" I asked, scooping up the last bite of rice. The curry had hardly made a dent.

"Fruit and cheese," replied Rory, and went to the fridge.

I sighed as she set a plate of Brie and melon on the table, stifling fantasies of...oh, coconut ice cream with chocolate sauce would've hit the spot. My sister, along with Mam, had a tiresome way of watching her figure like a prison warden eyes the inmates in the exercise yard. In lieu of a sweet, though, I'd something else to savor: the anticipation of telling Mam and Rory about my upcoming working holiday with the Gallagher family, even if it was on half-pay. Mam would appreciate it, since she was keen on sojourns to exotic, sun-drenched locales like the Aegean or Barcelona.

Sure, a cookie-cutter tourist condo might not seem all that glam, unless your last holiday was a rain-soaked weekend in Killarney.

Then I heard a discordant note: Mary Alice something something.

"What's Mary Alice doing these days?" I inquired politely, although MA didn't exactly inspire sisterly affection. We'd been forced to share a bedroom until Rory left home for university, and as Dad put it, we were like a pair of squalling cats. Afterward, despite our separate rooms, the situation deteriorated. When I'd just learned about sex and was extremely sensitive about the whole business, Mary Alice informed me that Mam and Dad only intended to have two kids—and I was an accident.

The disclosure not only confirmed that my parents actually did this nasty, icky *thing*, but that they'd been at it for reasons other than to produce a baby. Which cemented my Outsider status for good.

However, if the quick sibling update meant Mam was winding up this little get-together, it looked like I could escape relatively unscathed. "I propose a toast," said Mam, glancing at me.

Instantly disarmed, I berated myself for my undaughterly thoughts. Mam had called this family meeting to kick-start my birthday celebration—unprecedented! Suddenly changing my mind about the wine, I held out my glass as Rory topped off hers and

Mam's. I was the first to raise my arm, already hearing, *To Grainne, as we approach her thirtieth birthday!*

Instead, Mam sang out, "To Mary Alice, and her baby!"

Baby? I set my glass down so hard the wine sloshed over the rim. "Mary Alice—"

"Is pregnant," Mam finished, beaming.

My stomach lurched.

"She rang today with the news." Rory's face softened. "She and Jim have only been trying since New Year's, and her nearly thirty-seven! She's already three months gone."

"Imagine that," I said hollowly, then gulped down my wine. I'd heard Mary Alice wanted a baby, but I figured at her age, she'd her work cut out for her. I didn't get the American custom of actually announcing when you're *trying* to get pregnant either. It seemed rather tasteless, not to mention grossly optimistic. If things didn't go well, there you were, egg on your face, and no baby either.

Somehow, all this attention on Mary Alice only upped my sensitivity to Rafe Byrne's permanent exit from the fish market. So I sat, the curry like a lump in my stomach, as Mam chatted about Mary Alice wanting ideas about nursery-decorating, her morning sickness, which warranted a visit in July, and her plans for another trip when the baby arrived in the fall. I could live with Mam running on about a new grandchild. But what stuck in my craw was that she'd actually trouble herself to go all the way to America to visit it, when she'd never really appreciated the people right in front of her.

But why should I be surprised? All my life, Mam has focused on folk who are more interesting, more admiring, and more willing to do stuff for her than I am. I've tried telling myself I'm a petty, immature cow, that I'm no better than a resentful teenager when it comes to Mam. And that I should just grow up and accept my mother the way she is.

But I...can't.

"So then," I said. "Are we done?"

"Not quite," said Rory, looking tense as she leaped up to clear the table. I joined her, despite the ache in my middle. After all, Rory had a full-time job and Ciara and Brenny to clean up after.

While Mam toyed with her cheese, I gathered the take-away cartons, shoving Mary Alice's news to the back of my mind, and followed Rory into the kitchen. I'd hardly tossed the cartons into the bin before she finished loading the dishwasher and stalked back to the door. "What were you so grumpy about yesterday?" I hissed as we returned to the dining room. "Is Darren making more excuses not to see the kids?"

"Yes, but I can't get into it now," she said. It was too late to press her further, since Mam was breaking out a second bottle of wine. Rory cast a nervous look at her. "Since we're here, all of us…we'll… want to think about Grainne's birthday."

Mam looked at me again, as if perplexed, then she waved her glass. "Our little girl's not having another birthday? We'll want to do a party!"

I almost fell over my chair. "I'm hardly little, Mam," I said, trying to get my head around a pre-planned birthday celebration. Larkin birthdays tended to be rather spontaneous, since Mam generally forgot them unless reminded. "The way I'm getting on—"

"Makes me a battle ax," Rory said gloomily, who'd turned thirty-nine this year. She looked grim as she opened the wine.

"Oh, you've only a few gray hairs," I said, in a wee retaliation for Rory's crossness. "And your crow's-feet hardly show."

Refilling our glasses, Rory ignored that. Mam did too. She preferred to be ageless, and also preferred everyone around her to buy into the fantasy. "You'll invite Justine?" Rory asked.

"Wouldn't be a proper party without her," I said. How else would I get a birthday cake? Besides, having Justine close by would be the only way I'd survive two evenings in Mam's company within a week.

Mam's apparent enthusiasm for my birthday still seemed suspect—surely she had an ulterior motive. But I'd no interest in staying around to sort it out. "Well!" I said jovially. "Now that we've got all that settled, I'll be on my way—"

"Not so fast," said Rory. "We've one more item on the agenda."

"Agenda?" I curled my lip. "Shall I take notes?"

"You'll remember this, I'm sure," said Rory. "Mam is thinking…" Her voice trailed away.

"Glad to hear it," I said. "But I don't have all night." My skin itched with the urgency to end this visit—which, given Rory's crankiness and Mam's prattling on about Mary Alice, had been worse than I'd expected.

Rory began, "With Mam…*retired*…" Larkin code for living off the fruit of Dad's labor, "she's thinking about—"

"I'm starting a new project!" Mam said breathlessly. "I need a fresh start, you know, something exciting, that gets me to jump right out of bed first thing—"

"There's always an alarm clock," I said.

"—Like I can't wait to start the day, instead of lying in, then three cups of coffee over the *Irish Times*, until Doreen Hurley rings."

"Mam's been at loose ends," Rory said, ever the diplomat.

"I've the urge for a creative outlet, that's all," Mam said. "One that will bring in some extra cash. My new sofa was dearer than I planned, and I've been thinking about redoing the bathroom—"

"You might consider a budget, Mam." Rory said it in a rush, as if she couldn't help herself.

"There *is* a point to this conversation?" I asked.

Looking mutinous, Mam ignored me again. "Rory, you *know* your dad always said I was worth whatever I wanted to spend."

"Mam…" Rory's mouth tightened, but I knew she'd sooner walk on hot coals than cross Mam. "I wasn't contradicting—"

"Once my new project is underway," Mam interrupted blithely. "I'll have no need to cut corners."

"The thing is," Rory said, not meeting my eyes, "Mam's dead keen on this."

"This what? Give us a hint, will you?" I prompted, but Rory remained silent.

"Chrissakes, Rory, it can't be that bad." I reached for the Chardonnay, to keep my lovely blurred reality in place until I escaped. A painting class, and Mam could sell her artwork? A harmless fantasy. Or, given her window-dressing role at Dad's business, do interior decorating part-time? A stretch, but... "Spit it out, will you?"

Rory avoided my eyes. "It's...for the summer."

I gave my glass an extra splash of wine, feeling my tension dissipate. Whatever Mam's scheme, I'd be far from Ballydara, enjoying my fabulous holiday with the Gallaghers. "Mam? Don't keep us in suspense."

She clasped her hands together with an effervescent smile. "I'm turning the house into a bed-and-breakfast."

I dropped the bottle. It didn't break, simply fell sideways, glug-glugging wine onto the table. But the upended bottle was the least of my worries, as my sister wielded the coup de grace:

"And you're needed," Rory said to me, deftly righting the bottle, "to move back here to help out."

Five

"Jaysus!" I leaped to my feet, and tipped the chair over. "Are you fecking mad?"

"Oh, dear," said Mam, plucking at the wine stain. "Give us a hand here, will you love?" By "love," she meant Rory, who was already gathering up the wet tablecloth. "Good job it wasn't a Burgundy."

I've never been a crier—I've always found going ballistic a much better release, thank you very much. It's been my only defense against Mam's implacable charm. But with her uncharacteristically composed rescue operation, I could only curse silently, my chest heaving so wildly you'd think I was in the Olympic sprinting trials. "A B&B?" I finally managed, picking up my chair. "As if you'd want people you don't even know in your house!"

"What's the old saying? 'A stranger's only a friend you haven't made yet,'" Mam said gaily.

Speechless, I gaped at her. Mam hardly fussed over her bloody family, much less perfect strangers.

"And speaking of friends, Doreen wants my opinion on the room above the pub—Pat's thinking of renting it out. So I'd better be on my way." Too floored to back away from Mam's second air kiss, I nearly jumped when it turned into a real one. Mam smiled at me, and actually patted my arm. "You'll come back in about a fortnight? It won't be for long, Grainne, just through September."

She disappeared into the downstairs powder room for a moment, emerging freshly lipsticked, and gave me one last bright smile. "See you next week, for our party!"

If not running from a fight, Mam was certainly strolling from one. As the front door closed behind her, I turned on my sister. "The pair of you are having me on, right? A birthday joke! She can't be serious!"

"Oh, but she is," Rory said, wiping the table with a dry corner of the tablecloth. "Her heart's quite set on it."

"But you *knew* I wouldn't want any part of this! Why didn't you just tell Mam the B&B idea is something only a nutter would come up with, and be done with it? And the idea of Mam actually running a business is so completely ridiculous—"

"Maybe our mother's not the ninny you like to think," Rory broke in. "She once told me she'd had a bookkeeping job before she married Dad. But when she asked him if she could keep the accounts for the store, he said she was too pretty to fuss about business. Can you believe it?"

"Actually, no," I said. Dad *couldn't* have said that—he'd always encouraged we girls to have careers. "She probably imagined it."

"That's terribly unkind—just last week, Mam was saying the pair of you could have a great time, running her new place together."

"Sure, it'll be hilarious—Mam playing hostess, while I'd be the drudge." With difficulty, I restrained myself from kicking the nearest chair. *Since when did Mam want to spend time with me?* "No fecking way!"

Rory's eyes flashed. She bundled the tablecloth in one arm and swept into the kitchen.

I snatched the empty wine bottle and stomped after her. Believe it or not, Rory could actually be fun—at least, she had been, before her divorce. I suppose your husband leaving you and your kids to "find himself" would bring you down a bit, especially if he found himself a leggy redhead with a child aversion, but still. No one was forcing her to coddle Mam.

Our problem was, Rory and I not only engaged in the normal amount of sister arguments, but we also took on all the fights I *would* be having with Mam—if she'd deign to have one with me, that is. I slammed the bottle onto the countertop. "I said, I won't do it!"

Rory pitched the tablecloth into the sink. "You'd only have to help mornings and evenings. For pity's sake, she's your mother. And you're an ungrateful brat, when she needs you."

"She doesn't need me," I shot back. "She could hire someone."

"Didn't you pay attention? Money's tight," Rory sputtered, and wrenched on the taps. "And there's lots more reasons why you should stay here and help. Hasn't it been ten years since you left home? You and Mam could…get to know each other again."

"And why would I want to do that?"

"Well, you could find some common interests." When I muttered, "That would be the day," she added, "Besides, Dad would want you to."

Now *that* was below the belt. "Don't think you can bring Dad into this mad scheme!"

Rory dashed washing liquid into the sink. "It's not mad! And even if it was, it's up to us to be supportive!"

"You admit Mam's might be going off the deep end, then?"

"No!" Rory dunked in the tablecloth. "But if it wasn't for all the grief you've given Mam over the years, she'd be much stronger!"

"And if I never crossed her, I'd have the backbone of a caterpillar." Without Dad around to break things up if they got too ugly, Rory and I could go the full fifteen rounds. "Remind you of anyone?"

Rory's peachy-pink complexion turned papaya. "Ah, shut up!" She shut off the tap so hard I thought the handle would fly across the room.

"Or an earthworm," I added.

"Insult me all you like," said Rory, shaking the water off her hands, then she pulled out the coffee tin. "But you can't get out of helping this time, with Dad gone."

I stared out the window, biting the inside of my lip to gain control. I still missed Dad, and not only because he'd looked after Mam so I didn't have to. I often wished for a sign from him, beyond the grave, so we'd know he hadn't forgotten us. Like lights blinking on and off when no one's touched the switch, or moving the teacups round the cabinet. Although Dad hadn't lived here in Ballydara above a few months—he and Mam had moved house from Dublin after he retired—surely it had been long enough for his spirit to settle in nicely. It would be even handier if he'd haunt the place so thoroughly Mam would have to scrap her mad plan—nothing like a specter appearing in the mirror to scare off customers.

"Mam can't trouble herself to make a cup of coffee," I pointed out. "How in the holy hell will she succeed in the hospitality industry?"

"Because you'll be here." Rory measured out coffee, then programmed the machine for Mam's wake-up time.

"My cooking would poison the guests!"

Rory grabbed the broom next to the fridge, and thrust it at me. "Here—make yourself useful."

"Don't think you can ignore me." I whacked the broom round the kitchen. "You know I'm useless in the kitchen."

"Anyone can learn to scramble an egg."

The fact she was taking my involvement with this mad B&B for granted made my hackles—whatever those are—shoot upward. "If you think Mam's scheme is so great, why aren't you part of it?"

"With the kids, I can't take this on too. And you've already forgotten I'm to go to America to see Mary Alice?"

Rory, not Mam, was going for a visit? "So cancel! I'm sure her Jim'd be perfectly happy teaching Wally, the Wonder Dog to fetch her tea and saltines."

"I'll not cancel—the kids are thrilled, and I've lined up some holiday time, and bought the tickets. Everything's set."

"What a shame. Because I've tons of plans this summer."

"Plans?" Rory shoved the coffee tin back on the shelf. "Oh, that's rich—"

"I do!" I opened the kitchen door and swept the refuse outside. "I've been seeing a guy—"

"You can't help your own mother, because you're busy twisting your man what's-his-name round your finger until you choke the life out of him?"

"No!" Taking a deep breath, I closed the door without slamming it. I had to get Rory on my side, then maybe the pair of us could talk sense into Mam. "By the way, he's called Joe." She only lifted an eyebrow. "The thing is, I'm getting more...proactive about my life these days," I admitted. "Now that I'm nearly thirty, I've my future to think of."

"Thirty," Rory repeated. "Sweet Jesus."

"I can hardly believe it myself," I said, almost mollified, and returned the broom to its place. "It's a bit of a milestone, isn't it?"

"Milestone?" Rory pulled the plug from the sink. "I'd say it means we'd better brace ourselves, God help us."

"What are you implying?"

"You know exactly what I'm talking about—the way you create some big disaster for yourself every five years, like bloody clockwork. What have you in store for us this year—running off to join the circus?"

"I'm tempted," I said loftily, refusing to get pulled into yet another point of contention. "But I've been invited to join the Gallaghers on their summer holiday. To *Provence*."

"Hmmm," said Rory, squeezing water from the tablecloth. "A trip to France?"

I'd finally impressed her? "And you never know," I rubbed in, "I could meet some fantastic guys there." Rory hadn't been out with a bloke in months. If not years.

Rory didn't take the bait. "What about...Joe, is it? "I can't think he'd go for that."

Oops—maybe I'd mentioned him too soon. "Well, if he and I don't work out—"

"Sara Gallagher won't have any trouble finding a substitute helper for a fortnight or two," Rory said. "And if you're that keen on going abroad, you can pair up with Mam on her next visit."

When bloody pigs fly, I nearly blurted. "I am *not* missing a month in Provence," I said, trying to control my temper. "The Gallaghers are paying for the lot, you know. And the working holiday will look great on my resume."

Rory made an unladylike sound—a *snort*, if you can believe it.

"It will! People don't bring crap nannies on holiday—only the ones they consider part of the family."

"The Gallaghers aren't family," Rory shot back. "Mam is. So you need to do your duty."

"Come on—Mam's hardly a dutiful daughter herself. Hasn't it

been years since she's visited Granny, and her just a ferry ride away?" When Rory only shrugged, I clenched my fists. "And there's no way I can afford to go a month without a paycheck, while I'm scrubbing toilets around here."

Rory dried her hands, putting on a long-suffering look. "I'm sure Mam can give you a small allowance."

"Allowance!"

"If you earn it," she added smugly. My sister had somehow hitched a ride to the high ground, and left me wallowing at the bottom of a deep gulch. "It's past time you took a turn as a proper daughter."

Livid, I said the first thing that came into my head. "Too bad I'm not willing to be Mam's gofer-for-life to get her to like me!"

Rory's smug look vanished. I saw a sheen of tears in her eyes. "Rory, I..." Jaysus, did she have to be so sensitive? Blaming Mam— she always incited our worst arguments—I made to touch Rory's arm. "Really, I didn't—"

"Forget it." Shrugging from my hand, she stalked toward the door. "But don't think you'll get out of spending the summer in Ballydara. You're needed, and that's that."

THE GALLAGHER POST

Gai Lannigan's Girl Talk

Best Place to Meet a Guy

What's the most popular spot for meeting a mate?

You're probably thinking the pub, right? I mean, talk about your target-rich environment. A bar, however, is the last place you'll find your Dream Man. You'll run into lots of blokes to choose from, I grant you. But you and the guy will likely be the worse for drink, and because of the racket your conversation will be even more impaired than you are.

Sensible people will seek their soul mate at work, through friends, or at some high-minded activity like a night class. The success rate, however, isn't much higher than at the pub. At work, the decent men are either taken, gay, or hopeless. Via your friends, you don't fare much better—they've probably already had a go at any viable candidate and found him wanting. As for night classes, the few single fellows you'll find there are more of the white hair and dentures crowd.

You can always try those can't-fail strategies that dating experts have been promoting since the beginning of time. Like going to the frozen-foods section of the supermarket and keeping an eye out for the half-starved cute guy who's befuddled by all the frozen pizza choices. You know you're just the girl to advise him. But could you go for someone who gets confused so easily?

Those same relationship pros—or the storylines in romantic comedies—tell us the best place to meet a man is where he'll be feeling wistful and yearning for romance. Like a wedding. (Just make sure it's not his). There's the romantic ambience, and that *Four Weddings and a Funeral* mystique—but it's also terribly clichéd. Plus everyone's just as pissed as they are in a pub, and almost always paired up besides.

How about a wake? Any guy at a wake is sure to be full of longing and melancholy, most open to your womanly wiles. However, it's a state likely more inspired by the drink in him rather than you. In any event, would you really want a guy who's on the make next to a dead body?

There's always the option of meeting a guy online. What's not to like? You know he's ready for passion, or he'd have found something better to do than clicking personal ads. You can seek Mr. Dreamy in the comfort of your own home, in your dressing gown, with a packet of Tayto crisps at your elbow. The one inconvenient bit is that eventually, you'll have to venture out into the Real World and meet face-to-face. In which case all that sitting at the computer and those Taytos will have expanded your bum, causing you to avoid any possibilities of having it off with a man, Dream or otherwise. Count the Internet as a wash too.

So, what's a girl to do?

Like me, you may have concluded there is no best place—unless that place is actually a state of mind. So where can you find a great bloke, and at his most peaceful and receptive? My money's on a spot the experts never thought of: a cemetery. You can almost guarantee that anyone hanging round his loved one's grave has his heart in the right place. And unlike the pub or a wake, drink is unavailable. While you might not be perfectly sober—since you needed a stiff one before you ventured to such a creepy place—odds are, the guy is.

So there you have it: all you want is your man's true wistful and vulnerable state out in full force, so he's a veritable sitting duck for your charms...

Six

She's a vampire, that's what she is, I seethed, clumping up the footpath to our flat that night. *Mam thrives as long as she can suck the lifeblood out of everyone around her.*

During the interminable bus trip home, steam practically blowing out of every pore, I'd one consolation. Justine would have a dish of soothing carbs for me, and would let me watch whatever I wanted on telly, *and* listen to me vent about my horrible day.

Although the visit hadn't been an unmitigated disaster. Rory and I had managed to make up, after a fashion—once I remembered it was Mam I was angry with, not her. "Has Darren been up to his usual tricks?" I'd made myself ask her as we were leaving.

Her face averted, Rory looked ready to take off in a huff without answering. Then she sighed and turned toward me. "It's been a rotten week," she confessed. "Brenny's been having some trouble in school, and I thought Darren and I should meet with his teacher. But as usual, just when he's needed, he's not returning my phone calls."

"Bastard," I said in sympathy.

"Then I saw a new photo on his Facebook page, and it's clear why he's too bloody busy—he's panting after some new girl, while he's still 'in a relationship.'"

"Faithless bastard," I said. "Who actually cheats on his girl-friends!" I refrained from pointing out to that there were two easy solutions to her problems. If you wouldn't count on your eejit ex to be a proper father, you wouldn't be disappointed. And if you'd unfriend him on Facebook, you wouldn't have to see the evidence of his perfidy. "No wonder you're out of sorts."

"I'm used to Darren letting us all down by now," she said, locking the door behind us. Though if that were true she wouldn't have mentioned it. "Really, I can handle it if I don't have to worry about Mam too."

Ignoring that last ploy to remind me of my duty, I pulled out my mobile, to give Justine a heads-up on this altogether laughable family demand while I waited for the bus. "You've forgotten?" Rory said on the way to her car. "There's no mobile signal in Ballydara— or round the whole area. Except for one tiny spot somewhere over there." She waved toward the small line of shops.

"You're joking," I said.

"Would I joke about that, with no way to text the kids' minder when I'm here?"

Hundreds of cellular satellites circling Planet Earth, and not a bloody one of them could beam down a signal to this godforsaken village? I jammed the mobile back into my bag in disgust. So I was meant to be stuck here with Mam the Vampire sucking me dry, and no way to get some private pep talks or comfort from my best friend for an entire summer? I'll say it again. No Fecking Way.

"You'll never believe what my wacko family's come up with now." Bursting into our flat, I found Justine exactly as I'd hoped: lolling on the couch, a fettuccine-laden plate on her lap, another sure-to-be full pot of pasta on the coffee table. "Mam's gone completely bats!"

Her mouth full, Justine gave her head a tiny shake.

"It's true!" I wrestled my fleece jacket off and slung it onto a hook on the wall. "And Rory's enabling her—the pair of them are living in a fantasy world! Even worse than the one in yesterday's wed—"

"Cool it, will you?" Justine said.

I shifted my gaze to the corner of the room. There, half-hidden by our ficus plant, was a man, sprawled in our armchair.

"Your mam's gone mad, you say?" said Nate, Justine's brother. "I'll lay odds that these days, your worst day is still better than my best."

"Nate," I said weakly, and swallowed the ire I'd been storing up all day. Not easy, since I felt rather like a python trying to choke down a big juicy rodent. "What a...lovely surprise."

Actually, it was. Although Nate had an unfortunate tendency for practical jokes, I'd sort of adopted him as a surrogate elder brother. He was all I had, since adopting my two brothers-in-law had never entered my head. As we've established, Rory's ex is a proper gobshite, and as for Mary Alice's husband, anyone eejit enough to be married to her is no one I want to know.

I took a deep breath and leaned down to kiss his cheek. "What's a happily married man like you doing here on a Saturday night?"

"Just checking on my little sis," Nate said. "Mam got the idea Justine's job is getting dodgy and she wanted me to—"

"He's shamming," Justine said, picking at her pasta. "Aine left for Cork two days early, and he needed a proper meal."

Letting Mam's B&B insanity lie for now, I plopped onto the couch next to her. "A longer holiday than she planned?"

"She wanted to spend some time with her mam and sisters, since it'll be her last visit before the baby comes," said Nate.

As Rafe Byrne's closest friend, Nate was meant to have attended yesterday's wedding. But of course he couldn't go on a trip, on account of his wife's due date a fortnight away. Then *she* had up and left herself.

"Great idea—no nappies and carriers and things to lug around yet." I said brightly, remembering my sister Mary Alice's news. My stomach growled. Apparently an entire day of frustration had metabolized Mam's curry lunch in double-quick time. "Her family will want to give her one last round of childbirth horror stories before she goes into labor."

"Something like that." Nate squirmed in the chair.

"And if I know Aine, she'll force you to listen as she shares every last detail," I added. Not for nothing does the name *Aine* sound a lot like *Own-ya*. "Now where's my pasta?" I reached for the pot lid.

"I finished the lot," Nate said, looking a bit shamefaced. "Been living on crisps since my wife left."

As my face fell, Justine picked up her half-filled plate and thrust it at me. "You're welcome to mine."

I fell on the pasta with enthusiasm, not bothering to get a clean fork. As the infusion of carbs helped clear my head, I felt a definite narky vibe in the room. "What's up with you two?"

"I just found out why Justine's sitting home on a Saturday night," Nate said. "That bollocks Frank Kenny hasn't been in touch for over a week." He arranged his long legs over the chair arm. "So I told her, time to dump him."

"Good man," I said. "I've been telling her she deserves a proper boyfriend."

"Frank's all right," Justine said, sounding defensive. "He's working extra hours at the restaurant. And just because he doesn't ring—"

"Means you're missing out on the opportunity to treat him like shite," I said. "Then he'd probably come panting after you."

"I'm not up for playing games with guys," Justine sniffed. She picked up her mobile and waved it at me. "I've just read the new *Girl Talk* post—even a cute girl like Gai admits it's hard to find a new bloke."

Nate straightened up "How do you know she's cute?"

"For all you know, she could be a real hag," I added.

"Okay, there's no photo, but I can tell, just from the way she talks." Two bright red spots appeared on Justine's cheeks. "And if she's rather homely, I don't care, because I respect her opinions a *lot*. So will the pair of you just shut up?" She set her mobile on the table down a little too hard, and grabbed her new cookery book *Irish Puddings*.

To give the food photos time to work their magic—that is, calm Justine down—I leisurely swirled a forkful of fettuccine. "Too bad you've no opportunity to meet men on exotic, European holidays."

"Rub it in, will you, that you're going to France." Her book forgotten on her lap, Justine got a faraway look on her face. "*Toujours Provence.*"

"So you admit any French bloke's got to be better than Frank," Nate said.

"Justine's not on about the men, but the produce," I told him, laughing. "I'll bet she gets a bigger thrill from an unblemished cabbage, than oul' Frank Kenny."

"It's not fair," Justine complained. "If it were me, I'd be baking a fresh fruit tart every day—and oh, what I could do with French garlic, just picked—"

"I wouldn't want garlic breath, with all those handsome Frenchmen about," I said. "Picture me, will you?" I sat back, folding my arms behind my head. "Nibbling on a baguette at an outdoor bistro, wearing a lovely frock, silk scarf round my throat lifting in the breeze…"

Justine hooted. "Yeah, with your fashion sense, you'd look a mad article—"

"Right, so I'd have to hit the Paris shops first," I said, undeterred. Once in France, though, I'd instantly acquire the Frenchwoman's intuitive knowledge of how to elegantly do up scarves. "Once I get my glam on, though, I can lock romantic gazes with the holiday dreamboat at the next table, then hook up for a night of unforgettable passion."

If I actually did meet a hot guy in Provence, I'm not sure how I'd finesse spontaneous passion and have him tested for sexual diseases, but I'd work that out later.

Justine's giggles dwindled. "I can't believe you'd go for a holiday one-night stand." I took an extra big bite of pasta to avoid answering her. "Not after all those sex studies you were telling Sinead and me about."

"Sex studies?" Nate perked up even more.

"Dial it down, pal." I dug back into my pasta. "I've heard Aine's doctor put her out of commission."

"Until after the baby comes," Nate said morosely. "Seems like forever."

"Please, I don't want to hear about my brother's sex problems," and Justine opened *Irish Puddings*, shielding her face with it.

"Babies grow up fast," I told Nate. "Anyway, a little celibacy won't kill you."

Justine poked her head around her book. "Grainne should know—she's in the same boat."

"I am not!" I hissed.

"Are too! You said you and Joe—"

"Are great," I finished. "Terrific, in fact." I liked to give Nate the impression that I had a fabulous sex life. Just in case he passed it on to Rafe Byrne.

"Oh, Jaysus," Justine muttered and turned a page.

I needn't have bothered to put one over on Nate. He seemed lost in gloom. "It'll be months until we can have it off again."

"Spare us, Nate," Justine said warningly. "Or you're out the door—"

"That's if you have time for sex," I teased him. "In-between nappy-changing and cleaning up baby sick, that is. And if you're not so tired you'd much rather sleep."

"That'll be the day," Nate said. "Meanwhile, any Victoria's Secret catalogues round here?"

"No sense getting worked up so soon," I advised. "From what I hear, after giving birth, the last thing a new mother's interested in is sex. It lasts for months."

"Well, you've really cheered us up now," said Nate, and we all shared a moment of silence—inspired, I'm sure, by our misbegotten sex lives. Nate couldn't have it off, and I didn't want to—not with Joe, anyway. As for Justine, the only one of us getting any, she'd admitted shagging Frank on a very infrequent basis was nothing to write home about.

Better no sex than crap sex, I consoled myself, then Justine set her book aside. "So Nate," she asked, elaborately casual. "What do you hear from...Aunt Bernie?"

Justine's mother's sister led the sort of charmed life that tons of people found fascinating. Not me, you understand, but *tons*. Still, I smiled politely. "Right, what's Bernie up to?"

"In a real tizzy," Nate said. Justine and I didn't blink. Bernadette Byrne got into self-generated dramas regularly—the kind that made my mam seem like the Buddha incarnate. "You know, all that 'Mother of the Groom' shite. So, shall I put the kettle on?"

"I'll do it," I said, although after my carb-loading with Justine's pasta, I lacked the ambition to blink, much less get up. "When's

Bernie's next pilgrimage to the old sod?"

"Next week, isn't it?" asked Justine. "She told Mam she'd come see us right after the wedding, come hell or high water. She's keen to celebrate the baby's birth with us."

I frowned at Justine. "You never mentioned Bernie coming—"

"But now her visit's up in the air," Nate said at the same time. "She thinks she'd better not leave the...situation."

"That doesn't sound like the Bernie Byrne I know," I put in. Once the woman's made up her mind on something—or someone— her decision is set in stone.

"Mam would be crushed if Bernie begged off." Justine looked crestfallen. "After missing the wedding, she's been counting on having a high old time, with Bernie treating her to dinner and the theatre. And so have I," she added glumly. "If Bernie stays in the States, and with you off in France, Grainne, my summer is going to suck."

"Join the club," said Nate, no doubt thinking of the sexless months ahead.

Justine bent to retrieve Nate's plate. "Any news of..." She carefully stacked it on mine. "The other family?"

Knowing exactly who she meant, I took pity on her. "What's Ian doing?" I asked Nate.

Justine threw me a grateful look, as Nate shrugged. "The usual."

I felt Justine's silent prompt. "Like what?" I asked. Some might consider Justine's fancy for Ian Byrne, Rafe's brother, as sort of incestuous, but remember, he was her *step*-cousin.

"Got a new girlfriend, I think," Nate said. "Another supermodel type."

Justine's face took on her usual Ian-induced pensiveness. "And?" I said, fishing for something to give her hope.

"This girl apparently works in New York, some big PR firm—"

"Not the girlfriend—Ian."

"Still in graduate school," Nate said. "Hasn't a pot to piss in, with tuition and all that, and still won't take a cent from Bernie— or can't, I guess, the way her inheritance was made out. Not that it matters, since she's got her hands full with that eejit Rafe."

Hearing Rafe's name, Ian fled my mind entirely. "I must say, 'eejit' and 'Rafe' aren't two words you'll usually find together." Even if he'd been known to follow some…surprising impulses.

"Sensible and conservative, that's Rafe." Justine sighed. Probably wishing her heartthrob Ian had more sense about women himself.

"Not anymore," Nate said, and pushed himself out of the chair. "Bernie swears he's having a full-blown midlife crisis. That's why she's reconsidered her Ireland visit. She says she doesn't dare leave him alone in Seattle."

Bernie could even outdo her sister Helen when it comes to helicopter motherhood. But surely the woman could trust Rafe's bride to look after a grown man—especially on their honeymoon! "Midlife crisis you say? Don't tell me he's tooling round in a red Lamborghini, spending the Byrne fortune on diamonds for Lindy." I studied my fingernails.

"Isn't Rafe rather young for that?" Justine asked.

A man hardly needed a life meltdown to dote on his new wife, I thought, as an unwelcome image came to me. Rafe cozying up with Lindy on their secluded Hawaiian honeymoon, bringing her mai tais in their silk-sheeted bed, sneaking in a shag on a moonlit beach…

Reminded of his all-but-guaranteed golden future with Lindy, the golden girl, I realized discussing your ex's marriage was like heading down a rutted, pot-holed lane in pitch dark. Not the place you'd go voluntarily. "If he's gone off the deep end, Bernie'll have plenty of help from the Lucky Lindy," I said, determined to let go of Rafe, once and for all. "Now, how about we pop in a DVD?"

"Actually she won't," Nate said, heading for the kitchen. "Any pudding round here?"

Justine pushed her cookery book aside. "What do you mean?"

I held my breath, not daring to ask.

"Didn't Mam tell you?" Nate asked over his shoulder. "Lindy's filed for an annulment."

Seven

The first time I met Rafe wasn't quite one of those sexually charged, eyes meeting across a crowded room sort of things, but it was close. I'd recently experienced an initially disconcerting but ultimately rewarding surge in female development, gaining a stone or so in all the right places. My previous incarnation as an underfed waif whose face was all nose, and whose body was all legs (and stick ones at that), changed quite mysteriously. Almost overnight, I blossomed into what I considered potential siren material: my bosom finally trumped my legs (which miraculously, turned almost shapely), my bum became round instead of flat, and my face finally caught up with my nose.

Two days before my fifteenth birthday, I'd escaped from home to attend one of the Egan family parties. Nothing out of the ordinary there—I generally spent more time at Justine's than I did at our house—except I was even more furious with Mam than usual. She and Dad had been invited as well, but they were in the middle of one of their tiffs/major spats/World War III's, so they begged off.

Justine and I were charged with looking after the kiddies. So as not to scare anyone, I toned down my usual thick black eyeliner and deep maroon lipstick, adopted to get a rise out of Mam but had never succeeded. I was happy enough to be on nursery-duty, as I'd discovered my knack for child-minding was a great way to get a bit of respect—often in short supply for me at home. Soon after I arrived, Justine and I rounded up a small gang of Egan relations, and settled them round me for a story.

"There was once a wild Irish princess," I recited, to a gratifyingly spellbound audience.

"Who? Who?"

"Actually, she was a real-life pirate queen, Grace O'Malley." I tossed my long hair over my shoulder—I'd never really liked my unruly mane, but now, it came to me that it was sort of pirate-ish. "In English, she was called 'Grace' or 'Grania,' but in the Irish, she was called Grainne Ni Mhaille, leader of the sea-faring O'Malley's, up in the West."

A little girl raised her hand. "You're called Grainne too, aren't you?"

"I am." Really, it was much more fun telling this story than listening to Mam rabbit on about how she named her daughter after a legend.

"And do you know what the name 'Grainne' means?" Justine asked the group. They all shook their heads. "It means, 'she who inspires *terror*.'" The kids' eyes rounded as they looked back at me.

"Thanks," I muttered. "But you're not meant to scare the shite out of the poor things."

"I thought it would be a great way to get them to be good," Justine whispered back.

"Back to the story," I said to the kids. "Grainne the pirate was a tough one, all right. She was sailing the seas as a little girl, and she could hunt and fight with the best of them—"

"And she killed all the bloody English she came across," inserted a little boy wearing a vaguely satanic expression. "And the fookin' Spanish too."

"No swearing!" Justine hissed at him. She gave me a desperate look. "Tell them another story!"

I cast a sidelong glance at the clutch of parents nearby, just to make sure the mini-Satan's transgression hadn't registered, and found a young man I hadn't seen before staring at me. Or rather, at my breasts.

To my untrained eye—I was still a neophyte as far as sizing up blokes—this young man had to be at least twenty, with looks, presence, and a certain *Je ne sais quoi*. He'd a smooth, choirboy complexion and long-lashed eyes, which contrasted entirely with his craggy nose (thrice-broken, I'd discovered later). *And* he was much taller than I was. Tall enough, even, to stay taller, if fate was unkind and I kept growing (I did). His manly physique fed my romantic fantasies of having a guy who actually had the wherewithal to lift me into his arms, should we make it all the way to the altar and over the threshold.

Anyway, my boobs were still novelty enough, and I was still eejit enough, to be flattered by his stare. I caught his eye, smiling. He actually blushed, then melted into the crowd.

Needless to say, my story-telling abilities were shagged. Unnerved and excited by my first quasi-romantic experience, I looked round the circle of little faces and thought, *how about a romance.* "I've a new story—this one's about *another* Grainne."

"You?" asked the little girl, who still looked a bit bug-eyed.

"No, the goddess from Celtic mythology," I said, feeling like a goddess myself all of a sudden. "This Grainne had her share of adventures. With not one, but two magical guys fighting over her."

In my favorite version of the story, Grainne the Goddess, I told the kids, was forced into an engagement with a powerful, older god-bloke Finn McCool. Then she met a real hottie, the young and virile Dermot (or Diarmid, take your pick). As if she hadn't troubles enough, Finn threw Dermot a challenge: if he wanted to win Grainne for himself, he had to hunt down a wild boar. "The nerve of that Finn!" I pointed out. "Girls should get to choose what they do with their lives—"

Just then, Helen Egan set out a table of treats. Diverted—and probably bored by my feminist manifesto—the kids jumped up and stampeded for the food. I managed to swipe a handful of biscuits, then wandered away to the Egan's deserted parlor, unused except for wakes and Christmas. Seating myself at the piano bench, I set the biscuits in my lap. Despite my tin ear, I attempted to plunk out "Lanigan's Ball."

"So, Dermot killed the wild boar and they lived happily ever after?" Young. Male. American accent. Right behind me.

I whirled around, biscuits flying off my lap. There *he* was. The crooked-nose choirboy. Mortified that I'd strewn Helen's good rug with crumbs, I'd a near-instant recovery as I realized he'd been interested enough in the story to secretly listen in. "Hardly," I said with a boldness I hadn't known I possessed. "The boar nailed him, and your man Finn let poor Dermot die of his wounds."

"No kidding," he said, with what I could swear was an approving gaze.

"Sad, I know." His admiration making me braver, I reached behind me, pulling the piano cover down, then leaned back against it. "I generally let kids think the mythological Grainne spent the rest of her days longing for her lost love, but that's not how it works in real life, does it?"

"How *does* it work?" His eyes gleamed.

"Why, that life goes on." I crossed my legs, feeling quite the sophisticate. "And a girl can do perfectly fine without some man mucking up her life."

"Whoa," he said. "And what about the girl pirate? The first story?"

"It's true, actually." I held my breath as he approached the piano, then he actually sat next to me. Not so close as to be cheeky, but not on the edge either. "Grainne lived a life of adventure, back in the 1500s," I went on. "She even met Queen Elizabeth the First. And along the way," I added daringly, "she'd scores of lovers and devastated them all."

Incredible. I was channeling like, a Bond Girl. Or I was Scarlett O'Hara, bewitching the Tarleton twins.

He blushed again, then laughed. "Fighting words. What about you?"

"Well, I haven't killed any bloody English or Spanish yet, but the night is young," I said, feeling heat spread over my entire body.

"Then you inspire terror too...Grainne?"

Hearing him say my name made me dizzy. "Only when I'm crossed," I managed, then gave him a sidelong look from beneath my lashes.

"Crossed," he repeated, then he stared into the middle distance for a moment. I didn't like losing his attention, so I pulled my angora jumper a little tighter over my breasts—which did the trick. He snapped out of his reverie. "I'm Rafe Byrne, by the way."

"Oh," I sort of breathed. So this was *the* Rafe Byrne, the rich

American cousin Nate had been visiting all these years. Justine had never mentioned he'd the kind of thick hair your fingers could get lost in, or that his long black lashes made his eyes seem electric blue...They rather clashed with my mustard-colored ones, so who knew what color our future children's eyes would be, but...

I mentally shook myself. "Rafe, for Raphael, is it? Like the archangel?" Raphael definitely suited his angelic skin.

"I wish." He hesitated.

"Then what are you really called?"

"If I tell you, promise not to laugh."

"Okay," I said.

"Well...my name's, uh...Rufus."

I couldn't help giggling. "You're serious?"

"You said you wouldn't laugh!" But humor flashed in his eyes, like blue lightning.

"Yeah...well." I shrugged. "I'm no saint."

"Then..." and Rafe's high-voltage eyes were quite thrillingly fixed on me, "what are you?"

To be truthful, at fifteen, I'd no idea. "We were talking about you," I said with sudden inspiration. "So, then, who came up with 'Rufus?'"

"My grandfather," he said moodily. "And in my family, what Granddad wants, Granddad gets."

The Byrne branch was markedly different from the Egan crew, where traditionally, the women wear the trousers. "Why aren't you called 'Rufe,' then?"

"I think it's a dog's name."

"Too right." I giggled again. "You'd not want people snapping their fingers at you, trying to make you heel."

"They'll try," he went on darkly. "Though I'm already in the family doghouse."

I somehow got him to elaborate, don't ask me how. So amazed was I at my own aplomb, and at my subtle, yet previously unsuspected conversational skills, I nearly lost my powers of speech. But I was enjoying myself too much.

Rafe explained he'd come to Ireland for a break, since he'd just finished his university degree, in business and philosophy. "Although it took five years," he confessed.

So then—handsome, brainy, and well into his twenties! "No sense rushing the important things in life," I told him.

"The two extra years didn't go over too well with my family," Rafe said, "but being on the golf team took a lot of time. What's your major?"

Jaysus! He thought I was in college! "I'm into...journalism," I said. Which was sort of true, as I'd acres of journals in my closet. Rants about how I resented Mam, plus how much I hated my nose and Mary Alice, with a soupçon of despair about my flat chest. Which of course I wasn't writing about anymore. "At UCD," I added for believability. The secret of successful lying, I'd always heard, is providing good details.

"You're lucky." His grandfather apparently wanted him to buckle down and join the family business. "I don't mind working, but can't stand being shut up in a stuffy office all day. Besides, I want to play golf for a while," he said, and stuck out his chin. "What's wrong with that?"

"Nothing, if you're good," I said. "Though there's no sense wasting everyone's time if you're a duffer, says my dad."

"I'm pretty serious about it," he said. "My grandfather took me golfing as soon as I could lift a putter—said the game would come in handy when I was running the company. But if you ask me, making deals on the course and rubbing shoulders with hotshot CEOs is a waste of time."

I'd never understood pursuing the utterly useless goal of pushing a ball into a hole using horribly expensive sticks, but if Rafe did, I was all for it. "Then why keep playing?" I asked.

"I've been winning a few uh, amateur tournaments," Rafe said, and sort of blushed. "Or finishing in the top five."

"Tournaments, huh? Like...what?"

"The U.S. Amateur Championship." He scuffed a well-shod toe into Helen Egan's carpet.

It sounded like, really important. "Great," I said, trying not to show how impressed I was.

"It's a pretty big deal. I might try to get on the tour."

"Tour?"

"The PGA. You know. Go professional."

Jesus, Mary, and Holy St. Joe. I was in the presence of not just a fabulous guy, but greatness. "What does your dad think?" I rather liked this new role I'd discovered: Bosom Friend/Mother Confessor/Potential Girlfriend for Life.

"He doesn't," Rafe said, sounding rebellious. "He says and does exactly what my grandfather wants him to."

Not exactly a rebel's role model. "What about your stepmam?" I imagined all stepmothers to be pretty horrid, like Cinderella's.

"Bernie? She's great," Rafe said, surprising me. "But where money's concerned, she sticks to the family line."

"Well, you look old enough to be your own man," I said, then could've kicked myself. What if he asks *my* age? I felt a quiver of dread, then told myself Scarlett O'Hara would know how to put him off, wouldn't she? So I could too. "My advice is, do what you want."

"Anything I want, huh?"

"*Everything* you want," I emphasized. "Be free."

"You know, I think I will," Rafe said. Just then, Nate yelled for Rafe from the kitchen. If Justine's bloody brother found me sitting this close to with Rafe, there'd be no end to his merciless teasing, so I slid off the piano bench.

Rafe jumped up, then he knelt to pick up the biscuits, still fairly intact. *Double wow*, I thought. *Chivalrous too.* He rose to his feet, brushed off one of the biscuits, and took a bite. "You don't mind sharing?"

Not with you. "Be my guest," I said, and we strolled toward the door. A shame our idyll was ending. But I was still too exhilarated at the success of my first real conversation with an eligible male to let it get me down. Plus, I was suddenly convinced Rafe was my soul mate. So meeting him again was in the stars.

Rafe bit into a second biscuit. I liked that he wasn't overly fastidious, which could have a lot to do with his willingness to spend time with me. But I wasn't one to question an interlude that seemed at least as miraculous as the sighting of the Virgin at Knock, in County Mayo. Then he offered me the other half.

"As you can see, I steal cookies," he said. "You being named after a pirate—what kind of booty do you go after?"

"Whatever I want," I said, and we stopped in the doorway. As I looked up at him, I saw a desiccated bit of mistletoe that Justine's mam, not the best housekeeper in the world, had left on the lintel from last Christmas. "*Everything* I want," I said. I squeezed my eyes tightly for a second, daring myself. *Do it! Do it!*

I did it. "Happy Freedom," I said, and reached up and kissed him on the cheek.

Sure, kissing Rafe had been a mad impulse.

But I couldn't regret it—although the kiss, which I'd aimed thrillingly close to his mouth, hadn't appeared to go over well. Rafe had blushed yet again, then backed away. *What's your problem*, I wished I'd the courage to say. *You're a prude?*

Or, *I've more cooties than the carpet?*

Or, *too much garlic in Justine's mushroom canapés?*

However, life took a much better turn later that evening, when Rafe found me in the kitchen, helping Justine with the washing up. "Are we related?" he asked, point-blank.

Out of the corner of my eye, I saw Justine's head swing round, but I didn't care if she, or anyone, for that matter, heard me. "Only if you count...em, kissing cousins," I said, feeling a new and delicious triumph. "Isn't that what you call them in America?" Seeing Justine's back stiffen, I hastily added, "Justine's like my...*baby* sister, but there's no blood relation, really."

"Good," he said, grinning back at me. "Nate and I are going to the pub tomorrow night. Want to come out for a pint?"

Justine's eyes widened, with mixed shock and admiration. I stared back at her, daring her to interfere, then looked back at Rafe.

"Only if Justine's invited too."

So the next evening turned out to be one of those watershed moments. You know, when your life both ends and really begins. It's not what you're thinking...I didn't lose my virginity. Rafe hadn't tried anything physical, in fact. But we talked like we'd known— and been mad about—each other forever. So there it was: my first date (sort of), my first kiss (well, almost), and my first pint. Pints, rather.

It was the pints that led to my Year Fifteen birthday meltdown. I like to think I was entirely blameless for over-imbibing, since Nate didn't let on that I was underage, and he'd sneaked drinks to me with almost no encouragement. Naturally—as I was never one for half-measures—I'd gotten royally pissed.

It wouldn't have been so bad, except that the gig was up as soon as the lads dropped me off. Trying to stifle my convulsive giggles, I'd reveled in Rafe's supporting arm as he escorted me to the door. Amazingly, he'd leaned in close—then the door flew open and there was Dad, looking like the wrath of God.

"What's going on here?" he roared, as I was caught in another fit of giggles. Then he fixed a piercing stare on Rafe. "Young man, she's only fifteen!"

I abruptly stopped laughing, seeing the gobstruck look on Rafe's face. "Sir! I'm really sorry! I didn't know she was...Jesus Christ—I mean, I'm sorry—it'll never happen again!" Then he rushed off without a good-bye. As for me, a tidal wave of nausea hit me the minute I crossed the threshold.

Any lingering romantic daydreams instantly evaporated. All I could do was hang over the loo and expel what felt like my entire insides until the sun came up.

Eight

After that night, I'd gone off pints. Forever. And you'd think the experience would have had a similar effect on my feelings for Rafe. *Au contraire.* I became quite unfortunately, and apparently permanently, fixated on him.

Now, fifteen years later I stared at Nate's retreating back, as the word *annulment* still vibrated through the room.

Rafe was free! For one mad, intoxicating moment, I felt shooting stars explode in my chest, rushing to the top of my head. Unable to speak, I crossed my arms, trying to keep myself still lest I leap to my feet for an exuberant Tom Cruise couch stomp.

It's a good job Justine spoke up before I could move. "Annulment?" she squealed.

"That's it," Nate called from the kitchen, filling the kettle. "By the way, if you've no pudding, how about some biscuits?"

"Will you forget about food for just one minute?" Justine relaxed against the cushions. "Get back out here and tell us what happened!"

"Turns out, Lindy's dumping him," Nate said from the doorway. I tried to show a detached interest, as he talked about misunderstandings about the pre-nup and the money Rafe was funneling to the Byrne Foundation—details that somehow came out just as the wedding reception was winding down. "Mam said Lindy felt grossly misled about Rafe's inheritance, and told him so, then and there." Nate explained. "Apparently the state law doesn't allow for an annulment per se, but you can get the marriage declared invalid. That's what Lindy's going to do."

So Rafe wasn't married—or soon, he wouldn't be! The fact that Lindy had given Rafe the heave-ho before the marriage was consummated was icing on the cake.

"How's Bernie taking the new development?" Justine asked.

Hearing Bernie's name, I felt those lovely meteors inside me start receding. I didn't want to hear about Bernie, I wanted to know about Rafe!

"Not good," Nate said, settling back in the armchair. "Mam's been on the line with her for hours, planning strategy."

All my sparks fell to earth and winked out. "Bernie's going to talk Lindy out of it, isn't she." I crossed my arms tighter, to keep my misery inside.

"She'll bloody well try," Nate replied. He returned to the kitchen as the kettle boiled, and Justine switched on the DVD player.

Despite my overwhelming urge to drill Nate for any last shred of information regarding the Rafe-Lindy breakup, I kept my lips zipped. Quite a trick really, since I munched furiously through the biscuits Justine rustled up, while we watched *Downton Abbey*. Actually, it was Justine and Nate watching, and me pretending to— the state I was in, I couldn't even get pulled into all the star-crossed love affairs going on that ordinarily would keep me spellbound.

I told myself that Rafe being unattached again meant nothing. Zilch. Okay, so we sort of had a past. But it had ended years ago. Badly. And while people get back together every day, the inescapable truth was, there was Bernie.

Bernie Byrne, who was determined to keep the lovebirds wedded. And if Rafe's stepmam failed in her mission? Well, she was certain to plant another equally beautiful and well-connected heiress in Rafe's path. If there was one thing I'd discovered about people with money—it was that they were all for intermarrying. Especially Bernie, who was keen on squeezing a dollar or a euro until it screamed for mercy. Just because *she* had been a middle-class girl who'd married into money, doesn't mean she thought anyone else should be able to.

So, full of pasta and biscuits and misery, and working overtime to convince myself that Rafe was so yesterday, so last year... well, so five years ago, I mercilessly squished that tiny leap of hope inside me. And concentrated on the serve-him-right satisfaction that Rafe's life was looking a bit fecked.

"Why didn't you tell me before, about Bernie coming home this month?" I finally asked Justine, as we settled in at O'Fagan's Monday evening.

After brooding non-stop since Saturday night, about all the rich and gorgeous real-life Barbie dolls willing to be the mothers of Bernie's grandchildren, I was a mess. At work earlier, I'd raided the Gallagher's cupboards for every sweet thing I could get my hands on. In fact, I'd got so wound up on sugar I got rather addled—I tried to put Anna's princess knickers on Geoff, and stuck Ivy's bottle in her sister's mouth.

"She's not exactly one of your favorite people," Justine said.

I swigged my mineral water. After inhaling all that sugar at the Gallagher's, I'd even gone off lemonade. "More like, I'm not one of hers." But I'd a more important bone to pick. "Don't you think it's strange your mam didn't tell you about the annulment straight away?"

"Mam said she hadn't wanted to say anything, until all the information was in."

"Bollocks," I said. "She told Nate, didn't she? If I know Bernie, she talked your mam into keeping you in the dark about Rafe's split as long as possible, because she didn't want me to find out about it."

"That seems a bit far-fetched," Justine said, but her face went pink.

Which was all the confirmation I needed. "I can just see what Bernie was about—she was afraid that if I knew Rafe was free, I'd jump on the first flight out to America to get my hooks into him."

"Honestly, Grainne, you've some imagination," Justine said. "As for Nate being the only one in on it, you know Bernie's always been keener on the boys of the family. Now, what do you say to some darts?"

"Nice try," I told her.

Justine only rolled her eyes, then opened her handbag and dug out a small paperback, *Warming Herbs and Spices*.

Feck Saturday night's pessimism. I really, *really* wanted to believe reconnecting with Rafe was within the realm of possibility. Hadn't he been terribly keen on me before Lindy came along? Didn't that mean anything?

Actually, no, echoed in my mind. *If Rafe had really wanted to see you again over the past few years, he would've done it by now.*

Gripped by a savage urge to throw something after all, I was ready to lunge for the dartboard—until a nearby foursome burst into U2's "Still Haven't Found What I'm Looking For." *Don't you know that sort of crack is verboten at O'Fagan's?* I thought, glaring at them, as the real truth of the matter hit me. The way Rafe feels about family duty, especially how he dotes on Bernie, means he'd never do something as mad as look me up—A shadow suddenly loomed over us.

Actually it was no shadow, but a man. "I thought I'd find you here," said Joe Corrigan.

THE GALLAGHER POST

Gai Lannigan's Girl Talk

Do You Think I'm Fat?

If you think that *the* life-defining question in a heterosexual relationship is "Will you marry me?" you couldn't be more wrong. It's "Do You Think I'm Fat?"

This is, of course, a trick question—more on that later—but one that nearly every girl asks, no matter what her body type. (You lot with more self-control than the rest of us, who've never let "Do You Think I'm Fat?" pass your lips... well, we know you've still *thought* it.) Say you're slim to average—meaning, you carry a stone or four more than your average supermodel. It's completely normal to worry about the perfectly natural curve of your tummy or some pesky cellulite on your thighs, so you've asked "DYTIF?"

Or maybe you've been a bit Ruebenesque all your life. You're used to your family's subtle reminders about your imperfections. From your parents: "Only one piece of trifle for you, miss." Relatives: "You'll want to get rid of this (pinching your waist), else you'll never have a boyfriend." Or from siblings: the nicely understated, "Fattie." All of whom feel it's perfectly proper to comment on your body, since it's for your own good. So you couldn't help but ask The DYTIF Question too.

And what if you're in the third category: previously skinny, then a sudden metabolism change? After a few blissful decades of packing food away like a stevedore, and people saying, *you know, you could use a bit of weight here and there*, you look in the mirror one day and get the shock of your life. So any advice about your newly acquired pounds (however soft-pedaled) takes you by surprise, as you've been spending several hours a day obsessing about your bum and wondering how it got so big. You're *especially* vulnerable to asking the DYTIF Question.

And why, you may ask, is the Question life-defining? Well, it invariably arises at predictable situations—all involving sex, of course—that every girl can identify with. Like right after you and a guy have had your first shag. In the moment of faux-intimacy, you mean to say, *That was great,* but an involuntary *Do you think I'm fat?* pops out of your mouth. Secretly appalled, you quickly giggle, *just kidding* before he can say anything.

Or, when you feel your relationship curdling. Your fella only calls round when he feels like sex, and you know it's time to give him the heave-ho. Still, you go ahead and have it off with him, knowing he'll roll out of bed as soon as it's over. But instead of showing him the door, you snarl, *So, do you think I'm fat?* When he gives the wrong answer—"well, yeah," or a cagey but just as incriminating, "Does it matter what I think?"—you're ready to either fling the alarm clock at his head or crawl under the bed.

There's one circumstance, though, that's more complicated than all the rest. There's a special guy you're ready to trust, so after you've both had a lovely time in bed, you ask a tentative yet hopeful *Do you think I'm fat?* Of course, you feel like a complete eejit, and wished you'd been struck dumb first. But when he says earnestly, "I think you're beautiful," you think you can put your doubts about the relationship at rest. Emphasis on "you *think*."

Yes, you've put this narky, loaded question to them all: the men who loved you, the men you thought loved you, the men who love you and you wished they wouldn't, or the men who only want to get into your knickers. So why is this question a trick one? First, no girl really wants to hear the answer. And second, why are we asking someone else something we can answer on our own?

So when the inevitable DYTIF pops out, instead of feeling embarrassed, try this on for size: own your feelings! All you want is complete and total acceptance for who you are and what you look like. Too bad you haven't yet discovered the Shan-gri-la that lets you be you...

Nine

"Pass the spuds, Grainne?" asked Billy Corrigan.

Catching Joe's encouraging smile, I released my death grip on my fork, and reached for the platter. "Here you are," I said, then resumed swishing my food round my plate.

Billy piled what should be an unlawful amount of potatoes on his, then took a gigantic bite, his jaws working like an earth-moving machine.

There's nothing like dining *en famille* to put the kibosh on being propositioned. Since I was no closer to deciding if I should go to bed with Joe, I found myself knee-high in over-boiled potatoes and desiccated ham at the Corrigan supper table the day before my birthday.

I'd apparently been unofficially elected substitute mammy, since Mr. Corrigan kept planting the serving dishes in front of me, and the boys would look straight at me when their plates needed refilling. I was kept busy passing food round all through supper, and barely got in a mouthful. Luckily.

"You're not eating much, Grainne," observed Billy. "A slurp of tea'll help get that ham down the hatch."

"Thanks." I took a sip from my cracked teacup and tried not to grimace. I'd no sugar in my tea, due to the fact that the sugar bowl had several specks in it that looked suspiciously like ants.

"You're okay?" Joe, sitting next to Billy, looked concerned. Joe patted his jacket pocket, and I wondered if he'd some antacids stashed there. "You've not gone off your food, have you?"

Joe's four brothers and Joe Senior stopped chewing, and swiveled their heads in my direction. "Not at all." I tried to make myself take a second bite of potato, but couldn't, so I pushed it to the other side of my plate. "Had a big lunch." I smiled round the table. "Huge."

"That reminds me," Billy said with his mouth full. "Read an interesting bit on my lunch break."

"You?" hooted his younger brother (Mikey, I think). "Since when do you read?"

Mr. Corrigan roused enough to answer, "Billy never misses the hurling scores," then shoved another forkful of ham in his mouth.

"That's right," Billy said with injured dignity. "Actually, one of me work mates showed me this bit on his mobile, that his wife had e-mailed him. About girls always thinking they're fat. You don't think you're fat, do you, Grainne?"

"Eejit!" Joe elbowed Billy so hard the poor fella almost fell out of his chair.

"Feckit!" Billy rubbed his injured ribs. "What'd you do that for?"

"You don't ask girls that, you thick!" Joe retorted, as Mikey and the two other brothers leaned forward. With girls being in short supply round the Corrigan house, I'm sure they were keen to pick up a few pointers.

"Why not?" asked Billy, tucking back into his spuds. "The girl who wrote it—Gayle something—says girls are always asking their fellas if they're fat. But the fact is, they don't *really* want to know."

"Well, I've always liked a girl with a bit of meat on her bones," Joe said, dispatching a giant piece of ham. Then he winked at me.

I pretended not to notice, in case Joe thought a supportive wink for my un-skinny state might lead to a shag anytime soon. He patted his pocket again—a nervous tic, perhaps?

"Me too," said Billy. "Richie, down at work, well, his wife is sort of chubs, but you should see the size of their boy! He'll make a proper footballer."

"What's this girl look like?" asked Mikey.

"I've no clue," Billy said sadly. "There's no photo of her on the blog."

Joe Sr. bestirred himself again, enough to pronounce, "No way of knowing, if she's fa—"

"Dad!" Joe broke in, and Mr. Corrigan sank back in his chair, resuming his Sphinx-like pose. I suspected the slugs of Jameson's I'd seen him take before dinner had something to do with it.

In the Corrigan brothers' flurry of conjecture about if Gayle what's-her-name was a real looker, and if so, how to meet her, I met

Joe's eyes. By tacit agreement, we rose from the table and backed toward the front room. "We can make coffee, but I don't think Dad's got any pudding," Joe whispered.

"That's all right," I said. Joe Sr.'s puddings were probably just as bad as his potatoes. But inspired by hunger and a powerful reluctance to enter the kitchen, lest I wind up playing mammy again and get stuck with the washing up (if such a thing did go on in that house), I stepped closer to the door. "Any chance we can go out for something sweet?"

You might wonder, after a meal like this, why I left Joe in the Possible Contender side of the ledger. While Joe's long-term, single-minded and apparently unshakable attachment to me made him a guy with real potential, I was also sure that if we did become an item, I could talk him out of sharing holidays with his family.

The thing was, aside from Joe's personal worthiness, I *really* needed a boyfriend. Rory had rung me five times since Mam had dropped her B&B bombshell, asking for an exact date for moving in. What better way to get out of Mam's project than embarking on an intense love affair, upon which my entire future depended? Okay, one could hardly associate *intense* with Joe, since his pillow talk—judging from his non-pillow talk—was likely to center around his restaurant's profit and loss statements. But the fact remained: I would commit any number of crimes of passion to get out of indentured servitude Chez Larkin.

Joe and I were ready to leave when Billy waylaid us at the door. "If the pair of you make it legal," he said, his face flushed, "Dad says he'd move out of the big bedroom for you."

If memory served, Joe Sr.'s room shared a wall with Billy and Mikey's. Shuddering, I grabbed Joe's hand before he could cuff his brother, and scuttled outside before I cuffed Billy myself.

Naturally, Joe and I ended up at his restaurant, "Corrigan's Café & Takeaway." He'd fitted it up in a 1950s diner theme he'd seen in a restaurant magazine, with padded red-upholstered booths, shiny metal fixtures, and black-and-white checked flooring. He'd told me a half dozen times how he'd checked out the menus at fifty restaurants to get his pricing just right, while complaining about how much his market testing had cost him, ordering food he could've eaten at Corrigan's for nothing. And how he'd gone all out to make the place inviting—forcing the staff to polish all that chrome three times a day, according to Sinead. "Don't you know, customers who order in, instead of takeaway, run up a bigger bill." Well, duh.

Tonight, though, Joe seemed more attentive than usual, making me wonder if grabbing his hand had given him some unrealistic expectations. Especially once we arrived, and Joe pointed me out to his regulars. "Here's my girlfriend, Grainne."

I smiled weakly and waved back, blinking against unnatural shininess of the place. I was struck, as usual, that Joe could live amongst filth at home, yet keep his restaurant so spotless. Joe no sooner finished his schmoozing and slid into our booth when Sinead catwalked in from the back room and glided up to our table.

I tried not to grimace. "You're working the evening shift, now?"

"Trying to help a certain someone delegate," Sinead said, with a significant look at Joe. "Maybe my longer hours will impress the boss."

"Going for management, are you?" I asked.

Joe slapped the table. "Management! Everyone knows I'll always be hands-on round here."

"If you did let me run a shift or two, you'd have more free time," Sinead wheedled.

"To do what?" he chortled. "Spend my hard-earned money, taking Grainne to the clubs?"

She gave Joe the smarmiest smile I'd ever seen. "That's it, staying in is so boring. Let me give it a go, won't you? Pleeease?"

As Joe shook his head, still laughing, I looked up to see Sinead's beady gaze on me. "What'll you have tonight?"

"Two lattes—and have we any chocolate cake left?" Joe gave me a sidelong smile. His devotion could make me rather uncomfortable—except when he was feeding my sweet tooth.

"I'm sure we do," said Sinead. "You're celebrating Grainne's birthday, then?"

"I knew it was this week," Joe said to me. "Tomorrow?"

"Yeah, the big Three-O," I said before Sinead could.

"Your family's giving you a party?" Before I could answer, she sat on the edge of Joe's side of the booth. "Joe, if you take the whole night off, I could be in charge here, couldn't I? I'm not saying I want a promotion—"

"Em...our lattes?" I broke in. "And could you bring extra sugars?" I know, it was narky to remind Sinead she was meant to serve me. But it was either get rid of her now, or let the pair of them talk shop all evening.

"Ah, sure. Won't be a minute." She slinked into the kitchen.

"I suppose your mam's putting on a big do?" Joe asked. "With *all* your friends?"

Joe's hint could not have been broader. "Not so big," I said. "In fact, very small. Hardly a party at all. You know my mam—not one to make a fuss." Except over herself, of course.

"Actually I don't know her...but I'd like to." Another sidelong smile. "You know, turning thirty deserves a real celebration—I can do a party on for you, right here."

Oh, bollocks. I really *had* encouraged him too much. "Really, I couldn't let you do—"

"We could really put on the Ritz!" Joe rubbed his hands together. "After closing, that is."

"Wouldn't want to affect the trade, would we?" I said lightly.

"Sure, it would be late, but you could bring your Mam and Justine, and Dad and the boys'll come round—"

"Actually, I..." I admit, I was tempted. The thought of derailing Mam's butter-Grainne-up-party plan held a certain appeal. "That's really sweet—"

"Here you are," said Sinead, plunking a coffee and plate of cake in front of me—the smaller of the two pieces, I couldn't help noticing. Then she undulated to Joe's side of the table, and set his food down, standing so close to him I was afraid she would pierce his eardrum with her hipbone. "Anything else?"

"We're fine," Joe said, and absently patted her back as Sinead lingered.

Hmmm, I thought. "I could use just *one* more sugar," I said, whereupon she flounced off.

I'm first to admit I've envy issues: I'm jealous of girls with doting mothers, also of the ones who have a smaller bum than I do. And since food envy has no gender bias, I even get bent out of shape by people getting bigger pieces of chocolate cake than I do.

So it troubled me, that I couldn't feel jealous over Sinead's flirting. No, let's call it what it really is, out-and-out *crawling* over Joe. But I'd no one to blame for it but myself. Hadn't I all but admitted my ambivalence about him on the train last week? And worse, that we weren't having it off?

Since I always thought more clearly with some extra sugar in my system, I grabbed my fork, swirled it through the thick icing, and slid the laden fork into my mouth.

Savoring the cake melting on my tongue, I began demolishing the plateful. As a comforting sugar buzz set in, I considered Joe's party proposition…but not for long. If there was a craic party scale, one with Mam and Rory would rate a three out of ten, while a night with Dad Corrigan and the boys would get a minus seven. "About that party," I ventured, "I don't think—"

"I'll go all out," Joe said, leaning toward me. "In fact, let's not wait until closing—we'll include all the customers. They'll love it."

"Actually, Joe," and I took another bite, "I'm rather a private person—"

"We can have 'em all crowd round when you open your presents," Joe went on, flushing with excitement, and he patted his pocket again. "Just like those sing-along restaurants I've heard about, that are all set up for birthdays and anniversaries!"

"No, Joe." I wasn't at all keen to see my birthday turned into Joe's new marketing tool. "I've promised Mam. But it was a lovely idea," I added, to soften my refusal.

Looking crestfallen, Joe patted his pocket for the gazillionth time, then an expression I can only describe as resolute came over his face. "Then I'll give you my present now," he said, and reached into his pocket.

"Oh, really, you shouldn't have," I said. And meant it. In the past, Joe's gifts had included a coupon good for a free meal here at Corrigan's. And if you can believe it, a frying pan, "big enough to cook a breakfast for two," as he'd put it. My eyes on his pocket, I figured the gift would be something for the pair of us.

Theatre tickets? Too expensive. Passes to visit Dublin's unabashedly phallic Millennium Spire ("Stiffy by the Liffey"), to jump-start a shag? Sure, not even Joe would be that obvious?

So imagine my surprise when he pulled out a small box—and not any small box. A ring box.

THE GALLAGHER POST

Gai Lannigan's Girl Talk

Making Babies: Go Organic or Go Now?

In the old days, babies just happened. You married at the age of sixteen, and had three glorious decades of pregnancy until childbirth finished you off.

But in these modern times, things are altogether different. If you're tired of gazing enviously at other girls' babies or baby bumps wherever you turn, and you're ready for one of your own, you need a strategy. You may ask, what's the matter with getting pregnant the organic, all-natural way? All you have to do is find a nice boy and just let things happen. But hold it right there: Organic is great for food, but we live in a time-pressured world.

First off, you'll want to time the pregnancy just right, with your career and your most fertile years. If you're still in your twenties, and already have a plan, more power to you. But once you've turned thirty, you haven't much time to sort yourself out.

You're ahead of the game if you've already found a man who's ready, willing and able to father your baby. You may think your job is done, time to get on with the baby-making, but choosing the fellow is only the beginning. The real time suck is in all the intermediate steps.

There's getting serious with your guy, moving in—and if you're really into each other, you might want a child-free year or two of hot sex while you're still completely head over heels. Then once you're past all that, and you're ready to bring a third party into your life, there's building a nest egg before you can make so much as a peep about tossing birth control. Some might counsel that you should get married and buy a place first, but if you ask me, that's unnecessary paperwork. So marriage or no, you're looking at a three-to-five year stretch.

Then there's your worry that you're getting too old to be a proper mother. What if your child will be barely into toddlerhood, but you're such an oldster mammy your back hurts every time you lift her, and when she runs into the road, your knees give out before you can chase her down?

Then finally, there's the trying. Ideally, that's the fun part, but also completely unpredictable. Falling pregnant could be one quickie away. On the other hand, you might be having it off constantly for months, or even years with nothing to show for it, and sex has turned into a real slog. Then it's off to the fertility specialists, for exams and expensive injections and invasive procedures, and suddenly the lovely and natural act of starting a family has turned into a living hell.

So whether you've got the right guy, or you haven't even found him yet, you've discovered having a baby could take forever. And you start feeling desperate…enough to have it off with someone you don't care about, or you're even considering a one-night stand. At that point, you've turned into the heroine of a silly romantic comedy film—but all you want is your baby in your arms. Before it's too late…

Ten

It was shortly before my tenth birthday that I concluded marriage was fit only for eejits.

Rory had recently left home for university, and I was feeling rather...abandoned. Whether the extra tension in our family was due to Mam losing her most valued dogsbody, or the menopause hitting her early, her relationship with Dad deteriorated—from tempestuous to downright contentious. Mam would pick a fight over the smallest thing, and pretty soon there would be top-of-the-lungs giving out and slamming doors, then Dad, wearing the look of a Bassett hound, would take himself off to the store for days.

The worst was my realization that he loved her more than she loved him. So, armed with these insights, I chucked those bridal dreams little girls get brainwashed into, and simultaneously tossed the bride doll I'd got from Father Christmas in the bin.

This may sound like an odd justification for the Year Ten birthday mischief I caused. But at the time, all I wanted was for Mam to stop fighting with Dad long enough to notice I was alive.

Perhaps, at my tender age, my swearing off marriage forever was more of a vague notion I'd soon forget. But as I grew up, further observations of dysfunctional coupledom confirmed my worst suspicion: the unequal power—and love—I'd seen between Mam and Dad was the rule, not the exception. So, who would sign up for that sort of aggravation for life? Not this girl.

As Joe clicked the box open and a diamond flashed under the bright restaurant lights, that two decades-old epiphany completely fled my mind. You always hear about people getting a shock while they're eating, and the food turns to sawdust in their mouth. Well, when our man, in one debonair move, the likes of which I'd never suspected Joe capable of, slid the ring onto my finger, the cake in my mouth turned so sickeningly sweet my stomach rolled over and my teeth felt like I'd chomped on a piece of tin foil.

Before I could get my bearings, the staff and customers discovered the big goings on, and crowded round Joe and me. "Lovely!" "Have you set a date?" and "Grainne, you're a lucky girl." I also heard a sour, yet familiar, "How much did that set you back?" Had to be Sinead, but I couldn't tear my eyes from the ring to confirm it.

I've no clue how I got through the rest of the evening. I have a fuzzy impression of me sitting there, my vocal cords paralyzed, desperately trying not to tear Joe's ring off my finger and embarrass him in front of all those people. Then Joe driving me home, and kissing me goodnight more assertively than usual. Due to my shock, he got away with it too. As I made to go inside, he popped the inevitable question: "I'll stay the night, if you'd like?"

No, I don't like, I said silently, seeing in my mind's eye Vivian Leigh's/Scarlett O'Hara's sneer as she received a marriage proposal from that poor sap Charles Hamilton. "Em…another night, maybe."

Disentangling myself, I rushed into the flat. I headed straight for Justine on the couch, my face averted from the ring, and arm extended, like you'd carry a dirty nappy. "What the feck am I going to do with this?" I asked tragically.

Justine's eyes widened. "Jay-zus!" she breathed. "It's a beaut!"

"But I can't get it bloody off!" I made myself look at the ring, which I'd been surreptitiously tugging on since we'd left the restaurant.

"Joe, I suppose?"

"Who else?" I said, shaking my left hand, my finger looking dangerously swollen. "Do you think there's something to that bit about stress making your blood rush to your extremities?"

Justine jumped off the couch and led me into the kitchen. "If you'd been paying attention, you would've realized how much Joe cared. And stopped him before he proposed."

"Ah, sure," I allowed. "But Joe didn't really propose. He got the ring on me, then said, 'Well, what do you think?' I couldn't get a word out."

A good thing, or I'd have blurted, *Love of God, if I'm not tempted to sleep with you, I certainly can't marry you.*

Justine dabbed soap on my finger. "I hope you said something halfway proper to the poor man."

I wrinkled my brow. "After we left the restaurant, I think I said something like, 'I don't think I'm ready for a ring.' But Joe asked me to keep it for a few weeks, and think about things." As if accepting a diamond ring wasn't a social contract to marry him.

"Will you?"

"I already have," I said morosely, "so no need to wear this yoke a minute longer than necessary."

As we worked the soap under the ring, Justine said, "I've some news myself, from work—I can hardly believe the luck, but management wants to try putting some staff on temporary furloughs, you know, leave without pay, to build up their cash reserves!"

"Oh yeah?" I looked up, to see Justine's face shining. Normally, she never showed even a fraction of that enthusiasm where her job was concerned.

"It gets better—when they asked for volunteers who'll take a month or maybe the whole summer off, I didn't waste a minute!"

I went still. Wow, some dreams really could come true. "So, you'll have time off to cook." I gave her a congratulatory hug. "Just as you've always wanted!"

Her glow faded. "It is, but when I told Mam, she had the cow I was afraid she would. Of course she tried to talk me out of it. Then she got Nate to ring me, who lectured me about how the bank would discover they could do without me, and the entire corporate strategy was a sneaky attempt to eventually sack me and anyone else who'd volunteered. It took all evening to settle the pair of them down, and assure them I'd plenty of savings to see me through. So I'm a bit wrung out."

"Well then," I said, "as soon as we finish this business, I'll bring you a fortifying glass of wine. Then we'll sort out how to celebrate this momentous occasion."

With a second application of soap, we got the ring off. While Justine went to the fridge to see what we had by way of festive snacks, I rinsed the soap off the ring, entertaining a brief fantasy about "accidentally" dropping it down the drain to get rid of it.

Then another vision came to me—once the ring was down in the pipe, there'd be murky water swirling round it, and the ring would gather power like the haunted one in *Lord of the Rings*. So all I could do was dry off Joe's gift, stuff it back in the box, and for want of a better place, cram it into my handbag. And postpone deciding what to do about Joe the same way I put off everything else.

I blinked as Justine waggled her fingers an inch from my nose. "Sorry?" We were on the bus the next day, trundling across the country to Ballydara for my birthday dinner.

"So you're not in a coma after all." She sat back in her seat as the bus pulled out of Galway City. "I thought I'd have to ring 999 when I told you about the latest post on *Girl Talk—another* one about babies—and you didn't make one of your smart-arse cracks."

"I'm…em, not feeling too talkative," I admitted. "I'm just having a really bad…"

"Day?" Justine inserted. "Week?"

"Year," I said.

I'd begun my birthday in rather a filthy mood. With Justine's family having meltdowns over her job decision, she hadn't had time to bake me a birthday cake. Plus we'd need to stay overnight on the trip to County Galway, which would give Mam and Rory more time to nag me about spending my summer in Larkin purgatory.

My mood didn't improve upon my arrival at work either. While I brooded over how to give Joe his ring back without damaging any…future association, the three little Gallaghers, probably sensing Nanny Grainne's distraction, somehow conspired to help me take my mind off my ring problem. Ivy tossed up her breakfast on my jumper, Anna missed the potty twice, and while I was cleaning her up, Geoff got hold of a pair of scissors and cut up a dozen of Sara and Alan's wedding snaps.

I was also suffering from friendship-sin-of-omission guilt, for not letting Justine in on Mam's B&B insanity. Since Justine is so much nicer than I am, and puts family loyalty right up there with perfect rack of lamb I knew she would somehow talk, hound, or otherwise guilt-trip me into giving into Mam's demands. By keeping Justine out of the loop, I could be steadfast, and resist my mother's determination to ruin my life "Yeah, a really bad year," I said glumly.

"The proposal's got you in knots, then?" Justine squeezed my arm, sympathy in her eyes.

I shrugged. Joe's proof of devotion meant I could get him into bed without half trying. But I certainly couldn't go there if matrimony was the price. Even if you took the ring out of the equation, using a guy who's truly mad for you seemed really low, even for the most ethically challenged girl. Aside from my anti-marriage stand, try as I might, I still couldn't see being in an even semi-permanent relationship with Joe.

But there was a really big reason I was sunk in gloom. When Alan Gallagher came home early from work, so I could get the afternoon bus to Mam's, he'd looked uncomfortable. I wondered if he could smell the baby sick on my jumper, until he cleared his throat. "I've news about our holiday."

"Yes?" Anticipation filled me. Were the Gallagher's extending it? Upgrading their lodgings? I revisited my fantasy of a huge, sun-drenched villa in the middle of a vineyard.

"The thing is, my mother's asked to come with us," he said.

"Oh." I'd be sharing child-minding with Granny Una? Visions of the kids, mellow and well-behaved from my gentle but firm management, settling down for three-hour naps, and freeing me for extended recreation, began to disappear. Sort of like a Polaroid photo developing in reverse.

"Right," said Alan. "The thing is, she's keen to have the kids to herself, she tells us."

To herself? I'd been disinvited from Provence! What about my fantasies of sun and country walks and meeting virile, dark-eyed Frenchman for whom marriage was the last thing on their minds?

They'd turned to shite, that's what, confirmed when he added sheepishly, "But Sara says you're welcome to fly in for our last weekend."

"Fantastic," I said. "Can't wait." Giving the kids a quick kiss goodbye, and a "Cheers" to Alan, I let myself out. No holiday in France—wasn't that just bloody marvelous!

Now, on the train, I was *this* close to spouting off to Justine about Alan and Sara's betrayal when her mobile rang. "Mam," she mouthed, and took the call.

I stewed in silence. Instead of being an indispensable member of the Gallagher *ménage*, I would be an afterthought, joining their holiday for a crappy three days after Una ruined the kids with a solid month of junk food, unlimited telly and no naps. And Sara hadn't the nerve to tell me herself.

Worse, my excuse for why I absolutely could *not* help Mam this summer had just disintegrated. As Justine's laugh trilled into her mobile, I felt a new wave of envy. She and Helen Egan talked nearly every day—mostly so the woman could nag Justine about her job and marriage prospects, but at least the woman was interested in her life. The pair of them actually had a mother-daughter date once a month. I couldn't imagine voluntarily going out with Mam once a year. As Justine rang off, a sudden insight hit me:

Whatever you do, keep the cancelled holiday under wraps. At least for the moment...

"New update on Bernie," she said, her eyes shining. "She's leaning toward a trip home—so Mam and I may have her spoiling us for weeks after all!" She stowed her mobile in her bag. "It's certainly taken Mam's mind off my job furlough, thank God."

My unsteady stomach sort of plunked, like a jarring landing in an old lift. "That's... lovely." I swallowed, not wanting to ask, but how could I not? "Rafe's wound up his mid-life crisis, then?"

Justine wrinkled her brow. "Mam didn't say—but apparently Bernie's in such knots over this annulment business, she just wants to get away."

Rafe must have reconciled with Lindy—Bernie'd never leave

him otherwise. But I resolutely shoved thoughts of Rafe away. He'd made his bed, and now he'd still be sleeping in it.

With Lindy.

Across the bus aisle, a baby I'd noticed earlier was now parked on her mammy's shoulder, gazing at me thoughtfully—she must've picked up my narky vibes. I smiled and waggled my fingers at her. When I got a toothy grin in response, a fresh sense of injustice spread over me like a rash. I'd be away from the little Gallaghers for over a month...the longest stretch since I'd started minding them.

I looked away quickly. Within days, Justine would be out every night having fun. While I would be spending my Frenchman-free holiday spinning my wheels and enjoying what passed for summer in Ireland.

"Back to Joe's proposal—I've an idea or two," Justine ventured. "To let him down easy."

Trouble was, Joe now seemed to be my only option. So how to give back the ring, but keep him in play? "I'm keen for inspiration," I said, digging in my handbag for the packet of peanuts I'd bought before we got on the bus.

"Well, Joe thinking you're engaged to him is...all right, it's a problem, but not the end of the world," she said briskly. "All you have to do is go see him, and be kind but direct."

"Kind and direct?" I tore open the packet. "Right-o. And what do I say?"

"Those nuts'll spoil your appetite," Justine observed. "And your mam's sure to have something lovely for your birthday dinner."

"I doubt that. And nothing spoils my appetite," I said, and popped a handful of nuts in my mouth. "You were saying about Joe?"

"You could emphasize that the ring really was too sudden, and there's no reason to rush into an engagement, but you're so flattered, etc., etc."

Sure, her advice was a terrible cliché. But with all the effort she was putting into my love life, I felt even guiltier for keeping so much from her. "I guess I could," I said doubtfully.

"If you say it nicely enough, he won't even realize you're rejecting him," Justine said. "You'll need to get on it soon, though. I mean, you still have the ring."

"Good point," I said, pushing my handbag off my lap. Knowing Joe's ring was inside it gave me the willies.

"So, if you truly don't fancy him, you should let him know before you go to France."

That was Justine for you. A great one for doing the right thing. I wondered how long I could, or should—if we're throwing in ethical issues here—deceive her about my cancelled holiday. Of course, she'd know the day I didn't get on the plane, but it wouldn't do to let her find out that way. "You know, in a pinch, you could moonlight as a proposal-rejection coach."

"Ah, go on," Justine said, blushing.

"It's true." I chomped the last fistful of nuts. "But with Joe's proposal still up in the air, no need to mention it to my family."

As the bus bumped along the country roads towards Ballydara, I realized I should have hidden the ring from her too. Then I could have rung Joe first thing this morning, and told him taking the ring felt sort of premature, and she'd have never found out. But Justine would never let me phone up a fellow only to break his heart.

I stashed the wrapper back in my bag and rubbed my forehead with the heels of my hands. If my rather murky plans of a future...em, collaboration with Joe wasn't the most eejit idea I'd ever had, then I didn't know what was. I mean, consider what I was up against: For some unfathomable reason (known only to God and Joe, and neither was telling), Joe had decided he wanted me—for a lifetime supply too. Getting Joe to cancel his order would be the real sticky point.

Look what had happened to Scarlett O'Hara's men. She'd had two husbands mad about her, whom she didn't give a crap about, and they'd had to die to be free of their unrequited love. But whatever getting rid of Joe entailed, of course I didn't want him to meet such a drastic fate.

So if you add my cancelled holiday and Mam's B&B to Joe's

proposal, I was caught in one ginormous snafu:

With no visit to Provence, I couldn't have casual sex with a hot Frenchman.

Wearing Joe's ring, I couldn't have casual sex with *him*. It wouldn't be casual then, would it?

Nor could I have it off with another guy either, while I still had the ring. Not that I care too much about what other people think, but I'm not that far gone.

And if Rory found out I wasn't going to Provence, she'd twist my arm into living at Mam's, being her slave, and there'd be no way to meet anyone for casual *anything*.

As the bus pulled into Ballydara and heaved to a stop, I knew I had to come up with something fast. But what?

Justine and I disembarked in front of Hurley's pub, and my gaze was pulled to the hills beyond the village, a vibrant orangey-green in the slanting sunshine. Just like my previous visit, I felt that same tug inside. In anyone else, I suppose it could've been their heart-strings...for me, though, it had to be indigestion.

Collecting my overnight bag for the short walk to Mam's, I could swear my load felt heavier than usual with all my new problems weighing me down. As we approached Murphy's shop, a stout, middle-aged matron in a Hello Kitty apron popped her head out the door, smiling in a gruff sort of way straight at Justine. "You're Eileen's girl? Do tell us how you like your birthday treat."

Birthday treat? Justine only laughed. "I'm told I resemble Mrs. Larkin, but this is Grainne," she said, touching my arm.

"I will, thanks," I said weakly, not sure if I liked the locals getting to know me. I could just see Mam telling everyone in Ballydara I was to help her with her new B&B, then I'd have to deal with all the pressure from the whole village on top of Rory's. As Mrs. Murphy disappeared back into the shop, a pretty, red-haired girl with a baby bump came out the door and waved to us too, her wedding ring catching the evening light.

In that precise moment, a solution to my problems burst into life—a way to juggle my aborted holiday and fake engagement,

and *still* get out of being Mam's gofer this summer! I half-heartedly
waved back at the girl, my mind racing. I could fine-tune my plan
before dinner, but first, I'd clear up my sin of omission. (Always
advisable before committing another one.)

"Justine," I began carefully, "You'll want to know my mam's got
up to something, which I'll explain in a minute." I shifted my bag
into my other hand. "But you've got to promise—whatever I say to
my family tonight, just go along with it, okay?"

Eleven

"You must really fancy Joe, if you're marrying him," commented my niece Ciara.

I hesitated only a moment. "Oh, madly," I agreed. Ciara and I had holed up in the front room, so I could give her a private showing of my ring, away from the other three in the kitchen. We were also free of any distractions from her little brother Brenny, who was staying the night with a pal. "But we won't be getting married for... well, *ages*."

Whenever you have to deceive people, A-list liars advise that you stick as close to the truth as possible. So, when I'd asked Ciara if she would share the news of my ring at dinner, I instructed her to use the specific phrase, "Aunt Grainne's got an engagement ring."

Sure, using a child quite shamelessly to further my own ends meant I was wading even deeper into the crap side of the ethics scale, but there were times when the ends justified the means. And this was one of them.

I was actually still pinching myself, the strategy I'd conceived just as we arrived was *that* good. With my Provence trip no longer in play, I would hang onto Joe's ring long enough to 1) to sort out whether to sleep with him, 2) pretend to plan our wedding, so I'd be far too busy to help Mam with her B&B, or 3) wait until she came into what few senses she possessed—whichever came first.

Brilliant, don't you think?

I got Ciara to rehearse her line twice, then she said, "When it's time to bring it up, give me some sort of signal. Like tug on your ear, or itch your nose."

"Right," I said, and stuck the ring box back in my bag. "Let's go with the nose." While I didn't plan to promote my sham engagement, if Ciara mentioned the ring first, I could pretend to blush. So bridal, you know?

"Have you a spare lipstick, Aunt Grainne?" She'd already lost interest in my ring, my phony fiancé, and my even phonier wedding. All of which made her a great co-conspirator. With no emotional investment in the entire Joe matter, Ciara wouldn't suffer the kind of pre-pubescent wedding fantasy letdown I had.

"I don't really wear lipstick, but I could take you to the chemist's," I said, then quickly added, "Though we'd have to ask your mam first."

"Come on," she pouted. "She won't notice if I just use a teensy bit."

"But I'm a *nanny*," I reminded her. "I'm meant to follow a professional code of conduct."

She looked at me suspiciously (not a thick, our Ciara), then shrugged, dimples peeping.

I admit my record for respecting my elder sister's wishes was a bit spotty. Still, I wasn't keen to aid and abet my niece's inexorable march toward the usual teenage obsessions with fashion, boys and sex. Ciara is very pretty, but at ten, she's still young enough to be unaware of her appeal—though that's not likely to last. She'll no doubt be a handful as well, but luckily, Rory is a surprisingly effective mammy. Good job too, since that gobshite Darren has been good for exactly nothing as far as fatherly guidance.

Her pout forgotten, Ciara dug into her jeans pocket, then produced a folded up piece of newspaper. "I've something to show *you* now."

"What's this?" I said, unfolding a page printed from the *Gallagher Post* website. "*Girl Talk*? I'm surprised your mam lets you read it."

"She doesn't," said Ciara, taking it back. "That's why my friend Nan gave it to me."

"I think the blog's more for grown-ups, love," I chided. "Especially this bit about girls thinking they're fat."

"Then it shouldn't be posted online for anyone to read," said Ciara.

"Good point," I said.

"With the way Mam goes on about fattening food and always trying to lose weight and all that, I wanted her to see this, so last night, I cellotaped it to our fridge at home. But Mam told me to take it off. She thinks Gai's sort of low-class."

I stifled a laugh. "And we know a better fridge for your printout anyway, don't we?"

"Granny'll never notice, right?"

We both snickered. "Not a chance," I said.

Rory has always pooh-poohed my contention that our mother has a touch of attention deficit disorder, but let's face it: Mam's no emotional Rock of Gibraltar. I'm not saying she's bipolar or anything, but she was a great one for changing: her clothing, her furniture, and most frequently, her mind. So I'd high hopes that she'd have already forgotten about her B&B idea.

As we sat down to dinner, I glanced at Justine's animated face. She liked it here, but I didn't bring her to Mam's often. I'd the usual reluctance of someone from a completely mad family bringing home a perfectly sane, fully functioning person. And to be honest, Justine fit in with Mam and Rory a little too well. In fact, they were a perfect triple-Yin dynamic.

I didn't mind that she'd a similar petite figure, fair coloring and modest appetite. I could even handle her paying rapt attention to everything Mam said, no matter how boring. What really put my Yang nose out of joint was that Mam was actually attentive back. Justine didn't know that Mam, so gay and charming with company, was entirely capable of acting like you're the center of her world, then pouf! Suddenly, she's forgotten all about you. Anyway, as usual with all the times Justine had visited, Larkin family stories were on the menu. And tonight being my birthday, you can guess who played a starring role.

"I can still see Grainne the day she turned five, her hair chopped like someone had gone at it with a meat cleaver," said Rory, taking a modest bite of chicken casserole.

"Somebody had," I said under my breath, as Justine went into gales of laughter, like she'd never heard the story before. "Never!"

"Hair all over the bathroom, filling the sink, piled on the floor. You'd never seen such a mess."

I smiled sickly. "Haven't we heard the 'Grainne does a Joan-of-Arc job on her hair' about a million times already?"

"It gets funnier every time I hear it." Justine's laugh was merry. "This family's a crack, all right."

Just before we'd reached Mam's stoop, I'd filled Justine in on the latest Larkin exploit—Mam's B&B. I'd also implied, at my most oblique, that the poor woman wasn't quite right in the head these last months—losing Dad had been too much for her. So I was entirely flabbergasted at Justine's reaction. "Jaysus, that's fabulous! You are so bloody lucky!"

I stared at her, my hand on the doorknob. Didn't she realize Mam and running a B&B was as incompatible as... well, Joe and me? "Whatever," I said, with no time to explain why it was such an insane idea. "But do not, I repeat, *not* mention the B&B."

"But—"

"Not one word," I warned. And if Mam broached the subject, I added quickly, just ignore the poor dear. At least until Rory and I got her a medical check-up.

Justine had cast apprehensive glances at Mam when we first got here. But once dinner started and Rory launched into the "poor wacko Grainne" stories, she'd settled right into the Yin energy. "I've never heard *why* you cut your hair, Grainne."

"Easier to take care of," I said, not looking at Mam.

A tiny line appeared between Justine's brows. She was probably wondering why I'd been concerned about hair styling at age five, when as an adult, I could care less. But my sister was already launching into her next bit, according to tradition.

"No one really batted an eye over the haircut," said Rory, sipping her wine, "since Grainne was always one to go her own way. But little did we know, five years later, she would—"

"Yeah, yeah, run away from home," I said.

"Would you listen to her, acting like it's nothing! Here it was her birthday, and Dad in a terrible state, white as a sheet, ringing the guards, tearing madly round town searching for—"

"And the whole time..." Ciara burst into giggles. "Auntie

Grainne was just across the road, hiding in the shrubbery!" How do you like that? I thought my niece was an ally.

Mam laughed too. "Can you picture it?" I could tell she didn't remember one scrap about the incident but was trying not to let on. "She was such a fierce child, her dad always said thank the saints Grainne wasn't a boy."

"Right," said Rory. "Think of what she would've got up to then!"

"Gaol, at the very least, ha, ha," I said. Soldiering on with my casserole, I figured the public humiliation of having every eejit thing I'd ever done used for a cheap laugh was a fair trade for not discussing the B&B.

"Boys'll take years off your life, my mam says," Justine told her, then looked at me again. "Think of poor Mrs. Corrigan, Joe's mam—"

"Joe?" Mam lifted one elegant eyebrow.

Justine frowned. "You know, Grainne's…friend."

"Oh, that Joe," Mam said vaguely, scraping about a milligram of butter on her bread.

Justine looked bewildered. Helen, her own mam, not only knew what all her friends *and* boyfriends were called, but their jobs, likes, dislikes, and if she was related to them in any way. "Anyway," Justine went on, "Joe and his four brothers, all completely helpless with housekeeping, could have a lot to do with their mam going to an early grave."

I think it was all six Corrigan men and their collective screams at the football matches on telly that did her in, but I made myself say, "That must be the reason he's such a fantastic guy."

"What?" Justine narrowed her eyes at me.

I gave her a hard stare right back. *Remember, you're meant to go along with whatever I say.* "You know—losing his mam when he was in his twenties gives him lots of potential to…" I swallowed hard to get it out, "…be a great family man."

"Right. *Loads* of potential." Justine gave me a cheeky smile, then turned back to Rory.

"When it came time for Grainne's fifteenth birthday," Rory was saying as she took a second serving of broccoli (I ask you, don't normal people take seconds on meat?), "I'd got the inkling we'd better be prepared—God only knew what Grainne would come up with."

Justine pretended to hang her head. "With my brother Nate being her accomplice, shouldn't I take some blame?"

"No worries on that!" Rory reached over and gave her a friendly little nudge. "I'm sure my little sister didn't need any encouragement to get pissed." Lubricated with the fruit of the vine, Rory must have forgotten that Ciara was probably collecting tips for her own future misbehavior. "Grainne had such a head on her, she could hardly hold it up!"

I pretended to join the laughter—I could take the reminiscing as long as we didn't talk about...you know.

And so far, my luck was holding. I'd every hope that if Mam got distracted enough, her attention-deficit would kick in and she'd discard the B&B idea as she had so many other things.

"Now, Grainne's twentieth—wasn't that a birthday to remember?" Justine clasped her hands, looking eagerly around the table.

I frowned at her. Frankly, she was starting to concern me. Like I said, her first reaction to the B&B—like it was the best idea since the invention of the garlic press—was unnerving. But since then, the glow in her eyes and all-around air of suppressed excitement seemed completely over the top.

With her captivated gaze on Mam, then Rory, then Mam again, Justine gave the impression she'd a secret waiting to burst out of her. Was she going to race back to Dublin and ask her mam if *they* could start a B&B? If they did, maybe I could beg Helen to hire Mam...

"Her twentieth?" Rory shook her head. "A double-whammy is how poor Dad put it. Happened right before the birthday dinner."

"It's the Gemini in her," Mam said. "Sign of the twins, you know."

"Right, my one evil twin breaking it off with her fiancée." I stabbed my fork into my salad. "My other one dropping out of college."

"Wouldn't you call them evil triplets?" asked Ciara. "Since you left home the same day?"

I pretended not to hear that.

"Your dad's cooking went completely off," said Mam, who had her priorities. "His lovely birthday pork roast, burnt to a crisp."

"There was your poor fiancé, crying, and Dad looking like he was ready to," said Rory, pushing her plate away. "Although I think Donal got over the split before Dad got over you abandoning your education and getting your own flat."

"It *was* one short engagement," Justine agreed.

"Then I'm surprised anyone remembers it at all," I said sourly. Although I give my sister credit for not mentioning how fast Donal had found someone else. "But you can't have forgotten the stone I put on, after I sent Donal packing." One of the Laws of Sudden Weight Gain is to always mention those extra pounds before someone else does.

"Well, there was that," Rory said uncomfortably.

"Looked great on you, though," Justine said loyally. "Still does."

"Anyway," said Mam—notice she didn't agree. "Better to have broken off an engagement after three weeks, then marry and realize you're not really suited."

Mam actually knew how long my engagement was? "Some *marriages* are even shorter," I said, to get everyone off the Year Twenty drama.

"Yeah," Justine agreed. "Like my cousin Ra—" She broke off as I gave her a warning look.

"Back to Grainne's birthdays," said Rory in a determined voice, probably keen to avoid anyone mentioning her own unfortunate choice of husband. "Year twenty-five wasn't much to speak of, though. Grainne, didn't you spend every cent you'd saved, on airfare from Seattle to come home that day?"

"Something like that," I muttered.

"And two months before you'd planned." Mam *tsked, tsked.* "Sure it's highway robbery, what the airlines get away with when you change your reservations at the last minute. You know, it occurs to me that sharing travel experiences is a great way to chat up new custome—"

"Say, is there any pudding?" I broke in. The most I expected were biscuits from the shop.

"I almost forgot!" Rory jumped up from the table. "Mam, don't forget...you know, and Ciara, get the plates, will you?"

"Grainne, before the pudding, I've a little something," Mam said smiling. She produced a glittery gift bag from beneath the table and handed it to me. Looking inside, I pulled out a gorgeously-bound anniversary edition of *Gone With the Wind.*

Astonished, I said, "How did you..." *How did you know it's my favorite book of all time?*

"Seems I recall your dad telling me you loved the book when you were young," Mam said.

"It's great...fantastic." I'd read my long-ago Christmas gift so many times the paperback had nearly disintegrated. But I'm not sure she heard me say "thank you"—she'd already turned to Justine, telling her about a book she discovered in Galway City, about building customer relationships.

She broke off as Rory re-entered the dining room, bearing a double-layer cake—a chocolate one. Beaming, she said, "Mam hired Mrs. Murphy to bake you a birthday cake!"

Aghast, I stared at the cake—and not just because I'd gone off chocolate after last night with Joe. Mam acting so out of character—buying me a lovely gift, studying business, *and* actually ordering a cake for me—was freaking me out. Time for the heavy guns—my big announcement. I gave my nose a rub.

Unfortunately Ciara's attention was on passing round the plates of cake, and sucking stray icing off her fingers. Justine was telling Mam about her summer holiday she'd be spending with her aunt from America, if all went well. "What'll you do this summer, Mrs. Larkin?" she asked, then looked at me, stricken.

Oh my God, she'd done it. I rubbed my nose frantically, but Ciara, inhaling a massive chunk of cake, was oblivious.

"I've lined up something much better than a holiday," Mam said, nibbling her cake. I practically scrubbed my nose right off my face, but Ciara was now eating her way over to the telly. "I'll have Grainne here, helping me with my summer project. My new bed-and-breakfast!"

"No, you won't," I muttered, trying to avoid an argument.

"But Grainne'll be in Provence," Justine said at the same time.

"That's right," I said. It wasn't a lie when you were only agreeing with an untruth. Not saying it yourself. "I'll be completely unavailable."

"Oh, she'll be here," Rory said gaily to Justine, as if I wasn't there. "Even if we have to tie her to our new B&B sign!"

Justine looked at my mulish expression to Rory's smilingly determined one. An effervescent smile spread over her face. "So let Grainne do as she likes. I'll help you instead—as your chief cook and bottle-washer! And I know just the person who could be your first guest!"

In between Rory's "We're looking into a website," and Mam's "had a lovely chat with the Tourist Board people," I managed to drag Justine into the kitchen. "How could you?" I hissed. "Encourage *poor* Mam like that?"

Justine hadn't the decency to look sorry. "Can't you see?" Her eyes shone. "While I'm on my work furlough and you're in France, I can help your family. It's perfect!"

"Perfect for whom?" I snarled. Already so frustrated with my ring problem and no Provence (we won't even mention Rafe Byrne's marriage), I was struck by a childish rage. I could see Mam and Rory turning Justine into the favored youngest surrogate Larkin, while I'd *really* be out in the cold. "Won't you be busy looking for a temporary chef's job, like you've been hoping for?"

"Why? I'll be working here!" She glanced round the kitchen. "The cooker looks adequate, and your mam's got a nice big fridge.

Shouldn't be a problem to cobble together breakfasts for a few visitors."

"Justine!" I wanted to shake her. "You're missing the point! This is just another one of Mam's hair-brained schemes. If we just let it die a natural death, she'll forget about it and be on to the next thing so fast our heads'll spin right off our necks."

"Bollocks!" Justine was undeterred. "She's already getting things lined up. She's no more unbalanced or irrational than—"

She broke off as the kitchen door banged open. "Justine, we never did hear your suggestion for our first guest," said Mam, her face pink with excitement.

Rory trailed behind her, bearing a giant piece of cake. "Here," she said, and shoved the plate at me. "You've not even touched it."

"Yeah, and happy birthday to you too." I set the plate on the countertop, too irate and confused to be tempted. Which tells you the state I was in. "Tell us then," I said to Justine, "who'll be the first Larkin House victim?"

As Mam and Rory looked expectantly at her, she flapped her hands, like little Anna Gallagher anticipating a treat. "My aunt Bernadette!"

"God help us," I muttered. A reverb from last night's sugar attack hit my middle. As if I didn't have enough problems, Bernie Byrne could enter the picture? "But hold on—isn't her trip to Ireland still undecided?"

"Well, she's almost ninety-five percent sure to come. And she's terribly rich," Justine said. "She can afford a nice long booking."

"Lovely!" said Mam, but it was Rory who put her finger on it. "Wait a minute—I mean, it's great and everything, but isn't someone like her used to five-star city hotels?"

"Nothing else but," I said. "With all the amenities." Rory didn't know the woman wouldn't want to pay for them.

"She's a bit on the mean side, though," Justine said apologetically, as if she'd read my mind. "But if you gave her a low rate—"

"A really low rate," I put in. "Rock bottom. You'll not make a penny off her."

Rory looked from me to Justine. "I'm not sure that'll work, Mam, with those figures we worked up." She opened the kitchen jumble drawer. "Here are the notes..."

"Forget the budget," Mam said gaily, and banged the drawer shut with her hip. Rory yanked her hand out just in time. "My husband always said, in business, you've got to spend money to make money."

"Mrs. Byrne will never go for it anyway," I said. "She's a bright lights, big city sort."

"Well, for the right price, she might be persuaded to stay here," Justine said, but she sounded doubtful.

"Let's get a grip here," I said. As the lone voice of reason, I gave Justine a sharp look. "It's incredibly generous that you want to be part of this project," and I slathered it on thick, "but really, you can no more help with the B&B than I can. Or ask your aunt to stay here."

"Why not?"

"Right," Mam and Rory said at the same time. "Why not?"

I ignored them. "Have you already forgotten? Bernie and your mam have big plans with you this summer, to live the high life in Dublin. You'll not have a spare second for being the kitchen drudge here."

"The high life?" Justine's laugh went all tinkly. "Mam'll probably be too busy with the new baby to go out much. And for me, shopping and going to the theatre gets old after a while. I'd much rather cook—and I'll do it for free."

Mam looked perplexed—the idea of preferring kitchen work was a foreign concept to her. But the word *free* got her attention. "You're hired!"

"I'm not going to look sideways at a gift horse either," exclaimed Rory. Never much of a hugger, she actually put an arm round Justine and gave her a squeeze. "We'd love to take you on," she said. "Can you check with your aunt, see if she's interested?"

"You'd be mad to have Lady-of-the-Manor Byrne as your first customer," I pointed out. "She'll run everyone off their feet—you won't be able to take care of your other guests."

"That's all right," said Mam, with an anticipatory smile. And why shouldn't she smile? *She* wouldn't be working her arse off. "You know what they say about a bird in the hand."

Mam and Rory's cliché-quoting was more than I could take. "Well, this bird's a corker," I said. If there was one woman in the world more high maintenance than Mam, it was Bernie Byrne.

"We'll manage," Rory said. "With you *and* Justine as staff, we'll be so attentive she couldn't consider staying anywhere else."

I gave Rory an exasperated look. "What's with the royal 'we'? You'll be safe in Chicago."

"Ah, get over yourself," she replied. "Mam, you were right not to worry about giving Mrs. Byrne a super-low rate. We could use her as sort of a…a…test."

"Beta customer?" Justine asked.

"Exactly!" Rory squeezed her again. "I'd love to settle things straightaway—how soon can you contact your aunt?"

Justine bit her lip. "She's rather…occupied at the moment—my mam would probably like it if I checked in with her first anyway."

Mam took the kitchen phone off the hook and handed it to Justine. "Then why not call her now?" she said, more sparkly than I'd ever seen her. "You can take it into the dining room."

A moment later, Justine was saying, "Mam, I've a new travel tip for Aunt Bernie!"

"And Grainne," Rory said, her voice noticeably cooler, "How soon can you move in?" We've tons to do before we open for business."

"I can't." By now, I was practically frothing at the mouth. Justine had completely balled up the works. Her offer to help *and* lining up Bernie as a customer would only prolong Mam's insanity—

"Never!" Justine squealed into the phone from the next room, as Rory grabbed my plate of cake off the counter and thrust it at me for the second time. "Here. Eat your cake. And get used to it—you're staying here."

I clutched the plate automatically. "No way!" My imaginary

mentor Scarlett O'Hara would never let people order her about. And here it was, my bloody birthday, and my wishes still didn't count for one fecking thing round this place! "No bloody way!"

"Ah, knock it off." Rory wagged an indignant finger in my face. "If you think that swearing and giving out is going to get you out of helping, in fact, get you anywhere—"

"Shut up!" I shrieked. Caught in an emotional tailspin, I couldn't stop myself. "I'm marrying bloody Joe, I'm going to bloody Provence, and I won't stay here and surrender my bloody life to bloody Mam!"

Mam and Rory stared at me, jaws agape. With matching distasteful looks on their pretty peach faces.

Still tasting my two big, bad lies in my mouth, I'd never felt more like the big, gawky Larkin changeling that nobody had any use for. Until now. As I choked back an instinctive, *I didn't mean it, I'd help if you'd just want me for who I am*...Justine burst into the room, still clutching the handset.

"Aunt Bernie's coming home, all right, and you'll never guess what else?"

"What, what?" chorused Mam and Rory. They simultaneously turned their backs on me, clearly relieved not to be dealing with The Problem Child. As Ciara bounced in, carrying my handbag, I pressed my lips together before another mad something came out of them.

Justine looked straight at me. "Rafe's coming with her!"

Twelve

Wildfire hopes streaked through my chest. "Rafe's coming to Ireland?" As Justine grinned, I pressed my hands to my heart—you know, the ones holding my cake plate.

"Bloody hell," I muttered, feeling the squishy sensation against my boobs. As Mam, Rory, Justine, and Ciara stared at me, goggle-eyed, I set the plate back on the counter, and chunks of cake fell off my shirt to the floor, circling me like a fairy ring.

"What on earth is wrong with this child," Mam said, the same rhetorical question she'd posed about a million times since I was born.

"It's one of her five-year birthdays, mind," said Rory, as if that explained everything. She took the plate from my hands and handed me a towel. "Why else would she act like this?"

"Love," Ciara said wisely, holding out Joe's ring box. "Aunt Grainne, you'll want to show Granny and Mam your engagement ring, won't you?"

There's something about making a complete eejit of yourself that takes your mind off any guilt about deceiving people. After I changed into an old shirt of Dad's and cleaned up the cake, the delayed Showing of the Ring ceremony was rather an anticlimax. Especially since Justine hardly bothered to hide her skeptical look as I slid the ring on.

Typically, Mam's response was underwhelming. "Engaged, are you? Lovely. What's the boy called?"

"Joe," Justine and I said at the same time. "The guy I mentioned like, an hour ago," I added.

"Joe?" Rory said incredulously. "That one you thought might not work out?"

"That's right," I said, and stuck my chin out. "People do change their minds, you know."

"It's a woman's prerogative," Mam said coquettishly.

"What's a 'prerogative?'" asked Ciara.

"Means a person can do whatever they want," Justine said, with a significant look at me. "By the way, you've buttoned your shirt all wrong."

"Well..." Rory looked relieved. "We could do worse for your thirtieth, than have you get engaged. It's an improvement over your un-engagement birthday, at any rate."

"I feel I've disappointed you," I said, redoing my buttons. "You expected something more spectacular?"

"Joe's quite a catch," put in Justine, though I could still feel her suspicion like an extra person in the room. "Has his own business."

"Great," said Mam. "We'll have him round for dinner. Now, about our test run with your aunt?"

Justine looked confused. Mam hadn't exhibited one jot of wedding-related maternal ecstasy. Nor had she bombarded me with the typical Mother-of-the-Bride quiz about dates, colors, flowers or dress-shopping. Neither of which surprised me, but clearly, Justine had a lot to learn about my place in the Larkin Universe.

We stayed the night at Mam's—Justine, as befitting the Larkin House savior, in the second-best guestroom, and me on the couch—with no opportunity for a private chat. All smiles the next morning, Justine told Mam, "I'll be in touch as soon as I talk to Aunt Bernie." But once we'd said goodbye and settled on the bus back to Dublin, she gave me a stern look. "What the hell are you about, showing Joe's ring to your family? An hour before, you were in the horrors about it."

I looked out the window. "I'm...still too knackered to talk. I hardly slept a wink on Mam's new couch." Which was true, but it wasn't because the cushions were too stiff. With so much to work out, I closed my eyes and pretended to nap all the way home.

So Rafe was coming to Ireland. But how could I un-announce my trip to Provence, after vowing to go so vociferously? Then there was the bigger issue of Joe's ring. It was too soon to retract my newly revealed engagement. Besides, the only way Bernie would allow me anywhere near Rafe was if I was committed to someone else.

I managed to hold Justine off for the entire bus trip, but shortly after we got back to our flat, she rounded on me. "Let's have it—are you engaged or not?"

Remembering my earlier vow to stick as closely to the truth as possible, I said, "I think I'll keep the ring—at least for now."

"You're having me on, right?" Justine tightened the belt of the tatty dressing gown she always wore when we stayed in Saturday nights. "I mean, you've never even had sex with him!"

"I'm thinking seriously about...things." Well, I was. "Giving Joe, I mean, *it*, some time."

"That doesn't sound like you." Justine looked dubious. "And nobody changes their mind about a man that fast. Especially a fella like Joe."

Evidently the big scene at Mam's still hadn't convinced Justine I was flaky enough for a 180-degree change of heart. "And what's wrong with Joe?" I asked. "He's a decent guy, his heart's in the right place. Maybe I haven't appreciated his finer qualit—"

"Mother of God, spare me," said Justine. "What about...you know."

"No, I don't," I lied.

Justine rolled her eyes. "The perfect guy, who's now free, and will be Ireland within days! Rafe, of course."

"What about him?" I still hadn't worked out how to balance my ostensible engagement to Joe against the chance to ensnare Rafe, but I figured I'd make it up as I went along.

Justine scowled at me. "I'm no eejit. A few years ago, the pair of you had a big thing for each other."

"Old news," I said airily. "We've both moved on, obviously. Anyway, who wants a guy on the rebound—"

"I won't lower myself to argue with you," Justine interrupted, and opened the fridge. "You're no more engaged to Joe than I am to Colin Farrell—"

"Well, I like that," I sputtered. "You couldn't be more supportive?"

"—But if you want me to pretend along with you," Justine went on as if I hadn't spoken, "I will." She pulled out a carton of eggs. "Because I am a true, loyal friend. Now then, how about a veggie frittata for our tea?"

She didn't mention Rafe again all weekend—and I didn't dare, what with keeping Joe's ring and all—nor in the days that followed. By the Friday following by birthday, when my curiosity for more news of Rafe had me ready to burst, Justine's mam rang.

"They're here?" Justine exclaimed, and my heart trip-hammered *Rafe really isn't married, Rafe's in Ireland!* While I tried not to hover, it was all I could do not to grab her mobile and quiz Helen Egan myself. After the call, though, Justine took pity on me. "Turns out, Rafe's the one who decided to come to Ireland, and Bernie had to tag along," she said. "Apparently he wanted to get away from it all, so he and Nate are going fishing this weekend, before Aine gets home."

Just hearing Rafe's name made me shiver. Outwardly, though, I was calm as a saint, if I do say so myself. "A fishing trip, then. Where?"

"Lough Corrib—they'll be staying in Oughterard," Justine said, opening the fridge. "The salmon fishing's meant to be fabulous there, almost the best in Europe."

Jaysus, I thought I'd faint. Oughterard was like, a stone's throw from Ballydara.

"My mam thinks some fresh air will be good for Rafe—he wasn't in his best looks, she said." Justine set out a pair of chops. "I told her he's probably despondent after being left at the altar, but according to Bernie, he's handling it well. You don't think he's over Lindy already?"

Now *that* would put me in good form. But to keep things real, I suggested, "Maybe he's putting on a good face." The thing was, Rafe had never been that good an actor…

"Apparently the lads will be staying at some little lodge," Justine said. "They turned down Bernie's offer to put them up in some fancy digs in Wicklow. Rafe told my mam he wanted the more rustic experience he'd get in Galway—it's time he got used to scaling down his lifestyle anyway. Naturally, Mam couldn't see why he wouldn't just stay with Bernie."

"Besides needing the psychic space?" I said.

"That wouldn't occur to Mam. She asked me, 'He hasn't lost all his money, has he?'"

We burst into laughter at the very thought of Rafe, living on the cheap—even if he gave away millions, he'd have plenty left for himself. "Can you picture him in some narky fishing kip?" I said. "Shivering in a dusty rug like Scrooge, eating yesterday's porridge."

Justine chuckled again, rustling in the cupboard for a head of garlic. "He'd probably think some breathing room was worth it. Although now that the annulment's in process, Mam said that Bernie's eased up her pressure on Rafe to make up with Lindy. She realized a greedy cow like Lindy Holmes would've run through the Byrne fortune in record time."

Am I the only one who's not surprised? Justine's mobile rang again. "Aunt Bernie!" She set down the garlic. "Good to hear your voi—" Pause. "I'm free—tomorrow would be grand." A longer pause. "Oh, really?" Her eyes widened. "A little...okay, I'll give it some thought."

She rang off, a gleeful look on her face. "Here I was wondering when I'd get the opportunity to pitch your mam's B&B to Bernie, and she invited me to lunch! And that's not all—I was ready to ring off, then she says, 'Rafe's got a request.' Though Nate's invited him to stay with him, with three being a crowd once Aine's home, she said he'll be looking for a small country hotel, doesn't matter where."

I swear I stopped breathing for a minute.

"Did you hear that? A small hotel! I'd have to be a complete eejit, not to drop a hint about a lovely B&B he could stay at. And wouldn't Bernie *luuurve* having him in the next room, to keep tabs on him?" Her grin turned saucy. "Just like someone else we know—" Then her smile quickly faded. "I just remembered...you'll be in France."

I could hardly speak, my mouth was that dry. "Didn't I tell you?" I finally managed. "Provence isn't on. Alan's mother decided to go—she wanted to be the one to help out."

She looked at me suspiciously for a moment, then her face brightened back up. "So you'll be free to work at your mam's B&B with me! Won't that be fantastic?"

"It'll be a great crack," I agreed, a tingle of hope rising in me, from my toes to my throat. "And the place is sure to be a go if we could line up two bookings instead of one."

Rafe bunking under our roof was the kind of synchronicity I couldn't have conjured up if I tried. And if I played my cards right, he wouldn't dream of staying anywhere else.

THE GALLAGHER POST

Gai Lannigan's Girl Talk

Moving Back In With The Parents

We've all been there: He's left you. You've left him. The job has fallen through, or your flatmate's moved out to get married, and the rent's become too dear. There can be a million reasons why your life's taken a wrong turn, and you're out of options. So, hat in hand, your dreams drooping about your knees, you ask your mam and dad, "Can I come back home for a bit? Just till I'm back on my feet."

You get two possible reactions. The parents smile delightedly and say, "How soon?" Which is bad news, since they're thinking you're still twelve. Or, they exchange an appalled glance, and say, "How long?" Which is also bad news, since now you not only feel you're a total failure, but unwanted too.

If you've a Sensible Family—heads are screwed on reasonably well—you sit down together and lay out a few ground rules. Cooking and laundry. And (your dad clearing his throat), how late you'll be staying out. The big question doesn't get asked, but it's on the table too: sleepover guests. Of course, you'd never sneak a man in, would you? You're a decent girl.

If your family's not sensible, over we go to the dark side: the Loose-Screw Family. The sort where you can't sit down and discuss, because you've already shown up on the stoop with a bedraggled suitcase that doesn't close all the way, and a couple of boxes taped together. It'll be pouring rain of course, and you hope your parents mistake the tears on your face for raindrops.

The scene gets off to an auspicious start. Your dad gets red in the face, and roars, "Why are you bringing all that shite?" Your tentative answer is still stuck in your mouth when your mother starts to shriek. "What's happened?" Pretty soon there's a fight on, angry words flying round the room, and Uncle Larry joins in, you know, the one who's living in your old bedroom and hasn't had steady employment for years.

With the realization that you're no better than your Uncle Larry, you make a run for the loo before you break down. Naturally, there's only one, and Larry's soon pounding on the door, hissing "Open up, for feck's sakes, before I piss myself!" But you're thinking, to hell with the lot of them. All you want is to be left alone. Luckily someone's left a *Marie Claire* in there (Oh, God, Mam's reading sexy magazines?) and wouldn't you know, you find a great self-help article.

You start reading. And soon, the clouds part, the sun shines down. You have a plan! Find job/save $/ring old friend with the extra bedroom. And while you're at it, you'll lose weight/cut back on the drink/keep your roots colored, then chant keep-your-spirits-up affirmations.

While reminding yourself that your parents' place will do until you launch a new life, you can't help squirming at the constraints. All you want really, is what you've given up. Your pride, which you've swallowed, your independence, which received a kidney punch, and your self-identity, which got sucked into a void, as if your mam has turned her new Hoover on it.

So you gather up the tatters of your former life, vow that someday, you'll have a *real* future and stare at what's become of your present in the face. Instead of following your own star, you're a kid again. And back to thinking, what do I want to be when I grow up?

Thirteen

"You can still get out of this lunch," Justine said the next day, as we headed into Temple Bar on foot.

"Are you mad? Like I'd turn down free meal at the Siobhan Hotel," I scoffed, though I felt my palms go damp at facing Bernadette Byrne again. But I felt even nervier about sorting out how soon I could see her newly unattached stepson.

"You know what I mean—you and my aunt don't exactly see eye to eye."

As we hurried along Fleet Street, I straightened my pencil skirt, which seemed to have shrunk since the last time I wore it. "I did think you were having me on, that Bernie rang this morning and asked if you'd bring me along. I can just hear her—'you can bring that great cow of a friend, if you must.'" While I'd years to accustom myself to being that large, strange one of the Larkins, I hadn't grown the same thick skin where Bernie Byrne was concerned.

"Bernie doesn't think anything of the sort," Justine said. "Could you lighten up, please?"

"All right, Bernie may have her heart in the right place," I allowed. Wasn't it was the decent thing, to give a mother's love a free pass? Then I gave Justine a playful jab with my elbow. "Unless she tries stiffing us when the lunch bill comes."

"She wouldn't do that," Justine insisted. "Because Rafe would hear about it and make her pay us back. Anyway, do pull it together. An *awful* lot depends on this meeting—" Her mobile chirped. "Hold on, I've an alert," and she stopped walking and pulled her mobile from her handbag. "Great! A new *Girl Talk!*"

She slid her thumb over the screen, then suddenly glanced up at me, reproach on her face. "Say, have you told your family about your change in plans?" When I didn't answer, she said, "Didn't think so. I'll just take a quick look at this post while you ring them."

She kept giving me the eye until I sighed, and pulled out my own phone and pressed Rory's number. "It's me."

"Grainne?" She wasn't used to me ringing her.

"I've given Mam's B&B lots of thought," I said, a quasi-apology in my voice. "With all the help she'll need to land Mrs. Byrne as our first guest, I believe I can…help out after all."

"Really." Rory was silent for a moment. "What does Joe think?"

"Whatever I decide, he goes for," I said. Altogether true. While I hadn't got round to mentioning the B&B to him, I'm sure he would think it was great. Though I didn't give a feck if he did or not.

"And your boss Sara Gallagher?" Rory asked quizzically. She wasn't used to me being cooperative either. "She found a substitute minder for the Provence holiday?"

"They're all set," I said, with an entirely clear conscience on that too.

"Very decent of them," Rory commented. "When do they leave?"

"Wednesday next," I said, manufacturing a regretful sigh. "They've asked me to visit later this summer, if you think Mam could do without me for a weekend."

"Once everything's up and running, it would seem she could," Rory said, sounding pleased. "So, you and Justine will be coming to Mam's…when?"

"Tomorrow? Is that all right?"

"That'd be grand," said my sister. "You're the best."

"Cheers, then." So although I felt a bit of a fraud, peace, or at least a temporary cease-fire, reigned with Rory and me once again. In my current mood of making nice, I waited until Justine was through reading the post. As we started walking again, I asked, "What do you think our chances are, really, of getting Bernie to stay at Larkin House? She won't be thrilled at staying out in the boonies."

"True, but she's fair sick about all the money wasted on Rafe's wedding," said Justine as we turned onto Cope Street. "Odds are, she'll be dead keen about saving on her lodging."

As we climbed the imposing steps to Bernie's hotel, I had to wipe my palms on my skirt to keep my hand from sliding off the railing. But if I couldn't swing sucking up to Bernie, and finagling a meeting with Rafe at the same time, I didn't deserve the terror-inspiring name of Grainne.

The Siobhan Hotel had all chic elegance of Temple Bar's other boutique hotels, only without a quayside view, a hip, in-house club, or the cachet of rock-star ownership. But I hardly saw the glossy wood and granite interior, or smattering of *objets d'art*, as I picked Bernie's coppery head out of the lunchtime crowd.

If Justine was the sister I'd always wanted, Bernadette Byrne was the kind of mother-figure I'd once secretly longed for. While the way she'd raised Rafe as if he was her own nursling had first piqued my interest, her romantic personal history cemented it.

After emigrating to America in her twenties, Bernie had promptly married Henry Byrne, a divorced Protestant with two sons. Imagine, her husband was not only *not* Catholic—Jack, his Irish-American father, had been black-hearted enough to turn Episcopalian because it was better for business—but was a bigamist in the eyes of the Church. According to Justine, however, the family's discovery that Henry was really loaded and had no objection to his second wife's frequent trips back to Ireland, pretty well cancelled their disapproval of the marriage.

By the time we first met, Bernie had been widowed for years. And with the millions her husband had left her, answerable to no one. That is, except her father-in-law, who controlled the family business and purse strings with iron fists. I suppose having a bossy father-in-law watching every penny you spent could account for turning into a skinflint, but he'd been dead for several years. Plenty of time for her to get over it. You'd think.

Anyway, when I started seeing Bernie at the Egan's family gatherings, back in my teens, I'd been a sitting duck for someone who gave me the time of day. I couldn't help but be drawn to Rafe's stepmother, who had the delicate features of my own mam, and a gift for making you feel like you were the most fascinating person on earth. And though she'd no children of her own, she practically oozed motherliness. Unfortunately, first impressions, like looks, can be deceiving.

I'd managed to kid myself for nearly ten years. Bernie's attentiveness, I discovered, was simply a habit—cultivated to charm other captains of industry at cocktail parties. And her maternal fondness for Rafe was revealed as the fierce love of a she-wolf.

Don't get me wrong. A mother's meant to look after her child's best interests. But Bernie was hard at it long past the time she should have let her pup out of the den and into the big bad world.

Now, approaching Bernie's table, I was practically dragging my feet. Still, whatever I privately thought of the woman, I'd a job to do: Goodwill Ambassador for Larkin House.

"Girls!" Bernadette Byrne held her arms out to Justine. Then turned an only nominally false smile on me, and extended her hand. "Grainne. We meet again."

Thirty-five years in America hadn't made much of a dent in her Irish accent. Nor in her pretty features. Although anyone could see she'd "had some work done"—her eyes, nose, and lips were just a little too... perky. In a scary way.

"Wouldn't have missed it, Mrs. Byrne," I said as she shook my fingers. Given the damp state of my hands, I was relieved at the finger thing. Until it occurred to me that she just didn't want to touch me.

Justine turned an approving smile on me as we sat down, and I tucked my handbag securely in my lap. "We're all so thrilled you came home after all," she said to Bernie, who immediately started nattering on about Justine's family and what to order for lunch.

Bernie seemed to be in a bit of a state, though. I wasn't quite sure what to make of the woman—chirpy and upbeat one moment, then distracted and restless the next. Normally, she was nothing if not focused—you didn't get on with marrying millionaires by not paying attention.

"How do you find Ireland this time round?" I asked Bernie after our food arrived.

"Horribly expensive," she said, her smile tight. She must have had that bit done where they scrape the wrinkles right off your face. "My hotel room is costing the earth!"

Justine and I exchanged glances. Talk about a perfect opening. "The service here must be worth it," I said, trying not to jump the gun.

"Not at these prices," Bernie complained, peering at her soup as she swished her spoon through it. "They call this shrimp bisque, but I've yet to see one."

"You've likely got your serving from the bottom of the soup pot," Justine said.

"Here, you can have mine," I quickly offered. "It's full of the little buggers, and I've just had one spoonful."

"I'll take it," Bernie said immediately.

With great regret I passed my bowl over. "The soup's lovely, but nothing like Justine's," I said. "She could cook circles round the lot here."

Justine and I shared another glance as Bernie dived into the bisque. We'd cast the lure—all that remained was to get the woman to take the bait.

Pausing mid-slurp, Bernie sighed. "What wouldn't I give to have you cook for me, Justine."

"Actually...you can," said Justine. When Bernie said, "oh?" it was all Justine needed. She gave Larkin House such a grand promo I thought any minute a raft of celebrities like David Beckham and his Spicy wife would ring for a booking. "And it's fairly close to Rafe's fishing spot," Justine added. I didn't dare look at her, lest a premature grin of elation break out.

"Hmmm—with Rafe on holiday in Galway, it would be grand to stay close by," and Bernie gave me a sidelong look. "In case he... needs me. How much?"

Justine quoted a rate so low that anyone other than a cheapskate like her aunt would've wondered what sort of hut they'd be staying in. But Bernie's eyes gleamed. "It sounds perfect."

"Mam's plan is to have just one or two very special guests at a

time, so you'd have plenty of privacy," I said. Who knew I'd such a
talent for sales! "Larkin House will definitely be an exclusive sort
of lodging."

"Ah. Exclusive, you say?"

"Absolutely," Justine said, looking like she could hardly contain
her excitement. "Mind, you'll need to decide soon, since…since—"

"There's a waiting list," I broke in, to save Justine from a fib.
The right job for the right people, I always say.

Bernie wore that sort of dazed, yet calculating look of a career
bargain-hunter forced to make decisions on the fly. However, we'd
one more critical factor to put into play.

I clutched my handbag. "You'll want to know that Larkin House
has room if you want to bring…someone else to stay with you." All
three of us knew exactly the someone I'd in mind.

Bernie looked at me doubtfully—as I knew she would. "Did
you say you'll be on the staff too?"

I could see her weighing the upside of the cheap lodgings, with
the downside of my presence—meaning Rafe and I would run into
each other. "But I'll be more like the invisible sort," I assured her.

"You'll hardly see her, in fact," Justine said. "Just like you never
really see the staff at the best hotels."

"When I'm not needed, I'll be out," I said, digging in my bag.
Beneath the table, I closed my hand around my ring box, opened
it, and surreptitiously slid on the ring. "I just got engaged, and my
fiancé will want me to…" I raised my left had and fluttered it a
little. "Spend *all* my free time with him."

Bernie stared at my ring, then turned a glowing smile on Justine.
"Let's book the Larkins' before someone beats us to it!"

Reeling in Bernie Byrne had been such a taking-candy-from-
a-baby experience I felt a definite letdown, that had nothing to do
with the woman being too mean to stand for dessert. (My gone-off-
sweets period hadn't lasted the week.) In fact, Bernie had been so
keen on dumping the Siobhan for Larkin House, she'd had Justine
ring Mam on the spot.

Savoring the last bite of my turkey sandwich, I had some teensy second thoughts about my fake engagement. I was all for fudging reality when the situation called for it. But bringing an innocent party—Joe—into the business raised the potential for complications.

But really, wasn't our success a sign that Bernie staying at Mam's B&B was meant to be? So who could worry about niggling little details like a conscience? With mine in the clear, I decided to leave right after the meal. Bernie's company was like her plastic surgery— a little goes a long way.

"I've got to run—thanks for the delish lunch." I refrained from making a token offer to pay, as Bernie would take me up on it, and there would go my new Larkin dogsbody allowance. "You girls have a grand afternoon together."

Bernie looked relieved. "My sister's joining us for facials later." Then she pressed her lips together for a moment, looking torn. "Grainne...what did you say your fiancé is called?"

"Joe. Joe Corrigan."

"He has his own business," Justine said reliably. "And he's positively *mad* about Grainne."

Bernie gave me, then my ring, a probing look. "Well, then," she said, unwillingness in every syllable, "...might you chat with us a bit longer?"

"Sure," I said, foreboding filling me. Bernie requesting my company was only slightly less worrisome than Mam doing so.

Bernie looked from Justine to me, and back again. "I wanted to consult with you girls about something."

If Bernie requesting my company was out-of-character, her actually asking for my opinion was still more bizarre. But hey. I was all for racking up brownie points with the woman.

Bernie dipped her head, casting her eyes right, then left, like an actor in a really bad melodrama. "It's a matter requiring extreme discretion."

"Grainne can keep a secret," Justine said. "But shouldn't we talk somewhere less public?"

"That's it." Bernie slapped the table. "We'll go to my room."

With the slap, our waiter materialized at her elbow, bill in hand. Bernie quizzed the discomfited man about the charges with the toughness normally given to murder suspects in the dock, then signed her bill with a flourish. "Right, girls—upstairs. We haven't a moment to lose."

Entering Bernie's hotel room, I immediately saw she wasn't as into euro-pinching as we'd thought. Unopened Jo Malone products covered the dresser, and a new Louis Vitton makeup case rested on the desk. Brown Thomas carrier bags were strewn on the duvet, alongside another huge bag exploding with baby items from Mothercare, obviously for Nate's baby. Tossing her handbag into the middle of the mess, Bernie said, "Why I've brought you up here— well, I won't beat round the bush. Girls, I need your help."

Justine dropped next to the Mothercare bag. I was equally mystified, but I managed to back into an armchair. Sitting on Bernie's bed seemed like too much cheek. Even for me.

"What's the matter, Aunt Bernie? Do you need us to…" Justine gazed around at the maelstrom of merchandise. "Help you pack up for Ballydara?"

I looked at Bernie cynically. Since when did packing someone's clobber require extreme discretion?

"I'm in trouble," Bernie said, her voice shaking. "No, *we're* in trouble."

Jaysus above, had she smuggled some contraband goods into Ireland and needed us to cover for her? Then I remembered something about Bernie. Whenever she said "we," she always meant—

"It's Rafe—we have *got* to save him."

Fourteen

I'm not a great one for regrets—my motto is, whatever's happened, get over it, and get on with it. But if there's one thing I'm sorry for, it's that I didn't save myself for Rafe.

Admittedly, I was a late bloomer...in all respects. At nearly twenty, I'd no clue what to do with my life. The one thing I'd determined was that whatever Mam had done with hers, I'd do the opposite.

For me, that meant leaving college for a job, and finding a fellow I liked. But not loved. I'd spent the rest of my teenage years mooning over Rafe, despite the fact I hadn't set eyes on him since the night I'd gotten so pissed. The fanciful side of me had decided that since he was my top choice, why shouldn't I go after him, full stop? Okay, any sane person would consider my plan wildly optimistic, even if we'd lived in the same country. But a girl can dream, can't she?

Rafe had actually ended up playing professional golf after all. Just like he'd wanted—which seemed like a miracle to me, since I *never* got what I wanted. And being the scion of such a prominent Irish-American family, with his real mother Irish-born, he'd got a fair amount of Irish media coverage. Throughout my teens, I'd mystified Dad by my daily immersion in the *Irish Times*' Sport pages, but I was hungry for any mention of Rafe.

After nearly five years of my worship from afar, though, the practical side of me took over. I had to admit my fixation on Rafe would get me nowhere. Donal seemed like a good risk, and he said he loved me. So when he brought up marriage we went to bed. It wasn't awful, but it wasn't transporting either. I should be ashamed to say that having it off with Donal was probably improved because the whole time, I pretended I was with Rafe—but I'm not.

Naturally, fate conspires to present you with the opportunity you've been longing for... after it's too late. In my case, the Powers That Be brought Rafe to Ireland for a golf tournament hardly three days after I'd pledged my troth, my body and my ring finger to someone else.

Poor Donal. I'd managed to attach the pair of us to the Egan family contingent that had turned out to watch Rafe play at the Royal Dublin. At a crucial putt for Rafe, I'd fixed my eyes upon him, willing him to see me.

And it worked! He looked up, his eyes going straight to me. And presumably, to Donal, who had his arm round me. Before I could move, or even smile, he bent back to his putter. He hovered, motionless for a long moment, then as he putted, his body twitched.

He missed the cup by a mile.

As the crowd heaved a disappointed, "Oooohhh," the entire Egan clan, realizing who had caught Rafe's eyes before The Twitch, looked at me accusingly.

I thought Rafe's putting malfunction would be a one-off. But when he missed every remaining putt in the tournament—well, let's say that if looks could kill, the Egans were out to murder me. Worse, Rafe had blown his standing from the top five to the lowest three. He left Ireland directly, and soon after that, quit the tour entirely. I learned that he'd developed what every golfer dreads—the Yips—uncontrollable, jerky movements that devastate your game.

Needless to say, Rafe went on to put his academic training to good use. I went on to enter the nanny business. But not before sleeping with Donal every night for three weeks, then splitting up with him two hours after I got my period.

Now, ten years later, I found myself clutching the arms of my cushy Siobhan Hotel chair so hard my hands ached. "Save Rafe?" Given my history, I was a poor candidate for the task.

Justine gaped at Bernie. "What's happened to him? Besides that cow Lindy throwing him over?"

Bernie dropped onto the bed. "I'm at my wits end with him—why I need you girls."

Honored as I was to be part of the "we" meant to rescue her

stepson, with my heart racing like greyhounds at the track, I was ready to shake her for dragging this out. "Tell us—what's Rafe done?"

"He's gone mad!" Bernie clasped her hands, looking tragic. "Resigned from the family firm with no explanations, the business with the wonderful stock evaluations that his granddad built, brick by brick, with his bare hands, when it would've been much easier for a tough one like Jack Byrne to be a policeman, and enjoy himself cracking people's heads together, and now Rafe's given away his fortune, practically every bloody cent of the hard-earned money Jack and my poor Henry, who was the best president of Byrne Enterprises in the company's history, earned by the sweat of their brows—"

"That's terrible, I'm sure," I broke in, prying my hands off the chair arms. Now that I knew Rafe's life wasn't in danger, I could take a breath. "How exactly are we meant to help—"

"—With no explanation for funneling everything into the Byrne Foundation either!" Ignoring me, Bernie took a deep, sucking breath. "Now Rafe's in the poorhouse with no career either, and Nate said to leave him be, but I can't, especially now that he's lost the girl who'd seemed so ideal I couldn't have picked a better wife for him myself!"

You did pick her, I wanted to say, as Justine consoled, "Really, Aunt Bernie, Rafe will sort himself out—"

"Wasn't Lindy from the best family," Bernie burbled on, "the daughter of my dear friends the Holmes, who really couldn't help losing all their investments. This terrible recession—"

"Aunt Bernie," Justine broke in again, as Bernie's face was developing a blue tinge from lack of oxygen, "You wouldn't want Rafe to have a wife who married him for his money."

"Well..." Pinching her chin, Bernie stared into the middle distance, apparently struck by the idea, that a girl could love a skint Rafe just for himself. Then she said, "Still, he'll ruin himself. Unless we can stop him."

Bernie was a great one for trying to save Rafe from himself. "But Mrs. Byrne," I said, "hasn't he always been a sensible person?" *Well, almost always.*

"Not anymore. Some terrible things turned up in the U.S. media, that made him look simply awful, like he's not quite right in the head—"

"You did say he's gone mad," Justine reminded her.

"He's perfectly sane," Bernie snapped, contradicting herself. "But he's a laughingstock—"

"I don't think Rafe's annulment could be that newsworthy." I tried to keep my eyes on Justine, but my gaze was pulled unerringly to the Mothercare bag. "People split up every—"

"It was on ESPN!" Bernie steamrollered right over me. "And in *People*—the wedding was Seattle's social event of the year! And now that horrid Lindy has turned up in the media—"

"Didn't you just say she was ideal?" Justine pointed out.

"Not anymore!" said Bernie, looking incensed. "She's taken up with some gobshite baseball fella who was caught with the steroids, and of course they always mention Rafe."

So Lindy had morphed from an obscure former debutante, to a semi-notorious party girl with a taste for loser athletes? Made me look positively stable by comparison.

"And if that isn't bad enough, when we arrived in Dublin, a few people recognized him despite that scruffy beard of his, and practically stalked us out of the airport, taking photos. It won't be long before he turns up in the Irish press, looking like a fool here too."

"Even if he does" Justine said, "surely he'll be a one-day wonder."

"Well, I won't have Rafe's image tarnished, not even for an hour." Bernie waved a beringed hand. "The Irish media have always been good to us, but what if they turned as cutthroat as…" She chewed her lip, then looked at me for a long moment, eyes narrowed. "Grainne, Justine tells me your employer runs a news website."

Ah. I hadn't been invited to lunch for the pleasure of my company, but my connections. "Sara Gallagher, owns *The Gallagher Post*," I said. "But she's going on holiday abroad soon."

"I'd like you to put me in touch with her, then, before she leaves. If that's not on, perhaps you could put a bug in her ear, to do a story on Rafe?"

As my nerves went all tingly, Justine asked, "You're looking for some positive press, Aunt Bernie? Like...crisis control?"

"Whatever we call it, we've an uphill battle." Bernie's stretchy mouth turned upside down. "Rafe's turned so stubborn lately, he'll have nothing to do with publicity *or* public relations."

My conscience warned, *Then I'll have nothing to do with it either*, but sure, there was too much at stake to be scrupulous. "Okay," I said, "if I've got this straight, hiring a professional publicist is out. But you're thinking Rafe needs some media exposure, someone who'll write a lovely bit about him?"

"Exactly!" Bernie brightened. "But not a 'bit'—I want a grand media splash, to show that Rafe's future is—"

"But that'll only bring Rafe more attention," Justine pointed out. "He'd be furious."

"What about some mention in the media that's more subtle?" I ventured. "To get Rafe's reputation back on track, you could line up someone who'd be perfectly happy just to plant a few small seeds, an *organic* sort of publicity campaign—"

"Organic," Justine repeated, frowning. "Grainne, where'd you come up with—"

"And by the time Rafe's sorted himself, gotten out of this mood of his, he'll likely be ready for a big-time interview!" Bernie wore a triumphant look. "That's absolutely perfect! Would this Gallagher woman know someone like that?"

"I...think so," I said, my voice suddenly croaky.

"Wait a minute, Aunt Bernie," Justine interjected. "You can't hire just anyone. This person might say 'oh, sure, I'll do just a little blurb, you can count on me.' But what if they give in to temptation to write a ruthless exposé? A story full of Rafe's Yips and his golf career, ditching a Fortune 500 company, Lindy's ballplayer, every shred of dirty laundry. You'll want someone who'll totally respect Rafe's privacy."

"And," I couldn't help adding, "Especially someone who won't hound him about his unfortunate taste in women."

Bernie looked sharply at me. "I suppose..."

"Problem, Auntie," said Justine. "That's exactly the sort of stuff people like to read about."

"But..."

"Justine's absolutely right." I twisted my fingers together to keep my hands from shaking. "Most writers would consider it professional suicide to avoid the juicy stuff."

Bernie folded her arms, scowling like little Geoff Gallagher when you pull him away from his mud pies. "And your point?"

My heart was suddenly beating so fast I felt sick. "You need a media insider who gets read, but no coldhearted hack who'd sell their story to every tabloid in the country. You want one you can trust to write exactly what you want."

Bernie's perfectly waxed brows met over her formerly stubby Irish nose. "*You* know someone?"

"I do," I said. "Me."

Justine couldn't have looked more bewildered than if she's been a drunken atheist stumbling into High Mass. "Grainne, you've gone mad as Rafe. Madder."

"*You?*" A horrified expression crossed Bernie's face before she got control of herself. "That's...em, lovely, I'm sure, but we need someone with...with—"

"Credentials," Justine said baldly.

"I've a few," I said. Digging into my bag, I drew out the notebook I carried everywhere.

"Your bloody journal?" Justine gave me a baffled look, then a high-pitched giggle escaped from her. "Those are your credentials?"

"Hardly," I said. Wishing I could laugh too, I produced my mobile.

Out of the corner of my eye, I saw Bernie's frown deepen, until I thought her eyebrows would turn inside out. I flipped the journal to the last scrawled pages, and set it on the low table next to my chair.

Then I pulled up a favorite website on my mobile, and placed the phone next to the journal. "See? Credentials."

Justine crawled off the bed, sidling over to the table as if there was a crocodile beneath it. She peered at my journal, then at the mobile screen showing *The Gallagher Post's* latest *Girl Talk*, then back to the journal. The heading of the scribbled page read, "Moving Back in with the Parents." She gasped. "Oh. My. God."

I scrabbled in my bag one last time. Despite the turkey sandwich churning in my stomach, I coolly pulled out a crumpled pay stub from the *Post* with a flourish. "Good enough for you?"

"Holy. Fecking. Jesus." Justine's jaw dropped, then sort of hung there, like knickers on a clothesline. "Aunt Bernie, get over here."

"I've no time for this nonsense," Bernie muttered, but slid off the bed, and yanked a pair of reading glasses from the bedside. Ramming them on, she approached the table. "What's this?"

"She's Gai Lannigan, that's what." Justine turned an accusing stare at me. "You're fecking Gai Lannigan!"

Fifteen

Grabbing my mobile off the table, Justine crammed it into Bernie's hands, without taking her eyes off me. "You're her!"

"The very same," I admitted.

"Who's Gai Lannigan?" asked Bernie, frowning over my *Girl Talk* blog.

"Her," said Justine, pointing a menacing, Grim Reaper's finger at me. "That one, my fecking best friend, who's been fecking living with me for years, and never said a word about being the most popular young blogger in Ireland."

"I wouldn't say *the* most popular..." I said modestly. "But I—"

"Shut up!" Justine snatched my mobile from her aunt, which was completely out of character, and shook it at me. "How could you? How could you keep this from me?"

"Justine, please." Bernie pressed her hand against her middle. "All this giving out makes my stomach hurt."

Justine tossed my phone onto the bed and grabbed my arm. "Excuse us, Aunt Bernie," she said. She trundled me into the blindingly white, shiny hotel bathroom, slamming the door behind us. "I can't believe, I just can't *believe*, that you would keep this a secret!"

I flicked on the privacy fan. "Well, I—"

"Shut up! Haven't we been friends and flatmates forever? Haven't I told you everything about me? Didn't I tell you the time I lied to Mam about having cramps, so I could get out of—" she frowned. "Well, I can't remember what it was, but what about all the other stuff? Didn't I tell you all about losing my virginity? And when Frank couldn't...you know, perform?"

I turned on the taps, full blast. "Your aunt can hear—"

"Who cares?" Justine snapped. "And haven't I shared everything about fancying—"

"Justine! Watch it!"

She pressed her lips together, looking frustrated, then whispered, "Ian Byrne." Shutting the water off, she added, "When I know good and well he's taken?" She folded her arms, anger back in her eyes.

Besieged by Justine's gimlety stare, I considered making something up. Tell her Sara Gallagher had wanted to keep Gai's identity a secret? Or when praise for my blog had started rolling in, I was too modest to let on I was the writer? But Justine would eventually discover the truth of the former, and would never believe the latter. While she might sympathize with my fear-of-rejection silence when I'd submitted my blog to Sara Gallagher, she wouldn't understand why I had to keep Gai to myself after the *Post* took me on—

"Tell me something!" Justine folded her arms. "All the times I'd blathered on about Gai, how smart she was, how much I liked her, were you laughing at me?"

"Of course not!" I grabbed a hand towel, and rubbed at the water spots on the otherwise immaculate mirror.

"Oh, really? You were probably hysterical the whole time, thinking, Jaysus, I've something on that eejit I'm living with—"

"No!" I left off wiping the mirror. "What if...what if I didn't want anyone to know I was Gai because..." Trying to look penitent, I twisted the towel in my hand. "Because what if I told people and no one believed me?" It seemed as good an excuse as any.

"I'd have believed you! Because *I* am a true and loyal friend." She gave me a sharp look. "You know what your problem is?"

"Well, I..."

"You're too secretive, that's your problem," she said before I could prioritize my multitude of faults. "Too bloody secretive. But whatever for? What sort of secrets do you have that anyone else couldn't top six days of the week and twice on Sunday?"

She had a point. But Justine slagging me was so out of the natural order of things, that I needed to restore the equilibrium of the Universe as soon as possible. "What if..." How to make up for not confiding in her? "What if I promised to tell you all sorts of things from now on?" A new inspiration hit. "And I'd really like it, if you could brainstorm topics with me, for Gai's...I mean, my blog."

"Really?" Justine's eyes began to sparkle. "I could give you ideas...help you—" She suddenly frowned again—deliberately, I was sure. "I'll think about it." She yanked the towel from me, arranged it on the nearest rack, then flung open the door. "And you're not forgiven."

We found Bernie peering into the mirror, patting the underside of her suspiciously taut chin with the back of her fingers. But as soon as she saw us, she straightened, meeting my eyes in the mirror with a razor-sharp gaze. "So, then. You're a famous blogger, writing under a pen na—"

"You have got to hire this girl," Justine broke in. Evidently she wasn't angry at me enough to sabotage my moonlighting endeavors. "*Got* to."

Bernie turned round to lean against the bureau. "Give me one good reason."

Now the woman was making no bones about her previously concealed antipathy for me. I longed to make a scathing remark, then do a Scarlett O'Hara flounce out of the place. But this gig had Gai Lannigan all over it.

I took a deep breath. "As I said, you need someone who gets read, who you can trust to show Rafe in a good light. Not go for the jugular so they could sell it to the highest bidder." *And if you're especially sweet to me,* "I'll..." I swallowed, "I'll even let you read the posts before I turn them in."

"Harrumph." Bernie folded her arms.

Apparently compromising every shred of my professional integrity wasn't good enough. "Since I'm a friend of Justine's, I wouldn't dream of embarrassing your son by asking nasty, snoopy questions." Really, I'd plenty of other ways to embarrass the man.

"Harrumph." Bernie said again.

"And," I said, not letting Bernie's reaction put me off, "since my editor gives me a free hand on subject matter, I can put some lovely, fluffy bits about Rafe in the next few posts without pressure to put a tabloid-ish spin on them."

"Everyone in Dublin reads *The Gallagher Post*, Aunt Bernie," said Justine.

Even Billy Corrigan, which really does mean everyone. "But it's no rag," I put in.

"And you can set the record straight about Rafe straightaway," Justine added. I sent her a grateful look, which she pretended not to see.

"Well..." Bernie looked sideways at her reflection, caressing the tip of her newly pointy nose. "You realize," she said to it, "your little website isn't quite what I had in mind for Rafe. I was thinking *Image*, here in Ireland, then move up to *Vanity Fair*. Or *GQ*."

I didn't think I was half-bad looking, but if I ever started making love to my proboscis, I'd tell Justine to give me a good clout on the head. "But it's a start," I said, overlooking her insult. I didn't want to point out that because of the surfeit of celebrity stories, Rafe's life implosion would be stale news in three days. But who was I to inject reality into Bernie's fantasy world. "I won't let you down."

Bernie sighed, dropping her hand. "Now, how does this work? I take it that this *Post* site compensates you when they publish your blog. So if I paid you for mentioning Rafe, you'd be paid twice? Seems like a bit of a racket."

Bernie might adore her stepson, but not so much if it cost her. "You don't have to pay me," I said. "*Journalists* don't take money from their sources."

"Right then." Bernie seemed to relax. "If you can put a positive spin on Rafe's life, I'll let you write about him."

Let? I gritted my teeth, but staying on Bernie's good side was absolutely critical. "Looks like we have a deal."

"Fantastic!" said Justine. "But who'll tell Rafe?"

I hadn't intended to reveal my alter ego for a very long time—perhaps never. Although in the past, I was sorely tempted when my sister Rory, concerned about my choice of career, would ask, "what'll become of you?" Then she'd harp on my having a job like nannying, with built-in obsolescence and no pension. And Mam would add,

"Please God you'll get a better job when you finish your degree."

But when an irresistible opportunity lands in your lap, you've no choice but to grab it. And coming out as Gai to Justine and her aunt was the smartest thing I'd done in a long time. Now I had a Bernie-sanctioned reason to hang out with Rafe, with no worries she'd try to derail it. Even better, I would face him as an up-and-coming media professional, not a temporarily unemployed child minder. My spirits soared, until—

"No one will tell him," Bernie said.

I shot a fierce frown at Justine. *Say something!*

"Are you sure about this, Aunt Bernie?"

"Positive," she said. "I don't want him refusing to cooperate."

"Rafe?" Justine asked, astonished. "But he's so easygoing, and likes to make you happy—"

"Not lately." Bernie's disgruntled look was back. "So we can't risk him ruining our blog plan—everything must be completely confidential. As soon as the first post is published, I'll present the entire business as a *fait accompli.*"

"Wait a minute," I said. "I'm sure he'll come round, with the right persuasion. Perhaps Nate could talk to him?"

Bernie looked insulted. "If he won't listen to me, he'll hardly listen to Nate."

"Right, right," I said hastily. The woman was clearly mad, thinking she could keep this scheme from Rafe. But I'd already come out on top about lining her up at the Larkin House, *and* featuring Rafe in my blog. Why tempt Fate?

Justine looked from me to Bernie. "But how is Grainne to write about Rafe, if she can't interview him properly?"

Bernie scrabbled round the desk and pulled out some hotel stationary. "I'll make a list of things you'll want to include in your blog."

"But—" My jaws ached with all the clenching to keep my mouth closed. If Bernie thought a potential media personality like myself would consider creating posts with whatever scraps of information she chose to feed me, she needed to be set straight. "That won't quite work—"

"The posts won't feel authentic, Auntie, unless Grainne gets things straight from Rafe," Justine said.

I could have kissed Justine, but I don't think she'd have let me. "How about, the pair of you can give me whatever background I need?" I suggested "The rest, I can fill in with…conversation."

Bernie chewed her lip. "I'm for visiting Larkin House before I check in—since Rafe and Nate will be done fishing, perhaps we could all gather in Ballydara Monday?"

"For lunch!" Justine's face glowed. "I could do a lovely—"

"And I could ask him a few questions," I broke in, elated. "Subtle ones. He'll never guess."

"Well, all right," Bernie said grudgingly. Shoving the stationary aside, she pressed her hand to her chest. "I don't think that shrimp bisque agreed with me." She gave me an accusing stare, as if *my* portion, which she'd practically commandeered, was the culprit. "Justine, will you be a love and see if the concierge has some antacids?"

"I'll go with you," I said, eager to escape. But Bernie wasn't done with me yet.

"Remember, Grainne, our plan must stay completely under wraps."

"Right," I said, already at the door. Besides, who says I couldn't tell Rafe about *Girl Talk* anytime I chose? I could just neglect to mention that I was writing about *him*.

Justine and I got into the hotel lift in an uneasy silence. Knowing I hadn't much time, I pressed the Lobby button, sneaking peeks at her impassive face as the lift glided downward. "That was grand, the way you got Bernie on board," I said. "You were a regular font of wisdom." No response. "Really, I couldn't have done it without—"

"I *have* decided to forgive you," Justine interrupted. "Since we'll be sharing a room at your mam's starting tomorrow, we'll need to get along."

Relief flooded through me. Although I wished she hadn't

brought up Larkin House. Now that fame and fortune were just one or two blog posts away, I was ready to focus on *my* future. Not Mam's. To get Justine to smile again, I said, "And because you're my true and loyal friend?"

It worked. "Well, yeah," she said, breaking into a grin. "But make that Gai Lannigan's friend. Wait—BFF!"

"Yeah—but as Gai's best friend," I said, feeling all was right in the world once again, "your job is to make sure you or Bernie don't mention my being Gai to *anyone*. Not a living soul—"

"You mean, except your mam," Justine said. The awe on her face was gratifying. "She must be terribly proud, to have a daughter who's a famous—"

"Of course Mam hasn't a clue." Who'd want to admit you didn't tell your mam something important, because you knew she wouldn't be interested? "I'll let her know when I'm ready."

"Oh," said Justine, looking bewildered. "Of course I won't breathe a word!"

"Or to your mam either," I said.

"As if," Justine said. "I'm the first to admit Mammy would have half of Dublin in on it before nightfall..." She stopped, an arrested look on her face. "Wait a minute—if your mam doesn't know the first thing about you being Gai, who exactly does?"

The lift bell dinged. As the door opened to the lobby, I took a deep breath. "No one."

"Never!" Justine's eyes widened. "Are you actually saying no one on this earth knows except Sara Gallagher?"

"Now there's the beauty of email," I said as we exited the lift. "Sara doesn't know either."

I thought Justine's eyes would pop out of their sockets. "Jaysus," she breathed. "You're like a spy, living a double life—minding Sara's kids by day, and writing for her by night."

I grinned. "It's not like I'm blogging about the Gallagher family secrets." At least, unless I ever ran out of material on my family, and had to start in on hers. "But actually," I said, pausing to admire a baby elephant-sized floral arrangement near the desk, "I've decided to tell Sara."

"Sara! But won't she sack you when she finds out the truth?"

I shrugged. If I could handle Sara's kids, I could certainly handle their mother. "I always knew that if I wanted to build my Gai brand," whoa, that sounded good, "I'd have to tell her eventually. And now that this Rafe deal has fallen in my lap, it seems a perfect time."

I could also clue Sara in on my impressively close and personal family connection to the Byrnes. I admit, I probably should have informed Sara about Gai long ago. But the knowledge I'd something over on her was too enjoyable to contemplate giving up until I had to. Like sometime in the distant, murky future.

And it looked like that murky future was now. I had a brief fantasy of Sara's awe-struck look as I 'fessed up, and her throwing the *Post's* entire budget on its ear to give me a huge rise in pay. "Sure," I went on, "telling her after all this time is somewhat risky—"

"Yeah," Justine agreed. "She'll probably make you sign a privacy waiver."

"Make me?" I laughed. "I don't do anything I don't want to. But *you'll* want get those bloody antacids before Bernie sets the security staff after you."

We agreed to meet up in Ballydara tomorrow evening—I'd be taking the bus to Mam's, while Justine was spending the rest of the weekend in Dublin with her mother and Bernie, then her dad would drive her over later on Sunday. Exiting the Siobhan Hotel, on my way to the Dart station, I had a lovely vision of showing Rory and Mam my posts about Rafe and seeing the esteem dawn in their eyes—that their Problem Child was actually *somebody.* Rory would likely change her mind about Gai being low class too.

On the way home, I also anticipated the utter fabulousness of Sara seeing me as a valuable commodity, instead of a piece of furniture in her house that she didn't always pay on time. Since I'd planned to call round to the Gallagher's for my paycheck before they left for their holiday, I could tell Sara about Gai then. That way, she'd have plenty of time to work out the inevitable tension arising from my change in status—that is, from being her underling to a respected colleague—before we saw each other again.

Once home, I packed my most slimming black ensembles, and rewarded myself for surviving the afternoon with Bernie by eating the four lovely biscuits Justine had left for me. Settling onto my bed with my laptop to check email, I happily occupied myself imagining several scenarios of meeting Rafe, where I looked spectacular and sophisticated in them all.

I smoothed my seen-better-days duvet—that had never had a man on it, or under it...yet. While I created a mental to-do list of *put fresh sheets on bed, buy lacy knickers*, and *price new duvets*, my euphoria only increased as I envisioned my plans for this bed and waded through email.

Right up until I found the one from Sara Gallagher.

Sixteen

I can count on the fingers of one hand the times I've shared a bed with someone else the entire night. Besides Rafe, that is. Mam hadn't been the sort who brought her kiddies into the marital bed with her. I doubt Dad would've been keen on it anyway, since looking after Mam was really time-consuming and kept him perennially short of sleep.

I'd never bunked with my sisters either—although when I was small, I'd often creep into Rory's room to curl up on the floor. Any occasions that called for doubling up, like our forays to County Galway to visit Mam's relatives, I always got a spot to myself. Rory asserts I was such a viciously restless sleeper—you know, sleeping crosswise, flinging my arms and legs about—that she, Mary Alice, and our cousins would out-and-out refuse to sleep anywhere near me.

You might ask, what about my first big affair, with Donal? Hadn't I slept with him for three weeks?

Technically, no. I'd still been living at home, and since I wasn't really tempted to sneak Donal into my bedroom, why risk hurting Dad by doing it? My feelings for Donal weren't strong enough to sleep at his place either. So I'd no reason to bother with it, then be forced to lie and say I was with Justine.

The night before my twentieth birthday, though, I was prime for a breakout. Dad was away visiting his brother, and not expected back until lunchtime the next day. It seemed a golden opportunity to stick it to Mam. So, at bedtime, under her startled gaze, I pulled Donal up the stairs.

She didn't say anything, which rather took the fun out of it. But I'd got all the fun I wanted when Dad came home late that night instead, and bumped into Donal making a nocturnal trip to the loo. "You're not married yet, young man!" Dad bellowed, and he all but collared Donal and shoved him out the door. I felt so ashamed of myself I packed my things, and at daybreak, slinked out to go flat-hunting. By mid-day, a set of keys in hand, I'd realized I'd need to

get a job so I could afford the flat. When my period came that afternoon, I knew I had to jettison Donal too. So, at my birthday dinner
that night, Donal in attendance despite the donnybrook with Dad,
I announced the lot:

I was leaving home, college and Donal at one fell swoop.

Looking back, I'm thinking my precipitous series of decisions were influenced by monthly hormones, but I can't say I'd do
anything differently. Except the next time I thumbed my nose at
Mam, I'd have the sense to make sure Dad was out of the way, and
would stay out.

Justine and I settled Sunday evening into the spare room Mam
used for storage—which resembled a jumble-drawer, except it had
four walls and an old bed borrowed from Doreen Hurley. Given my
sleep history, we made a deal: one of us would get the bed and the
other what space we could clear on the floor, then trade alternate
nights. Being the perfect hostess, I offered, not too grudgingly, to
give Justine the bed that first night. Curled in my bedroll, I knew
I'd get little sleep.

For one thing, after a quarter-hour I was already stiff as a
corpse. And there was Joe. When I rang him yesterday, to say I'd
be in Ballydara for the summer, he said, "I'll drive over and see you,
then. How about sometime next week?" I managed to put him off
by giving him Mam's phone number, but now I'd one more worry—
Joe would turn up while Rafe was here.

Then, Justine kept us both up late perusing all of *Girl Talk's*
back posts. After a particularly intense session of giggles and "oh,
right!" she said, "If you're Gai, does this mean you're writing about
yourself?"

I rolled over, so my back was to her. "I mostly try to come up
with ideas that'll entertain people."

"But aren't bloggers meant to share their *own* opinions?" She
sounded disappointed.

"I suppose." I pulled the blanket over my eyes to shut out the light. "But for my blog…I just look round at the people I know, and see what inspires me."

Justine was silent for a moment. "Then who inspired those weird posts about babies?" Before I could answer, she laughed. "Oh, I know—your sister Mary Alice! Rory told me she was trying for a baby, and got up the pole in no time." She read the most recent post aloud for the second time, stopping to chortle now and then. "I didn't know you had an Uncle Larry."

"I don't," I said. "It's creative license—now, can I go to sleep?"

"You made him up too? Fantastic! I'd have never thought you're so…well, *wise*."

"Thanks," I managed, shifting onto my back. If I hadn't enough to keep me from falling asleep, I was still fuming about Saturday's email from Sara Gallagher.

> As you know, I leave on holiday Wednesday, and Dad will be in charge of editorial in the interim. I was quite keen on running *Girl Talk* while I was away, but there's been a hang-up. I know it's our most popular feature, and we get great feedback on it, but the truth is, your posts make Dad a bit nervous. :-(

I'd glared at the screen. Why Sara was allowing her dotty father to play managing editor was beyond me. And if her dad couldn't handle the content side of the *Post*, including my blog, he could always shove it up his—Then I caught myself. *Stay calm…You'll need the practice, with Rafe showing up Monday.* I took a deep breath, and kept reading.

> I've got one more post in the pipeline, then we'll take a few weeks' break. You'll have time to play with lots of ideas, and I'll expect a really fantastic piece upon my return. :-) Sara

A day later, I still couldn't believe Sara was putting my blog on hiatus. Granted, her message had been unusually conciliatory, but I couldn't help muttering, "And you know what you can do with your bloody smiley faces too, don't you?"

"Are you referring to me?" Justine said from the bed, sounding injured. "I know, I've been laughing a lot—I didn't realize my being here would—"

"I wasn't," I said hastily. "Just talking to myself—Sara Gallagher's just pulled a fast—" I broke off, as I realized how completely Sara had turned my new blog plans upside down.

If her incompetent dad wouldn't run my posts, this was hardly a good time to reveal my alter ego to Sara. It would be even less strategic, to tell her about Rafe Byrne appearing in my blog, if she wouldn't be publishing squat from me until she was back from Provence.

And now that I thought about it, was it smart to let Justine know Sara had blown off *Girl Talk* for the summer?

Really, I'd have preferred to be honest. But I couldn't deny how lovely it was to have Justine admire me. And who'd want to disillusion her best friend? Especially a best friend who might inadvertently spill the beans about the *Girl Talk* hiatus to Bernie, whom I needed to impress with my savvy and connections?

Not me, I told myself. And if my blogging career was going to be temporarily in the loo, that was just one more thing I'd keep to myself.

With my mind crammed full that night of how I'd manage Sara, Joe, Rafe, and everything else, I couldn't sleep. Finally, my eyes sandpapery, I peered at the rubbishy clock on the wall. Barely six a.m. Ugh.

"You're awake?" Justine chirped, and poked my leg with her toe.

"No." Rolling onto my stomach, I covered my head with the pillow. "Completely dead to the world." I shivered suddenly, remembering the morning I'd awakened spooned against Rafe. *He* hadn't complained about my reluctance to get out of bed...

"Too bad—time to rise and shine!" Justine poked me again. "Today's our debut Larkin House lunch, so we've tons to do."

"Isn't it bad enough," I mumbled, "I have to share a room with you, and you no sooner wake up and abuse me."

"Well, you're in luck, since I'll be after you all summer!" Laughing, she quickly straightened the bedcovers. "Come on then—Bernie's hired a car *and* a driver to get here by lunchtime. And she's used to the best!"

I pulled the pillow off my head and threw it at her. "Not all of us are keen to leap out of bed, and be disgustingly cheerful about playing scullery maid."

"But I'll be the *chef*," Justine said loftily. "Your mam's keen to test recipes later, and my spinach quiche is in the running for the first guest breakfast."

"Super," I grumbled. "I suppose porridge is all the hired help will get."

"And what's put you in such a mood?" asked Justine. "Rafe coming, I suppose."

"You suppose wrong," I said grandly, climbing out of my bedroll. Then ruined the effect by tripping over it.

Her gaze sharpened on me. "You *are* nervous about Rafe!"

"Me? His comings and goings have no effect on me whatsoever, except as they pertain to my blog," I insisted. "And I'm engaged, remember?"

"Right," Justine said drolly, and smoothed the dusty duvet.

I didn't answer. There's nothing like insomnia to focus your worries, and I realized I'd plenty of new ones. Now that Justine was in on Gai, I'd have to watch the *Girl Talk* self-disclosure. And with Sara's bad news, and the necessity for delaying the posts about Rafe, I was in a bit of a jam. Maybe I'd want to give a true and loyal friend like Justine a hint that things might not go as smoothly as we thought? And prepare her aunt too? "I've been thinking—Bernie's plan for keeping Rafe in the dark might be a problem. I mean, how can you interview someone without them knowing?"

Justine pulled out two nearly identical white shirts and discarded one. "You don't think hanging around him and asking casual questions will work?"

"I don't want to look like I'm stalking him," I said, and dug in my case for some black jeans and a top. "And I'm sure Joe wouldn't like my spending too much time with Rafe either."

"Joe again? Give me a break." Justine grinned. "Gai Lannigan will know what to do," she said, and headed for the door.

"She's not real," I pointed out. "Remember?"

"She is too," said Justine. "She's you. So you'll think of something. You always do."

THE GALLAGHER POST

Gai Lannigan's Girl Talk

Reunion with the Ex

Whenever you run into an ex—boyfriend, fiancé, husband, even a friends-with-benefits guy—a million things go through your mind. If not seeing each other anymore was his idea, it's rather rough going, isn't it? You're wondering, does he ever think about me? Or regret our breakup? And more painful, was the next girl better? In looks, money, or bed?

On the other hand, if splitting was your idea, it's not so bad. Sometimes you're embarrassed. *Ewww, I can't believe I slept with that one.* Or relieved. *Just think, I almost married him.* You might find yourself on the defensive, like when your girlfriends say, *How could you ever dump a nice fellow like that?* Or have the laugh, when they ask, *Well, then, mind if I have a go at him?*

Which brings us to an altogether different sort of break-up: when you've been with a guy you thought was The One, but you've realized it'll never work. Maybe you want more than he's offering. Or he wants more than you are. So you break off the relationship, knowing in the long run it's the best thing to do. Although best for you or him is debatable.

But whatever the situation, after it's over, every time you see him—and trust me, given the perverse way life works, you *will* see him—all you want is to show him a calm, friendly attitude. Show you're totally over him, unconcerned over who did what to whom. That you aren't the least affected by the past, or your memories. The trouble is, there will always be a man you'll never quite get over. And you can't help but remember…everything.

Seventeen

Dad and I had never been particularly close. Although I always knew he loved us, frankly, he'd always been too caught up in Mam's toils to dote too much on his daughters—especially a troublesome one like me. But since he died, we'd become proper mates. In a way.

Every time I visited Ballydara, I'd mosey up the road to St. Macdara's graveyard, and consult with Dad about life's thornier dilemmas. And today's was about the prickliest one I'd had in the last five years.

With Rafe, Nate and Bernie due to converge at Mam's house any minute, and Mam, Rory, and Justine covering the welcoming committee, I decided I wouldn't be caught dead (pardon the pun) hanging round Larkin House. If Rafe wanted to see me alone, he'd find a way.

To make myself scarce, I strolled round to Dad's grave. The shaded ground was too damp to sit on, and plunking onto the stone next to his seemed awfully disrespectful, since I believe the deceased had been a Clare Sister.

Crouching next to it, I stared down at *Matthew Xavier Larkin* carved into the polished granite. "Well, Dad, what do you think? Will I be able to pull it off?" I waited for Dad's gruff, familiar voice.

A long moment…then, *Seems like a long shot*, I could hear him saying in my head. Dad wasn't a betting man, but he did like a good horserace. Or golf tournament.

"It does, doesn't it?" I told him. "I thought I'd my hands full, with taking Joe's ring and Mam's project, then this blogging opportunity fell right in my lap."

Couldn't have fixed that bit of luck better myself, said Dad.

"But if being around Mam all summer isn't bad enough—"

Now then, I won't hear you criticize your Mam, Dad interrupted.

I rolled my eyes. If he'd said that once, he'd said it a gazillion times, despite how undeserving Mam had been of his devotion. "Fine," I sniffed, then thought for a moment. "How about, if pretending to help with her eejit B&B experiment isn't knotty enough—"

That's not much better, Dad chided.

If he was alive, he'd have given me one of his stern looks, salt-and-pepper beetle-brows meeting over his glasses. But what can I say. We'd never agreed about Mam. "—Pretending to be engaged to Joe is even more complicated."

Sounds pretty mad to me too.

I tore at some long grass covering one corner of the stone. "But when Joe slid that rock on my hand before I could move, I was stuck," I said morosely. "Then I had to keep it, to throw...em, any interested parties off the scent."

Which looked plenty fishy from up here, let me tell you.

I couldn't bring up Rafe—I mean, there's only so much you'll want your dad to know about you. "Then there's Gai...I don't regret telling Justine, but things really got out of control when I agreed to go along with Bernie. You know, keeping the posts a secret. I've got to get round her, but how?"

I waited for Dad to make a suggestion, but nothing. So I prompted, "Like I said, I thought I had everything worked out. But now I'm not so sure."

I listened hard, but I no longer heard his voice in my head...just the rustling of leaves in the beech tree overhead. Wishing I'd appreciated him more when he was still around, I reached out and traced the "X" of the "Xavier" on the stone. *I miss you, Dad.*

"You, not sure? I thought you were always sure of everything."

I jerked my hand back, wobbled on my haunches, then banged my knee on the gravestone. Pressing both palms on the stone for balance, squeezing my eyes shut. Love of God, how far had my voice carried?

And who cares about that? said my unruly heart. *It's you. You.*

I opened my eyes. "Not everything," I said, faking a light tone, and rose gracefully to my feet—Dad must've helped me, as I don't know how I managed it on my own. Ignoring my throbbing knee, I turned to see Rafe lounging against the churchyard gate.

He still had that lanky grace. Like he was relaxed, but in an instant all those muscles you didn't know he had would spring into action and you discovered he was way stronger than you could ever dream of being.

But the look of him…that had changed. It wasn't just his untrimmed hair, shot with gray, or that the lines round his eyes and mouth had deepened. Or that he sported at least four days' worth of ungroomed stubble on his chin, when he'd always been clean-shaven. He also looked…Jaysus, this sounds dead silly, but he looked dangerous.

Still, while you might not take him for a high-powered CEO, he was no Howard Hughes. "So," I said, "what brings you here?"

"Your mother sent me to tell you lunch is on."

Mam had known where to find me? I was surprised into silence. Being me, though, not for long. "I meant, here to *Ireland*," I said with exaggerated patience. "'The land of mists and widows.'"

"Or 'saints and scholars?'" Rafe quoted right back, and crossed his arms over his chest.

Despite his jaunty pose, he looked tired. Jet-lagged? Or suffering the Annulment Blues? But remembering what had happened between us five years ago—or rather, what hadn't—I wouldn't feel sorry for him. "You must be the scholar. You can't possibly be the saint."

"That makes two of us," he said coolly.

Feeling a funny pain in my chest, I couldn't speak. Our re-encounter in a cemetery, one of those best places to meet guys, should have been a good omen. But he was meant to be the wistful, vulnerable one, not me. "I call it as I see it," I said finally.

The creases in his face deepened. "I'm no scholar either, as you probably know. Not anymore."

"Er…yes," I hedged. The Egan grapevine had not only kept me apprised of Rafe's crash- and-burn as a professional golfer, but his subsequent short-lived career in academia.

"What else have you heard?" He sounded morose.

That your life has turned to crap. But suddenly I relaxed. Perhaps the man simply needed a bit of cheering up. I gave him a cheeky smile. "They say you've gone quite mad."

A spark came into his eyes. "Oh, yeah? *They* also say you've gotten engaged. Again."

Suppressing a smile, I held out my hand to admire my ring, wiggling my finger so the diamond caught the light. "Any reason I shouldn't?"

"We both know you're not the marrying kind."

"Really," I said. "What sort am I, then?"

He gave me a hard stare. "As I recall, the kind who won't settle for anything ordinary. For instance, a conventional relationship."

A lot you know, I wanted to say. What could be more ordinary than pursuing what women have been made for? "You think so?" I gave him a wide-eyed look.

"I know so," he insisted.

"I'm quite fascinated, how an upper-crust Yank with so much money it falls out of his pockets can read the mind of a middle-class Irish girl."

"Cut it out." Rafe flushed. "You never played the class card before—"

"There's a first time for everything," I returned.

He squared his jaw. "Maybe there is. Like when you spend most of your life trying to make people happy, then suddenly decide to go cold-turkey. Because you realize you can only please other people so long."

"Maybe *you* do," I said, "but *I* don't try to please them in the first place." Although I would cooperate fast enough when I'd no other way to get what I wanted.

Rafe kept looking at me, and narrowed his eyes. "Nice that you've had that freedom. Unless you've just been kidding yourself. Either way, once you break loose, you know what'll happen? No one will understand you."

Actually, no one has ever understood me. Except you. But that was a long time ago. But I didn't want to remember that. "How do you come up with this blarney, anyway?"

"It's no joke. Everyone's saying I'm crazy, for not toeing the family line. But I forgot—you don't have that problem. You've always lived your own life…right?"

I took a tiny step backward. That intense way his eyes looked into mine—it was like he knew what I was thinking, knew *me*—and a lot better than anyone else ever would. I could hardly tell him I've been living my own life, when it's been a total reaction to Mam's.

"Whatever," I said airily. I hadn't been prepared to take Rafe on quite so early in our new relationship—that is, our Gai Lannigan-stealth-interview relationship. "My life's great, actually."

Rafe shoved his hands in his trouser pockets. "Unlike mine, is that what you're implying?"

"Well, on top of the bit about you losing your mind, *they* say you've just lost a wife."

"Did *they* tell you why?"

"I'm afraid not," I lied, with an inviting smile. "Care to give me your side first?"

"No," he said shortly. "Unless you're willing to give me yours."

I frowned. "My side of why you split up with—"

"Forget about me and Lindy." He sprang away from the gate toward me, his eyes suddenly glinting, like a wolf's. "I want your side of why you changed your mind about us five years ago."

Rafe must have forgiven me for wrecking his golf career. Because five years later, the spring I turned twenty-five, hardly two minutes after we saw each other again, we were a couple.

After hanging up his golf clubs, Rafe answered the siren's song of academia. He earned his Ph.D. in double-quick time, then accepted a post at ultra-exclusive Bennett College in Vermont, as their vegetarian business philosopher-in-residence. He'd no sooner attracted a macrobiotic, Zen-inspired following and published a few business management papers, than his ailing granddad, Jack Byrne, summoned him to Seattle and Byrne Enterprises.

It was right about the time Justine and I decided to follow the typical Irish girls coming-of-age tradition: taking a summer job in America. We did the sensible thing and decided on Seattle—as if I'd argue—where we had our pick of Justine's family connections.

I signed on as an au pair for one of Justine's cousins, who'd just had her first baby, while Justine did freelance kitchen help for Bernie and her friends' dinner parties.

We'd just settled happily in Kate Carey's McMansion (two parents and an infant, five bedrooms—only in America, right?), when life took an intriguing turn. Justine and I got roped into a mad plan of Bernie's—kidnapping a load of home furnishings from her father-in-law Jack.

Bernie had called round at the Carey's, her knickers in such a twist they were practically inside out. "Rafe—he's off his head. Completely off his head!"

We'd already heard from Nate that Rafe was utterly miserable in the corporate career his granddad had foisted on him. I still didn't get the part of why someone would trade a career he enjoyed for one he hated, but that was rich people for you.

Now, horror-struck, I almost burst out, *Rafe hasn't jumped out of Byrne's penthouse office windows, has he?*

Instead, Bernie pronounced, "Rafe's making trouble again— throwing money away!"

As it turned out, Rafe hadn't taken up Internet gambling, day-trading, yacht buying, or any other rich guy's spending sprees. He was simply moving out of the family mansion in Seattle's Denny Blaine neighborhood to a compact flat downtown. "A terrible waste of money," Bernie pronounced. "He's often on the East coast for weeks at a time. Why should he let his own condo, when he has all the room he needs at Jack's?"

Trying to look sympathetic, I wished I could say, *Because…he's nearly thirty-five, and those apron strings of yours are strangling him?*

"He's planning to buy all new furnishings too!" Bernie's face was red with indignation.

"I don't think your father-in-law's furniture will fit through modern doorways," Justine pointed out.

"But Rafe has no need for new rugs and linens and things, when Jack has loads of extras that he'd never miss." When Bernie started calculating aloud the cost of the custom-made window treatments her stepson was ordering, I thought she was going to cry.

Instead, as she hit the mid-five-figures, she suddenly gasped. "I've got it! I'll kit out the flat myself, with Jack's stuff, while Rafe's away on business!" She turned a 200-watt smile on Justine and me. "Girls, you'll help me, won't you?"

Help with something that underhanded and possibly illegal, just so the Byrne's—including Bernie, who'd jet all the way to New York for a facial—could save a few farthings? While my first instinct was to say, *no fecking way*, I wasn't entirely opposed to the scheme. I rather liked the idea of putting something over on Jack Byrne, who'd been on Rafe to join his business for the last ten bloody years, the narky old autocrat. And I had a bit of a mammy-crush on Bernie, and was eager to do things to please her, in hopes of becoming one of her posse. Which, I hardly need to mention, would vastly increase the odds of running into Rafe.

So the following Saturday, dressed in a rather festive sundress, I reported for duty to the Byrne's Victorian mausoleum with Justine. All week, I'd asked myself why I'd do such a nutty thing. In exchange for enabling the Byrne's acquisitiveness in general, and Bernie's cheapness in particular, the woman might take us to dinner. No, probably lunch. To save money. Then there was Rafe. Justine's family always said he was terribly indulgent toward Bernie, loved her enough to call her "Mom." Still, wouldn't he be angry with her taking over his life like this? But the chance of seeing him overcame my admittedly shallow scruples.

As Bernie showed us round the place, accompanied by the overtly disapproving Oscar, Jack's caregiver and major-domo, I had to take care not to show my astonishment. I'd heard the Byrne place was immense, but my first glimpse of its vast polished wood floors and wainscoting, and ginormous claw-footed furniture—not to mention several generations of utterly useless and terribly ugly bric-a-brac—left me just about speechless.

Bernie started us off scarfing up items from a linen closet the size of a small garage, then on to the kitchen to pack up one of the spare sets of family china. With twenty-four place settings, mind.

Before Bernie left for some appointment, she chose several Persian rugs for Justine to roll up, while I was to dismantle the library's old bronze velvet drapes that she planned to make over for Rafe's flat.

The library was stop-in-your-tracks impressive, with its soaring ceiling, ten-foot high windows, and wall-to-wall bookcases, with those brilliant ladders attached to horizontal railings you see in English manor houses on BBC. The ladders came in handy, since I could roll them to the end of their rail, and lean right over to the windows, and no need to ask the supercilious Oscar for a proper stepladder.

My outfit, chosen to impress old Jack, should he emerge from his third-floor self-contained apartment to meet us, turned out to be wildly impractical for hanging off ladders. I couldn't help laughing to myself, thinking of Scarlett O'Hara, pulling down her mam's green velvet curtains—which matched her eyes—for a fancy dress. Though my humor didn't last, as I began the tedious process of lifting drapery hooks off the rod, and slinging the heavy velvet over my shoulders.

By early evening, my legs and back ached. And my spirit of charity toward the Byrne's, *and* my visions of life as Bernie's bosom pal began to fade. "Jaysus, I'm parched," I called to Justine, collecting embroidered throw pillows from a wee alcove across the hall. "We've not had a break since lunch."

"Right," Justine said. "I'll ask Oscar to put the kettle on."

"Bring biscuits," I commanded from my perch, and slung yet another twenty pounds of bronze velvet over my shoulder. Climbing up two more rungs, I struggled with the swathe of fabric draped over me. I'd already tons of it bunched round my legs, and another length hanging off the ladder frontward, past my feet, like a backwards dress train.

Hearing Justine's footfalls, I laughed. "Say, I need a new ball gown—you think Rafe would miss a few acres of this velvet?"

The door shut with a clunk. "You steal curtains too?"

I jerked my head down to see Rafe, standing not three feet away, face expressionless. *Five years have passed, but you've not forgiven me for the Yips at all, have you.*

"I'm no thief," I muttered, my face on fire. Not only from my Yips-guilt, but because anyone below me with two eyes could see up my dress. I tried to shift some of the material round to my back-side, then took a step down. But with my balance already impaired from the weight of the drapes, the velvet tangled round my feet. I felt myself slip.

"I was kidding!" I heard Rafe say. Sensing his leap toward me, I clutched fruitlessly at the ladder, the bookcases, anything to save myself.

"Grainne! I was kidding!"

"Get out of the—" I yelped, bronze velvet billowing all round me, and I tumbled off the ladder.

Straight on top of him.

My not inconsiderable weight drove us both to the floor, Rafe grunting at the impact. In our jumble of arms and legs and fabric, I could feel my breasts jammed between his neck and underarm, my knee between his legs, but I don't think I was hurt. And though I'd heard that the adrenaline rush from highly emotional situations—for instance, being pretzeled into a Kama Sutra sort of position, albeit fully clothed, with the man you've been dreaming about since forever—can mask pain, I'm sure I wasn't feeling any.

No screams from Rafe either, which was a good sign. But before I could get a thrill from our intimate contact, I heard him gasp. For an awful moment I thought I'd kneed him...you know, *there.*

Panicked, I thrashed round, then shoved one hand against his chest and the other against his thigh, flinging us apart. Then I crabwalked back along the smooth floor, my dress hiked almost to my bum.

Kicking the fabric out of the way, I snatched my dress down. Rafe's eyes shot to the flash of my knickers as he pushed a hunk of velvet aside and sat up. Given that look, and the fact he wasn't clutching his...you know, it appeared that we hadn't harmed his ability to father children. In fact, after a tiny peek there, I thought I detected a hint of a bulge.

"You're all right?" In my relief—I guess all that material had broken our fall—and at the absurdity of our reunion, a giggle escaped me. "Nothing's broken?" Clearly, not the Byrne family jewels. I laughed harder.

Rafe shook his head. He didn't take his eyes from me, a serious, almost poleaxed look on him. Then a faint grin appeared on his face, which morphed into chuckles, then he exploded into laughter. Soon, clutching our stomachs, we were howling together, sprawled all over the bronze velvet, when the door was hurled open.

"Jaysus, Grainne, I heard this awful thump—"

Our laughter trailed away as Justine stopped dead in the doorway. "Rafe—you were meant to be in New Yo—"

"Canceled it," Rafe said, not looking at Justine. "Heard there was a pirate around, who needed to be dealt with." I didn't look at her either, just smiled back at Rafe.

The pair of us hardly noticed when she said, "I'm thinking I'm in the way here," and backed out of the room.

"Canceled?" I breathed, almost mesmerized. I'd forgotten how blue his eyes were.

"I figured I'd have a much more *interesting* summer if I stayed closer to home." He bounced to his feet, and extended a hand toward me.

Unless I was completely delusional, it seemed clear Rafe hadn't left because of me! Deliberately, I reached out with my left hand. He appeared to examine it carefully, then and pulled me upright, smiling into my eyes. "No ring, huh?"

"Gave it back years ago," I said. Rafe didn't release my hand. Or take his eyes from mine. "Good job I didn't kill you," I finally added, to fill the silence.

"Sure is." Rafe eyes turned even bluer. "Because you're having dinner with me tonight."

Eighteen

And tomorrow night. And the one after that, I could still hear him saying.

Five years later, I didn't want to be reminded of those first, heady days with Rafe. I turned away from those sharp blue eyes and stalked past him, toward the churchyard gate. Sensing him close behind me, I was still stunned by his cryptic comment just now, *why you changed your mind five years ago.*

Either he had a bloody nerve, trying to pin our break-up on me, or he was so clueless he hadn't realized he'd been using me to rebel against his family. In any case, I knew, even if he couldn't see it, that if I hadn't been roped into helping her, Bernie would never have let me within a hundred miles of Rafe's family home.

Still, the rush of memories was hard to hold back…especially the one of Rafe and me, really alone for the first time. *I've heard all Irish girls have freckles,* he'd said as he unzipped my dress, and on the pretext of looking for one, kissed his way up my spine… Do *not* go there, I told myself. Instead, I ruthlessly focused on not tripping over the stones hidden in tufts of grass.

"Damn it, Grainne," Rafe growled behind me, "tell me—why'd you leave?"

I didn't answer Rafe until we were a few doors down from Mam's. "Don't tell me you quit Byrne's and came all the way to Ireland to ask me that," I tossed over my shoulder.

"What if I did?"

"I'd say you took your time."

"What if I said I couldn't ask you before," Rafe said as we strode up the walk, "because I couldn't call my life my own after my grandfather asked me to take over the company."

"And what if I said, you had plenty of bloody time for bloody Lin—" I broke off as Justine appeared in the front doorway, wielding a wooden spoon big enough to flatten somebody. Rafe immediately grabbed my arm, to stop me from going inside.

"And what's taken the pair of you so long?" Justine said. "The meat's going dry!"

Not answering, I stuck my chin out at Rafe, then looked pointedly down at his hand. He loosened his grasp without letting go of me. "I was just telling Grainne that...that..." Then he stuck his chin at *me*. "That I'm sorry her dad passed away."

"And I," I tried to tug my arm away, but without success, "was just telling Rafe that *I'm* sorry he lost his granddad."

Justine suddenly giggled. "Yeah, you look really sorry," she said, and disappeared inside.

"Do you mind," I said to Rafe, and shook my arm, again.

Wouldn't you know his gentlemanly manners were too ingrained for him to be a first-class Woman-Restrainer. Just when I started thinking, wouldn't it be grand if he went the masterful route and yanked me into his arms for a reunion snog, he dropped my arm.

But as I met his eyes, it was obvious snogging was, if not *the* last thing, one of the last things on his mind. "It's true, I *am* sorry about your dad," he said, a stubborn jut to his chin.

"Yeah, well, likewise," I began, "but—"

"But you're still not off the hook about why you left."

"If that's the best you can do to charm an answer out of me—"

"Grainne..."

"—You'll gather a lot of dust before I give you one."

"Look, do we have to arg—"

"Yes, we do," I snapped back, though scrapping with Rafe was the most fun I'd had with a man in...well, in the last five years. "I'm not one of your bloody subordinates, you know."

"Grainne, if you can't give me a straight answer, I'm going to—"

"Ah, hold your shirt on." While Rafe in a temper could be enthralling, I told myself, now was not the time "Why I left..." I thought fast. Perhaps a little air-clearing would help us both face the family meal. "Well, the relationship wasn't going anywhere."

Rafe looked blank. "Not going anywhere? But I'd brought you to meet my grandfather—"

He was clueless—just as I'd suspected. "Yeah, but your granddad wasn't too impressed with me." I faked a careless laugh, remembering how Jack Byrne had squinted at me, like I was some strange species of bug that wanted squashing. He'd said, "Your eyes—they're yellow!"

"It's the jaundice," I'd told him blithely. "Mild but chronic, I'm afraid." I wouldn't let the old goat hurt my feelings, since I'd been told I'd lovely golden eyes. Even once by Mam, who hardly ever noticed anything about me.

"I'm sure he liked you…" Rafe looked uncertain.

"As the household help, maybe," I retorted.

"Oh, come on. You're exaggerating—"

"I'm not!" I hated when people told me I was exaggerating—even if I was. "You've conveniently forgotten you'd invited me to dinner with your family, then your stepm—" Shite! I couldn't go there either. I'd only see Bernie's triumphant face again, when she'd made it clear that I'd never belong with the Byrne family. "Forget it."

Rafe's eyes flashed. "Forget what?"

"Nothing."

"Don't give me that! The day after the dinner, you just upped and left Seattle with no explanation. No return phone calls or emails—nothing."

I avoided his gaze. How could I explain? That since I'd been last on Mam's list all my life, I had to come first with him? But it sounded terribly unreasonable. Childish even. I steeled myself, and shrugged. "It was time to move on."

Rafe stiffened. "All of a sudden, you decided to 'move on,' just like that?"

"Just like that," I agreed, thankful that those Old Testament rules about liars no longer applied. If they had, God would've struck me dead by now.

Rafe glowered at me. "That's all you have to say about it?"

With effort, I stood my ground. "'Fraid so," I said, wringing the last drops of satisfaction I had, being in control of the situation.

"Really, it's past history, isn't it? We've both moved on." Before he could answer, I opened the front door and escaped to safety—the family lunch.

The gathering promised to be tense, with Rafe alternately ignoring me and scowling at me over the appetizer, and Bernie darting suspicious glances at me and anxious ones at him during the main course. But between Justine's peerless lamb, Mam's imperturbable hostessing, the child-free table (Rory's Ciara and Brendan were at school), and fellow-fisherman Nate's presence, lunch turned out to be a rather festive affair.

I'd managed to finesse the seat across from Rafe—the better to watch his face. Which was a mixed blessing, since the better he could see mine. With our row still fresh in my mind, and the fact that Rafe was evidently over it already—chatting up both Mam and Rory, the nerve of him—the first mouthfuls had been hard going. But Justine's pudding invariably focused my thoughts.

Forking up her apple tart, I realized stonewalling the man was hardly the way to soften him up, for my posts or...anything else. In the midst of brainstorming a few buttering-up Rafe stratagems, I almost missed Nate saying, "So, mate, what'll you do while you're on holiday?"

"I haven't given it much thought," Rafe said. "Read, relax—I don't know."

A vengeful imp made me say, "Hit the links?"

Rafe's eyes went wide, as Nate, Justine and Bernie turned appalled gazes on me. Bernie asked dangerously, "What did you say?"

"It's all right, Mom," Rafe said, then he gave me a level look. "You think I should play golf?"

The tension was so thick Mam actually noticed. "What's that?"

Nobody answered.

Mam looked round the table again. "Is there something terrible about Rafe golfing?"

Just when I thought I'd have to get a garlic necklace to ward off Bernie's venomous glare, Rory finally said, "Rafe used to play professionally, Mam, but he's not keen anymore." She gave Mam a grimace that said, *please, drop it.*

Unbelievably, Mam must've sussed out the situation. Or simply couldn't delay her own agenda another second. She gave her tummy a well-bred pat, and rose from the table. "You know, I don't have room for pudding. Mrs. Byrne, what do you say we leave the sweets for the young people, while I show you round Larkin House."

Bernie seemed reluctant, but of course she'd have to see if our place was Byrne-worthy. "I won't be long," she said to the table in general, though I sensed a warning glance in my direction as they left the room.

"Any more of this tart?" asked Nate, as I said to Rory, "I didn't know you followed sport."

"I used to," she said defensively. "You know, when I was…em…"

Married. "Right," I broke in, to spare Rory the need to mention Darren or her divorce, which still embarrassed her. Besides, I wanted to keep the conversation on Rafe. "So then," I said, watching him carefully, "have you considered it?"

Rafe didn't seem discomfited. "Taking up golf again?" Still looking at me, he leaned back in his chair. "I might—there's even a golf course near the fishing lodge. Care to join me?"

"I would," I said, thinking, *what the hell, I'll butter Rafe up later,* "but I'd hate to muck up your game."

Now it was Justine glaring at me. Nate said, "Christ," under his breath, then louder, "Justine, did you say you've more pudding?"

Rafe only took a leisurely bite of tart. "I doubt you can…muck up my game any more than it already is. But how about you? I understand you're great at games."

"You mean sport?" Rory asked. I could feel her bewildered gaze. "Our dad gave Grainne a few pointers on darts."

I leaned back in my chair. "I guess I'm not half bad at games, here or there. If I've a worthy opponent."

I knew I was being a complete eejit, risking the chance that Bernie would overhear this and sabotage our blog plans. But Rafe's and my Mexican standoff—as in, who-can-go-the-longest-without-blinking contest—was the best *craic* I'd had in ages.

And Rafe was definitely up to par. "What do you think I should do for fun, Grainne?"

I allowed the tiniest of Mona Lisa smiles. If Scarlett O'Hara's motto had been all about catching more flies with honey than vinegar, I'd already given my fly—Rafe—the vinegar treatment. Time for the honey. "If I wasn't so busy with my fiancé, I'm sure I could help you think up a few things."

Rory wore a gobsmacked expression. Nate finally said, "Well, if no one's going to eat this…" He quickly spooned up the dregs of the tart himself. I caught Justine and Rory exchanging a look, then the pair of them jumped up simultaneously. "I've a lemon curd in reserve," Justine said breathlessly.

"I'll get the coffee," said Rory. "Grainne, help us." And before I knew what she was about, she grabbed my arm and hustled me to the kitchen.

Crossing the threshold, my sister-captor pulled me to the back of the kitchen as Justine pushed the door shut. "You know him!" Rory said in a loud whisper, releasing me. She pressed the start button on the coffeemaker— to drown our voices, I guessed, more than make coffee.

Who? I was tempted to ask, but really, why waste everybody's time. "Well, Rafe and I have had…em, a previous acquaintance."

Justine snorted. Rory's brows rose as the coffeemaker began gurgling. "Previous acquaintance my arse." Rory being vulgar—she really *was* surprised. "How long have you known him?"

Forever. "Actually, about fifteen years, but sort of intermittently—"

"Never." Rory's eyes shone.

So Dad must've kept Rafe's part in my Year Fifteen drunken episode to himself. Wishing I could thank him, I managed a flippant, "I've actually impressed you?"

"Ah, shut up," Rory said cheerfully. "Here my sister never let on she was a number with Rafe Byrne, the sport sensation."

"Sport has-been, more like," I put in, and retrieved more dessert plates from the cupboard.

"Don't be catty." Rory pulled a clean knife from the drawer and set it on top of the plates. "And now Rafe runs some hugely successful company," she marveled, turning pink.

"Not anymore," I pointed out. "He's unemployed."

"Rafe is *not*," Justine corrected. "He's sort of...retired."

"I'd have thought someone like Rafe Byrne would be a horrible snob," Rory commented. "Who'd have guessed he was such a lovely man?"

Except when he's playing interrogator, grabbing a girl's arm—but that sort of he-man stuff had its own charm. "You don't think he's mad, then?"

Rory looked shocked. "Who says so?"

"Bernie," I said. "Him leaving his career, and all that."

"That's hardly mad." Rory's gaze sharpened on me. "You and Rafe seemed to have some... unfinished business. What will your Joe think?"

"He's not my Joe—"

Justine laughed, then covered her mouth.

"What?" I rounded on her.

Justine's eyes danced. "You've forgotten already, about that rock on your finger?"

Rory's eyes dropped to my left hand. "Some people don't know how lucky they are."

"Yeah," Justine added, "they can't help playing with fire, messing about with—"

She broke off as the kitchen opened and Mam glided in. "Who's being messed about?" She looked round at all of us. When no one answered, she lowered her voice confidentially. "Really, girls, you can tell me—there're no secrets in the Larkin family."

I gave Mam a hard stare. "Is that so?" I said, just loud enough for her to hear. Then I tried to laugh, but it didn't sound like me.

Rory whisked the coffeepot from the machine. "We were saying

Grainne's given me a bit of a surprise—turns out she and Rafe are… old friends," she said. "I'll bring the coffee in, then I'd better say my goodbyes—the kids'll be home from school, and we've still got some last-minute packing for our trip to America."

As Rory left, Mam looked at me as if she was really seeing me. "You *know* Rafe, then?"

Just like when I was a kid, I felt both a thrill at my mam noticing me, and a longing to retaliate because those times were so rare. "Not biblically," I said before I could stop myself. "But almost. Use your imagination."

Seeing the shock on Justine's face, I could hardly believe I'd said such a thing to my own mother. I braced myself for the reaction of any normal Irish mammy, a withering, "I'll thank you to keep the details of your relationships to yourself." Instead, what did I get?

"Maybe," Mam said mildly, "you didn't love him enough to go to bed with him."

I nearly choked. Who did she think she was anyway? My bloody sex therapist? But I managed a careless shrug. "Maybe I didn't love him at all."

Despite Justine's accusing glare, I waited for that lovely triumphant feeling, the one I used to get whenever I pulled something over on Mam, but all I got was a sour stomach.

Mam's gaze shifted. "Er…shall we bring out that lemon curd? Mrs. Byrne would like a taste."

My hand shaking, I opened the kitchen door, and Mam, bearing the curd, proceeded to the dining room without looking at me. Justine, on her way out with the plates, hissed in my ear, "It's a good job Rory didn't hear that."

Closing the door behind them, I stayed in the kitchen, trying to get my bearings. What was with me? For years, I'd been able to keep Mam at the distance she deserved. But I hadn't anticipated that living with her again would bring out all this…I don't know. Resentment.

I couldn't spend my energy sorting out my dealings with Mam, though. My future was what counted, and with Rafe here, I needed to get on with it. Tiptoeing to the door, I leaned in.

"So then, mate, what's next?" Nate was saying to Rafe.

"I thought I'd go back to my fishing digs, maybe get another day of—"

"Nate meant, after we leave for Cork today, dear," Bernie said anxiously. "And for the next fortnight."

"I know what you meant, Mom," Rafe said.

In the pause that followed, I slipped through the door and returned to the table. Taking some tiny nibbles of lemon curd—my stomach was dodgy after the run-in with Mam—I was determined to be on my best behavior. At least for the rest of the afternoon.

Concentrating on his pudding, Rafe finally said, "I could use some...time. You know, to do some thinking."

"Like a retreat?" Justine said eagerly. "Ballydara's a grand place for it, so quiet and all that. And I know a lovely lodging—"

"What about Dublin?" Bernie broke in, giving me a sideways look. "You could see the sights, do the tourist bit."

Typical Bernie, I thought. Wants to have it both ways. Get Rafe interviewed for the media, while trying to keep him away from the interviewee.

"He's seen it all before, Aunt Bernie," Nate put in.

"Actually, Dublin's not a bad idea," Rafe said, setting his fork aside. "I don't want to play tourist, but I've been thinking...I should meet with my Ireland banker. I'd like to expand the Byrne Foundation on this side of the pond—maybe look around for some Irish business opportunities while I'm at it."

"That's a wonderful idea!" Bernie's face shone. It was anyone's guess, though, whether she was pleased that Rafe was interested in some kind of career, or that he wouldn't be spending unsupervised time with me at Larkin House. "Tomorrow?"

"Why not?" Rafe said lightly. "Mrs. Larkin, is there anything I can pick up for you in Dublin?"

Rafe going to Dublin instead of staying in Galway was just the stroke of luck I'd been waiting for. Even if it was sooner than I'd planned...

"Why, what a lovely offer," Mam said. Nothing made her day like the attention of a good-looking fellow. Looking glowy again, she set her cutlery just so across her untouched dessert plate. "I'll give it some thought."

Rafe's smile broadened. "Anyone else? Justine, how about a day in the city?"

Justine shook her head. "Don't tell my mother, but the further away I am from the bank, the happier I am. Besides, tomorrow I'll be testing recipes."

I cleared my throat. "I could use a ride to Dublin—I'd like to pick up my paycheck before my employers go on holiday."

Bernie's mouth tightened. "You're sure to get carsick, Grainne. I hate to say it, but my son's a rather bad driver."

I felt a pinch of trepidation at that, before I realized what she was about: pulling out all the stops to get Rafe away from me. I thought fast. "If Rafe won't mind, while he's at his meeting, he could drop me at my fiancé's café." I flashed my ring in Bernie's direction to reassure her. "I haven't seen him since last week."

She looked torn, then gave Rafe another anxious look. "Son, they say solitude's good for the soul."

"I've had plenty of it, fishing in wilds of Connaught," Rafe said, leaning back in his chair. He didn't meet my eyes, but I detected a trace of that wolfish grin he'd flashed at the graveyard. "But who knows? The fishing could be better around Dublin."

Nineteen

Five years ago, when Rafe and I finally got serious about our mutual attraction, I hadn't put him off about sex just to be coy. There was a certain lack of opportunity, given my au pair job with Justine's cousin in Seattle. And Rafe was not only immersed in running the family company, but still living at his granddad's. Other the other hand, I'd no intention of giving the milk away for free. Not until I had some assurances that Rafe was ready to buy the cow—as in, commit to what I had in mind for us.

After my rather spectacular tumble onto Rafe at the Byrne mansion, I spent my days—in between caring for baby Madeline—dreaming about seeing him in my limited free time. After I tucked up the baby, we'd meet downtown for a couple of hours two or three evenings a week, either for dinner, if the baby was cooperative, or later, at O'Shaughnessey's Irish pub, if she wasn't.

Then the night before he finalized his condo purchase, Rafe invited me to his granddad Jack's place, ostensibly to help him pack up a few things from the old fellow's library, but in reality, to get in some uninterrupted snogging.

After a particularly passionate embrace, I broke away. "At this rate, we'll never finish your packing." Really, the thrill of teenager-ish snogging was starting to wear thin. Plus, I was keen to move our plan forward—the one Rafe didn't know about.

"Who cares?" Rafe kissed my hair, then backed me toward his grandfather's shiny desk, lifting me to sit me down on it. "Say, isn't your birthday next week?"

I only nodded, not wanting to appear to be angling for a gift. Over Rafe's objections, I'd studiously paid for all my dinners, and hadn't let him send a car to pick me up at the Carey's for our evenings together. I'd already worked out that a rich bloke like him was hit up plenty to pay for his dates with girls, and I didn't want to be one of them.

"Then a celebration's in order," Rafe said, his big hands clasping my knees. "Especially with my move to the condo. I'm ready to play hooky anyway."

"Won't Mrs. Byrne's get cross?" I asked, still a little in awe of his stepmother. "I got the impression she wasn't exactly thrilled you cancelled your East coast meetings to stay in Seattle."

"Bernie's a little overly invested in my career, but she could use some disappointment in her life." Rafe ran his hands slowly up my thighs. "I told her I was bringing you to meet Granddad, then I'm taking a little time off—think about life's big picture." He grinned at me. "Can you get a few days off and come with me?"

I looked at him from underneath my lashes. "Sounds like a grand idea. Wasn't it Socrates who said the unexamined life is not worth living?"

"I'd like to examine more than my life," he said meaningfully. "Well, will you? Join me?"

In between more snogging, I managed to convey I could get my birthday off, and was due to take a weekend. When we finally broke apart to catch our breaths, I smiled against his mouth. "We're disrespecting your granddad," and I wiggling even closer to him over the smooth surface of the desk. "But this is a fantastic way to keep the furniture dusted."

Before we could start up again, the measured footsteps of Oscar the house boss sounded in the hallway. Rafe made to pull me off the desk, but I quickly crossed my ankles round him. "You can't go until you pay the penalty."

"You really are a pirate," Rafe said, laughing. "And pretty soon, I'm going to go insane, unless you…"

"Show you my treasure chest?" I laughed back, squeezing his hips with my knees.

As the footsteps went past the door, Rafe tightened his arms. "I think we'd better find a way to be alone, or I really will go nuts. So next week, after you meet Granddad, let's go for it—celebrate your birthday…and us."

So Rafe and I planned our getaway—which would include,

after the weeks of waiting, a Big Night. Unfortunately, instead of us mutually satisfying our long-delayed lust, Rafe came to what I'm sure his family believed was his senses. And our Big Night turned into a Big Bust.

"You're not having me on?" Justine asked, moving her pint glass to position our mobiles for maximum signal strength. She leaned closer. "You've really never been to bed with Rafe?"

A few hours after Bernie and Nate had left for Cork and Rafe for his fishing lodgings, Justine and I were parked in the most coveted booth in Hurley's pub—this corner being the only place in town where you could get a mobile phone signal.

Taking a sip of Pat Hurley's version of chai, I wondered how technical I should be with the details, but decided to play it straight. "Sorry to disappoint you, but no."

"Oooh—I sense an intrigue." Justine said. "Who'd have thought it? The no sex, I mean."

As it turned out, Rafe and I *had* managed a night alone three days before our planned mini-break. When the Careys unexpectedly left to visit an ailing relative in Portland, Oregon, I broke my cardinal nanny rule about bringing a man to an employer's house and invited Rafe over. With the house to ourselves, we snogged our way up the stairs. But as soon as we bumped up against my undersized au pair bed, Rafe got an arrested look on his face.

"Say, do you, uh, have any protection?"

"I was hoping you would," I said, not entirely truthfully, then teased, "You didn't get around to asking Oscar to do a condom run for you?"

"Very funny." He sat down and pulled me onto his lap. "I was hoping you were on the pill," he said, then looked rueful. "Actually, I wasn't. But right now, it would have come in handy."

"I didn't need pills...until you," I whispered against his ear. "Maybe tonight, we could just..."

"Take things slow?" Rafe asked, then he smiled and kissed my neck. "Hey, I was a golfer. I'm used to going slow."

I slid off his lap and reached behind my neck to the zipper of my dress. "Three more days and we won't have to."

"It's going to be the longest three days of my life," Rafe said, his hands on my waist. He turned me around, brushed my fingers from my zipper, then pulled it all the way down. Slowly...

Now, in Hurley's, I found myself playing with the zipper on my fleece shirt. I quickly pulled my hand away. "Maybe Rafe and I were all about the meeting of the minds," I told Justine. "A cerebral sort of relationship, where you've evolved beyond the physical—"

"Puh-lease," said Justine. "I could've sworn you'd spent every spare minute with the man for weeks. I can't believe you couldn't work in a shag."

The night we'd had together, neither of us had slept. It had been, simultaneously, the longest night of my life, and the shortest... Picking up my mug again, I shrugged, trying not to remember the sweetness of it...not to mention the sweet nothings Rafe had murmured against my bare skin...

My mobile rang, just barely audible over the din of the pub. A far more lively spot than O'Fagan's, back in Dublin, Hurley's was *the* happening place in Ballydara. I quickly checked the display in case it was Rafe. Bloody Joe! Ringing for the third time since we'd arrived, and earlier, he'd left two messages on Mam's line too. I stuffed the phone into my pocket.

"Sorry to disappoint you, about Rafe I mean," I said. *We'd wanted our first time to be special...*

"Well, Rafe's always been a bit of a throwback," Justine said meditatively. "A gentleman, if there still is such a thing."

Gentleman? I stifled a reminiscent grin. "Haven't I told you, sex is no way to find out if a bloke is right for you?" I said. I'd known right away I didn't need to shag Rafe to lock my hormonal bond with him into place. "Back then, Rafe said he was...happy to wait, until the time was right." He'd also said, *Unless you drive me right out of my mind first.*

"What man is happy to wait?" Justine scoffed, then an alarmed look crossed her face. "Never tell me he's asexual?

"Jaysus!" I nearly dropped my mug. "Of course not!"

"Maybe that's why Lindy broke up with him! Aside from—"

"Rafe is perfectly normal! Now can we please drop the sex talk?"

Justine's eyes danced. "You're not meant to get all hot and bothered if you're going to interview the man for your blog. Or rather, Gai's not meant to."

"It would hardly be professional," I began, all dignity, despite the warmth spreading through me. I hadn't quite sorted out what to do about my blog, with Sara Gallagher putting it on hiatus, or how to work Rafe into it. But who could worry about that when I'd have the day with him in Dublin? And to expand Rafe's metaphor, with bigger fish to fry. "I would never mix business and—"

"Ah, spare me your shite." Justine poked my arm. "Think, you'll be spending the entire day with him tomorrow, all intimate in his car." She giggled. "The temptation, what with the pair of you never having it off—you could find yourselves pulling over for a snog without half trying."

Sometimes it was bloody inconvenient for your best friend to know so much about you. "Whatever," I muttered.

"And you, engaged!" she ribbed. Her smile faded and she leaned in close. "Speaking of snogging," she said low, "I still can't believe you said...*that* to your mam today."

Neither can I.

"If I'd said anything about having sex to *my* mam, she'd have clutched her heart and called an exorcist. While you throw the fact that you almost shagged Rafe right in your mam's face, and she hardly blinks."

It would take too long to explain why I'd said it. Nor did I want to confess that trying to shock Mam had had far less entertainment value than I'd hoped. But discussing my relationship with her was too...well, I just couldn't. "Didn't you say your mother took it pretty well, when you told her you'd lost your virginity?" I said, to change the subject.

She nodded. "Mam welled up a bit, then gave me a three-hour lecture about getting pregnant."

Compare that to the Eileen Larkin school of maternal connection—I couldn't even tell Mam when I'd got my first period. There's mother-daughter closeness for you. "Just showing she cares," I said.

Justine pushed her pint aside, her expression turning woebegone. "As if I'd ever take the risk with anyone but—" She sniffed. "Not that I have any chance in hell, to hook up with Ian Byrne."

It was a shame Justine hadn't developed my well-honed strategy of not liking someone unless it was a sure thing—them liking you first, that is. Otherwise, we shared the same problem: constitutionally unable to forget the Byrne men long enough to take any other guys seriously.

"What if Ian's ready for a change of heart?" Maybe I shouldn't have offered false hope, but any proper friend would at least give it a go.

"All he seems to change is his girlfriends," Justine said, staring into her pint.

Suddenly, the pub's low ceiling creaked. There was a thump, then a swishing sort of sound. "What's going on up there?" I asked Justine, to distract her. "I can't believe Doreen Hurley's cleaning the floor—I understand she's never lifted a finger round the pub."

Justine sighed, and looked back at me. "Actually, there's a local girl who's let the room to teach a yoga class. Aislin somebody or other, took yoga teacher training when she decided to have a second child. I think tonight's the first session."

"Yoga coming to Ballydara," I commented. "Ian coming to Ireland seems far more likely. You'd think Rafe and Bernie could have invited him along."

"That would be the day, Rafe and Ian traveling together," Justine said, still looking blue. "You know they really haven't anything to do with each other."

"Because of the family splitting up when they were young?" I wrapped my hands round my mug.

"The family's never spoken of it much," Justine said. "But I managed to put two and two together."

I'd learned years ago that Rafe's real mother, an Irish girl old

Jack had practically hand-picked for a daughter-in-law, had left her husband when Rafe was a boy, taking Ian with her when he was just a baby. Although Lydia, who'd clearly been one of Jack's rare miscalculations, didn't disappear entirely, despite Rafe's granddad granting her only limited access to her son.

"Bernie always said Rafe had been mad about his baby brother, that he took it hard, losing Ian so suddenly," Justine said now. She'd never spoken so freely about Rafe's past before. "And worse, Lydia had apparently used Rafe as a bargaining chip, to get a decent divorce settlement. Bernie could never forgive her for that."

"Who could blame her?" I said, for once in complete agreement with Bernie. Poor Rafe. Surely a history like this would give a man a powerful need for a life do-over, I mused. And who better than me to—

"I don't think Rafe had time to dwell on things, though," Justine said. "When he was younger, Bernie was a proper mother to him, then Jack sort of took him over—there was sport and prep school and university. And grooming him to take over the family business, of course."

"No wonder the poor man just wanted to hang out at the golf course," I said. "But if Rafe cared so much for Ian when he was young, what happened to the relationship?"

Justine looked pensive again. "I suppose they just grew apart."

My mobile rang again. Joe, probably. But just in case it was the man himself, I pulled my phone from my pocket to check.

Rory. Ready turn off the phone, in the event Mam had told Rory about what I'd said to her this afternoon, I remembered the gods of Fate had been kind to me: removed my sister from the house before she could witness my nasty behavior to Mam. Really, I'd an almost karmic obligation to take the call. "Hallo?"

"With our trip to America, I never got a chance to show you Mam's B&B paperwork," Rory began. "There's a folder of spread-sheets on the second shelf of—"

"I'm sure I'll find it," I said, not sure at all. But hearing about Rafe's past with his brother had made me appreciate my sister a little more—particularly since she wouldn't be around to bug me for the next few weeks. "You're not to worry, just have a great time." If the B&B fell apart while she was away, I'd make sure she didn't hear about it.

"There's...one more thing," Rory said, sounding reluctant. "Uncle Donald rang me today, and said Granny has a touch of bronchitis. If Mam wants to visit, will you go with her?"

"Oh." Jaysus above, even the prospect of visiting Granny O'Neill gave me the creeps. "Okay...be glad to," I lied. But the beauty of agreeing to go was I could stay on Rory's good side, while knowing that Mam never went to see her mother. Her excuse was that she'd always gotten horribly seasick on the ferry ride to the Aran Islands, where Granny lived with Mam's brother, so she'd given up on keeping in touch. My take was, if you loved somebody enough, you'd put up with any amount of discomfort or even misery to be with them...

"Grainne, you're still there? So you'll go?" Rory sounded surprised. "Look after Mam?"

"You can count on me," I said. Being so supportive of Rory actually felt rather...nice. "And...say hi to Mary Alice for me."

"Sure I will," she said. "So...see you next month," and we rang off on a high note. Feeling rather virtuous, I shifted to stow my mobile, but it rang *again*. Rory, for one last reminder to be nice to Mam? To get it over with, I quickly picked up. "You again?"

"Ah. Yes."

God save us. Joe. Sounding hurt. "Sorry," I said hastily, mouthing "Joe" to Justine. "I thought you were my sister."

"Right," he said, sounding hesitant. "I know it's late, but I'd rung...em, twice, and didn't hear back from you..."

Twice, my arse, I thought, but his fib made me feel better about ignoring his calls. "My mobile must have got turned off," I lied, as Justine frowned at me. "Everything all right?"

"I just wanted to know if...if..." Joe paused.

The oppressed feeling I often got around him picked up steam. "If what?" I said more sharply than I meant to.

"If you've decided to keep the ring," he said, fast.

I felt a squeeze of guilt. I hadn't *really* intended to humble Joe...A clatter of footsteps suddenly distracted me—the yoga people were coming down the stairs, and bringing up the rear was the teacher, the pretty, red-haired pregnant girl I'd seen before.

As she gave us a friendly smile, a brainwave struck me, full-stop: Joe was my insurance.

Everyone knows men will be more interested in you if they think they have competition. (Sounds heartless, but facts are facts.) So...in case my plans with Rafe needed a jump-start—not that I could imagine they would—but if they did, my engagement ring should remind him that there were other...*contestants.*

But whatever happened, Joe would be there for me. Just as he'd been for years. "What was that?" I asked. "I can't hear a thing in here."

"I asked," and Joe sounded a bit impatient, "if you decided to keep the ring?"

"Mam's kept us incredibly busy," I said breezily. "Runs us right off our feet. I thought I'd take the summer to think about it—"

"The whole bloody summer?"

Where'd he get off sounding belligerent? "Being engaged is an important decision," I said firmly, to hide my annoyance. "Not something to...take lightly." Or if you're wise, do at all.

"But wearing the ring isn't sealing your future in stone either," Joe said. "So what's the harm?"

I'd certainly be wearing it tomorrow, my day with Rafe. "I'll consider that too, and get back to you." I saw Justine's frown deepen.

"I'll call round to your mam's then, shall I? So we can sort it out. It's time I met her properly, anyway. How about tomorrow?"

"Sorry," I said, trying to sound regretful. "I won't have a spare minute for days." I sent Justine back a look that said, *well, it's true, isn't it?* "I'll ring you at the weekend, and we'll fix something then, okay?"

"But—"

"Talk to you then," I said quickly. "Bye!" I shoved the phone back in my pocket. "Let's go before he rings again."

Justine gave me a severe look. "One of these days, Joe's going to—"

Just then, a middle-aged fellow of not inconsiderable girth, who'd come down with the yoga class, shuffled over. "Say Justine, sorry to barge in, but any chance you girls can give me a go at the table shortly? I'm expecting an important call on a job."

"Sure, no problem, Bernard," Justine said. Our man turned out to be Pat Hurley's brother, a contractor handyman who'd been to Mam's house. After introducing us, Justine grabbed her own mobile off the table. "We were just leaving anyway—cheers."

As we wound our way through the tables, Justine nodded to the other yoga people. There was Bridie O'Donnell, who looked after her elderly mother, Mrs. Murphy, the shopkeeper, Mam's friend Doreen Hurley, and Maeve O'Donoghue, easily the most beautiful woman in town, despite being granny to two kids about the age of Rory's. Sitting with her was Edith Moore, a generation older than the rest but clearly still spry.

"I must say, you have your finger on the pulse of Ballydara," I commented to Justine as we emerged into the soft June darkness.

"You might try keeping your finger of the pulse of Joe," Justine said as we headed down the road. "If you don't watch out, he might get tired of you putting him off."

"Oh, yeah?" I suppressed a hoot of disbelief. "What's he going to do—find consolation with another girl?"

Justine yawned. "It could happen."

"I'm not worried." Joe's devotion was as constant and unvarying as the sun rising in the east. "Joe's never let me down."

We walked in silence for a few minutes. "Yeah, everyone knows he's mad keen for you," Justine finally said, as we approached the footpath to Mam's house. "But every fellow has his tipping point. Even Joe."

Twenty

"How do you like your new lodgings?" I asked Rafe in his hire car the next morning. "I suppose Larkin House wasn't quite up to your standards." I didn't try to hide my pique.

Rafe turned onto N59 to Galway City, then gave me an enigmatic look. "Larkin House seems great. But sleeping under your mother's roof didn't...suit my needs at this time." Steering with one hand, he polished off the sausage roll Justine had prepared for him.

After Nate and Bernie left for Cork yesterday, Rafe had checked out of his fishing lodgings in Oughterard, only to book a room at a place called Harmony Hotel, a few kilometers from Ballydara. In a last-ditch effort to lure him to Larkin House, Justine had packed us a lovely takeaway meal. Rafe had seemed impressed by the breakfast part of the B&B, but as far as the bed, he was sticking with the Harmony place. And now that we were on our way to Dublin, he had this rather...unpredictable aura about him. Which pleased me even less than his choice of lodgings.

I was also feeling jumpy about calling round to the Gallagher's to pick up my pay. It went without saying that with Rafe present, I could hardly tell Sara about Gai Lannigan. Not that I could sort out the sea-change in our working relationship anyway, when I needed to concentrate on Rafe. But whatever happened, I'd need to keep my game face on.

"What time is your appointment with your banker?" I asked him.

"Huh?" He took a slurp of orange juice from the flask Justine had provided.

"The appointment you mentioned yesterday," I said patiently, though with an effort. "The reason you're going to Dublin."

"Oh that," he said cheerfully. "I made it up, to get Bernie off my back. Does that interfere with your date with your...fiancé?"

Made it up? My grumpiness disappeared. In great form again, I said, "I've something to confess too—I made up going to see him."

Rafe gave me what seemed like a promising smile, then reached into our takeaway paper sack. "You want this last sausage roll?" he said, holding it out. The car veered toward the centerline.

"I'm grand, thanks," I said, tensing. "By the way, you're meant to stay between the lines on the road. If we're to get to Dublin in one piece."

"Gotcha," he said. Munching his roll, he leisurely corrected his steering. "You know what I've noticed about you?"

Oooh, I liked that. "What?"

He gave me a long look, which also didn't do much for his driving. "You don't act all that engaged."

I smiled inwardly, and held out my left hand to admire my ring. "Well, you don't act all that mad."

"Nice try," he said, and fumbled to turn on the car heating. "But we were talking about you. So...you're ready to commit to someone for life?"

"That's right." Who said it had to be Joe? "Being in love is... great." Well, if I *was* in love, it would be, wouldn't it?

Rafe glanced at me again, and the car swerved toward the verge. "But doesn't your fiancé mind that you're spending the day with an old boyfriend?"

Better and better. Rafe referring to himself as an ex. "Joe's very understanding," I said, clutching the car's elbow rest. "Could you watch the road?"

"The thing is," said Rafe, "at lunch yesterday, you were definitely—"

"The road's right *there*," and I pointed at it. Holy St. Joseph, but Bernie *had* been telling the truth. Rafe was a hideous driver.

"Flirting," Rafe finished, yanking the car back into the driving lane as we approached the outskirts of Galway City. "Since you're engaged, by most standards it's not appropriate to fli—"

"I suppose you're rather an expert on being engaged," I interrupted, still clutching the car door. "Wasn't it quite a long engagement?"

"About five years," Rafe said good-naturedly. "Almost a geologic era."

Shouldn't he be on the defensive? Especially after Lindy made a fool of him? "Rather a contrast to your three-hour marriage, wouldn't you say?"

"You got that right," said Rafe, apparently not offended in the least. He held out his mug. "Want a sip?"

I wasn't sure what to make of this pleasant, accommodating persona of his. I rather missed the spurned lover he'd played yesterday. But perhaps all this goodwill of his could work to my advantage...

I accepted the mug. "Such a short marriage hardly seemed worth that expensive wedding." As I handed it back, a light rain began to fall, misting up the windscreen.

Replacing the mug in the car's cup holder, Rafe shrugged philosophically. "Yeah—the money I laid out probably equaled the GNP of Lichtenstein."

"You paid for it?" I knew I sounded disapproving. Not so much because of the money, though. It had more to do with the way Rafe was tailgating this enormous SUV.

"Lindy's family didn't have that kind of cash," Rafe said, but didn't seem resentful. "But a fancy wedding was important to her."

I frowned. Rafe still loved the woman, faithless cow that she was? "Well, I can't picture wasting money like that," I said, feeling better as the SUV turned off the road. "Have you noticed you can't see through the windscreen?"

"Oh, yeah." Rafe twisted a few gizmos before engaging the wipers. "I'm just glad the whole episode is over and done with," he said, sounding rather cheerful.

Rafe managed to make it through Galway City without crashing the car—but just barely. When we were safely on the motorway to Dublin, I breathed a little easier, and relaxed my hold on the door.

"You do seem to be taking things awfully well, for a fellow who's just had his heart broken," I said daringly. "So what's the real story about you turning into a nutter?"

Rafe actually chuckled, which I took as a sign his heart was pretty well intact. "I wondered when you'd get back to that."

"Well, you seem reasonably sane to *me*," I said. "But as you're probably well aware, your stepmother dropped strong hints that you're in...em, delicate emotional health."

"Bernie worries too much." Rafe reached into the paper sack and pulled out one of Justine's freshly baked buns.

"If it makes you feel better," I said, "She seemed more concerned about the world's perception of your mental state, rather than your actual condition."

"Oh, I feel a hell of a lot better now." Holding the steering wheel with his knees, Rafe swiped at the foggy windscreen with his free hand, apparently forgetting about the interior air system. "What do you think? Do I seem nuts to you?"

"For God's sake, will you get your hands on the wheel!" When he obliged, I shifted in my seat to look at him more directly. "Well," I said with a challenging smile, "I've not seen enough of you to make a final judgment."

Rafe's hand tightened on the wheel. "Well, that's new." The cheerful tone was gone.

"Sorry?"

"You not rushing to judgment," he said.

My smile disappeared. He wasn't meant to get one step ahead of me like this. "How about this," I said, trying to sound pleasant, "if you're mad, then I must be too, else I wouldn't willingly go off with you. Especially with the way you're driving."

"Good point," Rafe muttered, and took a bite of his bun.

"So why not tell me the lot," I said, "and let me decide if you're off the charts, or the rumors just got out of hand." For a moment, I thought, these new insights could work for my upcoming *Girl Talk* post, but I quickly dismissed it. It was *me* who wanted to know.

He seemed to relax. "I think it all started in my golfing days. When I got the Yips. Ever try to control a full-body twitch while you're putting?"

"I don't golf, remember?"

"Oh...right," Rafe said. "You just like to watch."

So he hadn't forgotten that I'd turned up at that crucial

tournament with Donal and his ring on my finger. "Are the Yips a bit like performance anxiety?" I said, watching him closely. "Similar to…other kinds of masculine dysfunction?"

A muscle moved in his jaw, then he grinned unexpectedly. "Too bad there's no little blue pill for it."

"If there was, would you still be playing?"

Rafe shook his head. "I wasn't passionate enough about golf to work through the problem."

He'd been plenty passionate about me. But also not enough to work out the problem. "But everyone said you were so good."

Rafe shrugged. "Playing pro golf meant I could do my own thing, until I decided what to do with my life. Turns out, when my grandfather had his stroke, it was decided for me."

"Joining Byrne's?"

"I couldn't turn down my grandfather. And the pressure was intense from…everyone else."

Bernie? Lindy? I wondered, then the car swerved over the center line again. "Sweet Jesus, a lorry's coming!" I broke into a sweat.

He righted the car, then started to pull over. "Look, why don't you take the wheel."

"I…don't drive," I admitted.

Rafe looked incredulous, then accelerated back onto the road. "Why not?"

A knot grew in my middle, but I managed a careless, "With the bus or the Dart, who needs to drive in Dublin?"

"I suppose." Rafe adjusted the heating. "Now, where were we?"

"Family pressure…the business," I prompted, to get my mind off my queasy stomach.

"Right," Rafe said. "After five years, I couldn't take being CEO anymore. Although resigning so soon after Jack's death didn't go over too well with the investors. Or the board."

And even less with Miss High Budget Wedding Lindy, I'll bet. "So, what happened then?"

"How about a rest stop?" Rafe asked. "I could use some coffee."

Maybe some caffeine would help him focus on his driving. "Sounds great." Arriving at the next highway stop, I managed to pry my fingers from the elbow rest as Rafe parked the car. "I'm still keen to hear the rest of your story," I said, and as I opened the door, I shifted my shoulders to make my breasts jiggle, to see if I could get his attention.

Turns out I could. But Rafe quickly looked away. "I'm not that fascinating," he said, and bounded from the car.

While getting Rafe to look at my breasts was momentarily gratifying, it only proved he was a guy with a pulse—not that he harbored an undying passion for me. Of course, he didn't need one to participate in my grand plan, but given Rafe's driving, I was in no hurry to get back in his car.

I sipped the bottle of water I'd bought at the service kiosk, perusing the postcard rack. He approached with his own steaming cup, and said, "Ready to get a move on?"

"What's the big rush?" I said. I'd all day to finesse things with Rafe.

"We've got another sixty kilometers or so to Dublin. And after we stop at your employer's, the day will be half over. I'd like to maximize my time, since I've only got..." Rafe flicked through a row of cards then turned back to me. "Two weeks in Ireland."

"What?" My fingers slipped on my bottle, which Rafe captured neatly, his fingers touching mine. "Did you say two weeks?"

"That's...right." He handed the water back to me. "So, no time to lose."

Nearly choking on my own spit, I watched him head back to the car park. How could I have misread the situation? And subsequently planned on having two entire months with Rafe? Because bloody Bernie inferred he was on a summer-long "finding himself" holiday, that's why! Realizing I'd a shagging awful time crunch on my hands, I hastened to the car, a new, accelerated approach forming in my mind.

"Aren't Nate and Aine due back in Dublin this afternoon?" I asked as we returned to the motorway. "We could call round and say hi—"

"Maybe another time," Rafe said. "Nate was really tense all weekend—couldn't really focus on fishing."

"He *is* in the throes of expectant fatherhood," I pointed out.

"Huh?" Rafe reached into his pocket and pulled out a chocolate bar.

"You've already forgotten your best friend is about to be a father?" I said indignantly. "Aine must be about eleven months pregnant by now. You could be more supportive."

"Right," Rafe said, in a rather off-putting tone, unwrapping his chocolate with one hand. "Want half?"

What was with him? Shouldn't Rafe be fascinated by his best friend's imminent parenthood? Ready to upbraid him, I realized he could be feeling sort of threatened—that once the baby came, their friendship would go on the skids, and Nate would be too busy for him. Maybe it was up to me to show Rafe there could be some compensation in his future. I smiled to myself. Though I'd have to endure the rest of this knuckle-biting drive into town, I'd have the afternoon to help him investigate the...possibilities.

Right after I softened him up with the Gallagher kids.

Twenty-One

Rafe glided to the curb in front of the Gallagher's home in Rathmines, then ruined the effect by jerking to a stop. "This is where you work?" he asked, frowning. An overflowing kitchen bin sat on the stoop, Geoff's mud-splattered wellies beside it, with toys scattered on the lawn. "It looks like someone's house."

"It is." As we headed up the footpath, I saw a naked Barbie lying rather indecently in a border. "The Gallagher's are leaving on holiday tomorrow, so things are a bit...mad."

Alan answered the door looking harried, until he saw Rafe. His jaw dropped. "Jesus, if it isn't Rafe Byrne! The golfer!"

"Hey," Rafe said easily.

"I didn't think anyone in Ireland would actually remember you," I said to Rafe as he and Alan shook hands.

Alan looked scandalized. "Not remember an up-and-comer like Rafe Byrne? I was a great fan years ago, a great fan."

Rafe smiled gamely, and allowed his arm to be pumped so hard it's a wonder his shoulder wasn't dislocated. "Thanks, uh, Mr.—"

"That's Alan—no need to stand on ceremony, is there?" Alan finished with two mighty thrusts. "Grainne, you're a dark horse," he said, as Rafe furtively flexed his hand. "A friend of Rafe Byrne!"

"Family connection," I said smoothly, so Rafe wouldn't think I was presuming. Though we'd be a lot more than friends if I'd anything to say about it.

Without taking his hero-worshipping gaze off Rafe, Alan called, "Sara—kids! You'll never believe who's here!"

Geoff barreled pell-mell down the stairs, followed by Sara with Ivy tucked in one arm, brandishing a piece of paper like it was a royal proclamation. Thumb in mouth, Anna brought up the rear, dragging the ever-reliable Raggy.

As Sara looked round, perhaps searching for the people she was meant to be excited about, Geoff, a glob of red jam on his chin, rocketed into my arms. "Grainne!"

"Hi, little man." I lifted him up, feeling a pinch in my back.

The nights of sleeping on the floor were taking a toll—or I really was getting on. "Ready for your big holiday?" Avoiding his sticky chin, I gave Geoff a kiss, and smiled at Anna, who curled her arms round my legs.

"Hallo," Sara said to us, jiggling Ivy, then passed the paper to Alan. "This is my master travel list. You can start ticking things off."

"Hi, Mrs. Gallagher," Rafe said politely, although he looked sort of...confused.

"It's Rafe Byrne!" Alan said proudly.

Sara barely nodded. "Excuse us, will you?" She pulled Alan aside to consult The List with much muttering. In my peripheral vision, I saw Rafe sort of back away. Probably to give them privacy. Really, blokes didn't get much more polite than Rafe.

Concentrating on the kids, I said, "Having a grand time with your granny Una, are you?"

"Yeth," Anna said without removing her thumb from her mouth. "She giveths uth toast."

"With lots n' lots of strawberry jam!" added Geoff.

Ah. Una Gallagher's sucrose-loading programme was already in play. "Yum—I can see that," I said, and cut my eyes at Rafe for one of those shared smiles, as in, *ha, ha, grannies will be grannies, kids will be kids...* A frozen look on his face, Rafe didn't smile back.

"Geoff," and Sara looked up from her list, "You're allowed four DVDs. So go pack them in your case. Right now. Alan, can you help him? And absolutely only four, mind." Dutifully wriggling down from my arms, Geoff padded back upstairs, while Alan skulked after him.

Anna raised her arms to me. As I lifted her up and smoothed her hair, I tried another amused glance at Rafe, to say, *Sara's not usually this awful—pre-travel stress, you know,* but now he had a sort of desperate look about him. Not that I blamed him—Sara's tone could make the Prime Minister feel like a cipher.

Jiggling Ivy in one arm, Sara glanced at Rafe. "Do I know you?" Then to me, "Do I know him?"

"Possibly," I said, rather proud to be so well connected. "He's Ra—"

"Anna," Sara interrupted, with an exasperated look at her daughter, "Let go of Nanny and give her a hug goodbye—your granny's ready to tuck you up for your nap." She held up a haughty finger. "And Grainne, if you can hang on a moment…" She barked two more orders up the stairs to Alan.

Trying not to grind my teeth, I knelt down and put my arm round Anna. As middle-children often do, she seemed to get short shrift from her parents. "You've your special blanket all set to put in your case?" I fingered the shredded fabric.

"Ith my Raggy," Anna lisped, her thumb still in her mouth.

"So, then, Raggy's lucky, to go on holiday too." I kissed her hair. Of all the kids, I'd miss her the most—or maybe I knew she'd miss me the most. "Sweet dreams for your nap."

"I wove you, Dawnya," she whispered, touching my cheek with her thumb-sucking hand, and leaving a warm swath of spit on me.

"I wove—I mean, love you too," I whispered back. Swiping the wet spot away with my knuckles, I released her and rose, noticing Rafe's utter silence. But then, Sara hadn't yet acknowledged him properly. "Anna, upstairs now." As soon as Anna was out of earshot, she said, "Really, there's no way she's bringing that disgusting rag on holiday."

I wanted to say, *she's only three, let her have her damn Raggy, will you?* But Sara would soon discover her mistake. From the numerous occasions Raggy had gone missing, I knew that Anna wouldn't be fit to live with if her mam didn't bring it along.

In fact, should Sara be so foolish as to make good on her threat to ditch Anna's blanket, I wouldn't be surprised if she rang me from France and pleaded with me to Overnight it. Or even Same Day the Raggy, if possible. Time for another secret smile at Rafe, but before I could, Sara bundled Ivy into my arm, with another imperious, "Hold her while I get my bag, will you?"

Hoping Rafe wasn't offended at Sara treating him so cavalierly, I made a mental note to share her managerial quirks with him later.

I settled Ivy on my hip, enjoying her freshly bathed smell—which, thanks to Una, hadn't taken me two hours of hard bathroom labor to produce.

I could feel my Sara-related stress melt away. I'm always amazed by the number of people who take medication to settle their nerves, when in fact, cuddling a baby is a far simpler and all-natural path to serenity—the only side effect is that you might want one for yourself. I kissed Ivy's velvety little head, then looked up to see Sara returning with her bag in hand, Alan scrambling behind her.

"Sara," Alan was explaining, "I've been trying to tell you, this is *Rafe Byrne*. The *golfer!*"

"Rafe Byrne…" Sara frowned as she rifled through her bag, then pulled out her checkbook and a pen. "Lovely."

Love of God. The woman saw herself as a journalist, but there were times she couldn't recognize a newsworthy subject if it hit her in the arse. While she wrote the check and Alan muttered to her, I realized here was the golden opportunity to get Rafe in a receptive frame of mind before we left. "I know you'll have a lovely holiday," I whispered to Ivy and kissed her again, then I looked at Rafe. "You'll want to say good-bye to Ivy too?"

He took a step back. "Well, uh…not exac—"

"It's all right." I hid a tender smile. Perhaps Rafe hadn't held an infant since Ian's baby days, poor man. But Ivy would melt the most reserved heart. "Don't be shy," I coaxed, and turned Ivy in my arms so he could see what a gorgeous baby she was. "Have a cuddle."

"Rafe…*Byrne!*" Alan said to Sara. "Yank from Seattle, a pro golfer. Quit because of the Y—" He sent an embarrassed look in Rafe's direction. "There's been a bit of…" and he lowered his voice, "scandal in his personal life, and he just turned up on the *People* magazine Web site!"

"Byrne…Byrne…" Sara still looked blank, then finally, her face cleared. "Oh, God, that's fabulous!"

I froze, still holding Ivy, my arms half extended toward Rafe. Sara's sudden effervescence was a sure sign she was going to—

"How fantastic, to run into you," she said to Rafe. "By the way, I'm with *The Gallagher Post*."

I nearly dropped the baby. *Wait just one minute*—I managed to clutch Ivy close again as Rafe said, "Great," with a decided lack of enthusiasm.

"*GallPo*, we fondly call it in Ireland," Sara said, smiling so widely her molars gleamed. She captured Rafe's hand in an even more aggressive shake than Alan's. "I'd love to do a piece on you!"

Sara, write about Rafe? Feck! No way. No bloody way! I felt ready to burst—*he's my subject, for my post, for my blog, you bloody opportunist!* How had I not seen this coming?

"Well, uh...uh..." Rafe stalled.

Everything in me screamed to pull the woman aside, and say, *Great idea, Sara, but haven't you heard? He's mad!* But I could hardly warn her that the man was too unstable to be featured on the site, if I was submitting my own post about him. A post she wouldn't be publishing for weeks.

"Do say yes," Sara nattered on. "We don't do a lot of sport articles, but when a rising star, especially a Renaissance Man like yourself, does a bit of a crash and burn—"

"Sara," Alan said uneasily. "I don't think—"

"One problem, though," Sara went on, ignoring Alan. "I'm going on holiday tomorrow, so I'll ring you as soon as we get settled."

Rafe moved still closer to the door. "I'm...uh, not really giving intervie—"

"His...em, publicist will ring you," I broke in, as Rafe was obviously too polite to tell her he wasn't talking to the press. Except for Gai Lannigan, but he wasn't to know that. "Since we need to be on our way..." I gave the check she held a significant look.

"Super!" Sara said, handing it to me. "As far as photos—"

"His...ah, *people* will send a press packet." Juggling Ivy in one arm, I managed to stuff the check into my jeans pocket, and knew my window for softening Rafe was closing fast.

"We'll be in touch then," Sara said.

Seeing his rather sickly smile, I hadn't a minute to lose. "So then," I said to Rafe, and made to pass Ivy to him again. "Time to say goodbye."

I'd nearly relinquished my hold, when Sara threw in, "It'll be a brilliant article—that annulment of yours will really pull in the readers."

Rafe jerked up his hands, clearly in protest, and backed away, plastering himself to the door. I was forced to grasp Ivy again in an awkward baby shuffle. Sara, the overbearing cow, had completely ruined the moment.

Stumped for what to do now, I jumped as Geoff screeched, "Mr. Rafe!" He ran downstairs, straight for us, Una huffing right behind him. For an old girl carrying about five stone more than she should, she'd a lot of energy. "Mr. Rafe!" Geoff yelled again, and launched himself at Rafe. "Willya take me goffing?"

Wearing an identical beam to Alan's, Una plucked the baby from my arms. "Well now," she said to Rafe, who appeared to be frantically prying himself out of Geoff's limpet-like embrace, "My son says you're that mad golfer."

Twenty-Two

"Kids can be like cats," I said to Rafe as we drove away from the Gallagher's. "As soon as they sense you don't want to pet them, they're all over you."

He didn't reply. On our drive to Central Dublin for lunch, he seemed to have taken a vow of silence, taking frequent swipes at the jam Geoff had left on the front of his trousers. Which did *not* improve his driving.

I attributed his gloom to two things: that Ivy, taking a long, baby-serious look at him, had burst into tears, and that he found the prospect of the Sara interview as dismal as I did. "If you're worried about Sara's pursuing you for a piece, I'll get you out of it somehow," I offered as he parked the car near Temple Bar. "Since it's my fault you ran into her in the first place."

"Thanks, but I can handle the press myself," he said shortly. So Sara really *had* put Rafe's rather battered nose out of joint.

By the time we reached the pub I'd recommended—O'Fagan's, where else?—I'd already sorted out what to do about Sara: upon her return, I'd send her a blog post, with regrets that Rafe had suddenly left Ireland to go on a retreat. And in case she tried to reach him via e-mail, that he was on a technology fast in Tibet or somewhere. Leading Rafe to my favorite table, I put her out of my mind, then noticed the sticky spot was still on his trousers. "Maybe we should find a shop, and get some travel wipes for that—"

"You're a nanny!" Rafe burst out, and sat down with a thump.

"You might tone it down." I sat across from him. "We like things quiet in here."

"A nanny!" Rafe whisper-hissed this time. Was that an accusing note in his voice?

"Hey, Grainne," Eamonn the barman waved at me. "You're in luck—I've some fresh-baked lemon biscuits today. Will your friend have a pint?"

I waved back. "In a minute." I looked at Rafe, confused. "My job is news to you?"

"Back in Seattle, five years ago, you were a…a PA, weren't you?"

"You mean an 'AP'? That's what I was, an au pair to Justine's cousin Kate."

Rafe frowned. "I thought you were a personal assistant."

"I was," I said, feeling uneasy. "That's what an au pair does— you personally assist with the children."

Rafe was staring at me like he'd never seen me before. Hoping food would distract him, I gave him a disarming grin. "Shall we make it simple? Ploughman's lunch? It's Eamonn's specialty." Actually, it was the only menu item O'Fagan's offered.

He ignored that. "And now you're a…a *nanny*." Was that distaste in his voice? "Why?"

I stuck out my chin. "Why not?" Rafe didn't answer. "Okay, I get it," I said, feeling inadequate and hating it. "You're a snob."

"Don't be ridiculous—"

"A snob," I repeated. I never thought I could be so disappointed in a man. "A bloody elitist, just like the rest of your fam—" *Oh, no. Can't go there.*

"What are you talking about?" Rafe's brows knit together. "My grandfather was a penniless immigrant, for God's sake."

"I know, I know, pulled himself up by the bootstraps," I retorted. "But that didn't stop all you Byrne's from—" *Arg! Can't go there either.*

"From what?" Rafe paused, then, "Oh, I see—you're on the offensive, to avoid telling me why you've settled for a nanny job."

"I've no obligation to answer to you about anything!" I snapped. "And my job isn't 'settling,' you fecking—" Love of God, I had to calm down before anything else flew out of my mouth I'd regret. Taking a careful breath, I said, "All right then…maybe I'm…over-reacting." I forced a conciliatory smile. "Might we relax for a while before we eat?"

"You want a pint?" Rafe stood up.

"Actually," I looked up at him innocently, "how about a game of darts?"

"Darts?" Rafe's frown smoothed. "I don't know if I feel like—"

"Come on." I'd show him who was the real *crème de la crème*. I headed for the dart board before he could refuse. Feeling him behind me, I added over my shoulder, "Great way to work up an appetite."

The other great way was just not on. At least, not in O'Fagan's.

Having a dart in my hand actually did have a calming effect on me. Which I sorely needed when Rafe said, "I assume this nanny job is temporary, while you figure out a better—"

"It's not temporary at all," I said, and threw my dart with a bit of a vengeance. Predictably, I didn't score well. But from here on, I'd concentrate on the game.

When Rafe's first few throws were, in a word, crap, I relaxed even more. "I'm sure you're thinking I should go for three or four university degrees and a high-flying career," I said, nailing an inside pie. "I don't blame you, as one of the filthy rich and all that, but get used to it. I'm a domestic worker."

You'd have thought I said *sex worker*, the way his face went stiff. "You couldn't be more wrong," Rafe said.

I decided I'd do him and his game a favor, and not let this become an argument. "The au pair thing might sound glamorous, but perhaps what's confusing is the term." I said in a friendlier tone.

Rafe took his time before picking up a dart. "And 'au pair' means...what?"

"The loose translation? 'You work for peanuts, but because you're a foreigner, you're not meant to care,'" I told him. "But I *am* a nanny. It's what I do. It's who I am."

He hesitated, then threw. "But you're smart—you could be doing anything."

I blinked. He'd hit the inside pie next to mine. "Thanks," I said coolly, trying not to let his lucky throw rattle me. "But are you implying the only people qualified to take care of children are eejits?" I grabbed another dart. "Or that mothers who devote their entire lives to their kids are just as thick?"

I'll show him who's an eejit, I thought, suddenly incensed. If that's what he thinks of me, why not prove him right? I hurled my dart, barely hitting inside the circle.

"Hardly." Rafe weighed the dart in his hand before he threw. He actually hit the line of the outside bull! "Bernie pretty well dedicated her life to raising me, and as you've probably seen, she's very intelligent—"

"What I see," I hissed, forgetting my vow for serenity, "is why you kept our relation—" Jaysus! What was I saying? *Why you kept our relationship a secret five years ago.* I threw my dart as hard as I could.

And nearly missed the board. What the *feck* had happened to my game? I caught Eamonn's arrested look at me.

"What about our relationship?" Rafe asked leisurely, and threw.

I stared at the board. The dart was still vibrating, lodged quite neatly on the line of the inside bull. Crossing his arms, Rafe turned to me, smiling blandly.

I'd been had. Completely pissed about.

Rafe, the bloody hustler, had beaten the living shite out of me. "By the way," he said, "you were way off base, calling me elitist."

I stared back at him. *And how long will you keep that smile if I throw a dart up that crooked nose of yours?*

"You don't believe, me, do you?" he said, and proceeded to reel off a slew of employees' assistance programs he'd instituted at Byrne Enterprises. "And though only nine-point-two percent of the staff utilized all their personal days, nearly one hundred percent spent time in the company—"

"I hate to interrupt," I said, swallowing my ire with difficulty. "But we were talking about the caretakers of children, and their relative braininess, or lack thereof—"

"In the break room," Rafe went on, his grin widening. "Along with air hockey and Foosball, we had a dart board."

"You've obviously taken your share of breaks, then," I said, and realized what Rafe's con had revealed. Like dart-playing, his visit to Ireland was just another way to pass the time and enjoy his mid-life crisis. Well, I knew of a lovely way he could amuse himself…but how to get from here to there as soon as possible?

"Ready to eat yet?" Rafe asked.

I'd completely forgotten about food—which goes to show how this discussion about nannies being thick had sidetracked me. And I was too nervy to eat anyway. "Actually...would you be open to a minor change of plans?" My mind worked feverishly. "If you could...run me up to my flat before lunch, that would be great. I need to...pick up a few things, then we'll have the afternoon free."

"No problem," Rafe said easily. "We've got all day."

"Right," I said. I didn't have time to develop a...relationship with Rafe. What's more, if he thought I was a pathetic under-achiever, or that I wasn't good enough for him, there was no reason to have any scruples about my plans for him.

Now that I'd made up my mind—or rather, Rafe had made it up for me—it was all systems go. Full speed ahead.

On our way up to the flat, I had such a bad case of jitters I could hardly speak.

"Sulking?" Rafe asked me as we approached Howth, doing his usual lane straddling and weaving.

"Not at all," I said truthfully. I wouldn't complain about Rafe's driving, now that things were...unfolding just as they ought. "Just... thinking."

"Me too," said Rafe. "While we're in the city, what do you say to visiting a few tourist spots after all? I've never been to the James Joyce Center, or the Writer's Museum—"

"Are you planning to write a book?" I asked, relieved at the distraction. "Your memoirs? There are lots of people who'll want to know what happened with your errant bride—"

Rafe shook his head. "If I did write a book—and that's a big if—she wouldn't be in it."

Was the thought of Lindy too painful? "That would probably hurt her feelings," I said.

"Highly unlikely," Rafe said, jerking to a stop and nearly clip-ping the taillights of the car in front. "Lindy comes up pretty short in the feelings department."

Okay, so he didn't sound like a man pining for his lost love. In fact, Rafe didn't seem to give a flying feck about things other blokes in his situation would consider crucial: his golf game, his career, or his erstwhile fiancée. Even his so-called mid-life crisis seemed inert.

Well, I was going to give the man something to care about... A frisson of anticipation zinged though me as he turned onto my road. "It's that house." I pointed it out, feeling my hand tremble. "We live upstairs."

He cut the engine, and peered up at it. "Nice place."

I wouldn't invite him into the flat—it had to be his idea. Gripping the door handle, I swallowed carefully, so my voice wouldn't squeak. "I'll only be a minute." *Ask me if you can see it.* I thought the words so fiercely I was sure they'd pop through my skull. *Ask me, ask me, ask me...*

"Can I come up?"

The moment I'd been waiting for, and I was paralyzed. I couldn't remember whether our flat was fit to be seen—if we'd done the washing up before leaving for Ballydara, or if I'd even made my bed. Which was really important all of a sudden.

"Why not?" I managed. As we exited the car and climbed the stairs, my heart pounded hard enough to rattle my rib cage. If I hadn't been so nervous, I thought, unlocking the door, the sheer genius of my plan would take my breath away:

I would be just like Scarlett O'Hara, sallying forth, dimples a-twinkle, to charm, trick, or browbeat the man I'd chosen to give me what I'd no way of getting on my own. Something I wanted more than anything on earth. However, I would deviate from the Scarlett *modus operandi*—I'd ask Rafe for my heart's desire with no lies, deception or trickery either.

Closing the door behind him, I summoned all my courage. "So, then, Rafe," I said in a friendly voice, "how would you like to be the father of my child?"

Twenty-Three

Rafe's jaw went slack. "What did you say?"

"You heard me," I said. "I'm asking you to be my future child's father."

His cheeks turned a mottled red. "But...but—"

"Is that a yes?" I smiled to myself. I fully expected Rafe to resist—a little. Any sane man would. In fact, if he'd jumped at the opportunity to be my sperm donor, no questions asked, then I really would have doubted his sanity.

"You already forgot?" Rafe's jaw hardened. "I gave away the family fortune."

My grin disintegrated. "I don't want your fecking money," I said pleasantly, though my hands curled into fists. "I want your fecking...DNA."

Rafe's face suddenly relaxed. "You're kidding, right?" He burst out laughing. "Jesus, you can have a really perverse sense of humor, but you really had me going there—"

"I'm not having you on." His laughter broke off, like the laugh track on a telly that had suddenly gotten unplugged. "I want your baby."

He stared at me. "You're crazy," he said through clenched teeth. "Even more nuts than I'll ever be."

"If I was," I retorted, *really, this wasn't going so badly*, "I'd have tricked you into it."

"Trick?" Rafe looked like he'd never heard of the word.

"If a girl wants to get pregnant, and I do, wouldn't it be easy enough?" I said reasonably. "You bring a guy home, lie about birth control, then initiate a no-commitment-necessary shag. I mean, what a cliché."

"Oh, that's right." A tic began in Rafe's left eye. "You don't like to follow the crowd."

"Exactly—anyone could do *that*." I curled my lip. "I'm being spot-on straightforward."

Rafe reached behind his back for the doorknob, his hand

swatting air before he clutched the knob. "If you think," he ground out, "that I'll go to some clinic, and…and…" Now his face was a lovely rosy orange. "…Hole up alone in some cubicle to—"

"Have sexual congress with a plastic cup?" I said, and Rafe's jaw twitched. "I'm sure they'll give you a dirty magazine to help you—"

"To produce a sample of my—"

"Those in vitro things don't always take," I interrupted, cheered that he hadn't bolted straight out the flat. "Sometimes the…donors might have to repeat the process," I said with relish. "Until the little bugger's a sure thing."

Rafe's cheeks looked like they'd burst into flames. "I won't dignify that with an answer—"

"But I'd never put you through that," I said at the same time.

His brows drew together. "What do you mean?"

"I'm all for the all-natural, one hundred percent organic method."

His eyes bugged, and he turned the doorknob. I tensed for his imminent departure, but instead, he just stood there for the longest time, his color fading.

"You want to have an affair with me," he said finally, his eyes opaque. "Or more accurately, use me as your stud."

"That's the idea," I said blithely, though a niggling worry cropped up. A man off-balance, or even angry, is easier to get around. Whereas an emotionless one…isn't. See, I wanted Rafe frustrated, mad with wanting me—anything but controlled. So I said, "You can use me too. To get over Lindy. Or whatever. As long as you leave your…raincoat at home."

Well, that did it. Face blazing again, Rafe opened the door, gave me one last scathing look, and slammed out.

I'm not exactly sure when my vague longings for a child began. Like most girls, I'd thought I'd have kids…someday. Though I must have been in my mid-teens when I'd seen all I'd wanted to of Mam's mothering style, and said to myself, Jaysus, I can do better than *this*.

But I *can* tell you the minute I decided my life wouldn't be complete without a baby. And I realized I wanted one sooner rather than later. Dad and Mam had dragged me to Mary Alice's graduation, and to get my mind off my seething resentment at having to support the sister I couldn't stand, I turned to people-watching. In the row ahead of me was a young mother with a baby who was maybe seven or eight months of age. The baby was awfully squirmy, probably wanted to get on the floor for a good creep about the place. And she must've been hungry too, since she gnawed on her mammy's knuckle the minute it was offered.

Before long, she gave up on the finger, and started suckling on her mammy's chin. I watched, transfixed—how utterly amazing, for a human being to trust someone else so profoundly. To me, chin-sucking was an altogether higher level of connection from breastfeeding, where the baby got an immediate and yummy reward for sucking. Here, this baby clearly felt her mother was as much a part of her as her own thumb. I knew then that the mother-baby bond was more precious, more intimate, than other relationships can ever aspire to.

All I needed was the right, no, the *perfect* man to make it happen. And as soon as I met Rafe, I knew he was the One.

Watching from the flat's street-facing window, I saw Rafe dive into his car. Then an ear-splitting *Vrrooom* practically rattled the glass as he started the engine. I turned away. Rafe was actually going to break tradition and do the very ungentlemanly thing of abandoning me. Now I'd no ride back to County Galway.

My knees feeling unsteady all of a sudden, I staggered to the couch. Well, I'd done it—the cat was out of the bag. I told myself there was an upside to Rafe leaving me here—much safer to take the bus, even if riding in luxury with Rafe and his hired BMW had its own charm. I'd just slung my bag over my shoulder, to head down to the bus stop, when the front door banged open.

"Rafe," I said brightly, trying to hide my shock.

"You're engaged."

You could be completely deaf and not mistake the accusation in

Rafe's voice. "Well, I—"

"How could you ask me…ask me…what you asked me today, when you're going to marry someone else?"

"Good question," I stalled. "I…forgot?"

"Well, so did I," Rafe said grimly, still in the doorway. "Until about three seconds ago."

"I'm glad you didn't waste any time," I said, "to remind me."

"I've actually got a number of things to remind you about," Rafe said, a bit of the Angel-of-Death in his voice. "But if you want a ride back to Ballydara, I'm leaving in exactly two minutes." He slammed back out.

The fact that he was offering a ride was a good sign. Sure, after my proposal I'd have preferred Rafe to have taken me in his arms, say he'd be honored to have a baby with me and shall we get back to your mother's house asap and tell her to expect another grandchild? On the other hand, he hadn't actually said "no," had he?

Humming, I went to my bureau and stuffed a few pairs of knickers in my bag, locked the door, then leisurely made my way down to the car. "That was three," he said, checking his watch. "You're lucky I didn't take off without you."

And you're lucky you're still in the game. I settled into my seat as Rafe jerked the car into the roadway, and prepared to endure another knuckle-biting ride back to Galway. "So, what did you think of—"

"Be quiet," Rafe said grimly, eyes focused on the road like laser beams. "I don't want to hear one word out of you."

"Okay," I said, "but can I—"

"No!" Screeching to a halt so fast my teeth rattled, Rafe shoved the gear into Park. "I swear to God, if you so much as open your mouth I will dump you on the side of the highway. Understood?"

I nodded. Silence could be golden, especially when I needed to come up with a streamlined, yet honest way to lure Rafe into consensual, babymaking sex. Himself crashed the gear back into Drive, and we were on our way.

Although he was driving like a bat out of hell, Rafe was golden too, all the way across Ireland. He didn't once look at me, and for nearly four hours, not a word, not a peep came out of him—save for him taking one lone phone call just outside Althone. He said only, "Yes, I'll be there," and rang off. Weaving on the motorway, he stowed his mobile, and lapsed back into silence.

As we entered Ballydara, I took a sip from my water bottle, breathing a sigh of relief that this hideous trip was nearly over.

"So...what's in it for me?"

I jumped in my seat. Water dribbled down my chin. "What?"

"I can't believe you forgot already," said Rafe, his voice bland, "about that proposition of yours."

"Oh, that proposition." I surreptitiously blotted my shirt. Great—he was ready to talk turkey! "I'm allowed to speak then?"

"I'm a businessman," Rafe said, not answering the question. He turned the main village corner so fast I almost fell on top of him. "So—"

"*Were* a businessman," I reminded him, righting myself. There'd be other times to linger on top of him.

"Right," he agreed. "But I haven't forgotten about the art of the deal. Like you don't proceed without finding out what's in it for you."

"Funny you should ask, then," I said sunnily. "I should have thought it was obvious."

"Sex, you mean?"

I capped my bottle, not liking his ironic tone. "What else?"

Rafe glided to a stop in front of Mam's, then slung an arm across the top of the seat and looked me straight in the eye. "I can get sex anywhere."

I gritted my teeth, but managed sweetly, "Not from me, you can't."

"You'd be surprised," Rafe went on as if I hadn't spoken, "at the number of...offers a has-been professional athlete with a little money gets."

"I'm sure I would." Fighting the urge to smack him, I said calmly, "But *you* might be surprised to learn how many health risks you'd have with groupies."

"Risks I won't have with you?"

"*I've* a clean bill of health."

"How do I know?"

Now I really wanted to take a swing at him. "Because I say so," I said childishly. Rafe controlling the agenda this afternoon was definitely throwing me off my stride. Even more so, when he put his hand on my wrist.

"And you always tell me the truth?" Rafe asked.

"I will about this." I plucked his hand off me and gathered my bag. Wrenching the door open, I nearly fell out of the car. As I stumbled to my feet, Rafe said, "See you tomorrow."

"The hell you will," I said, and slammed the door.

Wobbling up the footpath, I heard the whirr of the car window. "Oh, you'll see me," Rafe called from the car. "And we both know it."

Twenty-Four

The nerve of him! Pissing me about like that—twice in one day!

I pulsated with fury. It was all I could do to not only bang the front door behind me, but go round and slam every other door in the house. Thought he'd see me tomorrow, did he? Well, he was fecking right!

"That you, Grainne?"

Justine—and her sympathetic ear—was home! I threw my bag and jacket on the floor and followed her voice into the kitchen, trying to compose my face into some semblance of normality. Although there was no way I could go raving to Justine about what, or who, had me boiling like the big pot she was stirring, but having her around made me feel better. "What's for supper? I'm famished." Rafe and I hadn't fit lunch in, what with our jam-packed day.

"Pasta," she said, voice more animated than usual. "We'll eat as soon as your mam gets back, and I find a spare moment to make a salad."

I sighed. "I'll do it." I plodded back to the entryway and put away the bag and jacket I'd slung onto the floor. Back in the kitchen, I washed my hands and began chopping the vegetables Justine had laid out. Mam hadn't actually ever asked me to do any house chore, nor Justine either. Justine would simply start doing it, along with everything else, and would thus guilt me into helping. "So, how was your day?" Anything to get my mind off Rafe.

"You'll never believe what I did! I've been waiting all afternoon, dying to tell—" Her eyes dropped to the carrot I was chopping. "That'd be easier if you sort of rock the knife over the—"

"Will you just let me bloody well cut vegetables the way I like? And while you're at it, tell me what's going on?"

"I saw Bridie O'Donnell in the shop," Justine said as she sliced a loaf of French bread. "Bridie mentioned a book that she'd got from her niece Deirdre. She said the book made no sense to her, but the young ones in Dublin seem to like it. It's all about taking charge of your—"

"Hey." I pointed my knife at the cooker. "You'd better take charge of your pasta—it's ready to boil over."

"Oh!" Justine turned the heat to simmer. "The pasta will get horribly soggy, but who cares?"

"This must be big," I said, "if you're willing to spoil your pasta."

"It is," Justine said. "Anyway, I spent the day reading how to be proactive about your destiny, and the power of ultimatums. So I rang Frank, and asked him to come out to Ballydara and visit me."

Frank Kenny, that tosser of a boyfriend? "You didn't!" I set my knife down before I did myself a harm. "Never tell me you're trying to have a long-distance relationship, when the short one was a disaster?"

"Hear me out," Justine said. "On the phone, I told him I was through being an afterthought to him, and unless he was ready to make a commitment—"

"Jaysus, you don't want to marry him!" I completely forgot about Rafe, being pissed about, *and* if you can believe it, having a baby. It was a grand gesture, Justine telling Frank off and everything, but if she took the man on for life, the world as we know it would be as good as over. "Please say you're not engaged?"

"No." Justine looked militant. "He tried to ring off 'cause he was busy plating a fish and chips, and with Joe around, he'd get in trouble. "'Too bad,'" I said, and I told him that unless he could be a proper boyfriend when I got back to Dublin—you know, regular nights out without canceling at the last minute, and treat me to the occasional dinner out, instead of me always picking up the tab—"

"I hope you also mentioned his ogling other girls in front of you wasn't acceptable either."

"I did," Justine said. "And if he wasn't willing to change, I didn't want to see him anymore. When he didn't answer fast enough, I rang off, with no goodbye."

Justine, rude? Now that was really showing him. "What brought on this fire-in-the-belly?" I asked, and started slicing the lettuce.

"Put that knife down," she said. "You'll bruise the lettuce—you're meant to tear it. Gently." She picked up a leaf and demonstrated.

"Back to Frank—of course I knew he'd never go for all my conditions, but that made it easy to split up with him—and consequently, create an opening in my life." She paused for a long moment. "For Ian."

That Justine was setting herself up for disappointment was the understatement of the century. "Justine—"

"It's like an energy thing," she went on. "You know, quantum physics or something. So, even if Ian doesn't love me, that's not to say he never could. He might have like this gigantic leap of consciousness, and realize that in the entire cosmos, I'm the only girl for him."

"It could happen," I said loyally, despite my misgivings. "But for this miraculous energy exchange to happen, it helps if the pair of you live in the same country. And didn't your brother say Ian's up to his ears in school and work?"

"That's true," Justine said, but I could still see the optimistic light in her eyes. "But if he did come to Ireland, and I was still in a relationship with Frank, he wouldn't look at me twice—he's too honorable."

"But Justine," I said, "you only dumped Frank today. And there's that new girlfriend we heard about…"

"Oh, her," she said, a defiant look on her face. "Bernie's implied she'd have to be a saint, to put up with Ian's schedule—he hasn't time to take her out. In fact, she could already be history, as we speak."

"But…" I needed to tread carefully here. "You won't deny yourself, like a proper relationship, because you decide to wait for Ian? I mean, he's a lovely bloke and all that, but didn't you say yourself he's a long shot?"

Justine eyes suddenly filled. Our conversations about Ian always ended up the same way, me trying to be supportive, yet talk sense into her, and her getting all depressed. "I don't care," she said. "I have to believe it could work—" she broke off as Mam breezed in.

"Well," Mam said, eyes bright, "we had a lovely book group meeting. That room above the pub Doreen organized has become the new village hot spot. And Justine, the girls loved the pastries you sent along with me." Without waiting for a comment, she turned to me. "So then, did you have a good day with Rafe?"

"It was…fine," I said sulkily. I could've been more pleasant, with her showing an interest in me, but I suppose I was trying to pay her back for all the times she hadn't.

"I had Justine ring Rafe and invite him to breakfast tomorrow," Mam said. "I want to show Mrs. Byrne we're looking after him while she's gone. And Grainne," my mother wore an oddly anxious smile, "while you were out, Joe rang."

Joe? "Oh…right—thanks."

"Three times," Mam emphasized. "We actually had a lovely chat."

"Great." You must've been really bored, I thought, and resumed tearing the lettuce.

"He asked me to tell you to ring him when you get a chance," Mam said, still watching me. "You will ring him, won't you?"

"Since when do you—" *Want to be involved in my life*, I almost sniped, then caught Justine's eye. "Take my messages?"

Justine scowled at me. Mam only laughed. "From your fiancé? Why wouldn't I?" She turned to Justine. "I'll put my things away and be right down for supper."

"You didn't have to be a cow to her," Justine said under her breath as Mam mounted the stairs. "She *is* your mother."

"I can't imagine why she's trying to chat me up," I said flippantly. Really, I told myself, defenses on high alert was the only way you could cope with Mam.

"Because you're living in the same house for the first time in ten years?" Justine said. "Not that it matters—it's just that you sounded so…cold." She sounded more sad than disapproving.

"We all can't be like you and your mam," I said. "Best mates and all that, you going along with whatever she wants."

Justine seemed surprised. "I just like to make her happy."

I weighed the notion of trying to please Mam…then swiftly banished it. She was plenty keen on doing whatever she needed to make *herself* happy—leaving no room for anyone else to take up the job. "If you were a halfway normal girl," I said, "you'd just tell your mam whatever she wanted to hear, then do what you liked anyway—"

"Lie to her?" Justine looked scandalized. "Lie to your own mam?"

I couldn't look at her. There was one perfectly acceptable excuse for lying to your mother. What if she lied to you first?

Later that evening, Justine and I were holed up in our cramped jumble room. Mam was keeping the best spare room pristine for her ladyship Bernie's booking, and ever the optimist, was saving the second best room in case Rafe should change his mind about staying at Harmony House.

I'd been reading my gorgeous edition of *Gone With the Wind*, hoping to get inspired by the part where Scarlett, ever ballsy in spite of her widows' weeds, takes Atlanta by storm. But all I could think of was how much later in the story, she'd unsuccessfully propositioned Rhett to get money for Tara's taxes—and wound up settling for homely ol' Frank Kennedy.

Too restless to read, though, I set my book aside. Had I been too overconfident with Rafe? Should I have waited until I'd got him into bed, then hit him with the baby thing? And when I saw him tomorrow, how could I regain the upper hand? Scarlett had done it by kicking Rhett out of the marital bed, but that was so not on, if I wanted to get pregnant...

I looked up to see Justine flipping though the pages of *GWTW*. "What *are* you doing?"

"Reading—"

"That's not reading!" I snatched the book from her. "You're meant to *savor* this novel—it's a work of genius, not a bloody cookery book!"

"Just looking for the hot parts," Justine said, unperturbed. She folded her arms behind her head. "You never did say—how'd you get on with Rafe today?" I bit my lip. How to be honest, yet not tell her what I got up to? "Let me guess," she went on. "Your not answering tells me you probably just tormented him all day."

"'Tormenting' seems awfully strong," I said in a mild voice. I lifted my legs straight up to point and flex my toes, my daily workout.

"Ha!" said Justine. "Given your performance at lunch yesterday, it's obvious you'd just as soon pick an argument with Rafe as look at him."

I made circles with my ankles. "Things between us are great, very friendly, amiable—"

"Did Rafe get you to play darts?" Justine giggled.

"You *knew*?" I let my legs drop. "You utter gob—" I resisted the urge to pitch the book at her head—those thousand pages would give her a concussion. "I'll overlook the fact you didn't warn me he could...hold his own, since I'm sure it's revenge for your own pathetic game."

Not insulted in the least, Justine laughed again. "He beat you, didn't he?"

The wretch! "We actually had a perfectly lovely time—"

"Bollocks," said Justine, and sat up. "From what I can tell, you and Rafe have something between you—you had it five years ago, and you still have it. It's like this...this static electricity around the pair of you."

"Really?" I asked, pleased by the analogy.

"Like a cat with its hair on end."

That didn't please me at all, but I said grandly, "You are so wrong." I much preferred to think we'd a magnetic current between us—the same current that had brought Rafe to Ireland just when I needed him most. "In fact, I really don't know what you're talking ab—"

"Save that shite for someone who'll believe it." Justine's gaze could've bored holes through a lead apron. "I've eyes in my head— the way you look at each other as if there's no one else in the room."

Did we really? "Your point?"

"The way I see it, you've two options: make your peace with Rafe and end it," Justine said, "or give into your mutual fate together.

Otherwise you'll just be in limbo, like the worst relationships—can't live with him, can't kill him."

"I don't want to *live* with him—" I pressed my lips together. I'd let this conversation get out of hand.

"But Grainne..." Justine suddenly looked serious. "Every time you're around Rafe, it's like you're...I don't know, dealing with some...some *thing*. I don't know what's with the pair of you, but I wish you'd settle it."

I resisted the urge to clarify the future I envisioned with him. We'd only start quarrelling, and in my current situation, going head-to-head with Rafe, and not letting Mam get the better of me consumed pretty much all my arguing energy. "You seem to have forgotten about Joe," I said, my deft attempt to change the subject. "But I haven't."

Justine snorted. "My guess is, Joe is a mere speck on the telly screen of your life. So why not put him out of your head, while you deal with Rafe."

"But that hardly seems fair to Joe," I said. Though to be honest, he *was* a bit of a dust mote in the general scheme of things.

Justine rolled off the bed to her feet, and began gathering her laundry. "What about being fair to Rafe?"

My throat caught—along with my conscience. *She's right. But what's fair to me?* I knew what I'd been to Rafe five years ago: his last chance at post-adolescent madness before his grandfather got his hooks into him. But now? Who knew? All I could say was, "Rafe can take care of himself."

"You think? I don't doubt Joe'll get over you," said Justine. "But I'm not sure Rafe will."

I'd heard once that sometimes you see things most clearly in the dark. Unable to sleep that night, I puzzled over what Justine had said. Rafe didn't actually...well, *like* me, did he? I got a funny ache in my throat, just thinking of it. And if he did, was my intention to hit him up for something he might not want to give me on his own, unworthy? Disastardly, even?

Not at all, I told myself resolutely. A girl's got to look out for herself. Scarlett O'Hara had been prepared to sell herself to Rhett for three hundred lousy dollars—but I was one up on her. *I* was prepared to give myself to Rafe for free, gratis, no strings—except a bit of sperm.

So it couldn't be my conscience keeping me awake…more like too much pasta, too much Mam, and too much uncertainty about my next move with Rafe.

I think I finally dropped off around three a.m. But what felt like ten minutes later, I was jolted awake by the house phone in the hallway. Clambering to my feet, I squinted at the time. Jaysus, it *was* ten minutes later.

"Chrissakes, can't you get that?" Justine mumbled.

"What sort of gobshite rings in the bloody middle of the night," I complained, then checked the phone display. Oh. *That* gobshite.

I cleared my throat a couple of times so I wouldn't sound as if I'd just been awakened, then picked up. "Rafe—lovely to hear from you—"

"I'll bet. Just checking to see—"

"Although you must have some emergency, to ring at this time of night," I interrupted. "Not that I care."

"Just making sure you haven't skipped town," he said calmly. "I'll see you at breakfast. Then we'll take a walk, pick up where we left off." He rang off.

"What the hell is Rafe about, ringing like this?" Justine mumbled.

I curled back into my bedroll. "He…needed to tell me something."

"Nothing that couldn't have waited until, say, sunrise?" Justine said into her pillow.

"He thought he should ring straightaway, in case he forgot to mention it tomorrow." Justine's only response was a delicate snore. Then I remembered something crucial—something I'd overlooked in the heat of the moment at my flat. And all the hours since.

Rafe hadn't said no.

I practically hugged myself. If Justine, the ultimate pragmatist, could see that Rafe was attracted to me, it must be true. So why not put it to use?

And I could revise my *Gone with the Wind* storyline entirely: Instead of slinking out of the Atlanta jail, Rhett's jeers still ringing in her ears, Scarlett (that would be me) would sashay out in triumph. With her man's three hundred dollars (that would be Rafe and his... cells) tucked safely in her reticule.

Twenty-Five

"Great breakfast, Justine," Rafe said the next morning, packing down eggs and rashers like he hadn't eaten for a week.

I watched approvingly. The full Irish fry was my idea—I'd heard meat was full of B vitamins, grand for preparing the body for conception—and I'd even persuaded Justine to include white and black pudding. Indulging in some lovely daydreams of hitting the jackpot with my first shag with Rafe, I lingered on his face and lovely crooked nose. When he met my eyes, I quickly looked away.

We'd been playing sort of eye contact tag since he arrived, without talking to each other. He'd come in, given me a meaningful look, as if to say, *we're going to have it out, whether you like it or not.* Which I returned with lifted brows, as in, *Yeah? We will if I feel like it, we won't if I don't.*

Justine had looked from me to Rafe and back again, then rolled her eyes, and focused on serving up all that protein. "Mrs. Larkin said to go ahead and start without her—she's not much of an early riser. But I didn't think you were either, Rafe."

"Early bird gets the worm," Rafe said cheerfully.

"If you like worms," I said.

"Mother of Jaysus," Justine said under her breath. "Anyway, Rafe, Grainne's mam invited you to have supper with us tonight."

I forked up a bite of eggs, feeling ambivalent about the invitation. Sure, I'd been all for Rafe staying at Mam's B&B, but I'd discovered I didn't think very straight when the three of us—he, Mam and I—were in the same room.

Before I could sort out how to disinvite Rafe, Justine said, "Grainne, I forgot to tell you—yesterday, when I was on the phone with Frank, before I gave out at him—he's my now ex, Rafe—Sinead was nearby, and she says to Frank, 'say hi to Justine and Grainne for me.' Then she said, 'Of course, Joe says hi to Grainne too.'"

I glared at Justine. The less said about Joe, especially in Rafe's presence, the less I'd have to lie. "Lovely of her, I'm sure."

"Joe is Grainne's fiancé," Justine explained to Rafe, "and Sinead works at his restaurant." She sent me a sly look.

Was Justine, emboldened by dumping Frank, trying to get me to 'settle things' with Rafe? "Your fiancé owns a restaurant?" Rafe asked, his first direct remark to me.

"It's more of a coffee shop." I gave Justine a warning look. *Enough about Joe.*

She only grinned, and passed round a pitcher of juice. "It's quite successful."

"In an average kind of way," I rebutted, setting the pitcher down with a thump.

"You don't sound too supportive," said Rafe, cutting his white pudding. "Even if his place is only averagely successful, I imagine this guy makes a good living." He gave my diamond ring a significant look. "He can support a family."

"I don't care about his money," I was goaded into snapping. "Or...anyone else's." Rafe only grinned, the shite-eating sort you'd want to smack right off his face. "I can take care of myself, with my *nanny* job," I added significantly.

Rafe suddenly looked pained. Savoring my zinger, I asked him, "So then, what...game are you playing today?"

"*Grainne,*" Justine said, like she was grinding her teeth. But Rafe said, "You mean, what'll I do today? Don't you remember, we're taking a stroll around Ballydara."

"That'll be one short walk," I said, "since you can see the whole village from Mam's front window."

"Oh, I'm sure we'll find a way to...amuse ourselves," was Rafe's riposte.

That sounded promising. And Justine played right into my hands. "I hope you'll be able to run back to Dublin before you leave Ireland, to see Nate and Aine's baby," she said. "It's due any day now."

Rafe didn't say anything. "I'm sure Nate'll be quite the proud papa, wanting to show off the baby," I prodded him. Sure, he couldn't ignore *that* hint.

When Rafe only forked up a massive chunk of black pudding,

I thought, *Right, ignore me at your peril.* I calmly pointed my knife at his plate. "You'll want a smaller bite of that. Especially if you're a black pudding virgin."

Rafe cocked an eyebrow at me, and lifted his fork. "You eat this stuff?"

"All the time," I lied cheerfully, then scooped up the last of my eggs.

Practically inhaling the pudding bite, Rafe chewed enthusiastically, then a strange look came over his face. "What's in this?"

"Well, it used to be called blood sausage," I told him. "For obvious reasons."

Rafe started coughing. Grabbing his water glass, he drained it and stood up. "Say," he croaked, "do you have a spare toothbrush, for your B&B customers?"

"In the bathroom," Justine told him.

"Thanks for the meal," Rafe said. "And that Frank's a real idiot for letting you go." He rushed out of the dining room.

Justine's expression took on a faraway look—the Ian daydream look—then she seemed to come back to reality. "You know, Rafe's acting a bit mad."

"In what way?" I said absently, mentally calculating how many times Rafe and I could have it off before he went back to America. But hadn't I read that a man's sperm count and quality could be reduced by too frequent sex? Better Google that.

"Jaysus, it can't have escaped your notice that the man acts completely out of character when you're around."

"Like how?"

"Like eating black pudding to prove his manhood," Justine said crossly. "Or ringing his girlfriends in the dead of night—"

"You think I'm his girlfriend?" I said, secretly elated.

"I don't know what else to call you," Justine said, and began clearing the table. "Although here you are, wearing Joe's ring. But I just remembered something else Frank said on the phone yesterday—Sinead was acting sort of weird."

"You and Frank always think Sinead's acting weird."

"But he said it was a new kind of weird," Justine said. "Like she owned the place."

"That's hardly new," I said. "You know she's keen on being the manager."

"You're not the least bit—ah, forget it. I've better things to think about. And I'm sure you know what you're doing."

"Concerned, you were going to say?" I asked. "Actually, I'm not in the least. And yes, I *do* know what I'm doing."

"Well, I don't." Heading for the door, Justine stopped, and gave me an inscrutable look. "Tell me I'm wrong, but it looks to me like you're pissing about both Joe *and* Rafe."

Meeting me in Mam's entryway, Rafe had hardly closed the front door behind us when he said, "Yesterday, you told me you wouldn't need to get tested." He set off jauntily along the main road. Lined with low stone walls, the road was bordered by thick woods on our right, pastures and the occasional house on our left. "That is, if I decided to take you up on your offer."

Matching his stride, I said, "The village is thataway," and I pointed back toward the shops. "This way takes us past the golf course—you don't mind?"

"I figured we wouldn't want our...conversation overheard by any passersby," he said, and kept walking. "And the sight of a golf course won't give me a Yips attack."

I lifted my face to the sun, peeking out from the puffy clouds scudding in from the west. With any luck, it wouldn't rain for the next hour or two, and I'd enough nervous energy to hike all the way to Lough Corrib, if he wanted. "Right then," I said, "about testing. I won't need to ask you either?"

"Let's just say my sexual escapades have been pretty limited the last few years."

"What about Lindy?" I asked before I could stop myself. "Your escapades with her?"

"There are a couple of things you should know," Rafe said. "One, we got tested. And two, they weren't escapades."

So sex had been on the tame side? "Can I have that in writing?"

"Are you going to pass it on to the tabloids?" he asked, grinning.

I couldn't smile back—not even a fake one. I'd pretty well put the blog post I was meant to write for Bernie out of my mind. At this stage of the game, getting pregnant was my Number One priority. "Look," I said as we followed the curve of the road, and the golf links, set on low, rolling hills, came into view. "This is all quite entertaining, but can we just get back to my...proposal?"

Rafe was silent. While my impatience mounted, I told myself to keep my cool. We'd reached the other end of the course before Rafe answered. "We've got some things to talk about first."

"We're talking now. Aren't we?"

"Hardly," Rafe said. He touched my arm with just enough pressure to compel me to look at him. "You have a really annoying way of answering my questions with a question."

"Call me naturally curious. For instance, why are we taking this walk, when we could be doing much more...interesting things?"

"I'm big on fresh air, nature, all that stuff." Rafe's mouth quirked.

"Well, what could be more natural than—"

"Since you've heard so much about my life," Rafe broke in, "it's only fair that you tell me about yours."

Now it was me taking my time. I told myself there was nothing to tell. Not much, anyway. "Fair is fair," I agreed, not meaning it.

"Well, I'm ready," Rafe said. "Entertain me."

"Entertain you?" I repeated.

"Yep. I want your life story. The highs, the lows, the fantastical, the dirt—"

"Forget it," I said. "I'm not going to be your personal shagging Scheherazade." When Rafe had the nerve to laugh, I added, "You've a point to all this?"

Rafe just stuck his hands in his pockets and looked round. "Nice country." We were walking past the other side of the deep woods. "This road'll take us back to the village?"

"Yes," I said. "But—"

"Hang on a sec." He seemed to be staring at a bedraggled "For Sale" sign at the edge of the woods, not far from the O'Donoghue place. "I wonder who owns this."

"I've no idea—that sign's been there a while," I said. "And don't try to change the subject—you'd a point to make?"

He turned back to me and picked up his pace.

"I've actually got three," he said. "The first is that if we're going to trade life stories, you've got some catching up to do."

I thought fast. "You can always ask Justine about me. Or Rory."

"Doesn't count," he said. "Because you'll talk Justine and everyone else you know into feeding me your version of what you want me to know. Then you'll be off the hook."

Rafe and his bloody upper hand and his bloody grin were getting bloody annoying. "Are you hoping the life stories come from me?"

"No, I'm requiring that they do."

"You're not the CEO of *me*," I said, sulky. "Since when do you have the right to make all these conditions?"

"Since you propositioned me," he said. "Learning what makes you...tick, will help me make my decision. So, for my second point, I'm telling you that I have no intention of considering... uh, *it*, without... without..."

I looked at him from beneath my lashes. "Without giving me a test drive first?"

"No!" He reddened. "If I'm going to even *think* about your proposal, I want to be as knowledgeable about the...situation as possible."

"Seems pretty straightforward to me," I put in. "We have sex."

He ignored me. "But my most important requirement..."

I resisted the temptation to say, *You want my firstborn? No problem—because it'll be yours.* "Yes?" I said politely. "Numero Uno?"

Rafe paused for a moment. "I want you to be truthful."

Truthful. I was relieved to see the village up ahead, and wondered if Pat Hurley kept any biscuits at the pub. I was starting to feel so muddled I needed a sweet in the worst way. "Are you calling me a liar?"

"No," he said, appearing to choose his words with care. "Just pointing out you have a certain tendency toward…uh…well…"

"Prevarication? Obfuscation?"

Rafe looked surprised, then he started to grin. "That's one fancy way of—"

"I may be a nanny," I interrupted, "but I'm not completely ignorant."

Rafe's smile disappeared. He took two long strides away, then stopped abruptly and turned back to me. "You know, with that giant chip on your shoulder we're not going to get very far."

I had to get Rafe in bed, and soon—before he got too attached to this life story shite. I stopped walking too. "So," I said in a sultry voice, "How far do you want to go?"

At this point, my Inner Yang was embracing what a great distraction sex could be. But on my Yin, shadow side, whatever I felt for Rafe, I would just as soon not know what it was.

Still, when Rafe narrowed his eyes at me, I quailed inwardly. Then he started laughing.

"What?"

He just looked at me, crossed his arms and laughed harder.

If there was one thing that drove me mad, it was being laughed at. "What's so fecking funny, then?"

"You!" He slapped his knee, roaring.

"If the folk who think you're mad could see you now," I said, "they'd be convinced of it."

Rafe snorted, and kept laughing. After a long moment, which I spent looking about to make sure no one had witnessed him going round the bend right here in public and had rung the local Guards, his laughter trailed away. "You know, I'm on to you now."

I resisted the urge to shake him. "Oh?"

"You'll do anything, feed me all kinds of bullshit to keep from being up front with me."

"My proposition wasn't shite," I retorted, and set off again. "I meant it."

"Exception to the rule," Rafe said. "The Grainne Larkin rule of All, One-Hundred Percent Bullshit, All The Time. You can't—won't—be straight with me."

Can too, I almost said, but Rafe stopped me with a look. "Okay, here's a test. You ask me something. I'll answer—truthfully—then I get to ask you something. And you can't answer me with a question."

"This is ridiculous," I sputtered. "I don't need a fecking test to—"

"Trying to weasel out of actually leveling with me?"

"Of course not—"

"Truth-telling will be our Marquis of Queensbury rules," Rafe said, an unholy gleam in his eyes. "Just like no kicking, no kidney punches, or hitting below the belt—"

"And why would I do that?" I asked innocently, "if I want you in primo virility—"

"Let's stick to the subject at hand," Rafe said. "You ask me, I ask you."

"Well, then, bring it on," I said brazenly, feeling anything but.

"You get to ask me something first," Rafe reminded me.

"Oh. Right." Before I lost my nerve, I looked him straight in the eye. "Did you come to Ireland expressly to see me?"

Rafe's gaze shifted infinitesimally. "Who else?"

"You're not meant to answer with a question," I said. Rafe's eyes had already told me Justine had been right—but I wanted him to admit it. "Queensbury rules."

"Yes, then," he said, and colored again.

With that blush, I felt an entirely unexpected tenderness. But I squashed the emotion immediately. Now that he'd admitted why he'd come all this way, getting him to bed couldn't be far away. "Your turn." I braced myself.

Rafe pushed his hands into his trouser pockets. "Okay—question: You're not really engaged, are you? Because if you were, why didn't you ask him to have a chil—"

"That's two questions," I interrupted. "You can't even follow your own bloody rules."

"See, you're doing it again," Rafe said. "Trying to avoid the question."

"Just going along with the one-question deal," I told him. As we re-entered the village, the pouffy white clouds I'd admired at the start of our walk were turning dark.

"Okay," Rafe said, and took a deep breath. "Are you really engaged?"

I winced. I had to tell the truth. "Not…officially."

Before I knew what he was about, he clasped my left hand and lifted it. "This rock looks pretty official."

"I regard it as more of a *pre*-engagement ring." I gave a nonchalant smile to Mrs. Murphy, sweeping the stoop of her shop.

He held my hand another moment, then dropped it. "You know, there's no use talking about this…proposition of yours at all, as long as you're with this guy."

"I'm not 'with' Joe," I said quickly. Hell, telling the truth really wasn't so bad. "If it makes you feel better, I'll stop wearing the ring." I pulled it off, and stuffed it into the pocket of my jeans. "See?"

"Not good enough." Rafe held my gaze in a disconcerting way. "If you're serious, you should give it back to him."

No way. Joe was my back-up. "I *could*," I said slowly. "Maybe the next time I see him." Out of the corner of my eye, I saw a man with a familiar profile climb out of a car. Oh, Jaysus, what'll I do now?

"Unfortunately," and Rafe clasped my hand again, running his thumb over my skin. "I don't want you to see this Joe. Or even talk to him."

Rafe sounded entirely serious. And how unlike a polite fellow such as himself, to make a chauvinistic request like that.

Panicky, I yanked my hand away. I knew about power plays, about asking for more than you can get—my strategy exactly when I'd asked Rafe to give me a baby. But Rafe's gaze seemed to imply anything but games.

"I'm afraid avoiding Joe isn't possible," I said as the man approached us. "I'll introduce you, shall I?"

Twenty-Six

I'm a great one for embracing your Inner Cavegirl.

So Rafe squaring his jaw in an ever-so-manly fashion, and Joe hunching his shoulder and cocking an arm, as if primed to throw the first punch despite Rafe being half a head taller, gave me a definite buzz.

The thrill evaporated as Joe suddenly un-hunched himself, and smiled uncertainly. "Say, you're that golf fella, aren't you?"

Rafe's face relaxed too. "Actually, I'm known as 'that mad golf fella,' but yes."

"He's called Rafe Byrne," I said quickly. "He's Justine's cousin."

"Rafe Byrne!" Joe's eyes shone as he shook Rafe's hand. "No kidding! I wish Dad could see this—he's dead keen for golf."

I stared at the pair of them, perplexed.

"We saw you on telly—what, nine, ten years ago?" Joe went on. "That tournament where you made a hole in one, before the Yips got you." A mortified looked crossed his face. "Jaysus, you don't mind I said that?"

"Hell no," Rafe said, with a rueful smile. "But the Irish sure have good memories."

"Ah, feck the gossips," said Joe. "You were fantastic, that's for sure—"

"Excuse me," I said. Rafe was meant to see Joe as his competition, not his pal! "I have to make a phone call."

They paid me no mind, already chatting about Joe's restaurant. Rushing into Hurley's—walking to Mam's would take too long—I nodded to Pat and made for the back booth, luckily empty, and pulled out my phone. "In the name of God," I hissed as soon as Justine picked up the house line, "what were you thinking, to tell Joe where to find us?"

"Don't you give out at me," Justine retorted. "You're the one putting off the poor man. Besides, it was your mam who told Joe."

"Mam?" I found myself squeezing the phone hard enough to crack it. Why the feck would *she* try to bollux up my time with

Rafe? Unless she was back to her old pastime, playing one person against the other...I swiftly pushed that thought away, picturing the two men in my mind's eye.

Who would I want my baby to look like? No contest. Joe was not only shorter than Rafe, but rounder. As in, everything: chin, cheeks, tummy, and bum, his roundy pug nose a sad specimen compared to Rafe's battered, roman one. While Rafe was all edges, craggy, sculpted, firm...

"Grainne...Grainne, you're still there?"

"Er...sorry. Of course you wouldn't have told Joe—you're a true and loyal friend." I laughed reluctantly.

"I am, aren't I?" She laughed too, then her voice turned serious. "I think you'll want to come home soon, though. Your mam's got me that worried."

"What's her problem?" I asked carelessly. "She's a hangnail or something?"

"Not funny." Justine's tone was disapproving. "We were talking about doing beef in Guinness for supper, and right in the middle, she broke off and said, 'I've a bad feeling.'"

"Jaysus, Mam and her dramatics—"

"Hear me out," Justine said. "From the look on her I knew she wasn't talking about supper. I asked, 'Do you have a stomachache or something?' But she said no, she just knew something terrible was going to happen."

"It has," I said. "Joe and Rafe have become mates."

"This is no joke—she really sounded in a state."

"Well, don't concern yourself," I said. "Mam often thinks she has the sight or whatever."

"I suppose," Justine said, sounding uncertain. "But there's something you should know..."

"What?" I sighed.

"She's invited Joe to dinner too."

Joe? For dinner? With Rafe?

Seething over Mam's latest stunt, I rang off. Jaysus, the nerve of the woman. What'd she think she was doing, messing about my relationships? She seemed to like Rafe, so how dare she stick Joe where he wasn't wanted?

I banged back outside, only to find Rafe and Joe discussing the grosses at the restaurant, and how much Joe's expansion plans would set him back. "Here's Grainne then." Joe glanced at his watch. "I'll have a quick word with her, then I'd better run—I've a conference call with my banker."

"You'll want to nip into Hurley's right away for your call," I said to Joe. "The hot spot won't be free for long."

"Right," said Joe. "Justine told me about that."

He made to take my arm. Feeling Rafe's eyes on me, I started to sidle away, but I knew Joe deserved some kind of explanation for my hanging out with Rafe.

"Any problems at home?" Joe asked under his breath as Rafe tactfully moved away. While Joe could still qualify for the finals in a Mr. Nice Guy contest, his voice had a bit of an edge. "Since you don't seem to get round to ringing."

Here was my chance: to come clean about Rafe. But really, would Scarlett O'Hara confess the lot? Or proceed with her plans?

Definitely the latter. "I've been showing Rafe round the village." I kept my voice low too. "Since Justine's been too busy cooking for my mam to look after him."

Joe's expression cleared. "You said they're cousins?"

"And really close," I said. "Like siblings. And with Justine practically my sister..."

Joe said, "Then you and Rafe are like family."

"Exactly." Rafe actually *would* be family, once he got me pregnant.

"And here I was thinking..." Joe sounded relieved. "Well. Enough said." Guilt kept me from a don't-be-silly laugh, then he leaned toward me. When I ducked, he drew away, looking chagrined. "Right. The banker's waiting, anyway."

He and Rafe shook hands again. "I'll see you later, at dinner," he said to Rafe, then disappeared into Hurley's.

Rafe watched him go, then said, "He'll be at dinner too? Nice guy."

I nodded reluctantly, waiting for him to ask me how soon I could split with Joe.

Instead, he said, "Joe's not too big on romance, though, is he? He'd rather talk business."

Pulling my scrambled thoughts together, I knew I needed to light a fire under Rafe. "Joe's plenty romantic," I said. "If the size of my ring counts for anything."

"Yeah, but he didn't kiss you goodbye—" Rafe broke off as Joe suddenly re-emerged from the pub. "The banker bloke asked me to ring back in five minutes." Then without even pulling me aside, he said straight out, "Something happen to your ring? You're not wearing it."

How unlike Joe, to put me in the hot seat. "Nothing's wrong with it," I said carefully, as Rafe strolled away. "It was…loose, and I was afraid it would fall off."

"So you put it in your bag?" He sounded reassured.

"Em…my jewelry case, at home," I said, praying Rafe wasn't listening. Right—like he couldn't hear me from three meters away.

"What do you say, you give it to me after supper," Joe said, "and I'll have it at the jeweler's for resizing."

"Great," I said, desperate for him to leave. "See you then."

As Joe went back into Hurley's, Rafe glanced at the sky. "It looks like it's going to rain—we'd better get in my car."

In Ballydara, it looked like rain about ninety-five percent of the time, but when Rafe grabbed my hand, I jogged willingly alongside him toward his car, in front of Mam's, more than eager to be alone with him again. We jumped inside, and he shoved the keys into the ignition, then stopped.

With no clue what Rafe had in mind, I ventured, "Shall we…go sightseeing or something?"

He didn't answer. Then finally, "Like I said, Joe's a decent guy."

I only nodded, wishing Rafe would just drop the subject. "In fact," he said, facing me, "He's such a nice guy I could never consider, for even two seconds, letting you break his heart. So there's no way I can be with you, as long as you're with him."

"I told you before, I'm not 'with' him," I said, feeling Rafe's gaze on my face—so intense I couldn't look at him. Suddenly, he reached out, tipping up my chin to force me to meet his eyes.

"You're not sleeping with him."

Those blue eyes of his rather pierced my defenses. *Why do I say all those eejit things to put you off, when I can have this?* I shook my head.

"Say it," he said, his thumb caressing my chin.

"No, I'm not sleeping with him," I said, while rivers of entirely unexpected lust ran through me. And with only the light touch of his hand on my face…what would it be like to have him touch me all over—

"That's what I'd hoped you'd say," Rafe said. Then right there, in the middle of Ballydara, he kissed me.

Of all the Rhett Butler/Scarlett O'Hara parallels I'd drawn with Rafe and me, this kiss had to be the closest. It was the kiss where our man Rhett, even burdened with Melanie Wilkes, half dead after childbirth, plus her mewling newborn baby, dragged Scarlett out of their narky Atlanta getaway horse and wagon, and still had the presence of mind to lay a big one on Scarlett—a kiss of legendary proportions, as the flames of Atlanta streamed and exploded against the black sky. This kiss was just like it—better than any I'd ever experienced, and that counted all the times Rafe and I had snogged five years ago.

Legendary or no, the pair of us finally ran out of oxygen and broke apart. "Wow," I said breathlessly, "that was—"

He kissed me again, his hands in my hair, then he abruptly pulled away. "Not here," he said, breathing hard.

I smiled to myself. Mr. Ivy Leaguer CEO had gone so far as to have a wild snog in full view of anyone looking out their windows. "So let's get out of here," I said, coyness be damned.

But he made no move to start the car.

"This is all happening a little too fast," he said grimly. "Especially with Joe still in the picture."

"But...there's your hotel—"

"I know there's my hotel," Rafe said, with an endearingly tortured expression.

"We could be alone," I said temptingly. "All alone. Just the pair of us."

"I know we could," Rafe said, sounding forlorn, "but I still want some answers from you."

"There's a time for talk" I said, leaning toward him, "and a time for action. Like now—"

"You still haven't told me what was up with you when you left me five years ago," Rafe said. "How do I know you won't pull the same stunt this time?"

It wasn't a stunt, I wanted to say, but that would only lead to more talk, so I traced my fingertip around the curve of his ear.

"I can't believe I'm doing this," Rafe muttered, and pulled me into his arms again.

A few moments later, when he was creating what was sure to be a blue-ribbon hickey on my neck, it was my turn to come to my senses. "I just remembered—Mam is having this dinner."

"Yeah," he said, still nuzzling me.

"And Joe will be calling round," I reminded him, although really, I could have stayed in this car and snogged with Rafe for the rest of my natural life. "Wouldn't it be distinctly tacky, for him find out about us this way?" I could cover the love bites with make-up, but Joe seeing us with our lips glued together would be pretty tough to explain.

Rafe drew away, his eyes at half-mast. "You admit it? We're an 'us'?"

"Why else would I be snogging with you?"

He touched my hickey, then sighed. "You'd better go in now—before we start up again."

"You're not coming to dinner?" When Rafe shook his head, I said, "But you've been invited. And what Justine can do with a decent cut of beef..."

"It would be even tackier for you to break up with Joe with me on the premises," Rafe said. "I'll call your mother, let her know I won't be coming."

"Good point," I said, and gave him a careless kiss on the cheek, though I longed to devour his mouth again. "Ring me later."

Rafe didn't speak, but his eyes promised...everything. Not bothering to smooth my hair or straighten my clothes, I crawled out of the car. I was done pretending I didn't want him.

So I'm not too proud to say that instead of walking inside without so much as a backward look, I lifted my hand as Rafe put the car into gear, and watched him drive away.

I lurched up the walk, and let myself in, still dazed from unsatisfied lust. In the front hall, I almost collided with a harried-looking Justine, slipping her mobile into her bag.

Her eyes widened when she saw me. "You're obviously back in Rafe's good books."

In my dancing-on-air/post-snog state, who could care if she thought I was a tart? "Well, if you must know—"

"I don't," she said, her voice sharp—in fact, very un-Justine-like. "I've problems of my own—my mam has rung twice, after me to come back to Dublin. Aine's in the early stages of labor, and Mam says she wants me to be on hand for the birth—family solidarity and all that."

I'd thought Mam was one to make a big deal out of nothing, but you'd think the Egans were mobilizing for an emergency airlift to a war-torn region. "Can't you tell your mother you're busy, helping my mother get this B&B off the ground? Besides, this could be a false alarm, very common, I understand, with first babies..."

Justine wasn't listening. "But what Mam really wants is for me to rush home to clean up Nate's flat and make a load of sandwiches so everyone can keep their strength up, then cook all kinds of casseroles for when Aine's laid up. But you know what? I don't want to get pulled into all that baby fuss. And you know what else? I'm sick of always doing what Mam wants me to—I'm a bloody grown woman!"

Ready to applaud Justine for this new show of independence, which really, was completely out of character, I noticed her face was pale, her eyes bloodshot. "You're…all right?"

"I'm grand!" she snapped, hitching up her shoulder bag. "So I'm asking myself, why should I clean up after my brother just so his wife won't get in a snit? He's a bloody grown man too!"

"Yeah, too right," I said, still not sure what was eating Justine. "Aine can be such a diva."

"That's a good one, coming from you," Justine flared.

"What do you mean?"

"Jaysus! You're the biggest diva I know."

"What a load of bollocks," I snapped back. "You've got me mixed up with my—"

"It's true," Justine stared at me, face pinched. "You're always on about getting your own way, which is exactly what you're doing with Rafe…" Her voice sort of burbled away, like a coffeepot done brewing. "With Rafe," she repeated.

I'd just about got my claws out, when I realized this wasn't about me. "What's happened? You only give out at me when something's really gone wrong."

"Nothing…" Then Justine sort of sagged, and dropped her bag. "When I was on the line with Mam, she gave me the other big news." Her voice broke. "Ian's getting married."

"Ah, now." I awkwardly hugged her. "The eejit."

She backed away with an accusing look. "He's not!" A sob escaped her.

"I meant his girlfriend," I quickly amended. "She couldn't be as sweet as you, or as good a cook either."

"She's no eejit," Justine said mournfully, a tear rolling down her cheek. "She's graduated from Vassar, or some such place. She's called 'Gennifer.' With a 'G.'"

"'G' for gobshite?" I said, trying to coax a smile from Justine

Justine shook her head. "I saw her on Facebook—she's full-on gorgeous, and built like a Barbie doll. And Bernie says she's really smart. Brains coming out of her ears."

"Jaysus, I hope not," I joked. "Horribly messy." Justine only sniffed. "Ian must be a bit deluded," I added loyally, "to go after her instead of you."

"I'm the real eejit here," Justine said, her tears spilling over. "To fancy him when he's getting bloody married."

"But we both know Ian's a serial fiancé—isn't this his fourth engagement?"

"Everyone knows," and Justine sniffed again, "he's too nice to string a girl along."

Only a fool thinks you've got to marry everyone you sleep with. "Yeah, but it probably won't last—just like all the others."

"Bernie thinks this girl's the one." Justine swiped her nose with the back of her hand. "Why can't I just face the facts? Ian's never seen me as anyone but a friend."

"Well, you'll always have *that*," I said, without the least idea what I was talking about. I'd never been real friends with a guy.

"Oh, yeah. We're keen friends. Friends forever." Justine dashed the tears from her cheeks. "So you know what? I'm not going to rush off just because Mam snaps her fingers."

"But you're going somewhere—"

"Just for the evening—to the pub, and I'm going to try that new yoga class." Justine gazed at my mussed hair again, looking envious. "I'm hopeless with men, but what girl doesn't need more balance in her life. Besides, Mam won't be able to ring me if I'm not here."

"Good girl," I said. "Just don't go near the magical mobile reception booth."

"Mam's got Aunt Bernie for support—*she* can afford to bankroll the takeaway dinners and a bloody house cleaner!" Justine let herself out, then immediately popped her head back inside. "I haven't the heart to cook tonight, so you and your mam will have to improvise for Joe's dinner."

Justine really *was* upset. But her declaration of independence, however out of character, came at just the right time. It completely suited my plans to have Bernie occupied in Dublin, instead of settling in here at Mam's fledgling B&B, with the leisure to turn her she-wolf killer instinct on me, the girl messing with her pup.

Now, I'd only one problem—besides working out how soon I could go to bed with Rafe. I had to give Joe his ring and *sort of* break up with him...but not completely.

And with Mam right in the middle of it.

Twenty-Seven

I went into the kitchen, ravenous—illicit snogging will do that to a girl. A shame there'd be no lovely beef and Guinness simmering on the cooker, but now I'd a perfect excuse to cancel with Joe. I could hardly invite him here and give him bread and cheese, right?

As I grabbed the house phone and pressed Joe's number, hoping he was still in the back booth at Hurley's, Mam came in, giving me the same searching look she'd given me the night before. Very bizarre, her noticing me two days in a row. I wiggled my fingers in her direction, and concentrated on my call. When I got Joe's messaging, I said, "Sorry, dinner's not on. Justine won't be cooking tonight after all."

I rang off, feeling Mam's eyes still on me, which unsettled me so much I rang a second time. "It's me again, in case you couldn't pick up in time—ring me as soon as you can."

"There's no reason we can't have Joe round," Mam said as I rang off. "With Rafe not here for dinner, we could pick up some fish and chips from Hurley's."

"I don't think that's on—"

"But Joe seems like a nice fella, he won't mind," Mam went on. "And he did come all the way from Dublin to see you." Her face brightened. "We could even have him stay the night in the second bedroom!"

The prospect of a cozy dinner with Mam, me, and my soon to be sort of ex, then having to sort out Joe straight after, was rather horrifying. "Well, he *should* mind," I said, ignoring her suggestion of Joe sleeping in the bedroom next to mine after I'd broken his heart. "Doesn't he eat enough restaurant food as it is? God knows what it's doing to his arteries—I shouldn't want him to have an early heart attack."

Mam rearranged the knickknacks on the windowsill. "Of course you wouldn't," she finally said, "if you're going to marry him." Long pause, while I wondered how to answer that. "You...*are* going to marry him, aren't you?"

I knew Mam's careless mothering had affected me—I mean, I wasn't that thick. But her taking an interest after all these years—and after it was way too late—made me burn. "And why should it matter who I marry?" I tried to keep my voice light, like releasing a bit of steam from a volcano, but all I felt was a big vat of hot, ugly magma roiling beneath.

"Joe'll make you a good husband," she said.

Since when was Mam a great judge of men? "Really," I said, opening cupboards as if I was searching for something to eat, but I'd suddenly lost my appetite. "Why should you care—"

"Grainne," she interrupted, not looking at me. "I...em, saw you and Rafe." I got a prickly feeling, like I'd a spider in my hair. "In the *car*," she added. "The pair of you were...em, well, you know."

"Oh, that's rich." I slammed the cupboard, trying to laugh, but it didn't sound like any laugh I'd ever heard. "*You* giving *me* morality lectures—"

"That's not what I meant at all." Mam—the nerve of her—seemed more bemused than defensive. "I just don't think Rafe is... right for you."

"Not right for me," I repeated, anger heating my insides. "I'm not right for a lot of people—I'm too tall or too fat or too mouthy to be any daughter of yours."

I hated it, that after all this time it hurt more than ever, that Mam wasn't a normal mother. But I hated even more that she was starting to act like one, and actually stretching her hand toward me. I moved away before she could touch me.

She dropped her hand. "I never said that."

"Not in so many words," I said coolly, though my hot resentment was heading for the boiling point. "But *I* knew what you thought—"

"Not in any words," she interrupted. "My mam might say that sort of thing. But not me."

"But I'm sure I...but you always—" I broke off, leaning against the cold cooker. Had my memory played tricks on me? My termagant Granny O'Neill had been the one saying those awful things?

No one, not even me, would dare tell off Granny. Maybe I'd

been furious at Mam instead, for not standing up for me? I was too gobsmacked to speak. "I never said that," she said again.

In the confusion swirling round me, I managed, "So you think I should settle for a guy like Joe."

"He's a decent sort. And every mother wants her girl to have a loving husband, be happy."

That, coming from Mam, completely overrode any suspicion that I might have misjudged her. "But you're not like other mothers, are you?" I couldn't believe I'd dared to say it.

"What...what do you mean?" Mam had the utter nerve to look surprised.

"When were you ever—" *There for me?* I couldn't get the words out. You see, my rare confrontations with Mam had never got this far. At the first sign of conflict, she'd throw up her hands and tell Dad or Rory, or anyone else who'd listen, several variations of *this child is impossible—you sort her out.*

So, Mam imagining herself an adoring mother-of-the-bride fair made me sick. Or that she'd ever been a blushing bride herself made me want to puke. Ready to burst out, *A "decent sort" loved you, tried to make you happy, but you didn't care*, I bit my lip just in time.

"Forget it," I finally said sullenly. I'd been doing just fine all my life without her. So why pick a fight with her now? "Whatever I do with Rafe Byrne is nobody's business but mine."

I wondered dimly if it wasn't past time for me separate myself from my mother's old story and work on my own, when Mam surprised me again. "Even though things ended badly with Rafe, when you went to America?" She seated herself gracefully at the kitchen table, like she was on a stage.

"Who says they ended badly?" I scoffed, despite the pinch in my chest. I hadn't realized she'd worked out that I'd been seeing Rafe back then. "I came back a bit sooner than I'd planned, that's all."

"Maybe," Mam said, "but you hardly looked like yourself."

Mam had actually seen my misery, when I'd rushed home to Ireland five years ago? Caught in illness and age, Dad hadn't noticed anything amiss. For some strange reason, her sensing my secret feelings infuriated me more than her neglect ever had. "You don't know what you're talking about—"

"So you see," she interrupted again, "why I'm thinking that if you and Rafe...that is, if you fall in love with him again—"

"I told you before, I never loved him," I spat. "And I've no intention of getting emotionally involved." As Mam's eyes widened, I added crudely. "I only want him for—"

I snapped my mouth closed. Sweet Christ, what in bloody's sakes was the matter with me? Saying—or almost saying—all the awful things I'd kept bottled up inside my entire life? I was so rattled I didn't know right from left or up from down.

There was no disgust on her face. Only a childlike hurt. I wanted to run away and hide. Not like when I was the age of ten, when I *wanted* to be discovered. Now, I needed a place where no one could find me. Not even me—

The bloody doorbell rang.

I stood, rooted to the spot. Mam looked down for a moment, and I saw a small circle of gray at the crown of her immaculately coiffed hair I'd never noticed before. When had she gotten...well, old? I felt a wave of pity for her, which so unnerved me an apology rose in my throat. Before I could say anything, she made for the front room.

I let her go, ashamed it was me that had caused her mouth to tremble, made her step carefully around me. *Would you look at yourself, all but abusing an older lady. Are you going to let yourself turn into Granny O'Neill?*

But Mam deserves it, I snarled inwardly. What of all the ways she's hurt people? And worse, not admitting it?

Doesn't matter, chided that inner voice. *It doesn't mean you have to act the same.*

But the only way I could avoid fighting with Mam was to avoid living with her. And with Rafe here in Ballydara, I wasn't about to go back to Dublin, which would also bring the wrath of my sister Rory down on me. Then I heard a man's voice. "Grainne didn't give me a time."

Joe! In between snogging with Rafe and fighting with Mam, I'd forgotten all about him. And here he was, right next to Mam on the list of people I couldn't possibly talk to right now. I grabbed my bag and ran to the entryway. First of all, to nip in the bud any idea that he was staying for dinner. And second, to get the hell out of the house the minute I got rid of him. I stopped abruptly as Joe gave me a shocked look.

Oh. No. I'd also forgotten what I looked like after my ardent snogging with Rafe. "Hallo, Joe," I said nonchalantly. Setting my bag down, I ran my fingers through my hair, tugging at my collar to conceal any errant hickeys. "You didn't get my message then? That supper was cancelled?"

"No," Joe said, his eyes narrowing, as Mam piped up, "We can always do fish and chips."

Having apparently recovered from our fight, Mam could be like a dog with a bone when she got attached to an idea—like takeaway from Hurley's. Or Joe being good husband material. Or else she was as appalled as I was at the pair of us alone together all evening.

"No we can't!" Joe frowned at me. "I mean...look," I said, turning to Mam. "Could you give us a minute?" Mam gave a dignified nod. As she left, Joe's mouth tightened.

"This is sort of...a bad time," I said.

"I can see that," Joe said with an unaccustomed irony. "What's going on with you anyway?"

Apparently Joe wasn't as blind or patient as I'd thought—which made me actually respect him. But this was a bloody inconvenient time for that discovery. "I...like I said, tonight's no good—I'm in the middle of a family...thing."

"Ah. Family." His look grew even more ironic. "You've plans with Rafe Byrne then?"

Crap. I'd said Rafe was family, hadn't I? "No, nothing like that," I said, relieved to be telling the truth, even if it was only to Joe. Without ceremony, I pulled his ring out of my pocket. "Here," and I thrust it at him. After kissing Rafe, I didn't even like the feel of it in my pocket. "You wanted it for the jewelers."

"Right," Joe said, giving the ring a little toss, then catching it neatly. I saw something in his face—hurt, I think, but I couldn't be sure. Besides, I was too off my head to make sense of where Joe and I were headed. As he stepped toward the door, he added, "You never asked how my phone call with the bankers went."

I said automatically, "How did it—"

"But I need to get back to Dublin anyway," Joe went on as if I hadn't said anything. "They want more paperwork."

"I'll see you round, then." I backed away. *Just go then, will you?*

Joe's face changed, and for one awful, but fleeting moment, I was afraid I'd said the words aloud. Then, as if an answer to a prayer I hadn't gotten round to, the kitchen phone rang.

"I'll see you round," I repeated. Mam could answer it.

"Sure," said Joe. "Ring me later, okay? After you've come to your senses, that is."

This wasn't the first time I'd treated Joe like shite. But you'd think I wouldn't do such a thing, since I knew what it felt like.

Five years ago, in America with Rafe, I hadn't seen the shabby treatment coming. Rafe had not only made numerous hints to our having a future together, but he'd shown me his new flat and asked me along when he shopped for a new bed. Even more evidence of his serious designs—to me at least—was his patience in the sex department.

And bringing me to meet Jack Byrne, the family patriarch, no less. "I can't wait to show you off to my granddad," Rafe had said at least twice. But the same night, Lindy Holmes and her parents had also been invited to the dinner, with Lindy presented as the fatted calf. While arranged marriages might be a thing of the past, I could see that's exactly what Bernie, old Jack, and the Holmes had in mind. So I'd no choice but to take my leave of the lot of them, and before the caramel flan was served too.

Then I promptly quit my job as the Carey's au pair and returned to Ireland.

Four months later, Justine reluctantly (I knew that because she'd tears in her eyes) told me that Rafe had given a certain someone a diamond ring. To stop the sting in my eyes, I'd bitten the inside of my lip until I tasted blood. "Let me guess," I said. "Goldilocks." The one sleeping in my bed.

Justine nodded. "I can't believe he loves her."

"Yeah, well, they'll make a grand couple," I said carelessly, though the bitter taste in my mouth made me queasy. "Producing lots of Harvard-bound progeny." With blue, not yellow eyes.

Telling myself I'd been right to get away didn't make me feel any better, so I'd dragged Justine off to O'Fagan's and promptly got pissed. Then rung Joe…

What with giving Joe the brush-off all over again, recalling how Lindy ruined my life, and the prospect of an evening alone with Mam after the biggest fight of our lives, all I could think about was running off to Hurley's. I'd my hand on the doorknob when Mam came in. "That was Rafe on the line."

"Thanks," and I was racing past her to the kitchen phone before the word was out of my mouth. Rafe picked up on the first ring. "Look—I know I said things were going too fast," he said, "but hell, I don't care anymore. You up for spending a couple of days here with me?"

Was I ever! "If Mam can do without me," I said demurely.

"But I have to ask—you broke up with Joe?"

"I gave him his ring," I said. "And he's on his way back to Dublin."

"I'll be there in fifteen minutes." There was a smile in his voice.

"Wait." I couldn't allow him anywhere near Mam. Even if she would never be so indelicate to repeat what I'd said about wanting him only for sex, I didn't want the pair of them to meet so soon after I'd said it. Besides, I'd better let Justine know where I was going. "Pick me up at Hurley's."

I rang off, then sprinted up to my quasi-bedroom and poured myself into a black slip dress bought several pounds ago. Still, it had a lovely slimming effect. Why I was keen to look thinner was pretty ridiculous, since Rafe would soon be seeing me naked, but there's nothing like a good first impression.

Certain Mam would be as anxious to avoid me as I her, I was packing my holdall when she appeared in the doorway, and me with a handful of lace knickers. "Where are you going?"

"Chrissakes, Mam, I'm thirty." I shoved the knickers into the bag. "Past the age where I'm meant to report to my mother." Then my conscience smote me. *You're getting a lucky escape—so you can stop being awful for the next three minutes.* "If you must know," I said, trying to keep the rancor from my voice this time, "I'm going to see Rafe. And I've got to rush."

"I can see that," she said. "What I meant was, what do you think you're about?"

Really annoyed now, and not inclined to keep it to myself, I said, "I told you, I'm off to see—"

"You know, Grainne," she said, "I'm thinking that just like Alice in Wonderland, when it comes to that man, as lovely as he is, you've no real idea what you're doing. Or where you're going. So how will you know when you get there?"

"Easy. I'll know when I'm—" *Pregnant.* I zipped up my bag with a jerk. For a minute there, she'd actually sounded like a real, wise, Helen Egan sort of mam, and I got a weird urge to beg her forgiveness. "When I spend a bit more time with him," I said instead. "Cheers." I walked out, pretending not to see the woebegone look on her face.

Striding down the road to Hurley's, I tried to forget the entirely bizarre impulse that hit me as I left. To run back to Mam and actually confide in her—why I wanted Rafe. But the pragmatic side of me knew that was so not on, no more than Mam magically coming to grips with her mistakes, then apologizing for all the wrong she'd done.

I banged into the pub, and managed to catch Justine following Mrs. Murphy up the stairs to the yoga class. "Joe's gone, and I'm off to Harmony Hotel," I told her. "I'm sure you can sort out the rest."

"That was fast," was all Justine said. "See you."

"I'll ring you," I said, disappointed she hadn't asked for details, even if I hadn't time to tell her any. A nod to Pat Hurley, and I was back outside just as Rafe pulled up.

He emerged from the car and caught me by the elbows, looking very much like he wanted to kiss me, right in front of Hurley's. Then he did a very un-Rafe-like thing, and did kiss me.

His color was high as he let me go. To show that I'd kept my side of the bargain, I fluttered my bare ring finger at him. "See?"

He caught my hand. "You're a free woman."

"Entirely free," I told him. Well, just about. "So what are you waiting for?"

Twenty-Eight

For once I was glad Rafe was such an erratic driver. It took my mind off my nerves.

As he turned the car into the hotel drive, the anxious flutter in my middle kicked into high gear. Like any girl, I'd some angst about getting naked with the man of my dreams. And while Rafe appeared to appreciate the sight of me five years ago, I'd gained nearly a stone since then. But I was more concerned about disappointing him: not wanting to inadvertently bond with the wrong guy meant I wasn't exactly a sexually experienced dynamo.

While I had every expectation that getting horizontal with Rafe would soon turn me into a proper seductress, I'd need to keep my baby goal firmly in mind, to get through the pre-sex jitters looming ahead.

My first look at Rafe's lodgings helped relax me. Surrounded by a grove of beech trees and a manicured lawn, Harmony Hotel was a mid-sized country place—big enough so we could be relatively anonymous, and not a cozy B&B where the occupants next door would hear us having it off, and the landlady would give us dirty looks over our Full-Irish-Guilt breakfast. Once we entered Rafe's suite, I said, "It's perfect." The sitting room hadn't a shred of chintz, nor a Sacred Heart of Jesus on the wall. With its bamboo flooring, an upright beige futon instead of a couch, and no art to speak of save a small gong on the dresser, the place was spare as a monk's cell.

"Great décor too," I teased, slipping off my sandals onto the cotton floor mat. I peeked into the nearest bedroom and saw that the futon was only window dressing—thank God, they'd real beds. With my back stiff after the nights on the floor at Mam's, sleeping on a futon would've probably finished me off. "And isn't that one of those chiming clocks on the nightstand?"

"The place is billed as a Zen-like retreat." Rafe grinned. "An escape from today's frantic pace, where you can get yourself centered and attuned."

I ran my index finger down his shirtfront. "Sure, I'm ready to be attuned…to you." I took off my sweater. "But who's the second bedroom for? Bernie, in case she hightails it back here to pull you out of my clutches?"

"No." Rafe's grin disappeared. "It's where I'm going to sleep unless I get some straight answers from you." He stepped away from me. "Since I never did get too many yesterday, when I got… off track."

I tossed my sweater onto the futon. "But isn't distraction what we came here for?"

Instead of kissing me, he retreated to the small bamboo table and chair set. "We've got too much to talk about, to uh, jump into… uh, *things* right away."

"Things…oh, you mean sex!" I said, swaying toward him. "We can always talk later, during the afterglow, when we're curled up together, all naked and buzzed—"

"Cut it out," Rafe wore that lovely tortured look I'd seen on him earlier, when we kissed in the car. "I haven't changed my mind about getting our baggage out in the open. I don't want it to haunt us later."

"Is this an ultimatum? No sex until we sort things out?"

"Not exactly, but—"

"You've got it all wrong," I told him, my jitters increasing. "It's generally the girl who says, 'We need to talk,' while the fellow either kisses her to shut her up, changes the subject, or sprints away, never to be seen again."

"I'm not most guys," Rafe said, and squared his chin.

"I know." I looked at him from beneath my lashes. "That's why I picked you. But isn't Zen all about living in the moment?" For all my teasing, though, my knees were starting to quake, so I backed into the futon and sat down. But I still had the presence of mind to cross my legs and hike up my dress a bit. "I must say, you've a novel approach to foreplay. But if you've something on your mind, I'm all ears—"

"Not so fast." Rafe held up a hand, looking endearingly earnest. "Remember our deal? I ask you, you ask me. And it's got to be the truth."

"*Your* deal," I said, feeling a film of perspiration between my breasts. "Since this is your idea, you go first."

He pulled out one of the wood chairs and sat down, resting his chin on his folded hands. As the silence lengthened, my hopes grew that he was reconsidering his entire eejit chat. Until he said, "Five years ago, did you mind that I got engaged to Lindy? Right after being with you?"

He would have to start with that one, wouldn't he? I clutched the arm of the futon. "You and I didn't actually get to the 'with' part."

"A mere technicality," he said. "And you're avoiding the question."

"Which is? I've forgot it already."

Rafe's brows drew together. "Just answer the question: Did you mind that—"

"Okay, okay," I said. I couldn't lie. "I suppose I had a…a mild curiosity about why you…took up with her so fast."

"Mild curiosity," Rafe repeated. His frown deepened, though he said calmly enough, "And why do you think I 'took up' with her?"

I pretended to carefully consider. "You…ah, needed sex?"

Leaning back in his chair, Rafe gave me an ironic look. "I could get that without marrying her."

The image of him in bed with Lindy rather made my stomach hurt. I jumped up, strolled to the bathroom doorway, and switched on the light. "Lovely," I said over my shoulder. "Did you know there's a big spa tub in here? And two kimonos—"

"Grainne!" Rafe warned, and I turned back to him. "Here's what I think—if you'd wanted to know about me and Lindy, you'd have asked Justine, who would have asked her mother, who would have asked Bernie. But you didn't. So you didn't *care* that I got engaged to her?"

There was no way I could tell the truth on this one. *I couldn't ask—because I was afraid you loved her...* Leaning one shoulder on the doorjamb, I aimed for nonchalance. "It was more that I...didn't want to know why you proposed to her." That was as close to the truth as I dared.

"Too bad—because I'm telling you anyway." Rafe jumped up, and started pacing. "When you didn't return my calls or e-mails, I figured, why not go for broke? I wanted to make you jealous. Jealous enough to come back."

"And how would that do me any good?" I asked reasonably, while my heart went off like a spanner in my chest. "If you were already taken."

Rafe turned that blue gaze on me. "But I wasn't taken. Not even when I was in bed with her—"

"I need a bath," I broke in. I'd already worked up quite a nervous sweat, with Rafe being too serious, too probing, too...honest.

"Not until you've answered my questions," he insisted, looking rather adorably mulish.

I had a sudden brainwave. "Let's make this more interesting, shall we?" Inside, I was shaking, but I couldn't take this soul-baring much longer. "Every time you ask me something, I take off something. Sort of a combination strip-poker and Truth or Dare."

Rafe shoved his fingers into his hair. "I'm trying to be real here—why are you making this into a goddamned game? Will you just let me say that if you'd—"

"That's two questions right there—this is already looking like a really short contest," I said. "So I should warn you, I'm wearing only three articles of clothing."

Rafe's gaze turned even more intense. "If you *had* come back, I would have broken up with Lindy! What do you think of that?"

"You're terribly heartless about her," I told him, and pulled my dress over my head before I lost my courage. "If you haven't guessed already, you've just used your first question."

"That's no answer," he gritted as I stood in the bathroom doorway, every muscle tense, and trying not to feel horribly uptight in my black bra and knickers.

Then his gaze ran up and down my body—maybe we'd finally get this party started after all. I stepped inside the bathroom, and switched on the taps full blast. As the tub began to fill, I turned back to face Rafe.

"Since you're still trying to avoid talking about our relationship, do you even know what you're doing here?" he asked, raising his voice.

I winced. He'd touched the same raw spot Mam had. "Of course I do—I'm having a bath, then I'm having y—"

"Since I haven't said yes to your proposition," Rafe broke in, a bit of a wild look in his eyes, "have you brought some birth control?"

"That's two questions," I said over the low roar of the water, "but I'll be magnanimous, and count it as one." With clumsy fingers, I undid the front catch of my bra and dropped it to the floor. "You're one question left."

Rafe's eyes blazed, and with three long strides he was across the room. He stopped suddenly, just out of touching range. "It was a trick question." His hands clenched. "Because I brought it."

"Very organized of you," I said, willing Rafe to forget this talking shite—surely once we'd got started, wouldn't I stop feeling on the verge of a nervous breakdown? "Do you mind if I try to make you forget about it?"

There was a long silence as Rafe just looked at me. "There's one more thing—why I didn't break up with Lindy when I knew you wouldn't be coming back." He seemed to swallow hard. "I should have—I didn't love her..."

Every muscle rigid, I held my breath. *Tell me. God's sakes, tell me why you married her—*

"But if I couldn't have you, I didn't care who I ended up with. So I thought I might as well make my family happy, and do the right thing by Lindy."

I stared at him, a lump growing in my throat. I wanted...no, *needed* to keep it light, *needed* an easy-to-leave Rafe as soon as I got a positive on a pregnancy test. "That's even more heartless," I managed, then remembered the tub was getting full. I reached for the taps at an odd angle, setting off a mild twinge in my back. "But you've not answered *my* question," I said. "Do you mind if I try and make you forget about birth contr—"

"Shut up," he said, his blue eyes burning. "Will you just quit screwing around and marry me?"

My trip-hammering heart seemed to stop. *You want me? For life?*

Rafe had broken one of the basic Rules of Relationships: that a fellow proposing marriage should give a few hints so the girl can see it coming. So, if it's not wanted, like a bomb, she can take cover.

With nowhere to run, I knew of only one answer.

"Three strikes and you're out." I shimmied out of my knickers a split second before Rafe yanked me into his arms.

I'd fantasized about me and Rafe having amazing sex, an explosive shag after years of suppressed sexual longing. But my quick shimmy had sharpened the tweak in my back, so I wasn't as into Rafe's kiss as I wanted to be. Feeling the cold porcelain of the tub against my calves, I broke our lip lock. A soak could relax my tight muscles.

"Three families could bathe...in the water we've...run for the tub," I said breathlessly, as the pain crept down my leg. "Think of the terrible energy waste—"

"Later," he said.

"But I really...want a bath." Besides the muscle-relaxation therapy, I was game for any way to deflect Rafe's marriage proposal, even if it delayed baby-making for a bit.

"Fine," Rafe said. I yelped as he suddenly picked me up and slid me into the tub, sloshing water on the floor. Before I'd hardly blinked, he had his clothes off and had joined me, creating another mini-wave over the side. "You get five minutes." He started washing me, with all the ardor of a doctor prepping for surgery.

"Wait," I protested, as Rafe grabbed my left foot and lathered it up. While I'd have liked to raise a silky wet limb, to lure him into my erotic toils, this impersonal scrub was hardly sexy. "I need more—"

"Time? Too bad." He captured my right foot, soaped it too, then sort of scrubbed up the length of my legs—like I'd wash little Anna Gallagher. Maybe Rafe was even better father material than I'd thought, but when he hit the tops of my thighs, heat surged through my body.

In a reflex, I slid backwards—I hadn't been touched round there for a long time—and more water lapped over the side of the tub. "Now just one minute—"

"Just trying to do a thorough job," he said, moving his soapy hands up my torso. Rafe ran them over my breasts, though a bit slower than he'd done the rest of me, which made the heat and tension in me rise even further. Quickly swiping down my arms, he splashed some water on me for a rinse, then stood up and hauled me to my feet.

Bundling us out of the tub, Rafe seized a towel, ran it over me, then himself, and tossed it on the floor. "We're still wet," I said as he yanked me into his arms again.

"We'll dry."

"But we've left a huge..." The feel of his bare skin against mine set off more interior earthquakes—only at this make-or-break moment, my back muscles tightened. "Shouldn't we clean up here, before the water leaks downst—"

"Later," he said again. We staggered out of the bathroom, still kissing, and into the nearest bedroom.

There's nothing like a bit of baby-making instinct to get you past the awkward stages when you go to bed with a man for the first time—no matter how many lovely things that man is doing to you, and you can't help doing them back. But my turn-on got a bit turned off when Rafe reached for the nightstand and produced a little foil packet.

"We don't really need one of those, do we?" I said, wriggling against him.

Rafe sucked in his breath. "Yes, we do."

Unfortunately, my sexy little squirm had set off a new tweak in my back. Trying to unclench things, I considered trying some Mata Hari-ish move where the last thing on Rafe's mind would be birth control—then reminded myself that trickery wasn't part of the deal. "Okay," I said with difficulty, as my banjaxed back was that painful. There was always next time. But at the moment of truth, as I drew Rafe closer, my entire back twinged. I gasped.

"What is it?" Rafe pulled away. "What's the matter?"

"I...can't quite move." I tried to breathe, hoping the cramp would pass. "You know those Yips that...that turned your golf career to crap?" My voice rose to a squeak. "I'm terribly afraid...I've caught them."

Twenty-Nine

There was sex, and there was *sex*, was my first thought early the next morning. Now I finally knew the difference.

Last night, when my gimpy back had nearly put me out of commission, all I could think was, *How will I get a baby if I can't have sex?* But in a split second, Rafe rolled me over and gave me a full-body, muscles-into-jelly massage. Which not only eased the cramp, but got me so eager to pick up where we left off I forgot that I'd felt almost paralyzed just moments before. He seemed in no rush to get me on my back again, stroking me slowly, from my heels to the top of my head. "Where'd you learn to do that?" I murmured into the pillow.

"From my imagination," he whispered against the nape of my neck. "Thinking about everything I've wanted to do with you the last five years." Which was all I needed to hear to pull him to me. Really, who could care about condoms or getting pregnant or much of anything at a moment like this?

But in the cold light of day, I reminded myself I'd a baby to make. And condoms that needed to be chucked. Hopefully, our finally having it off meant that Rafe was done with his relationship talkathon and we could move on.

Feigning sleep, I sensed Rafe was not only awake, but watching me. A rather bizarre shyness hit me—though you'd wonder how I could be shy after all the…em, interesting things we'd done to each other. Still, I braced myself and opened my eyes. Rafe was indeed watching me with a faint smile, his head propped on his hand. "You didn't answer my question last night."

Feck it. Too late to keep faking. I stretched my arms over my head, producing a credible morning sigh, then smiled back at him. "Which question was that? There were so many."

Rafe remained disappointingly calm. "You know," he said, his blue eyes intense. "The one about marrying me."

Shite. I was afraid that was the question he meant. "We've just proved you don't have to marry me to shag me."

Rafe narrowed his eyes. "I figured you'd say something like that. So how about this—if we're going to keep 'shagging' each other, I'd like it to be on a 'til death do us part' basis."

A strange sweetness rose in my throat. To counteract it, I said lightly, "Who gets married anymore?"

"I do."

Feck it twice. I should have known Rafe would go for marriage, after what he'd said about doing right by Lindy. "But you just got un-married—"

"I told you, I didn't love her."

I pretended I didn't hear that. "And why get married anyway, when you see crap marriages everywhere you turn? Prime example, my parents drove each other mad."

"From what I remember," and he still wore that narrow-eyed smile, "mine hardly spoke to each other. But we're not talking about them, we're talking about us."

"Could we revisit this after breakfast?" I said, thinking fast. "We'd no tea last night, and I've never been able to think straight on an empty stomach." I looked around for my phone. "I'll call room serv—"

"I don't want you to think straight," he said conversationally. "In fact, if I thought it would get me some answers, I'd pick you up, turn you upside down and shake them out of you."

"Good job you didn't," I said. "You'd get a hernia, trying to lift me—"

"Grainne—" He got this determined look on him, and for one moment I thought he was actually going to prove he could. Instead, he pulled the sheet down and proceeded to draw circles round my navel. Which felt lovely. And I didn't want it to.

"That tickles." I pushed his hand away, when I really wanted him to widen his circles. "You were saying?"

"I was saying, 'Will. You. Marry. Me.' I can't get much plainer than that."

Now my hands were shaking. I carefully folded them over my middle, and wondered how my plans could have turned upside down so fast. Rafe and his bloody condoms, and now Rafe and his bloody marriage proposal. I considered making a run for the loo, but I didn't really need to go. Then I considered trying to make Rafe lose his temper, but that seemed really inappropriate after a marriage proposal. Maybe I should just get this over with... "But we've spent...what—barely a fortnight together. Hardly long enough to consider a commitment—"

"I haven't stopped thinking of you since the minute I met you," Rafe countered. "And I know what I want. Besides, you've given me a hell of a lot of..." he gave me, then my stomach, a significant glance, "encouragement, so you must feel the same way about me."

Feck it again. I had, hadn't I? By asking him to give me a baby.

"But...why would you want to marry *me*?" I asked, feeling cornered. "I can't cook, my income is crap, I'm no good at communication, and have the PMS something terrible. One week a month, I'm totally unbearable to live with—"

"C'mon," he said, his tone playful, "you're unbearable most of the time."

"That's a fine thing to say," I sputtered, "to someone you've just proposed to—"

"And you just got rid of Joe," Rafe added, as if I hadn't spoken. "So I've got to take advantage of you being unattached—before you snag a new boyfriend."

This conversation was veering spookily close to the Rhett Butler proposal to Scarlett, when he said he had to catch her between husbands. That little catch in my throat returned. Which, like the condoms, had to be got rid of immediately. "I'm flattered, but I don't see myself getting married," I told him. "Though I'd rather shag you than anyone else," I added quickly.

"I'm flattered too," Rafe retorted. "But presumably, you would have been 'shagging' Joe, if you'd gone through with marrying him."

"Actually, I never really considered it," I said. "The...engagement was sort of a misunderstanding."

Rafe's jaw firmed. I sensed that in about thirty seconds, he would jump of this bed, and give me another separate bedrooms ultimatum. Before he could move, I pushed him flat on the bed, and slid on top of him. "But you can't misunderstand this."

He curved his hands on my bum. "Is this our future?" He laughed, but the sound had an edge in it. "That all our conversations end with sex?"

"You have a problem with that?" I asked, and kissed his chin.

"Actually I do," Rafe said, meeting my eyes squarely, "but frankly, right now I don't give a damn."

Call me superstitious, but Rafe's last words before we had sex again gave me the willies—too much like Rhett Butler's parting shot to Scarlett. Which also reminded me that not only had Rhett and Scarlett's marriage turned to crap, but their only child had *died*, for God's sake.

So as soon as we were done—and I made sure to be done well before Rafe, if you know what I mean—I scrambled out of bed. "I really *am* starving."

Rafe caught my hand. "What's the rush? You didn't...uh, you know, have a—"

"I'm fine," I said brightly, disengaging myself. I'd decided somewhere between me rolling on top of Rafe and him pulling out another one of his fecking condoms (actually two, since we did it twice), that I was getting too...involved. So I was done with climaxes for now. At least until the condoms were only an unpleasant memory.

"Well, I'm not." He slid his hand down my belly. "Why don't you let me—"

"Maybe next time," I said, careful not to wrench away like I was in a huff over the Big O going missing. Ever-so-casually, I rose from the bed, lest I show how peeved and well, *unnerved* I was, at Rafe's insistence on condoms.

Feeling weird and uncomfortable, and that being alone with Rafe was making me feel things I'd no clue how to handle, I spied my mobile, surrounded by condom wrappers. Was there some symbolism there? And what was wrong with me anyway?

Here I'd no wish to linger in bed with an altogether lovely man

who was really sweet to me between the sheets, and for some unfathomable reason, wanted to marry me? I mean, weren't all the signs
pointing to This Man Is Meant To Be The Father Of Your Child?

Only I'd have to kick the sex up a notch if I was going to get rid
of Rafe's birth control. And since I was in the far end of the fertile
part of my cycle, I hadn't a shag to waste. I couldn't look at him as I
turned on my phone. "How about breakfast? Downstairs?"

"I'll...think about it," Rafe said, sliding out of bed to turn his
phone on too.

I felt even weirder, with the pair of us traipsing round the
place naked. So I sped to the bathroom doorway, where I'd left my
knickers.

What now? I thought, pulling on my bra for good measure. It
was too soon to have sex again, and besides, I was a bit...sore. And
if I was going to have it off, I wasn't going to waste all that friction
against my tender parts without a potential pregnancy. So I had to
get Rafe onto the Daddy track—but I wasn't sure how to do that
either, since I didn't want to talk about his marriage proposal.

In fact, I didn't want to talk about much of anything, in case I
accidentally let on how horribly I'd treated Mam yesterday. "Shall
we eat in the town, then?" I ventured. "Play tourist?"

"I'll...think about it," Rafe said again.

Well, that was helpful. The pair of us seemed to have indeci-
sion-itus. "Do you mind if I ring Justine, then?" Anything to kill
some time.

"Be my guest," Rafe said, but I'd already pressed her number.

Justine picked up immediately. "I was about to ring you, but I
hadn't the nerve—I didn't want to interrupt anything—"

"You're not. So, any news of Aine? Isn't the baby ready to pop
out?"

Rafe practically sprinted to the bathroom. Watching him, I
almost missed Justine saying, "The pains stopped, and she's back
home. But it's Bernie I wanted to ring you about. She's *really* got up
to something."

Which didn't sound good, given my previous experiences of Bernie's schemes.

"A surprise, she says," Justine went on. "She's coming back to Ballydara and wants to tell Rafe all about it. So your mam and I are getting a lunch organized for one o'clock."

Was Mam not inviting me? Or had Bernie asked her to exclude me? "And what am I meant to do while you lot have your cozy family party?" I asked her, then Rafe emerged from the bathroom in his boxers—just in time for his mobile to ring.

And ring. And ring. "Hold on," I told Justine, and pulled my mobile from my ear, while

Rafe strolled to his phone. Weighing it in his hand, he appeared to be studying it.

"Aren't you going to pick up?"

"I'm thinking about that too," he said, rather inscrutably, as the phone continued to ring. Clearly, he was in as strange a mood as I was.

I rolled my eyes, as his mobile finally went silent, and said to Justine, "Well, are you going to—" I broke off, realizing the line had got disengaged.

I considered pretending she and I were still talking, but really, that was for complete eejits. "She rang off," I finally said to Rafe, feeling forlorn. "Who was ringing you?"

"Bernie," Rafe said, still staring at his phone, then I jumped as my mobile rang again. Justine, of course. "What happened?"

"Sorry," said Justine. "It was Bernie, all over me to contact Rafe. His phone must be turned off. Could you put him on?"

"What am I, Western Union?" I said irritably. I pulled the phone from my ear and looked at Rafe. "Would you please ring your stepmother?" Then to Justine, "Well, are you going to answer my question?"

"Jaysus," Justine said impatiently. "There you are, being a diva again. Of course you're invited. Isn't it your mam's house?"

I felt nominally better as we rang off. Meanwhile, Rafe was on his mobile, mumbling a series of, "uh huh, uh huh, yeah," then he tossed his phone on the bed. "Looks like it's a command performance at your mother's place. Bernie's got a big surprise…a family thing—"

"What is it?" I wasn't a great one for surprises.

Rafe shrugged. "I don't have a clue," he said, then he turned another one of those intense blue looks at me. "This lunch okay with you?"

I felt that odd tenderness again. Rafe was treating us like a couple—an actual *functional* couple, where one party asks the others' OK for social events.

Feeling more unsettled than ever, I said without thinking, "So, a family surprise? About your brother's engagement, do you think?"

Rafe's face changed. "That would hardly interest me," he said, and strode back to the bathroom and shut the door. Not quite a slam, but close.

"What'd I say?" I said to the door, then remembered. Rafe didn't get on at all with his brother. "Still, no reason to take your bad form out on me," I muttered.

But actually, there was. He'd asked me to marry him, and I'd put him off. And maybe he'd guessed that I'd no intention of discussing it either. Myself, I felt like I was back at square one as far as getting a baby out of the deal. So, a status report:

Justine, my only ally at luncheon, would be busy playing chef. Rafe was annoyed with me, and my fertility window was closing fast. Dealing with Bernie's disapproval after sleeping with her stepson would be bad enough, but now I had to face Mam too.

And I wasn't ready.

Thirty

"You know these sorts of displays of affection will be like waving a red flag in front of a bull," I said to Rafe as we entered Mam's.

His arm round me, he only shrugged. "Bernie'll have to get used to it—to us," he said, and gave me this rather possessive look. Already nervy about this gathering, I wasn't quite up for Rafe going a bit more Alpha on me than usual. But I kept my mouth shut, and we followed Bernie's tinkling laugh to the front room.

I stumbled in shock. On the couch was someone I'd met years ago, at an Egan family party—a fair, less-impressive version of Rafe.

His brother Ian.

Rafe's hand clenched on my waist. "Ow!" I said under my breath, stepping away from him, and saw his stiff expression. If he'd been a porcupine, his quills would be sticking straight out.

"Look who showed up on Nate's doorstep last night," Bernie announced, beaming.

"Rafe." Ian stood up, and held out his hand to his brother.

Rafe glared at Bernie for a second, then his jaw hardened. Like Rock of Gibraltar hard. "Hi," he said to Ian coolly, his handshake reluctant.

Ian and I exchanged a, "hey, good to see you," then the situation went downhill from there.

Rafe made grudging replies to everything Ian said, and Bernie's labored attempts to smooth things over, punctuated by nervous laughter, only made the atmosphere more stilted.

Already horribly edgy at having to face Mam, I couldn't handle a Byrne dust-up too. Before I could change my mind, I rushed to find a corkscrew for Mam's best Riesling. And find Justine.

I tracked her down in the lamb-scented kitchen, setting the roasting pan onto the cooker. And thankfully alone, as Mam appeared to be doing her flitting round thing in the dining room, doing place cards, for Godssakes. "What's with the pair of—"

"Grainne!" Justine squealed, with a radiant smile. "Isn't it fabulous? Isn't *he* fabulous?"

"He's grand," I lied, reaching for the nearest bottle of wine. If you ask me, Ian was actually a total Beta guy, and tended toward the insipid: dark blondish hair (not Rafe's intensely black), blue-ish eyes (not nearly as blue as Rafe's), tallish (but not rangy like Rafe either), and an okayish smile (and no sign of Rafe's quirky one). Lastly, his nose looked entirely intact—without Rafe's interesting dents.

All in all, nice enough, but definitely an "ish" kind of bloke.

"Ian back in Ireland—it's a dream come true," Justine gushed. As I sloshed myself a glass and took a substantial gulp, she gave the lamb an absent poke. "I was right, wasn't I, about telling Frank off? Letting the Universe know I'd an opening for a new relationship."

Not the time to remind her that the man in question was newly engaged. "I'm sure it's great altogether for you—but what's Bernie thinking, getting Rafe and his brother together, if they don't get on—"

"Bernie says after all these years, isn't it time the pair of them got to be friends? And I think she's right." Justine opened a cupboard, stretching up on tiptoe, then looked at me. "Could you get the platter, there?"

I reached over her head, then set it on the countertop. "Sounds a bit like playing God to me."

I suddenly wondered if I was trying to play God too, with the baby thing? No way, I told myself, taking another slug of wine to help me forget the idea had ever occurred to me.

"Well, Bernie's heart is in the right place." Justine got the lamb on the platter, and was artfully arranging the roast spuds. "After all," she said really low, "it wasn't Ian's fault that his and Rafe's mammy ran around."

I wrinkled my brow. "Ran around?" I couldn't be hallucinating from a half glass of wine, could I? I took another slurp to clear my head. "What are you talking about?"

"You can't have forgot," Justine whispered, cutting up some herbs, "that his mother had an affair and got pregnant with Ian."

I choked, nearly spewing wine all over the lamb. "What?"

"Do you mind?" Giving me a dirty look, Justine brushed off the top of the roast. "I know I mentioned it to you."

"Right," I managed. How had I missed the affair thing? Had I pretended I'd never heard it in the first place?

Justine rotated a potato, then adorned it with a sprig of greeny stuff. "You see why Rafe's mam wasn't allowed much time with him after she left his father."

"Shunning her sounds like something the Byrnes would do," I said, still in shock.

Topping off my glass, I remembered now what Justine had said the other day, that Rafe had never got over Ian being taken away from him. I got a tight feeling in my chest, thinking of a little boy being abandoned. But hadn't Rafe risen above the crap treatment he'd experienced? So no reason to feel sorry and aching for him. Was there?

"You'd think he and Ian would have bonded through adversity or something." Justine scattered more greeny bits over the platter. "But it's never too late, don't you think?"

Justine, as usual, was being wildly optimistic. In my opinion, there was no accounting for the way people acted sometimes, seemingly against everything sensible, or rational. And shouldn't I know that better than anyone?

"Now that Jack's dead, the oul' tyrant," I agreed, "no reason for them to stay away from each other." I took another slug of wine. "When did you say lunch would be ready?"

Justine didn't pick up the hint. "Exactly why Bernie wants to get them togeth—"

She stopped as Mam came in the door. "Hi," I said briefly, and quaffed another mouthful of wine to avoid her. When I lowered the glass, Mam had her arm round Justine as she admired the platter, her champagne silk suit coordinating perfectly with her hair. Except for those gray roots. "The parsley did the trick—the lamb looks every bit as lovely as in your cookery book."

Glass firmly in hand, I took myself to the table. I could already tell it would be a long meal.

Despite the lamb's impeccable presentation, I'd no taste for it. Or the potatoes or salad either. Truly a one-off, since after missing supper last night, and breakfast this morning, I was starting to feel weak. I had to wonder, had I gone on my food because of the tension between Rafe and his brother? Or that I was getting early-pregnancy food aversions even before conception?

The fact that Mam had placed me nearest the kitchen, the furthest from Rafe, *and* pretended I wasn't there, didn't exactly pique my appetite either. Shades of the Byrne dinner from hell five years ago—when Bernie had done the same.

Still, my vantage point had an upside: a clear view of Rafe's frozen face. I realized that if he'd never gotten over losing his little brother, like the family legends said, my plans for him would heal his childhood wounds! Rafe would see that I, unlike his own mam, would embrace motherhood as a lifelong job, providing our child with an altogether idyllic childhood. And she—I had my heart set on a daughter—would fill all those empty places in his psyche.

The more wine I drank, the more insights I had into Rafe's soul. Especially when Ian, who'd been talking with everyone except his brother all through the meal, looked squarely at Rafe. "May I speak with you after lunch? Privately?"

Rafe forked a big chunk of lamb in his mouth, taking his time. "We're all friends," he said finally, gesturing around the table. "Nothing you can't say right here."

Ian didn't shift his gaze. "I'd prefer to wait until a better time, thanks."

Rafe took a leisurely drink of wine, the Alpha guy in full. "But *I'd* prefer to hear what you've got to say now." His expression clearly added, *and get it over with.*

I'd never heard Rafe sound so...cold. And a thought came to me—*is that how I come across to my own mother?*

Ian flushed. "It concerns a loan. To me."

Rafe raised one brow. "From...?"

"You," Ian said baldly.

Their eyes locked, the pair of them staring each other down, like they were the only two people at the table. After an excruciating moment, Ian launched into what appeared to be a well-rehearsed speech about college loans and wedding bills, and that he would've never approached Rafe but for Bernie's encouragement. Only Rafe didn't even look at him. Instead, he contemplated his wineglass, rotating it slowly, as if it was much more interesting than his own brother.

Ian finished up with "...And I have some personal expenses I'll go into later..." As Bernie visibly held her breath, he asked Rafe, "What do you think?"

"No," Rafe said.

Bernie made an air-sucking sound. Ian said stiffly, "That's it?" He didn't look put out. He looked hurt.

"Did you forget?" Rafe said, and cut another piece of lamb. "I'm broke."

"Oh," Ian said slowly. "Right."

"Not technically," Bernie chimed in. "You've still got—"

"My ex-wife is sure to claim a large chunk of my personal funds," Rafe said, still cool.

"But Rafe," Bernie said, "there's the trust—"

"Bernie," Ian broke in firmly. "No." Apparently, he'd more backbone than I'd thought. Then he looked at Rafe again. "No problem," he said, though he'd gone a bit pale. "Just thought I'd ask."

Rafe's knife clattered on his plate. He frowned, as if he felt cheated that Ian had taken his refusal so well. There was an uncomfortable silence, until Mam said, "Mrs. Byrne, that's a lovely frock you're wearing—a designer original?" Bernie looked relieved, and launched into a raft of shopping-on-the-Continent stories.

I looked at Rafe, my amateur psychologist instincts definitely aroused. Was I the only one seeing the whole picture? Rafe being used by his mam, his granddad, his greedy fiancée, and now a half-brother he never saw. Jaysus, who wouldn't overreact?

Ian seemed to recover with admirable aplomb, chatting up Mam and Bernie, and asking Justine for another helping of meat.

As for Rafe, he began cutting his meat with such vengeful strokes the blade scraped against Mam's Wedgwood.

It was easy to see that Rafe's childhood baggage had come back to haunt him. In my wine-induced wisdom, I came upon the perfect, healing solution—for the short term, that is, since having our baby would be for the long. As a nanny, I was intimate with children's complex emotions. So it was up to me to help Rafe revisit the painful memories of his youth. Sure, I alone could heal the estrangement with Ian forever.

"So, then, Ian," I said, leaning toward him on my elbow. "Justine tells me you were on the go a lot when you were a kid, traveling and that sort of thing?" At least I think she'd once said something like that.

Ian smiled uncertainly. I wanted to say, *if you were as persistent with your brother as you must have been when you proposed to all those girls, you'd make Rafe see things your way,* but I hardly knew the man. Which would change, of course, when he was my baby's uncle.

"We weren't actually traveling," he said. "We moved around a lot. My mother and I, that is. After I left home, we sort of went our separate ways."

I didn't look at Rafe. With the wine giving me lightning-fast insights, I sensed that discussing his mother had to be painful for him. But this was for his own good. I asked Ian, "Your mam had a great career then, changing jobs, promotions, that sort of thing?"

"Not really," Ian said. "When she changed jobs, it was because she lost them. There were a bunch of boyfriends, but they didn't last either. I can't remember all the places we lived, until I went to prep school."

How do you like that? While Rafe was securely ensconced in the family manse, Ian and his mam were forced to take to the road like tinkers? Surely Ian should be the resentful one, not Rafe. And how did the woman afford boarding school?

Ian must've read my mind. "I had a lot more stability once I got to school, thanks to Bernie," he added, and raised his glass to her.

Bernie looked pleased, then leaned towards Mam. "I had to

push Jack, my father-in-law, for Ian's education," she murmured. "Took a lot of pressure, I can tell you, but he finally gave in."

Mam looked at her admiringly. "There's a mother's instincts for you," she said, like she knew all about them. "Takes a special woman to pull that off."

Hard as it was to agree with Mam, it was true—Bernie got full marks in the stepmammy department. But *I* would be helping Rafe through this dark time, not her. "So, Rafe, while Ian was going to school, what were you up to, besides golf?"

Rafe gave me a look eerily reminiscent of the one his granddad had turned on me, like I was an insect under glass. "Aren't you the one with the mysterious past? The one you don't want to talk about?"

I frowned. How had the conversation got on to me? "Oh, hardly mysterious," I said airily. He might intimidate his brother, but not *me*. I reached for my wineglass again.

"Is too," Justine said, coming in with the refilled salad bowl. "Your sister's always on about your five-year birthday meltdowns, but I've never heard the story behind them."

"Me neither," Rafe said, his gaze still pinning me. Hearing a certain implacability in his voice, I lifted my glass with a shaking hand. What the hell did he think he was about? Then his voice going even edgier, Rafe said, "Isn't open dialogue what family is all about?"

You're the one with the family problems here, pal, not me, I almost snapped. Then Rafe's eyes shifted to his brother for the space of a second, and I saw the bleak look in them.

Rafe was really hurting then. Which really hurt *me*. And the fact that I was upset on his account bothered me even more.

But...maybe, I thought hazily, I could help take Rafe's mind off his pain, and share *my* narky bit of history after all.

"All right," I said, in a muzzy sort of way, "but there's not much to tell. Like my mam always says, I was just a bit of a problem child." I didn't look at her.

"A bit?" Justine hooted. "That butcher knife haircut when you were five is hardly 'a bit.'"

"Butcher knife?" I felt Rafe's fascinated gaze on me. Ian's too.

I was bringing the brothers together already! "Oh, *that*. Just a trim that got out of hand."

Mam looked up from her chat with Bernie about the posh shops in New York, and smiled fondly in my direction. "Matt and I always said our Grainne was a force of nature."

Now there was a good one—Mam talking like she and Dad had been a team? After what she put him through? "Yeah, I was a real crack," I said, the old bitterness surging up like it was brand new.

"And she wouldn't take no for an answer, either," laughed Mam. "She'd a will of iron, that one—do just as she pleased, and take her medicine later."

I was suddenly so angry I could hardly see. Maybe this bit about taking the heat off Ian and steering it toward me wasn't such a good idea...

"And if Matt gave her a swat, do you think she'd cry?" Mam went on, oblivious to my reaction. "But not a tear out of her! Instead, she'd give out so her sisters would run for cover!"

And how would you know? I wanted to snarl, and felt the room sort of tilt. *You were too...busy to notice me!*

"And what the girl got up to!" Mam looked round the table smiling, obviously enjoying the spotlight. "If it wasn't putting a toad in Mary Alice's bed, or climbing out windows after Matt sent her to her room ..." Shifting her plate, she reached for the wine bottle, and knocked her fork onto the floor. "Oh!" she said, with another trill of laughter. "Grainne, run to the kitchen and get me another fork, won't you?"

Love of God, I thought drunkenly, it really was the Byrne's disastrous meal all over again. Me, the outsider. Part of the servant class, who didn't belong. "No, Mam, I won't get you a fork," I enunciated clearly. "Our guests are waiting on the edge of their seats, keen for all the highlights of my childhood."

Mam looked confused all of a sudden. But I wouldn't care. "Well?" I asked the table at large. "Aren't you?"

Bernie and Ian appeared to be on the verge of bolting, and Rafe had gone very still. Justine pushed back her chair. "Actually…why don't we have our trifle…"

"Ah, stick around, this'll only take a minute," I said, while another part of me said, *Stop it. Before this really gets out of hand.*

But I didn't care. What was going on here was no longer about Ian, or Rafe. Or even me. As always, it was All About Mam. Time for her to take *her* medicine.

"You asked, so I'll tell," I snapped. "On my fifth birthday, I wanted Mam to fix up my hair with slides, just like my friend Breda's mam did. But while Dad and my sisters were gone from home, a man called round to our house. To see Mam."

Justine said uncertainly, "Grainne, I'm sure there's no need to—"

"Oh, but there is," I said, as my rage swelled. "Because, before I could get Mam to do my hair, the pair of them went upstairs."

I sensed a collective, appalled breath round the table, all eyes glued on me. "I followed them, and rattled the doorknob to Mam's room. I yelled for them to open the door, that I needed my hair fixed. But she wouldn't come out—"

"Really, there's a time and place for this," said Justine sternly, "but not—"

"And she wouldn't answer me either," I said, ignoring her. "So I kicked on the door, and pounded it with my fists, until she finally called out that she was *busy* right now, she'd do my hair later—"

"For God's sake, Grainne," Rafe said, but I ignored him too.

"So I went downstairs, pulled the biggest knife I could find out of the drawer, and cut it all off, to save her the trouble."

A ten-stone silence descended on the room. But now that the wine had freed my tongue, why not share my Year Ten Meltdown too?

"Five years later," I said, and luckily my head was spinning so I couldn't look at Mam even if I'd wanted to, "Dad took me for a ride, to get a birthday ice cream. Not far from home, we saw Mam walking on the road. She was with a man, the man I'd seen before, holding hands. I said, 'Dad, stop! Make her come home!' but instead he gunned the engine—"

"Stop it, Grainne!" Justine warned. "It doesn't mat—"

"But Dad rounded a corner too fast and crashed the car into a lamppost. Luckily, we weren't injured, just banged up. So after Dad was done with the Garda, we went home, and the next day I ran away. But you know all about that—"

"Grainne—please—" said Justine, as Rafe broke in, "Chrissakes, will you stop this *now*—"

"You just said we're all friends here, so there's nothing I can't say," I said defiantly. "So, then, five years after that, just before my fifteenth birthday, I overheard Mam and Dad having a row—"

"Shut up, Grainne." Justine had tears in her voice. "Just shut—"

"He was telling her she'd have to give up Tony for good, or he'd leave," I said relentlessly. I was fast losing my taste for this, but I couldn't stop. "Seemed like a good time to go to the party at Justine's house, and an even better idea to let Rafe think I was of age. Then get as pissed as I possibly could—"

'Grainne!" Justine shouted. "Shut. Up!"

"I'm done anyway," I said faintly, the rage draining out of me. "But what it taught me was that except for my own children, I'd never lo—"

I broke off. What did I almost say? My dizziness dissipated a bit, and I finally looked at Mam. She was white, her hand clutching her wineglass. *I don't care! Why shouldn't I tell what happened? It's true! Mam's the one who should be feeling guilty, not me! And don't they say, The Truth Shall Set Ye Free?*

Funny, the way freedom turned out to be overrated. Ian and Bernie were gazing at me as if I'd grown an extra head, Justine looked gobstruck with horror, and Rafe—well, it could have been the drink in me, but if I didn't know better, I'd say his eyes were full of compassion.

I wanted to snarl at him—*don't you feel sorry for me! And don't think we're soul mates, just because our mothers cheated!* Then, I looked at Mam again, my guilt and confusion like a swirling caldron inside me, and I realized, truly realized, what I'd done. I'd tried to shame her, but instead, I'd shamed myself.

As the horrible, creepy-crawly silence lengthened, I dimly sensed a way out. I tried to catch Mam's eyes. *Tell them*, I pleaded silently. *Tell them I'm lying, or that I'm too pissed to know what I'm saying, and I'll back you up.* In fact, this could go down in the Larkin family lore as my worst birthday meltdown yet, my age-of-thirty spectacle.

But Mam didn't look at anyone, least of all me. Her face curiously blank, she moved her wineglass to the edge of the table and knocked it over, straight onto her silk suit. "Will you excuse me?" she said crisply, then rose, with nary a trace of the drama queen. "I need to change my clothes."

It would've been grand if my Big Confession was all a big blur—but I wasn't quite drunk enough. I was all too aware of Justine's accusing glare, and as for Bernie's expression, well, it defied description. If I hadn't been so numb, I'd have gone upstairs to Mam, to say...*something*, though I'd no idea what. But after I'd just outed her as a shite wife and mother, she probably wouldn't open the door.

So I could only sit there, pokers of guilt stabbing my insides, and shame filling me in a way the wine hadn't. As the room swirled round me, I hung my head over my still-full plate. Then Rafe stood up, took my arm, and began leading me out of the room. Disregarding his brother, he said to Bernie, "Be right back."

"Rafe—stop!" Bernie jumped up and followed us to the front door.

Rafe only tightened his clasp on my arm. "Mom—"

"In the name of God, what do you see in this girl?" Bernie asked as if I wasn't there.

"No offense, Mom," Rafe said without turning around, "but please, butt out."

He opened the door, helped me into his hire car, then went back inside, presumably to inquire after Mam, say goodbye to his step-mother and ignore Ian some more. In those few moments by myself, I didn't try to collect my thoughts—I'd too many of them. Like wondering how soon Mam would tell Rory what had happened, and when to expect my sister's blistering phone call. And how had I forgotten I'd no more head for wine than pints? Good job I wouldn't be tempted to touch drink once I got pregnant, because I'd just gone off wine for good.

As soon as Rafe joined me back in the car, I took one look at his set face and my scattered thoughts made a fist and gave me a good clout upside the head. First of all, I was off the hook as far as going to *real* confession ever again. I could never tell a priest how I'd humiliated my own mam in front of strangers. And there was no way I could top this sin anyway.

Second, I didn't have to worry about Rafe proposing again, because I'm sure Bernie would no sooner let him marry me than one of the Kardashian sisters.

And finally, I discovered that I'd got the whole venting bit all wrong. Expressing your rage helps nobody, least of all yourself. Because the anger invariably becomes a torrent that flattens everything in its path.

A decidedly morose air about him, Rafe didn't speak on the way to the hotel. And I couldn't. Too busy fighting nausea, though whether it was existential or alcohol-induced was open to question. As soon as we arrived, I collapsed on the bed (in the bedroom we hadn't used), before I either puked up all the wine, or rang room service—to ask if they could send up some hemlock so I'd never have to face Mam again.

Thirty-One

Now I knew why people drink. When you pass out, you don't have to think of all the shite things you've done.

I awakened hours later—thirteen to be exact, according to the Zen clock next to the bed—with a throbbing head, sandpapery eyes, and a horrible taste in my mouth. Crawling out of bed, I stumbled through the dark suite to the bathroom.

After I drank about a gallon of water and brushed my teeth, I took a scalding shower, which was not just therapeutic, but the one place I couldn't be reached by phone. The amazingly high-pressure needles of water—rare, indeed, in Irish lodgings—felt a bit like a hair shirt. Exactly what a gobshite daughter like me deserved.

When I finally staggered out of the bathroom, dressed in one of the hotel's kimonos, I wasn't that surprised to find the lights on and Rafe sitting on the couch. For one thing, any hotel plumbing worth its salt always wakes the dead. And Rafe seemed to have embraced this whole attunement thing with me.

"Feeling better?"

"Not really," I said, toying with my kimono belt. I couldn't tell him that along with my hangover, I'd recently acquired a foreboding cramp below my navel, indicating the imminent arrival of PMS.

"Do you want me to...take you anywhere?"

I assume he meant Mam's, so I could apologize. But if I couldn't face her drunk, I could hardly do it hung over. I was just glad he hadn't asked, *Do you want to talk about it,* like a girlfriend would have. "Not really," I said again, and collapsed on the other end of the couch.

"Then how about something to eat?" He opened the cover of a tray on the coffee table I hadn't noticed before.

Scrambled eggs and wholemeal toast! For a moment, I could only stare in wonder at the plate. No one had ever really fussed over me like that, except for Justine, and her cooking for me was mostly practice. "Fabuloush," I garbled, already biting into the toast, and I fell onto the food like I hadn't eaten in days. But I guess I actually

hadn't, had I? And it hardly mattered that the eggs were cool and
the toast was soggy.

"Feel better *now*?" Rafe asked as I finished the eggs. His smile
seemed rather forced, but I didn't care about that either. A smile was
a smile. I took it as a sign he didn't hate me for what I'd said about
Mam.

I nodded and popped the last bit of toast in my mouth. "Who
knew this place would have twenty-four hour room service?"

"They don't," he said. I gave him a questioning look. "I bribed
the concierge to make it."

"Before dawn? That must've been some tip," I said, resisting the
urge to lick my fingers.

"It was." Rafe's smile turned tender, and despite my certainty
about Bernie's vociferous objections, it was a look with a second
marriage proposal written all over it. I cast my mind over all the
ways to distract him, and settled on the easiest. I clambered to my
feet, sprinkling toast crumbs everywhere, and held out my hand.
"I'm ready to go back to bed again," I said. "But not to sleep."

Afterward, I curled into Rafe's arms with another funny ache
inside.

Rafe had kept his condom on, and I had kept my mouth shut…
counting on the law of averages. Surely sooner or later, we'd run into
a defective condom, or Rafe would get sick of wearing the narky
things. That seemed more promising, since he'd a sort of agonized
look when it was time to put one on. Although I was sure I wasn't
terribly fertile at the moment, I did my share of wiggling round a
little to see if he'd take the bait. But he didn't, and here I was, still
having protected sex.

He'd whispered his concern about my not having an orgasm
again.

"Maybe later," I mumbled.

"How about sooner," Rafe suggested, and began drawing
figure-eights round my breasts.

"No," I said, and before I could stop myself, I pushed his hand off me, and turned onto my side, away from him.

Silence. When Rafe said, "What do you mean, no?" I pretended I was already asleep.

Morning light was filtering into the room as I awakened for the second time. I cast a resentful look at the box of condoms next to the bed, which seemed to mock me. Then I crept out of bed to the bathroom, knowing I'd probably rouse Rafe—since we were so attuned.

Sure enough, when I returned he was fully alert, pulling the covers aside to invite me in. But instead of putting the moves on me, he fixed one of those very male, purposeful looks on me. The sort that had nothing to do with a marriage proposal.

I was right. I winced as he expressed—in a mix of loverlike concern, hurt male pride, and can-do CEO-speak—that if we had a sex problem, let's fix it now. With nary a blush in sight.

I met his eyes. "It's your narky condoms," I said. "They pinch."

"There are other brands," he said, as if discussing bath soap. "Or other...methods."

Well, here it was. Moment of truth. "Or no methods at all," I countered.

Rafe rolled onto his back, his hand shading his eyes. "Grainne..."

"I mean it." I took a deep breath. "I want a baby."

"Grainne." He took his hand from his eyes, but only stared at the ceiling. "As much as I want to sugarcoat this...I can't. Because I don't."

I rose onto my elbow. "But—"

"I don't want kids."

"Why not?" I asked reasonably. I was still in a reasonable frame of mind.

Rafe's apparent fascination with the ceiling continued. "I just don't."

"That's no answer," I said.

"That's my answer."

"But the other day, after I asked you to…" My throat tightened. "You said you'd consider a baby. But you wanted us to talk about things first."

"I was…okay, I admit it. I was stringing you along. I'm sorry."

I waited for fury to overtake me, but I guess I was still too hung over and too overcome by my own sins to give out about his. Still, I was convinced you can talk a man into anything if sex is part of the deal—and since I'd gotten him into bed, I'd won half the war. "Come on. Every halfway normal person wants kids. Including Nate, your bloody best friend."

Rafe jackknifed up to a sitting position, and swung his legs over the other side of the bed. "From my perspective, being a kid is really shitty," he said, his back to me. "My mother left. My father went to the office every day, all day, including Christmas and Easter. Granddad took me under his wing, but I knew my value to him was as his high-achieving heir."

"You're worried about your parenting skills?"

"No. I just can't see…it. Creating a child to experience the same misery."

Seeing the tension in Rafe's back, I had the sudden urge to lay my face against his skin, kiss the sad little boy inside him to make it better. But I might never get another chance to work on him, so I hardened my heart. "People can get over a crap childhood—look at me."

He glanced at me over his shoulder, one brow lifted. "And you've coped with it? Your mother may not agree."

Just what I needed, a reminder of Mam. I took a breath. "I'll make sure my child has a wonderful childhood. So don't you think it's time you got over this hang-up?"

He turned to face me, the lines around his mouth pronounced. "I don't have to justify myself, to you or anyone. I don't want kids. I never have, and I never will."

"You can't mean that—"

"I. Don't. Want. Kids. How much clearer can I get?"

Resisting the urge to panic, I leaned back, and let the sheet fall from my breasts. "You don't have to want them. I want them enough for both of us."

His eyes drifted downward, but didn't linger long enough to suit me. "That's not how it works—"

"I'm actually quite keen to be a single mam," I broke in, glossing over the fact that he'd asked me to marry him.

Rafe recoiled, like he'd just uncovered a nest of spiders. "But what would your family say?"

Probably a lot. Like I cared. "I don't live to please my family."

"You can say that again," Rafe muttered, and cut his eyes toward my breasts. "But—"

'And just think," I told him, "wouldn't fathering an out-of-wedlock child show that you're serious about your big mid-life rebellion?"

"I can't believe you'd think I'd deliberately abandon you—"

"And after the baby's born," I interrupted, "you'd have no obligation to come round. You wouldn't even have to see her. I'll take care of everything."

"You have got to be kidding!" Rafe looked apoplectic by now. "My grandfather would roll over in his grave if I had a child and didn't take responsibility!"

"Your granddad's dead," I reminded him. "He'll never know."

"But I will!" Breathing hard, Rafe ran his hand through the hair I'd mussed up a few hours ago. "You're acting like I never asked you to marry me, that marriage isn't an option—"

"Can we just focus on the baby here?" I couldn't worry about how he was taking it—that I'd rather have his baby than him.

"Look," Rafe said, frowning, "I figured we could be one of those couples who don't feel the need to have kids. Who could be… everything to each other." Then his face changed. "Am I missing something here? Like…money?"

I clenched my fists. "Is that all you bloody Byrnes ever think about?"

Rafe's eyes drifted back to my breasts. "Well, no—"

"Not funny!" I pulled up the sheet. "You think I want a baby to get my hands on—Jaysus! I told you I didn't want your fecking money." I was starting to feel desperate. "What'd you think, that I'm trying to blackmail you? Get your baby, then file a paternity suit? Or fake getting your baby, and go after your money anyway? Everyone's made it abundantly clear you're broke!"

Rafe looked harassed. "That's been kind of...exaggerated. True, I'm no multi-millionaire, but if we got married, I'd take care of you."

"Forget it!" I snapped, as a small voice inside reminded me, *he already does take care of you. In every way.* My emotions whirling, I scrambled out of bed, feeling terribly ungainly—but really, who had any dignity whatsoever when they're standing naked in front of a man they're fighting with. "Haven't you heard the old Scottish proverb?" I asked. "'Never marry for money. It's cheaper to borrow.'"

"Aw, Grainne," he said, grabbing my hand. "Why does everything have to be a fight with you?"

"It doesn't—not always." I couldn't help curling my fingers round his, and let him pull me back into bed. Running my finger down his chest, I said, "Give me a baby and you'll see how accommodating I can be." As the words left my mouth I knew they were horrible. Far worse than the way Rafe had treated his brother. But I couldn't help it. I *had* to settle this baby thing once and for all.

Rafe curved his hand round my hip. "I love you. Why can't that be enough?"

Oh God. The dreaded "L" word. The one I'd hoped would never come up.

I swallowed hard, resisting the urge to leap out of bed. "I don't want you to love me," I said in a small voice.

"Tough," Rafe said. "You want to control everything, don't you? But you can't control the way I feel about you."

"Your feelings are none of my business," I said, and was instantly ashamed of myself. Why was I doing this to one of the few people who cared about me?

"That's right," Rafe said, and I had to look away from the bleak look in his eyes. "All you want is a warm body."

"It's your warm body I want." I shifted close to him. "No one else's."

"Oh, I feel a helluva lot better now," Rafe muttered, and abruptly rolled me onto my back.

I pulled him over me, closing my eyes to avoid the grim look on him. I knew I was losing the battle, but I wrapped my arms round him as tightly as I could...As if I was tumbling headlong down a cliff, and he was the last-ditch handhold keeping me from falling into a chasm.

But what did I whisper into his neck when he reached for another condom? "If you love me, you won't use that."

Rafe lifted his head. "What's going to happen to us if I don't give you...what you want?"

I reminded myself that Joe was just a phone call away. My grasp on the security of Rafe slipped, until I was hanging on by a mere finger. I took a shaky breath I hoped he couldn't feel. "I'll find someone who will."

I felt every muscle in his body tense. "Then here's something to remember me by." He threw the condom box across the room and slid down my body, his mouth right *there*. Before I could push him away, sensation rose in me, overwhelming me, and Rafe made that thing happen that I'd been avoiding. In fact, he made it happen three times.

But afterward, I didn't feel glowy or satisfied. I felt haunted, by the shameful way I was treating Rafe. *We could be everything to each other*, he'd said. That's how I'd felt about my baby, that I could be the moon and the stars to her. But...could I?

The misery grew inside me, squeezing my throat, pricking my eyes. To stop it, I could pull Rafe inside me, one more time. But instead I mumbled, "I don't feel well," disentangled myself from him and grabbed my mobile. Closing the bedroom door, I bolted for the bathroom.

Where I turned on the fan, the bath taps full-bore, and buried my face in the nearest towel. And celebrated my *real* five-year birthday meltdown by crying for the first time since Mam went upstairs with a man who wasn't Dad.

Thirty-Two

If I'd been queasy with drink and self-disgust after outing Mam yesterday, being stuck in a hotel suite with Rafe after rejecting him, and his love, was excruciating.

In the wake of my crying jag, I shivered in the bath, wishing I could puke up all the pain and anger inside me. Being reduced to my backup plan—that is, replacing Rafe with Joe—was the most depressing prospect I'd ever faced. Except for having to leave the bathroom—and soon. Not only so Rafe could have a go at the loo, but to tell him we needed to take a break from each other. Although I'm sure he'd be as keen as I was, after my insulting, "I'll find someone who will."

So, no help for it—I dragged myself out of the tub. After drowning my reddened eyes in cold water to reduce the swelling, I searched my brain for a legitimate way to escape Rafe's company. Where could I go? With a flat on the other side of the country, no job to get to? I wrapped a towel round myself. One thing was for sure, I couldn't bear to face Mam yet.

I could use a hand here, God, I told Him. *If You could help me get as far away from Rafe as possible, and straightaway, I'll…I'll…* I couldn't decide on an appropriate trade-off, as a wave of guilt nearly overpowered me. *What are you about?* I stared at myself in the mirror. *Hitting up the Almighty for favors, after you've ground the feelings of everyone you know into dust?*

Then my mobile rang. Not checking the ID, I seized it, desperate for distraction.

"Put your clothes on," said Justine. "And tear yourself away from Rafe. I'm downstairs. In the lobby."

"Why'd you come all this way, when you could have rung?" I said to Justine with a tad of grumpiness, so she wouldn't know how overjoyed I was to escape from Rafe. Although if God had actually heard my request, but had only got me as far as the hotel lobby, He'd come up short in the prayer-answering department.

"I realize I've interrupted your lovely romantic getaway," Justine said without a trace of apology in her voice. She seemed a bit... different today.

"That's all right," I said as we entered the dining room, half-full of no doubt harmonizing couples. "We've had our romance and our getaway." *And I've turned them all to shite.*

Moments ago, I'd dressed in seconds, then sprinted through the suite, tossing a "Justine's downstairs and needs me" through the bedroom door. I stopped as Rafe opened it, his face impassive, his trousers half unzipped. I hated that I noticed how adorably tousled he looked. I also hated that I noticed a flash of hurt on his face.

"You're leaving?"

"Just popping out for a bit," I said, clutching the front doorknob. *Please, God, can we make this quick?*

"'Popping out. For a bit,'" he repeated. Long, awkward pause. "If you were anyone else," he said finally, his voice dripping irony, "I'd assume that means you'll be popping back *in*. But then, we know you can't be counted on, that you'll pretty much do whatever the hell you want. Without giving a crap about anyone else."

Stung, I opened the door. Part of me wanted to run to him, say, *I'm sorry, you're all I want, I wish I didn't have to go,* but I just couldn't...be around him right now. "Really, I won't be long," I said, and fled.

Now, prying myself out of my self-absorption, I looked across the table at Justine. She looked pale today—even her freckles seemed faded—but there was also a new vibe coming off her. "I suppose you're here to give me hell," I said. Anything she could dish out would be easier to deal with than Rafe. "About the lunch. And...my mother."

She fixed a severe look on me. "I'm tempted, but I asked myself, do I have the right? I mean, she's *your* family. Not mine."

Maybe I was off the hook. "True, although—"

"Granted," she said, her gaze sharpening, "the pair of you have serious issues to deal with. Like five-years-with-a-counselor-and-you've-barely-scratched-the-surface serious."

The thought of being in therapy with Mam, sharing *feelings* and all that, would turn my hair shirt into a bed of nails for sure. "Ah, go on," I tried to scoff. "I didn't know what I was saying, I was pissed—"

"No excuse," she said, looking disgusted. "You were horrible, to air your dirty laundry in front of—"

"It was Mam's laundry, not mine," I retorted, fidgeting with the flatware. Still, I knew I couldn't get out of asking after her. "How... is she?" Devastated? Had she taken to her bed?

"I'll tell you what your mam is—dead right." Justine fixed an unrelenting, guilt-tripping gaze on me. "Don't forget, two days ago she said something bad was going to happen—and sure enough, it did. And you're the only one who can make it right. After you apologize, ask what you can do for her. Tell her how much she means to you."

I felt a sharp pain in my stomach, like a dull knife twisting in it. "But I—"

"No buts." Justine said. "I have to say, though, you've one strong mother. After you'd done your worst, which would've laid low the toughest person, she came back downstairs in a fresh outfit, and was the perfect hostess. Bernie was ready to find new lodgings, but your mam managed to talk her out of it without a hint about her personal problems. Later, I tried in a roundabout way to ask her if she was okay, but all she'd say was that she'd plans with Doreen."

I stared at Justine. Here I was, suffering agonies of guilt (well, not quite agonies, but you get the picture), while Mam was treating her checkered past like so much water off a duck's back. *Well, I don't need her*, I told myself, ignoring the hurt rising up inside me. *I'll have my baby*. Maybe not Rafe's, but I'd have *a* baby, which was everything I wanted.

I looked round and spied a waitress. "Well, since you're here, shall we order some—"

"I'm not done with you—after you made such a spectacle, I came to give you this." She handed me a piece of familiar-looking stationary.

I unfolded the cream linen, seeing the *EAL* monogram at the top. For one horrible minute, I thought Mam was informing me I'd no longer be welcome in her house. But the note wasn't in my mother's hand.

> *I've reconsidered our arrangement regarding a blurb for the media and I am no longer interested in your services. If I see my son's name in your little column I will notify my attorney.*
>
> *Bernadette Byrne*

So Gai, and I, had been royally sacked.

With all that had happened with Rafe, and Mam too, I'd all but forgotten my agreement with Bernie, my blog, and even my Gai persona. "You know what this is about, I take it?" Justine nodded. "Well, no great loss," I said, though I felt a moment's regret for the lovely recognition I would've gotten from my exclusive piece on Rafe Byrne. "It was an eejit idea in the first place."

Ready to tear up the paper, which I knew would earn me yet another disgusted look from Justine, I refolded it and stuck it in my pocket. I really was off the hook with marrying Rafe. Here was the absolute proof that Bernie would never, ever, let it happen. "So then," I said, keen to move on, "If Bernie's still here in Galway, I take it Aine still hasn't gone into labor?"

"Actually, it's looking like she is," Justine said. "I already let your mam know we're heading for Dublin as soon as possible."

I realized when I gave birth to my baby, whoever the father was, I'd be lucky to have one person—Justine—with me. There'd be no loving husband, or doting granny. Nor in-laws, or sundry other relations on standby. No sister certainly. As soon as Rory got wind of what I'd said to Mam, she'd disown me for sure.

Not that I wanted a crowd hanging about, I told myself stoutly. Getting in the way, taking videos of your bum and all that. "Let's hope your sister-in-law hops to it soon, then, before Nate and the rest of the family gets tired of waiting," I said, firmly turning my mind from all the cosseting Aine was getting. "But you didn't come here to talk about Aine either, did you?"

I felt that new vibe from Justine again. "Right before you and Rafe took off yesterday, things got really...complicated," she said, her face softening.

"With Ian," I said. It didn't take a genius to figure that out.

"You remember he asked Rafe for a loan?"

It all came back to me. "Rafe said no, and Ian seemed to take it in stride. Why is it complicated?"

"Believe me, it is," Justine said. "After your liquid lunch, you weren't so jarred you forgot Rafe helping you to the car, then coming back into the house?"

"Of course not," I said. "He was gone a few minutes. Why, did something happen?"

"It was closer to an hour." Justine got that melty look in her eyes again. "While your mam was upstairs, Ian rather cornered Rafe, though he was polite—"

"Polite?" I tried on a grin. "Is that why he asks all those girls to marry him?"

Justine stiffened. "I can't believe you can joke about this, when you know how important he is to me—"

"I take it back," I said quickly. "So then...?"

"Ian *made* Rafe listen, and stressed that the loan wasn't only for the wedding and his college debts. He'd a much more important reason for asking."

"Good man, himself," I said, wondering how soon we could wind up the Ian drama and I could start figuring out what to do about Rafe. And my baby. "Ian grew himself a spine—then what?"

A look of misery crossed her face. "Ian being Ian, he had to be completely honest. About those personal needs he mentioned. He'd just found out that his fiancée—I mean, the one before Gennifer..."

"And she's called...?"

"Isabelle." Justine looked ready to cry. "She's French—she was a guest instructor at his university."

"A teacher's pet?" Really, what had the man been thinking?

"No, she wasn't his teacher, but—"

"And now this Isabelle wants him back? She saw Gennifer in Bloomingdale's picking out her bridal gown and oul' Izzy went for her throat?"

"No!" Heads turned. Silverware clattered. The waitress froze, then gave us the evil eye. "Must you go for the laugh with every fecking thing?"

I blinked in shock, then leaned closer to her. "Christssakes, can you keep it down?"

"And why should I?" Justine hissed, but much lower. "I know how much you hate for anyone besides yourself to be the center of attention."

I drew back, and stared at her. The kitten had turned into a tigress. Before I could ask, "What the feck's got into you?" two things happened. My mobile vibrated in my bag, and as I pulled it out to check the ID, a man appeared in the doorway. Tallish, blondish. Ian-ish.

"I can't believe you brought him here!" I snapped at Justine.

"He actually brought me," she said baldly as I glanced at my mobile. Oh, Jaysus. Rory. Ringing because of what I'd said to Mam. She'd be guaranteed to rake me over not just your common everyday coals, but red-hot, nail-embedded ones. I stuffed my mobile back into my bag. Then Justine added, "And Bernie came with us—she wanted another go at getting her boys together before we leave."

Great. Bernie and her big dramas had to follow me here. "Well?" I said, as Justine gave Ian an encouraging wave. "What's he doing here?"

"I think you know," she said, but with a shamefaced air. "I was hoping—"

"Oh, I get it. You want me to talk to Rafe? What about Bernie? Isn't she working on him as we speak?"

"She's actually waiting in the car—she wanted her boys to sort it out themselves."

"Well, that's clearly not happening," I said, feeling bitter. "So you're depending on me, to convince Rafe to hand over the cash."

Isn't that just lovely. Justine hadn't come to Harmony Hotel to be supportive of me, she was here for *Ian*. Telling myself that awful feeling inside was hurt pride, I scooted my chair back a few inches. "Trouble is, Rafe won't listen to me." Men generally didn't listen to girls who told them to go to hell.

"He will, I know he will," Justine said, pleading in her voice. "The thing is, what I was trying to say a minute ago is that Ian *really* needs the money. Turns out, his fiancée—that is, his ex, Isabelle—had a...a..." Justine couldn't seem to get it out.

"A what?" I was so done with this conversation. Didn't I have enough troubles without taking on Justine's?

"A...a...baby!"

A baby! "Ho-ly God," I muttered. Someone fecking *else* who'd got a baby. And who'd have thought a weenie like Ian would get up to that? "Boy or girl?" I couldn't help asking.

"Boy," Justine said. "But Isabelle kept it to herself. Until a few days ago. Now Ian needs to pay her child support, along with his other—"

"Talk about a soap opera!" I interrupted. I looked back at the doorway, but Ian had disappeared. Probably to skulk around until Rafe showed up. "So Ian wants a handout—"

"But he doesn't!" The words poured out of her. "Just a favor. See, there's a trust fund for Ian that Bernie made Jack Byrne set up years ago, but he can't touch it until he's thirty-five. He told Rafe he only wants to borrow against it. But he'd hardly got the story out about the baby before Rafe gave out at him for getting a girl pregnant. Especially a foreign one, who wouldn't be staying in the States. Then Bernie got into it, shouting at Rafe about why couldn't he do this one little thing, and Rafe said, "I'm not listening to this," and stomped out the door. So, since we haven't much time, can you please talk to him?"

Me. Talk to Rafe. If he didn't want *my* baby, why the feck should I deliberately help put another one in his path? "If you aren't setting yourself up for a fall, I don't know who is," I said. I tried to sound calm, but the injustice of it all really got to me. Now, bloody

Ian (and some eejit French girl) had a baby. And I still did *not*.

"I'm not," Justine insisted. "I know what I'm doing. Helping Ian—"

"Will get you nowhere—" I broke off as my mobile rang again. Rory, of course. Though naturally, I had to check, just in case it was Rafe, telling me that he'd changed his mind, he'd give me a baby to make me happy. But no. It really was Rory. And I really was fecked.

I let it go to messaging. With Justine, I'd have to be ruthless if it would make her face the truth. "Look," I said. "You want to help Ian marry someone else, and set up yet *another* girl who's got his baby. Aren't you reading the signs here?"

"Signs?"

"The ones shouting, 'there's no room in his life for you.' Why do this to yourself?"

"I can't help it," Justine said, the misery back in her face. "Sure it's hopeless, but I love him."

Love. I thought I'd choke on the word. What was love but another meaningless, manipulative impulse between consenting adults. And hadn't I learnt at my mammy's knee (that is, I would have, if she hadn't been off with the infamous Tony, so I'd learnt it at my father's), that love was really all about hurting other people.

Rafe had said he loved me, but he didn't want a baby with me, so he clearly didn't.

And Justine "loved" Ian, thereby setting herself up to be his doormat—just like Dad had been Mam's. "You love him. Him with the fiancées and the baby and the no money. Jaysus, let's get out the viol—"

"Shut up," Justine snarled. "What would you know about it?"

Justine, snarling at *me*? "Plent—"

"Shut. Up," Justine said with a cold fury I'd never seen in her. The kitten/tigress had just morphed into a bloody cobra! "I'm talking now, and I'm saying you don't know the first fecking thing about love."

I opened my mouth, but couldn't seem to muster a sound.

"All the time I've known you, you've laughed at it, said it's all bollocks, and that it'll never happen to you." Justine picked up a fork and jabbed it toward me. "Well, bloody good decision. Because here's what love is like. Sometimes you fall for the wrong guy. Sometimes it hurts. And sometimes you do something—or maybe a lot of somethings—to help the man you love, even if he'll never be yours.

"So go ahead, laugh at me, and never let a man touch your heart." Justine's voice trembled. "But I'll have the last laugh. Because when I'm old, I might end up as alone as you, but at least I'll remember what love felt like. But you'll just be alone." Long pause. "And by the way, feck off."

I felt like I'd been mauled. By the girl as formerly sweet as Hello Kitty. I wanted to scoff, *so you're the expert on love now?* But with the bleak picture she'd painted, the words stuck in my throat. Justine, of all people, turning on me. Betraying me.

Yet another betrayal, in a long string of them. Mam had done the unforgivable, but now *she* was the victim. Dad had loved me, only to die on me. Rafe had messed me about by saying he loved me, but not enough to get me pregnant. And now, Justine.

I knew my voice had to be around here somewhere, but I couldn't seem to find it. Finally, I mumbled, "But I won't be alone—I'll have a—"

"There's one more thing," Justine snapped. "I also came here because I'd some news for you—and I thought it was only right to tell you in person. Break it to you gently."

Were those tears in her eyes? She cared about me after all—the soft, tenderhearted, and understanding Justine I knew was back.

"That's decent of you," I said, "but I've guessed already. Mam wants to disinherit me? Too bad, I'm going to disown her first—"

"It's not your mam. It's Joe. And Sinead."

A warning bell—in fact, an entire cacophony of them—went off in my head. "What's Sinead got to do with—"

"She's pregnant, that's what," Justine said with satisfaction. "And guess who's the father? But you don't care about anyone, so what's it to you, right?"

Sinead. Pregnant. Head whirling, I wanted to be sick, right there in the white-linen sea of Harmony's peacefully attuned dining room. "Joe?"

"It's Joe, all right," Justine said. "I'd seen her flash her bum at him, skinny though it may be, although you never did. But can anyone blame Joe for going for it, when you wouldn't give him the time of day?"

"*I* can," I managed through stiff lips. "How could he...?"

He could. And had. With Sinead, that total and utter cow, while he was still ostensibly engaged to me. Stunned, I could only sit there, as Justine pushed back her chair and stood up.

"I think we've said it all. So have a great old time shagging Rafe or playing mind games with him or whatever the feck you've been getting up to after you broke your mam's heart."

But Mam doesn't have a heart, would have been a lovely rejoinder. If I'd been able to speak, that is. "And it's a stroke of luck Aine's having that baby," Justine snapped. "Because I've had enough of *you*." Then she stalked out of the dining room.

I'd obviously imagined her tears just now. The fact that she hadn't the decency to cry on my behalf was salt in the wound. So Joe, that faithless gobshite to end all gobshites—actually, worse than a gobshite since he'd pretended to be so nice—wouldn't be part of my fallback plan.

Trying to pull myself together, I took a Harmony Hotel-calming breath. Justine wouldn't stay angry for long. So right now, I had to accept the new reality: No Joe. Well, then. Good job Rafe was just upstairs. Our taking a break could wait. All I had to do was get rid of Bernie, because Rafe would no doubt make short work of Ian. Again.

I stared into the middle distance. Rafe, you're the man after all. And no matter how much persuading, sex, or whatever—yes, I was ready to resort to out-and-out trickery—you're not getting out of being the father of my child.

Thirty-Three

The concierge sent me a malevolent glance as I entered the lobby. Not that I could blame the woman—Justine and I had not only brought disharmony to the hotel's breakfast, but had multiplied our faux pas by not ordering any food. So I sauntered outside, where a light mist fizzed in the cool air. Intent on not running into any of the Byrnes before they left, I headed for the tiny park round the back—the one I'd seen in the hotel brochure, but had been too busy having sex to visit.

I popped off an apology text to Justine, then breathed deeply, letting the fresh air clear my thoughts. I'd yet to work out what I'd do for the next day or two, since being in Ballydara alone with Mam was so not happening. At least I still had Rafe. After a fashion.

I felt the first drops of rain as I came upon an entirely unexpected feature—a labyrinth! A good, no, fantastic, omen, wasn't it? Walking the labyrinth, I would obtain all the spiritual insights necessary to show Rafe the error of his ways.

Feeling a bit silly, I crunched along the twisty gravel paths, telling myself to be open for celestial inspiration. About ten minutes later, my mobile rang. Mam. God, no. Not ready. I jammed the phone back into my bag and kept walking. But after another quarter hour, I realized I wasn't getting any spiritual insights. Actually, I wasn't getting any insights of any sort.

I was, well…not just wet, but bored. So when my mobile rang again, I considered taking the call just to relieve the tedium…and to keep from thinking about Justine. It would have to be either Mam (still not ready) or Rory (No. Way.).

But it was Rafe! There was something to this labyrinth bit after all! Really, you'd think the heavens were working in perfect tandem with my plans. "Yes?" I said cautiously, making my way to a nearby bench. I wouldn't take anything for granted for this second-go-round with Rafe.

"Where are you?"

"Just outside," I said, my confidence rising like a hot-air balloon.

Poor man. He'd been worried I'd gone and left him. So I'd want to show him I was interested in his problems. "Did you end up seeing... your brother?"

"For a couple of minutes. But that's not why I called you."

Rafe sounded...odd. The strain of seeing Ian, no doubt. "I'm glad you did." I said, trying to sound soft and supportive. You know, show him I really was great motherhood material. "Because I've been doing some thinking."

"So have I," he said brusquely. "I've changed my mind." Grand! Happy Days are Here Again, he was ready for a baby! But his distinctly unloverlike tone struck me. "About...?"

"About you. Us."

My new confidence plummeted. This definitely did not sound promising. "And...?"

"This morning, you said if I didn't give you a...what you wanted, you'd find someone who would."

I had said that, hadn't I? Rather horrible of me. "Em...yes, but I—"

"I imagine that someone will be Joe," Rafe interrupted coldly. "So do it."

"What?" The person on the other end of the line couldn't possibly be Rafe—who'd never been cruel or awful to me. Had my labyrinth walking put me on a more elevated plane, where I was imagining things? "What did you say?"

"You heard me," Rafe said, and I knew I couldn't have conjured up the ice in his voice. "Go find Joe, or whoever the hell you've picked for your next victim, and do what you need to do."

I heard a strangled sound, then realized it had come from me. "B-b-but you said you lo...I mean, cared—" I broke off, appalled at the pleading in my voice. I sounded like any other pathetic girl who's been turned down.

"My mistake," Rafe said. I dimly heard the tiredness in his voice, and wondered if I'd worn him out. The same thing Mam always said about me. "I realized you were just a...distraction."

Distraction. Incredulous, despairing, I wondered what had

happened to Rafe's lovely mid-life crisis? The state of him being amenable to all sorts of un-Byrne-like behavior? "You're splitting with me over the phone? Did your stepmother talk you into this?"

"Sorry it has to be this way," he said, not sounding sorry at all, "but I've been putting off getting my life together. And no, Bernie had nothing to do with this. I just know it's time I faced reality."

Now, I wasn't even worth Rafe fighting with Bernie over me. "What we've been doing seemed pretty real to me," I said, trying to sound provocative, instead of depressed.

"What I'm trying to say," Rafe said carefully, "is that it's over. We're done."

This couldn't be happening. Not to me—*I* always called the shots with people. Always the dumper—never the dumpee. Ever the optimist, I made a last-ditch effort to salvage the situation... I'd be blithe. Funny. Make him realize what he was giving up.

"So then," I said lightly, but clutching my mobile so fiercely my hand hurt, "How about one last shag for the road?"

Another pause—I just knew Rafe had to be thinking it over, that he'd been *way* too hasty... "No thank you," he said coolly.

I felt each word like a blow, the three of them knocking the wind out of me. Unable to move, I felt the horrible tingling in my nose, pressure behind my eyes, and clenched the phone harder, fear and loneliness like a void inside me.

No way. No way no way no way would I cry over him again. But I had to come up with a final *hey-it's-been-fun, a good-bye/good luck/ God bless*, and not let him know how he'd hurt me...

Then, a miracle happened—another phone call. Rory.

Saved, I thought dully. "Sorry, got to go." If I could remember what happiness felt like, I would have been glad for the excuse to ring off. "My sister's on the line."

Sunk in misery, I clicked over, ready to endure any tirade from Rory. Even embrace what was sure to be an exponential rise in guilt over Mam, if only to get away from Rafe's rejection. "Rory?"

"Where the hell have you been? I've been ringing you for *hours*—Christ Jesus, we've a crisis here, and you've got to—"

"Okay, okay," I interrupted, trying to recover. Sure, picking a fight would be just the ticket. "Mary Alice broke a fingernail? No, don't tell me, it's Willy the dog that's broken one?"

A silence, then, "That's not funny!" Rory burst out, and I realized she was crying. "Mam's in trouble, and you've got to ring her, right now—"

"Wait," I said, as yet another call came in. Rafe? To apologize? To say he did love me—

No. "It's Mam," I said to Rory. "I'll ring you back."

Feeling ruthless, I cut her off, and held my mobile in my lap for a moment. It was awful of me, when she was in tears, but you know, after what Rafe had said, anything my sister or Mam could dish out would be mere pinpricks.

And judging what this morning's phone calls had brought—disasters, across the board—I knew Mam's wouldn't be any better. But Mam being in the throes of one of her big dramas was probably just what the doctor ordered, to get my mind off Rafe. I forced myself to lift the handset to my ear.

"Ah...Mam?"

"Grainne, could you come home?" Her voice seemed to crackle, like a tune on an old vinyl record. "Straightaway?"

I'd been right—clearly, a big whoop-de-do in the offing. But what about me? I thought self-righteously. Don't I get one bloody minute to dwell on my own troubles?

"You want me for something?" I said, feeling the old resentment that she wouldn't be ringing me if Rory hadn't been out of the country.

"Yes," she whispered. "My mammy's dying."

Thirty-Four

It can be bloody inconvenient, when God actually *does* answer a prayer. While I give Him full marks for arranging my speedy exit from Rafe's hotel suite, I thought that would be it. I never thought He'd go so far as to knock off my granny.

On the bus back to Ballydara, I was lost in gloom, unable to make sense of what had happened: Rafe didn't want me, Justine had told me to feck off, Joe was an unfaithful gobshite, and Sinead was having *my* baby. And did I mention Rafe didn't want me?

The injustice of it made me feel like I'd a big hole in the middle of my chest.

I'd been too proud to try and find Justine and Ian at the hotel, to ask for a ride—my temporarily ex-best friend would probably spit in my eye, which depressed me even further. But when the bus pulled into Ballydara, my low feeling evaporated—in my rush to leave Hotel Harmony, I'd left my holdall in the suite, and I was suddenly furious with myself. What if Rafe thought I'd done it deliberately so he'd have to contact me?

Bollocks. If he did ring me, I'd be the one doing the spitting. How dare Rafe treat me like crap—I didn't want him anyway! And if he wanted my case out of his room, he could bloody well give it to Justine!

But that new humiliation lost its sting when I let myself into Mam's house, to find her sitting on the edge of the couch, arms hugging her middle, rocking herself. Mam looked dreadful, like a blow-up toy with all the air let out, eyes sunken, her face as gray as her roots. In fact, I couldn't remember her ever looking this flattened, not even when Dad had died.

With trepidation, I'd searched her face for her reaction to me, hoping for mere dislike...and preparing myself for hatred. But Mam didn't seem to actually *see* me. "Your granny's dying," she said, her voice rough as gravel. "But I told you that, didn't I?"

I'd bit back a flippant, Jaysus, Mam, she's been dying for five years. D'you think she means it this time? Instead, I said, "You did.

On the phone."

Mam just kept rocking. "I knew something bad was going to happen."

Dead right on that—I'd just experienced the Perfect Storm of misfortune. But of course she was talking about her mother. "We'll be all right," I said, hoping I wouldn't need to bodily pull her out of the chair, to get her to Inishmore Island and Granny. "We'll be at Uncle Don's house before you know it. All we have to do is catch the bus."

Sitting next to Mam on our way to Rossaveel, to catch the ferry, my hollow feeling returned. I was exhausted, and the day wasn't half over. I'd had no word from Justine, despite another two texts and an e-mail. And now an ache was growing behind my eyes, and I'd a cramp in my belly where a baby ought to be. I wished I could forget all the horrible things Rafe had said to me. But I could still hear his voice. *Next victim…my mistake…* and the awful finality in his voice, *we're done.*

You're a fine granddaughter, I reminded myself. Here your granny's on her deathbed and all you can think of is your own problems. But in my own defense, I should say that Granny hadn't much fondness for me—actually, none at all.

Once we'd arrived at the ferry landing, I'd sneaked away from Mam to ring Rory. "How soon can you get here? We're ready to board the ferry."

"I can't," Rory said quickly. "Brenny's got an ear infection and can't fly."

Rory never lied, but the speed of her response told me she was overjoyed for the excuse. She hadn't liked our granny much either. "But you've got to—"

"Grainne, you're just going to have to deal with this."

"But if you can't come, Mam will want Mary Alice, then," I said.

"That's not on either—she's had a bit of spotting, so her doctor's put her on…bed rest."

A likely story. I didn't put it past my middle sister to put herself on bed rest for a stubbed toe. "I can't believe you're not going to be here, to support Mam in her grief," I said, putting as much hurt in my voice as I could muster—that is, what little I'd left after Rafe dumped me. "You know I can't manage her."

"You'll have to," Rory said. There was no mistaking the satisfaction in her voice. "And if you don't know how, it's time you learned."

Strangely enough, on the ferry, Mam didn't show much evidence of her famed seasickness. True, she did look a little green, but she sat unnaturally straight, swaying with the boat's motion, and clutching her handbag with clawed hands. I realized that for the first time in my memory, Mam had none of her usual glamour. In fact, she looked an awful lot like Granny O'Neill.

"When did you say Rory will be here?" she asked.

"She can't," I said, the unfamiliar pity I felt at odds with my resentment. Here I was, trying to be a proper daughter, and as usual, Mam was focused on someone else. "Remember, I just told you she couldn't leave Chicago."

"That's right." Mam rubbed her forehead. "I can't imagine how I forgot."

"It must be the grief," I said. Maybe it would help her forget how I'd wrecked her luncheon the day before too.

"I think you're right," Mam said in a voice just above a sigh, and actually reached for my hand. "Sure, it makes you absent-minded."

I tensed as she touched me, then stared down at my hand, a virtual prisoner in Mam's. We hadn't held hands since I was five— and let me tell you, this was one surreal experience. Suppressing the reflex to yank it away, I wondered how Mam could act so sad, when she'd pretty much avoided Granny for the last decade or two.

Then an entirely new thought occurred to me. What if her relationship with her mother was as complicated as mine with her?

Granny O'Neill turned out to be a terror in death, as she'd been in life.

One of the neighbors met us as we disembarked, and brought us to my uncle and aunt's house in Kilronan, where Uncle Don, stout and ruddy-faced, met us at the door. Without the benefit of all his sister's youth- preserving beauty-routines—hair-dyeing, brow-waxing, and skin-tightening creams, not to mention her diet regime—he looked ten years the elder instead of the two younger that he was.

"I'm afraid you've just missed her," he said. As if Granny had called round for tea that evening, then took off, instead of being ensconced in his back bedroom since the beginning of time. "She left not two hours ago."

Mam clutched my hand again. "She's gone, then."

"I've just rung the undertaker," Uncle Don said sadly. "But Father Lynch made it in time for the last rites."

His wife Orla sat at the kitchen table, a tumbler in her hand and a half-filled bottle of Jameson's at her elbow. "He made quite a dent in the whiskey, that one," Orla said.

You'd probably need a bit of a tot if you had to pray over dead folk regularly too, I wanted to say. "Who'd have thought Granny would go so fast," I put in quickly.

"Fast?" Uncle Don said incredulously. "I...suppose you could say that."

The years with Granny in the back hadn't exactly rushed by, then? "Still," I said, "it's a...terrible loss."

Ha," cackled Orla. "Sure, I'll be sad to lose the rough side of her tongue." She waved her glass. "D'you know, her last words were of you, Eileen."

"Shhh!" hissed Uncle Don.

Mam let go of me to clasp her hands at her heart, gazing at Orla eagerly "She did! What'd she say?"

"We...forgot," Uncle Don mumbled, looking daggers at Orla. "It was the day before yesterday, after all, when she slipped into the coma."

Orla took another slurp of Jameson's. "The pair of you'll want to see her, I suppose."

Actually, I was dead keen to take a pass on this part of the process, but even I knew I couldn't get out of it.

We made a small procession going down the hallway, me, of course, bringing up the rear. All I wanted to do was sleep—really, was it too much to ask? A crappy eight hours of blessed oblivion, to forget the insults Rafe and Justine had heaped on me? But no. I had to visit a dead person.

I hung back, not wanting to be near Mam lest she grab my hand again, and forced myself to look at Granny. Uncle Don or the priest must have closed her eyes, folded her hands just so. I tried to feel compassion at the slightly shriveled look of her, but all I could think was that she'd never had a kind word for me.

And felt awful for it. "Did she go peacefully?" I asked, for something to say.

Uncle Don made a choking sound, while Orla hooted, "Did she ever do anything peaceful in her life?"

Mam paid us no attention. As she touched Granny's face, tears dripped down her cheeks. She'd always said crying ruined your looks—seeing her weep, then, I was so unsettled I had to fight the urge to light into Orla. *Did you have to mention that now, you harpy?*

"Actually, there was that time..." Mam said in a faraway voice, then, "Ah...no." She frowned, and the furrow between her brows looked as deep as the one between Granny's.

I found myself lifting my hand to smooth it. Realizing what I was doing, I snatched it down, my protective impulse toward Mam freaking me out even more than her tears. When a knock came at the door, I turned away eagerly. "I'll get that."

"That'll be the undertaker," Uncle Don said behind me, and the four of us trooped out of the room.

When Dad died, I'd managed to avoid meeting with the mortician blokes. But now, there was no getting away from Mr. White, the undertaker, and his beefy-looking sidekick, who easily could've doubled as a bouncer in a North Dublin pub.

Mr. White (great name, wasn't it, for a guy whose professional attire was anything but) managed to simultaneously ooze sympathy and talk serious money. Mam didn't say a word. And as I inhaled the sandwiches Orla had set out for us—I ate Mam's too, since she didn't touch a crumb of the food—there was also no escaping the weird emotions prompted by what was basically a business transaction.

Is that what it all comes down to at the end of your life? I wondered as Mr. White rhapsodized about the solid oak urn that would be perfect for Mrs. O'Neill, urged on by Mr. Beefy's uh huh, uh huh, uh huh. Folk dickering over the price of your urn and interment fees?

"Is that what she wanted?" Mam asked suddenly. She'd been paying attention after all, then. "To be cremated?"

"She'd left no direction for her funeral," Orla said resentfully. "And it's cheaper."

"Really, Eileen," Don put in, "she won't know the difference."

Mam still looked forlorn. Did she regret not visiting Granny more? Then I recalled a conversation she and Dad had years ago, when Granny's health began failing.

"Maybe we should ask her to stay," Mam had said.

"With us?" Dad looked aghast. "I don't think that'll do."

"Why not?" Mam wasn't used to Dad not agreeing with her. "The doctor'll be easier to get to, and with the girls having their own places—"

"She…ah, would likely prefer to stay at Don's," Dad said quickly.

"Well…" Mam didn't speak for a moment. Then, "He *is* her favorite, isn't he," she finally said, with a strange sort of laugh, and changed the subject.

Later, I'd asked Rory why Mam and Granny hardly saw each other. "Granny really doesn't like Mam much," is all Rory would say. *How can she not like her daughter?* I'd wondered at the time. *When I have mine, she's going to be my favorite person in the world…*

Now, trapped at Don and Orla's kitchen table, I stared at Mam, who was visibly drooping. I wasn't her favorite person—but then, she wasn't mine either. Then remorse hit me again. Was that any excuse for being such a gobshite daughter that I had to have my bloody arm twisted to help her in a crisis?

But when Mr. White brought up plans for the wake, my inner gobshite had the upper hand. Instead of sticking by Mam's side as they discussed what to dress Granny in, and should they curl her hair, or even give the old girl a dab of lipstick, I ditched the lot of them and fabricated an urgent trip to the loo.

I hid out until I heard the front door close, then re-entered the kitchen in time to see Mam's pleading look at her brother. "Try and remember what Mammy said about me, won't you? You know, the last thing, before she died?"

"It's slipped my mind entirely," Don said quickly. "Yours too, Orla, right?"

Orla only clattered the dishes into the sink. "It's late," she finally said. "I'll show you to your room."

Room? Surely she didn't mean the singular?

I'd forgot how small Uncle Don's house was. I got an ominous feeling as our hostess led us down the hall, Uncle Don clumping behind us with the cases—a dread that was entirely justified when Orla opened the door to their son Donnie's old bedroom, the width of which was taken up by *one* double bed. "Here you are, then."

"But..." I was sharing a bed with *Mam*? Despite my newfound filial guilt, I was Not. Ready. For. *That*. "What about the couch?" This bed looked tiny, nothing like the king-sized one Rafe and I had at the Hotel Harmony

"Donnie's offered to take it," Orla said. "He'll be here in an hour or so. And I'm sure you won't want to sleep *there*." She bobbed her head toward Granny's room and cackled.

"Ha, ha," I said weakly.

So, I was to be spared no indignity with minding Mam. Even sharing a bed with her—when I could hardly stand to have her touch my hand.

An hour later, Mam slept soundly beside me. You'd think I would have too—this had been one of the longest days of my life.

But the horrible bits with Rafe, then Justine, then Mam and the long trip here, preyed on my mind, like your tongue unerringly poking at a sore tooth. For a minute, I pretended I was walking the labyrinth again, hoping to find my inner peace. Instead, I felt a fresh spate of misery for the way I'd treated Rafe. And Justine.

I tried to tell myself that with Rafe, I was only standing up for what I wanted. And someone needed to stop a grand girl like Justine from being Ian Byrne's doormat. But dwelling on what a crap daughter I'd been, to deliberately humiliate my own mother, I'd no real excuse. If Mam had been a crap mother to me, I'd more than evened the score.

I rolled over, away from Mam. I couldn't help thinking that if Rafe and I had been together, if only I'd never hurt and insulted him, things would've been entirely different. He'd have done the gentlemanly thing and escorted us on our trip. Then he and I would have been cozily ensconced in a lovely little B&B.

Instead, I was stuck here at Don and Orla's for the next few days. Not only forced to endure the cacophony of snoring emanating from their room *and* knowing my granny's corpse was just down the hall, but tucked up in a miniscule bed with the woman I'd resented all my life. And knowing I was utterly and completely trapped.

Although I managed to doze off, despite the racket, something roused me while it was still dark. I found myself facing Mam, an unfamiliar pressure on my arm. She was hanging onto me in her sleep.

I didn't shake off her hand. Or move away. Feeling raw and aching, I forced myself to stay where I was, and pretended again.

That she was the mother I'd always wanted, instead of the one I'd got.

Thirty-Five

Whoever says Irish country funerals are a great crack doesn't know what they're talking about. Instead of rip-roaring music, drink, and high-jinks to send the dear departed on their way, Granny's wake was a rather sedate affair.

The second evening, a few of Don and Orla's neighbors joined the four of us, Donnie, and Father Lynch. Apparently they'd concluded that the sharp edge of Granny's tongue couldn't reach beyond the grave. So they'd be safe enough to pay their respects, say a quick "God rest her soul," and get a cup of tea and a sandwich out of the deal. I myself paid a quick visit to Granny's bedside, straightened up the prayer cards and relit a candle that had gone out, and told her I hoped she'd be a lot bloody happier where she was now than she'd been here on earth. Then I skulked back to the front room, with the goal of staying as invisible as I could until after the funeral Mass, the day after tomorrow.

The limited mourning contingent was also due to the fact that Mam's four other brothers had emigrated—two to the States, two to Canada—and had begged off, with excuses that held about as much water as Rory's and Mary Alice's. Clearly, if conventional wisdom dictates that a doting mammy will produce fond and dutiful offspring, Granny O'Neill had not been a doter.

By the next day, the strain of having to act grief-stricken over Granny's death, or at least nominally sad, started to really get to me. I wish I could say my cousin Donnie—who didn't seem all that sad either—was sort of an ally. But he was a younger version of Don, who'd got middle-aged and boring before his time (not leaner and craggier and wittier like Rafe). Donnie spent most of his time talking to Uncle Don about the best investments for the small inheritance Granny would be passing along to her children.

Sure, a bit of cash wouldn't make up for her having all the warmth of a banshee on a bad day, but Mam could probably use some money for her B&B. But when Granny's will was pulled out for a look, we discovered she'd left a small bequest to each of her surviving sons. And none to her daughter.

Don looked miserable. "Her memory went, these last years," he said to Mam, but anyone with half a brain could see he was reaching. "It probably just slipped her mind."

A lone tear trailed down Mam's face. "It's only money," she said. "But Mammy never forgot anything."

"I'll..." Don looked at his wife. "Orla and I could spare..." his voice trailed away as Orla's mouth tightened like a knot. "Well, perhaps we'll discuss it later."

"She was trial to the end, that one," said Orla. As if anyone needed reminding. "And she never gave us a penny for looking after her all these years."

Sensing the effort Mam made to keep smiling, I almost said, *You're welcome to it—my mam doesn't need or want one crappy euro of it,* then I felt a sudden cramp in my belly. For a moment, I thought it was an excess of sympathy for Mam. Then I realized what was happening and rushed to the loo.

My period had arrived, and way early too.

I admit it. I'd secretly hoped for the saving grace of birth control malfunction. I'd heard condoms had a statistically proved, if small failure rate—surely, out of all the times Rafe and I had got it off, hadn't there been a good chance one of the condoms would spring a leak?

Then something really bizarre struck me: In a strange way, I was *glad* about my period coming—it wouldn't have been right to get a stealth pregnancy over on Rafe.

I got that achy feeling behind my eyes again. How could this be? Just days ago, I'd vowed *nothing* would get in the way of having a baby—like Scarlett O'Hara, I'd lie, cheat or steal, whatever it took, to get what I wanted. So what was I about, waffling like this?

I couldn't *really* be growing a conscience. Could I?

The next day, after Mass, the same crowd that had attended the wake partook of refreshments and idle chit-chat in Don and

Orla's front room. I nursed a lemonade, sitting as far away as I could from Mam with her grief, Orla with her Jameson's, and Donnie and Uncle Don with their fecking mutual funds and the rest of them. I still felt crampy and out of sorts, but it wasn't period-related. Last night, I'd been awakened by Mam sobbing softly into her pillow. I knew what to do for a crying child, but I'd no idea what to do with my own mother, so I'd pretended to be asleep. And felt wretched for it.

Today, though, Mam seemed to be in fairly good form, sipping a glass of Orla's whiskey, some distance from a group of women her age. She knew them from years ago, Don told me, but you wouldn't have known it by the way they ignored Mam as they talked amongst themselves.

I remembered Dad saying how all the boys had been mad keen for Mam when she was a girl. Comparing the gray-haired, shapeless, mustachioed crones, I thought, *you jealous old cows.* In that moment, I felt proud of my glamorous mam.

Then a Mr. Power, Don's closest neighbor, took a careful look at the group—his wife was among them—then sidled closer to Mam.

"Don said his mam's last words were of you," Mr. Power told her in a gallant tone. Mam had that effect on men still, even if her looks weren't up to their usual. "Lovely to know she was thinking of you at the end, eh?"

Mam seemed to brighten—had to be either the male attention or the Jameson's, though her drinking spirits at all was very unlike her. "It is," she said, smiling tentatively, "but I've not heard the particulars."

"You could hardly forget them," Orla said in a loud voice.

A sudden intuition made me set down my glass. "Granny's last bit was probably very personal," I said. I figured that the lot here were your typical Irish people, terrified of emotional stuff. "Innermost feelings sort of things," I added.

"I wouldn't exactly call it innermost," Orla persisted in a grumpy voice. "She sat bolt upright, and—"

"Does it matter?" I said quickly. "She's gone, and we'll...miss her." I just about choked on that bit, but my aunt's antipathy, only an undercurrent until now, made me uneasy.

"Maybe *you* will," Orla said bitterly to me, then she looked at Mam, whose smile was pinned on tight. "Ah, sure, Eileen, you can smile, but where were you all this time, when you were needed here?" Mr. Power took one look at Orla and backed away.

Mam's smile faltered. "She didn't want—"

"She didn't want me either," Orla snarled. "But with the other boys abroad, someone had to look after her."

I looked round frantically. Shouldn't someone stop Orla? But as the conversation rose and fell all round us, everyone else seemed oblivious. Panicked, I thrust a biscuit at my aunt, to soak up the drink. "No one could've done any better, Aunt Orla."

She pushed the biscuit away. "But I'd have liked a bloody break from her. And isn't it just like you, Eileen, to avoid your mam, even in her last moments?"

"Really," said Mam, "I didn't mean to avoid—"

"It's my fault," I said hastily, "that we got here so late, I was tied up with—"

"Her last words were," Orla said, "'Isn't that good-for-nothing Eileen here yet? She always was worthless.'"

Mam's tremulous smile collapsed. The hum of the crowd broke off into appalled silence. As Don said reproachfully, "Orla, did you have to?" everyone shuffled their feet, with a *Jaysus, how soon can we get out of here* look on their faces.

"Well, it's true," Orla said defensively. "And who can blame her for wondering where in the hell her only daughter was in her dying moments?" Still no one spoke. Or moved.

I could've slapped Orla. Searching my mind for a way to lessen Mam's mortification, I stood up and grabbed a fork. "Hey, now." I tapped the utensil against my glass to get everyone's attention. "I've heard it's a lovely thing, to trade anecdotes about the deceased." I ignored the odd snicker from the herd of old cows. "Let's all of us...em, honor Granny..." I about choked on that bit myself, "...by sharing a special memory about her."

I glanced at Mam, seeing that she didn't seem quite so crushed, then looked round to pick out the first victim. Unfortunately, people were looking at me as if I'd gone mad. "They do this all the time in Dublin," I improvised.

"Ah...Dublin," nodded one of the crones, then Donnie walked into my sightline. "So then, Donnie," and I gave my cousin a look that said, *say something or I'll make you sorry you were ever born,* "you'll take the floor?"

"That's it, Donnie," Uncle Don said in an anxious, fake-jovial tone. "Stand up and give us a good story."

Donnie cleared his throat. "A story," he repeated. "Well..." He produced a stilted bit about the time he was a kid and Granny had made some sort of tart—a rare occasion indeed. "She didn't believe in pudding for everyday, you see."

I kept an eye on Mam. She appeared composed as my cousin droned on, though the Jameson's she was sipping may have helped the process.

"When I thought she wasn't looking, I tried to steal a fingerful of cream from the top," Donnie was saying, "and she gave me a good smack on the knuckles with a wooden spoon. Jesus, did I howl, so she smacked me again to shut me up. My hand hurt for a week."

A spurt of uneasy laughter came from an unknown source. Uncle Don looked pained. "That the best you can do?" he asked Donnie.

"Em...she gave me a spoonful of the sweet later, I think."

Then I looked at Mr. Power, the kindest person in the room. "How about yourself?"

He came up with something about Granny sending round a loaf of bread, thirty years ago when their youngest had the croup. "Fresh-baked too," he said.

A likely story. My self-appointed emcee bit was already feeling old, but I said, "Anyone else?"

I suddenly sensed the restlessness in the room, as if folk were about three seconds from trampling each other to get out the door. The only question was what brave soul would make their move first.

That's when I saw Mam's fingers tighten on her glass. "I've a story."

The female bovine ranks turned to her, their supercilious, unplucked eyebrows raised. Their look said, *So the flighty, nose-in-the-air Eileen has something to say about her neglected mammy?* "What's that, Mam," I said brightly, before the cotton-dress brigade got anything out.

"When I was a girl, we lived near Limerick," Mam said. "There was a time, not long after Mick was born, when Mam was rather in a state—she'd snap your head off one minute, then be silent for hours. One day, she gave me enough chores to keep me busy for a fortnight, cleaning and cooking and washing nappies until the skin on my hands split. When I was outside, picking cabbages, she said she was going walking."

Mam's normally light voice had become an odd monotone. But strangely, instead of being bored, everyone in the room seemed to strain forward, as if not wanting to miss a word.

"I'd never heard of Mam taking a walk in her life. She'd always told me they were a waste of time, when I wanted to get away from all the work round the house. And all of a sudden, I got this awful feeling that something bad was going to happen."

Seeing Mam looking gray round the edges, like she had when she told me Granny was dying, now I was the one getting the bad feeling. "Uncle Don?" I prompted. "I think Mam isn't up for her story after all. Why don't you give it a go?"

He opened his mouth, but before he got a word out, Mam said, "I tried to ignore the feelings, since whenever I told Mam about them, she said I was being wicked. That only God is meant to know what's going to happen. But after a little while, I told Don to mind the baby and followed the footpath I thought she'd taken."

By now, my intuition was screeching, *This story is definitely Not. Sounding. Good.* Did I have some new mind-body connection thing with Mam? "Really, Mam, you don't have to…"

But Mam kept going. I tried to close my ears, but her soft voice was relentless, and I could no more leave the room than anyone else could. "...I found my mam in the river, in up to her waist, but of course she wasn't swimming. It was October. She'd a queer, blank look on her, not like herself at all.

"Right away, I knew what she was doing. I'd heard stories all my life about folk drowning themselves, that the River Shannon was a graveyard. I said, 'Mammy, don't, it's a sin!' She looked straight at me. 'I don't care,' she said. 'Go away home and get the tea for your dad.'"

I felt my throat swell. *It's all right, Mam,* I wanted to say, *you don't have to tell the rest,* but my mouth wouldn't cooperate. Mam kept going.

"The water was up to her armpits now. 'Mammy, you mustn't!' I begged. Over and over, I cried, 'don't do it,' but she was stepping deeper into the current. 'I don't care what you say,' she said. 'I don't care about anything.'

"I scrambled down the bank, my voice nearly gone from the shouting. 'If you go under,' I cried, 'I'll come in after you, then we could both die. And who'll mind the boys then?'"

My mother's voice was like a little girl's now, high and so scared my heart ached for her.

"Finally, my mammy stopped, the water swirling round her neck. I guess she cared more about the boys than me. After a long time, she waded to the riverbank. She said, 'You're not to tell anyone,' with a look that said she'd flay me alive if I did."

Mam took a long, spasmodic breath. "And I didn't. I never told a soul."

My gaze went blurry, but oddly, Mam's face was as clear as a photo. "You'd have thought she'd have been grateful," she went on, "but instead, she hated me. All my life." She sighed, and I felt the decades of hurt escaping from the depths of her. "Maybe I should have let her go." Her face twisting, she began to cry.

The crowd was still caught in horrified silence, until Orla started blubbering. "I didn't know...I didn't..."

Nobody paid attention to her. I wanted to...I don't know, go to Mam—hold her hand, even hug her. But before I could move, the dowdy old cows turned toward Mam, and with a collective, *Ahhh,* every last woman surrounded her, clucking sympathy. *Poor thing... It was the post-natal depression, don't you think? Eileen, you mustn't take it so hard...*

Borne by their soft murmurs, Mam was carried off to bed. I knew what had happened. She'd just become one of them—old, defeated by life. They would look after her the way I couldn't.

I jumped out of my chair, tore out the front door, and climbed over the low drystone wall on the other side of the road. Then my knees gave out. Eyes stinging, I crouched against the wall, regret like a vise round my neck. No wonder Mam had looked for love in all the wrong places, despite having Dad, or we girls. I saw now that she didn't trust the love she'd had in all the right ones.

I huddled there, my arms round my middle, and the tears I'd shed in Rafe's hotel bathroom were only a warm-up for the sobs that shook my insides, waves of them battering me like the sea lashes the cliffs.

Feeling the cold stone against my wet, swollen face, the truth hit me: *I wasn't fit to be a mother.* All these years, I'd harbored a grudge against my own mother, and had almost enjoyed it. But I couldn't bear it, if my child felt about me the way I'd felt about Mam.

I wasn't fit to be a mother. And maybe I never would be, because I was just like her: I *had* found love in all the right places—with Rafe—and I'd thrown it away.

Thirty-Six

Don and Orla rather tiptoed round Mam the next two days. So did I, still seeing the defenseless look on her face as she told the terrible story about Granny. But we'd so much to talk about, even if neither of us knew how to start. Yet.

You see, I was hopeful that when we did get round to actually communicating, I might find it in me to be a proper daughter to her. Try to understand her a little, and...you know. Forgive her. And hope that she could forgive me. And as one day in Kilronan blurred into another, I sensed that if Mam was facing herself for the first time in her life...well, so was I.

I hadn't any reply from Justine all this time. I had to finally accept that I really had reduced our years of friendship to rubble... Justine, who'd always been there for me. Justine, who knew me through and through like my own family didn't. But now, it seemed, family was all I had left.

One week after our arrival on Inishmore, Mam and I were lying in bed, silvery moonlight pouring over us. (To show the progress I'd made, Donnie had left and freed up the couch, but I didn't really want to sleep on it!) Anyway, I knew the time had come for us to pick up our lives again. "Will you give Larkin House another go when we get home?" I asked, breaking the silence.

"I think so," Mam said. "It was a good decision, don't you think, to have a business?"

"It's great," I said loyally, in my new role as supportive daughter. "I'm..." I didn't have much practice with apologizing, especially to Mam, but I forced myself to go on. "I'm sorry I rather spoiled things with your beta customer."

"Who?"

"Mrs. Byrne."

"It's all right," Mam said in a dismissive tone. "Doreen said I probably shouldn't have offered her such a discounted price. 'Charge your full worth from the start,' Doreen said."

"Doreen?" When did she enter the picture?

As if I'd asked the question aloud, Mam said, "I was thinking of asking her if she'd like to help with the B&B, like a partner."

"Oh," I said. Mam was doing her usual, considering other people more important. But if that meant I could get off the hook... Only I found myself saying, "I was still planning to stay and...be your assistant this summer."

"That'd be grand," said Mam. "Then I won't need to ask Doreen. Of course, we'll still want Justine to make puddings for us, don't you think?"

After I'd tried so hard not to think of Justine, just hearing her name felt like a whack in the chest. I didn't have the heart to tell Mam that she probably wouldn't see Justine again. Because I wouldn't. "There's nobody better."

A long silence. I thought Mam had fallen asleep. Then she said, "Speaking of decisions... God knows I've made some...bad ones."

I held my breath. "Like...what?" I asked cautiously.

"Poor...choices," she said, her voice lowering. "Things I shouldn't have done."

Oh, God. This was it? Mam was ready to Confess All? I wasn't up for this! "Really, Father Lynch'll hear your confession, you don't have to say anyth—"

"Mistakes I've made," Mam interrupted, her tone ominous.

As I cringed inwardly, my heart—and the rest of my insides— rose to my throat. "Mistakes?" I croaked.

"Terrible ones." Another long pause, in which I died a thousand deaths. Was she was going to tell me about sex with Tony, or details of hers and Dad's marriage? Then she said, "But you know, what's past is past. And I've never been one to make the same mistake twice."

"You...haven't?" Mam's lightning-fast mood shift left me disoriented.

"Not me," said Mam. "No, I learn from them and go on."

"I'm...glad to hear it." I almost laughed. Could anyone be more self-deceptive than Mam, or better at glossing over the bad stuff? But given her experience with Granny O'Neill, who could blame

her. Now that I saw Mam in a new light, I realized it was part of
her charm.

"Grainne, you'll organize our bus back home, then?"

Apparently if Mam was going to make her confession, I'd just
heard it. "Be happy to," I said. Sure, I needed some purpose to my
life.

"Actually, a car trip would be lovely," she said. "Could your
friend Rafe come fetch us?"

Despite the knot that squeezed my middle, to speak of him, I
couldn't help thinking, wasn't this just like her! In Mam's world,
everyone had their uses. "I'm...not sure where to reach him."

"Justine would know," Mam said confidently. "Could you ring
her?"

I couldn't quite get out, *no, she broke up with me.* "I can't ask
Rafe. We...split up. For all I know, he's gone back to America."

Mam made a distressed sound, and rose to her elbow. "That's a
terrible shame." In the dim light I saw regret on her face. Whether
it was because of no comfy motoring back to Ballydara, or on my
account, who knew, but I chose to believe the latter. "He's a lovely
man."

"You think so?" I couldn't help asking.

Mam lay back down. "I rather liked him. And I thought you
did too."

"I did," I admitted. "A *lot.*" Funny, the things you can say in the
dark.

"Anyone could tell he was mad for you," Mam added. "A shame
the pair of you didn't work things out."

"I thought you were all for me marrying Joe," I said, tensing.
"Did you really think he'd make me a better husband?"

"Not really," she said. "But if you married Joe, you'd stay in
Ireland. If you and Rafe got serious, I knew you'd leave me, like
Mary Alice did. For America."

The air was altogether fraught with feeling. Mam really did
love me. In her own World According to Eileen sort of way, of
course. But you know, sometimes you had to take what was offered,

and not cry for the moon. Like Rhett had accused Scarlett of doing, come to think of it.

Before I could help myself, I leaned over, and kissed Mam's hair. Then quickly lay down again, before she could wonder what had got into me. "I'm not going anywhere. In fact..." I swallowed hard. "I'm looking forward to us working out the next step for the B&B. Until I leave for my holiday in France with the Gallagher's, that is."

"I'd like that," Mam said, as I closed my eyes. If hope didn't quite spring eternal in my breast, I felt a tiny spark. I wouldn't have Rafe. Or his baby either—the only one I'd really wanted. But I had Mam. Sort of. And that would have to do.

The week I'd been stuck in Inishmore, and focused on Mam, I'd been able to avoid pondering all the ways I'd turned my life to crap. Every time I wondered if Justine was looking for a new flat-mate, or if I should kill off Gai Lannigan for good—since I didn't care about her anymore, Justine probably didn't either, and I probably hadn't any readers left anyway—I'd push my worries away. The same goes for any time I'd think of how Rafe was enjoying reality. Whatever it was, I'd tell myself I'd think about my problems later.

Maybe... tomorrow.

Once Mam and I had settled back home, however, I knew it was past time to make amends to all the people I'd hurt, insulted and otherwise made really uncomfortable. She'd received a sympathy phone call from Justine, who'd pointedly not asked to speak to me. So I'd nowhere to go but up.

E-mail being the path of least resistance, I pulled out my laptop, typed Justine's address, with the subject line:

Don't delete! Please forward to Ian

Hi Ian... I began by telling him I was terribly sorry for the way I acted the day he came to my mother's house, and though it was an isolated episode, I'd gone off drink forever. (True.) I added that I'd completely reconciled with my mam too. (Also true. At least

I hoped so.) And would he please accept my best wishes for the future.

Ian's reply, which came hours later, was a simple,

> I heard your grandmother passed away. Sorry for your loss. Thanks, and good luck.

So Justine really had forwarded it! That had to mean something—not that she still cared, but...*something*. Like maybe she hadn't told Ian what a gobshite of an ex-friend I was, even if his message was no more personal than one of those auto respond e-mails. But still. He hadn't told me to feck off, had he?

Bernie next. Same drill: Justine's e-mail address, subject line,

> Don't delete! Please forward to your aunt Bernadette

Dear Mrs. Byrne...I jump-started with the same message I'd written Ian, with my apology, that I'd gone off drink forever, etc. Then came the hard part. See, if I hoped to have any sort of relationship with Justine, even as a distant acquaintance, I'd have to give Bernie her due.

The other thing was, Bernie could have been my mother-in-law—in a different universe, that is. The sort of universe where, when you get a proposal of marriage from the perfect man, you actually have the sense to accept it. So if there was any way to help her see me as more than a drunken wanton who'd treated her son like crap, I had to give it my best shot.

> Please let me know if there's any way I can make it up to you and your family for the terrible scene I made with my mother. Although we've sorted things out, completely reconciled in fact, I know I will regret my behavior until my dying days.
>
> I will be in Ballydara for the next few weeks (I wanted to let her know I wouldn't be chasing Rafe down, wherever he might be), to give my mam some extra support after my granny's death.
>
> I understand you have a new grandson. I wish you the greatest

happiness, now and always.

I had to admire the message before I sent it off. Sure, it was a bit over the top, but it was real.

I received a reply the next day. Even through e-mail, the message had all the warmth of January in Ireland.

> Regarding your ill-conceived confrontation with your mam, you could have picked a better time. And place. And I really can't imagine any way you can make up for the discomfort you caused.

The woman definitely had a way of making me feel small, which, given my size, was no insignificant feat.

> However, if your mother has forgiven you, who am I to hold a grudge. I understand that mothers and daughters have their struggles that we mothers of sons don't have. Please God Aine will have smooth sailing with her new baby girl.
>
> Good luck with your future endeavors.

Well, that was a lot more gracious than I would have ever suspected. Had Rafe told her to...? No. It wasn't possible. Still, the fact that she'd passed along the family baby news, and more importantly, hadn't conveyed any out-and-out hatred felt rather...nice.

Two down, two to go. Since I'd no word from Justine—not that I expected one—I did the next easiest thing. I took the bus to Dublin and Talbot Street, and walked into Corrigan's Café.

Seeing Sinead waiting on a corner table, I stepped back, ready to duck out again. Then Joe spied me. "Hallo," he said, looking uneasy.

And well you should, I thought, but I pasted on a smile. "Hi yourself," I said amiably, deciding to face this pregnancy bit head-on. "I hear congratulations are in order."

Reddening, he stepped behind the cash desk. "Justine's told you, then. You've come to give out at me?"

"Not at all," I said. "Who'd have guessed you were so keen on fatherhood."

Grabbing a handful of receipts, Joe muttered something about Sinead lying about being on the pill.

"Really," I said, and waited, as Joe's face turned a mottled red. Hey, I'm only human—and I was frankly enjoying this.

"It's true, she did."

"And you'd nothing to do with the whole business, then?"

Joe suddenly looked like a lost little boy. "Okay, it's the oldest trick in the book, but she said she'd always been mad about me."

I relented. Didn't I know how that felt? "I'm sure she meant it," I said kindly, with the presence of mind not to say, *I'll bet she's been lusting after a half-ownership in Corrigan's a lot longer than she's been lusting after you.* "I'm sure she'll make a...lovely mother."

"You're wishing us luck then?" he said, shuffling his receipts.

He sounded disappointed, which did give my recently ravaged ego a boost. You'll need all the luck you can get, I wanted to say, but settled for, "Seems the least I can do, given the circumstances."

"You mean..." Joe paused, "going off with that Rafe fella. Because it's him you really want."

Before I could answer, I saw an odd movement in the corner of my eye. Sinead, naturally, slinking toward us, triumph written all over her. "Well, if it isn't Grainne!" she said, and rubbed her still-concave stomach. (I felt a mild urge to slap her, but she was pregnant, after all.) "You've heard our news?"

She took Joe's arm, and gave him an adoring look, but not before flashing her left hand in my direction. She was sporting a diamond ring that looked a lot like the one Joe had given me. I peered more closely at it. Actually, it *was* the one he'd given me.

I wanted to laugh. A frugal businessman, Joe knew how to cut corners, but really! Still, I could give Sinead her moment, since God only knew what pregnancy would do to that weak back of hers. "I'm happy for you, really."

Sinead made a show of looking toward the door, a cat-like smile on her face. "Where's that Yank, the one Justine told us about?"

I saw a hint of misery in Joe's face. "I don't know where he is," I said calmly, though admitting it made my insides twist. "But I'm sure he'd wish you happy too."

I turned to go, feeling sort of pukey after all this phony well-wishing. And trying not to mind that it would be Sinead, and not me, who would be shopping for maternity clothes and picking out onesies. Then Joe suddenly shook off Sinead's hand. "I'll walk Grainne out."

Sinead tossed her dreadlock—with her left hand of course, to give me one more flash of her rock—waggling her skinny arse back to her customers.

Joe held the door open for me. Once it swung shut, he said, "You're not with that Rafe bloke any more then?"

Had I actually thought I could settle for Joe, after Rafe? I shook my head, since it hurt too much to say "no."

Pause. "I don't suppose..." He reached toward me, but I side-stepped just in time.

"It's...ah, better this way," I said. He had to know he'd ultimately be happier with someone who would love him. And his restaurant. Not to mention all those bloody sport-mad Corrigans.

On to my next errand. But as far as making amends, though, I wasn't quite done.

Thirty-Seven

Walking toward the Dart station, I rang Nate. Since I'd come all the way to Dublin, I couldn't resist the temptation to see his and Aine's new baby. But I'd wanted to make sure I wouldn't run into any other family, if you catch my drift.

Nate invited me to call round, and upon learning the coast was indeed Bernie-clear, I took the northbound train. "Grand to see you," Nate said as he opened the door. In just a few days, fatherhood had indeed changed him. He was unshaven, with bed hair and a spot of baby sick on his shirt. Instead of his usual smooth expression, he looked exhausted, freaked out, but...happy. Following Nate inside, I found Aine on the couch, hair done, face made up, wearing a fresh outfit, and I thought, *Nate, it's going to be a long eighteen years for you.* Then I forgot all that as the new mama pushed the blanket aside to show me little Mae.

"She's beautiful," I said, melting inside. Of course, all babies were gorgeous—one of nature's tricks was that even the homely ones were. As we chatted about the birth, how the pair of them were coping with the new demands of parenthood, I realized how empty my arms had felt since the little Gallaghers went away. "I've a cramp in my shoulder," Aine said. "You want to hold her?"

"I thought you'd never ask," I said, and carefully lifted Mae into my arms. I ran my finger round her velvety wee ear, and gently touched her soft spot, where her little baby pulse beat.

I could sense the pride coming off Nate—the guy who hadn't been all that excited about fatherhood. Babies were so easy to love, I thought, and had to swallow hard against the swelling in my throat. Easy to open your heart to. How I wished I'd done it, when I'd had my chance with...

"Seen Rafe lately?" I nearly jumped—not good when you're holding a newborn. What was Nate, a mind reader?

"No, why?" I said as calmly as I could, and eased Mae back into Aine's arms. Would it ever stop hurting, to hear his name?

"Apparently he's gone on walkabout," Nate said. "Some kind of nature cure, he implied before he disappeared."

"Bernie would be completely frantic," Aine said. "But with Ian still here in Ireland, she's got him to fuss over, thank God, or we'd never hear the end of it. Would we, Mae?" she cooed to the baby.

I couldn't stay for long, with the baby lust near overtaking me. But I found the presence of mind to ask, "A nature cure—he wouldn't be back in Oughterard, for more fishing?" And right in my neighborhood? Hope rose in me so fast I was almost dizzy.

"He's really not a great one for angling," Nate said. "Before, it was just an excuse to—" He broke off, looking flustered. Then he said, "Rafe could be anywhere. Ireland, Seattle—"

"New Zealand," Aine put in. "I remember him mentioning it. But who knows? He's always had an unpredictable streak."

"Right," I said, and knew I'd better leave. Talking about Rafe with a baby in the room was choking me up. "It was lovely of you to let me pop in."

As I turned to leave, out of the corner of my eye I saw Aine shift the baby in her arms. She hadn't quite supported Mae's wobbly little newborn neck. Then Aine set the baby on the couch, leaving Mae there as she and Nate walked me to the door. *Oh dear*, I thought as soon as I got outside, *the pair of you might learn the hard way, how fast new babies can learn to roll over, and you'll find her screaming on the floor.*

Then a real epiphany came to me. It's a good job babies are so resilient, because really, mothering could go all over the map. There was Granny O'Neill, who'd clearly been emotionally abusive, but hadn't it been love that had made her walk back out of the River Shannon and join the world again? Then there was the Bernie end of the spectrum, with her smothering, but even I could see real devotion in it. And there was Mam, who could be a pretty hands-off sort of parent, but give her credit. She hadn't followed her mother's example.

Sure, Nate and Aine would occasionally make a muddle of parenting, like everybody else did. But the baby would be loved. By both a mother and a father.

Our flat—and possibly Justine—was only a short ride away.

Ready to grovel, I screwed up all my courage and stepped back on the northbound Dart. Once I arrived at our house, I could see some lights on. Justine indeed appeared to be home. To show how willing I was to humble myself, I knocked on my own door.

Justine opened it, eyeing me with disdain. "So." She crossed her arms. "It's you."

"Yes," I said meekly. "Can I...come in?"

She shrugged. "It's your flat too."

Hardly encouraged, I followed her into the kitchen. Where, by the looks of the ingredients strewn about, a mouth-watering pudding was in production.

"As you can see, I'm a bit busy," she said. "So if you're here to ask me about Rafe, you've wasted your time. I've no idea where he is."

"That's not why I came," I said, though I'd secretly hoped Justine might know something about his whereabouts. "You've probably heard that we..."

"Split? Yes, he told Bernie." If Justine felt sorry for me, she wasn't showing it. "You've called for your holdall then? He gave it to me before we left the hotel."

I'd no use for all those lacy knickers anymore, I thought mournfully. "Actually, that's not why I'm here either—"

"So," she went on, "if it's not for your holdall, or to get your claws into Rafe, why talk to me?"

I didn't know how to begin. "I...wanted to thank you for passing along my emails to Ian and Bernie," I finally said.

"I didn't do it for you, I did it for them."

Justine's coldness was unnerving. "I really came to say I'm an utter gobshite," I blurted, before I lost what little nerve remained. "A rotten friend."

Justine scooped up a cupful of flour, then whacked a knife across the rim, raising a cloud of white dust. "Is this like, a new discovery or something?"

"And to tell you how much I've always...valued your friendship," I soldiered on. "I should never have said...well, all those things I said to you. At the hotel."

Justine only curled her lip.

"And that I appreciate...all the things you did for my mam, and for her B&B."

She shot another derisive look at me. "Speaking of, how's she been keeping since the funeral? Though I doubt you've even noticed."

I didn't know how much longer I could take Justine's cold shoulder. "She's bounced back pretty well," I said. "Lots of grand schemes for the B&B."

Justine's eyes narrowed. "How would you know? You never talk to her."

Jaysus, I never knew the girl could be so hard. But I was determined to let her act as horrible to me as I had been to her. "Actually, we're getting on. I've helped her on the computer, and she's shown me some fabulous angles for placing mints on pillows."

For a moment, I thought I saw the corner of her mouth tilt, but she only said snidely, "So, you've magically turned into a proper daughter?"

"I'm trying," I said simply. I could tell her later—if she was interested—about how we reconciled. "Finally...I also wanted to say, that...Ian's a prince. I totally get why you care about him."

"Is that so." Turning toward the cooker, she stirred something in a pan, and the scent of melting chocolate filled the kitchen. "I thought you'd an entirely different opinion of him."

"I realized I hadn't given him enough credit," I said, trying to sound properly contrite. "Here he'd been trying to do the right thing by his child—"

"He was." Justine pointed a chocolate-covered spoon at me. "And he cared enough to face Rafe, who rather treated him like shite." She threw the spoon back into the pan.

"If that's not being a hero," I agreed desperately, "then I don't know what is."

Yanking a steel bowl from the cupboard, Justine clanged it onto the counter. "Tell me something I don't know."

"Ian...he's...well, a far better man than Joe, that's for sure." I'd never dreamed it would take so long to get Justine's forgiveness. I mean, I'd pretty much exhausted my appetite for crow with Sinead. "All Joe had to do for his future was swap his engagement ring from my finger to Sinead's."

Justine pulled eggs out of the fridge. "Some folk might find that interesting, but I'm afraid I'm not one of them." Justine had always found my life dramas fascinating. "In fact, you deserved to have your ring *and* your fiancé given to someone who'll love them."

"I know." It hit me that I should let go of following Scarlett O'Hara's example. She hadn't had a best friend—she'd only pretended to be friends with poor Melanie Wilkes. And look at the hash oul' Scarlett had made of her life. Justine's friendship was so much a part of me that I'd say anything, do anything, to have it again. "Maybe you think I'm just putting all this on, but I really am trying to be a better person."

Justine's face changed, looking bemused instead of skeptical. And I knew I might never have another opportunity to make her understand why I've done so many eejit things in my life. "But speaking of fiancés," I ventured, "you remember, ten years ago, that thing with Donal—"

"Poor man." With one hand, she deftly cracked an egg over the bowl. "I never did believe what you told me and Nate—that you split up with Donal out of respect for our family. I mean, really, how could one look at you actually give Rafe the Yips? It was just you, being heartless again."

Justine really did want to extract her pound of flesh, so I'd no choice but to give it to her. "The truth is that...I wanted...you see, I'd got it in my head that I wanted a baby. I mean, *really* wanted one."

Justine's eyes widened. "So those *Girl Talk* posts about babies—you really *were* writing about you."

"Yes." Was it my imagination, or did she actually seem interested?

She broke another egg. "But at the age of twenty, you thought you were ready for parenthood?"

"I was sure of it," I said. "But when I didn't get pregnant right away, I decided Donal wasn't the right man for me."

She gave a short bark of laughter. "So you dumped him."

I wavered, but I *had* to come clean. "I'm afraid so."

"Now that, I believe," said Justine coolly, wiping her hands. "Sounds just like you."

"I know, it was a terrible thing to do..."

"You're still not telling me anything I don't know," Justine broke in, and retrieved a hand-mixer from a drawer.

I could feel that awful tightness in my chest again, that meant tears were too close for comfort. But if Justine wanted something really worth confessing... "Here's something then..." Jaysus, this was way harder than I thought it would be. "You remember the night five years ago, when... when you told me Rafe got engaged to Lindy?"

Justine paused. "You got pissed, as I recall."

"I didn't stop with the drink. I acted rather...badly."

"And what's new under the sun?" Justine asked no one in particular.

It took me a long time to answer. "I...ran into a bloke I knew, and I...well, I had a one-night stand with him."

Thirty-Eight

"A one-night..." Jerking her head up, she clutched her mixer. "Anyone I know?"

I nodded miserably.

Justine searched my face. "Was it...Joe?"

As I nodded again, feeling a bit sick, Justine's expression softened entirely. "Holy Mother, you really do lo—" She clunked the mixer onto the counter. "Ah, come on, now," she said, pulling me close. "Sure, it wasn't your finest moment."

I sniffed, wrapping my arms tight round her. And though her face was awfully close to being squished into my boobs, in that moment, I finally understood the point of girl hugs. "They say 'what goes around comes around,' don't they?"

"Poor Grainne," she said, patting my back. Probably leaving floury handprints, but this was no time to be fastidious. "And now Rafe's gone."

I nodded, and my chin dug into the top of her head. "I'm... all right." I actually *did* feel almost all right, knowing Justine had finally forgiven me. "It—the split, I mean—wasn't...easy, but we both knew we could never make a go." I wasn't quite ready to confess how horribly I'd treated Rafe either, but maybe someday...

"Wow, that sounds so mature." She gave me one last pat and let me go. "Grounded, even." Justine suddenly giggled, giving me a playful jab with her elbow. "Which is grand, since we wouldn't want you to have another one-nighter with Joe."

I had to laugh too. "You cow, to throw that in my face."

"But you've no reason to feel guilty about him any more." Justine plugged her mixer into the socket. "Because Joe has some bloody nerve. Yesterday I popped into the restaurant, to give Frank an old shirt and phone charger he'd left here, and our man hinted that he'd go for you again in a second, if you wanted it."

As I was still eating humble pie, it seemed rather egotistical to mention Joe had said the same to me. "Oh, Sinead's got her hooks in him deeper than he thinks."

Justine snorted. "Every time I see her, she's got some disgusting new thing to share about being pregnant. First, it was the enormous veins in her boobs, which are twelve times bigger than they were before, then it was her throwing up all over the restaurant loo. The last time I was in, she told me she makes Joe massage her...," and she pulled a grotesque face, "...her you-know-what, so the birth will be easier."

I produced a half-hearted chuckle. "Poor Joe." Good job I'd written him off, since any man willing to perform such a service for Sinead was far too enslaved by her dubious charms to stray.

Justine giggled again. "You've ruined him for other women."

"Guess I can tick off that goal," I said, trying not to sound dour. Because Rafe had spoiled me for other men. I'd never get a baby now...

But my self-pity thing was getting old, and besides, Justine's melting chocolate smelled quite fabulous... "Is that cheesecake you're making? What's the occasion?"

Justine looked defensive for a moment, then, "Ian's coming round tonight."

I kept my face neutral. I would be supportive if it killed me. "How is he, by the way?"

"Things have been rather...challenging for him," Justine said slowly. I tried to look fascinated. "See, Gennifer, his fiancée, didn't take the news well about Ian's baby, and made a real strop when she found out he and Bernie and...well, they went over to Paris last week to see the baby, Jean-Michel. But when Ian told her Isabelle was going to be studying at the Sorbonne, and wanted Ian to share full-on custody, she really went ballistic."

"Poor man," I said.

"Since then, Gennifer's been a total Bridezilla, ringing Ian all hours of the day and night, saying she needs more deposit money for flowers or the caterers, and how could he be flying to Paris all the time when he can't afford it!"

"Jaysus, what a cow!" I said. "Poor baby, to be having a step-mammy like that." I was already feeling terribly sorry for little

Jean-Michel.

"And Ian's heading back there tomorrow, to Paris, I mean, to pick up the baby. Bernie's persuaded him to stay in Ireland with Jean-Michel for the next few weeks while he and Isabelle work out a custody thing. It's looking like he might have his son more than half the time. So I invited him here so he can catch his breath, before he dives into fatherhood."

I couldn't blame Ian for laying low on this side of the pond, if that Bride from Hell was waiting for him on the other. "He's lucky to have you, then, for a bit of support."

"You think so?" Justine looked a bit incredulous. "You're not having me on?"

I shook my head. "Remember, it takes a village," I said solemnly. "You know, to bring up a child."

Which reminded me of Rafe—and his reaction to Ian's baby news made it all too clear he'd no intention of being one of the villagers. Of course, I couldn't help myself, and had to ask, "I suppose there's no news of..." I swallowed. "Rafe?"

"Oh!" Justine rushed to the cooker. "I almost forgot my chocolate!" She pulled the pan off the burner and set it on the countertop. "Last time I saw him was at Nate and Aine's, when we all got together after she came home from hospital. Rafe only stayed a few minutes, then he kissed Bernie, told her not to worry, that he'd ring her every once in a while."

Well, that told me exactly nothing, except that Rafe had relented enough to call round at Nate's.

"Bernie worries he's still in the throes of his mid-life crisis." Justine cradled a huge bowl with three blocks of cream cheese in it, and began thumping the cheese with a wooden spoon. "But she perked up when he actually did appear in the media."

"No kidding," I said, rather mournful it wasn't my *Girl Talk* exclusive.

She looked at my face, then setting down the bowl, rummaged in our jumble drawer and pulled out a computer printout. "He turned up in the *Galway City Tribune*, can you believe it?" She handed me the paper. "Bernie made copies for everyone."

Being a glutton for self-punishment, of course I had to read it.

American Businessman primed to invest in Ireland

I skimmed the brief interview, a frothy bit about Rafe's golf and business career, with the usual fluffy quotes.

"I'm not really suited to helm a Fortune 500 company," Byrne said. "Endless meetings, stuffy conference rooms, trying to keep the investors happy. It's not me. I'm more hands-on."

You got that right, I thought.

"Being a dual citizen, with family here, I'd like to be part of helping Ireland get back on her feet, post-recession. So I'm putting out some feelers out for investment opportunities—nothing concrete just yet, but I've seen several with real potential."

There was Rafe again, playing the white knight. I loved it. My throat tight, I read the last of the article.

"Golf? I don't think I'll take it up again, not seriously. Maybe I'll play a round now and then, at some quiet little country links. But it took coming to Ireland—in fact, right here to County Galway—to show me how much I enjoy the great outdoors."

He must've been talking about his short-lived passion for fishing. My eyes lingered on the photo, of Rafe standing in Eyre Centre in Galway City, squinting into the sunshine, the flags in the background. So he hadn't the decency to fall apart after splitting with me. Rafe had looked better—like when he'd been in bed with me—but an improvement on the wedding photo I'd seen of him a few weeks ago. I handed the clip back to Justine. "It's not the *Image* article Bernie hoped for, but I guess it's something."

"She was actually over the moon. With the new grandchild to settle her down, she's come a long way from her mad-mammy bit, the day we had lunch with her in Dublin."

No doubt, Rafe dumping me put her in great form.

Justine added, "As you've probably guessed, Rafe is much more financially solvent than she was ranting about."

Seemed like ages ago, that Bernie and I had made that ridiculous arrangement. Same goes for Rafe and me reuniting in Ballydara. For a while there, I thought I'd the world by the tail. But now, my life looked like a series of dead ends—except for my upcoming trip to see the Gallaghers.

"Would you look at the time!" Justine exclaimed, and pushed the bowl into my hands. "Here, work this cream cheese for me. Ian'll be here any minute."

I paused, spoon in hand. "You want me to leave? I don't mind, I understand if you want to be—"

"Alone? With Ian?" Looking self-conscious, Justine smoothed her hair, leaving a floury streak at her temple. "I don't, actually— since you're here, maybe you could give him some pointers on baby minding. You're just the person to give him tips about feeding and nappy changing."

"Don't forget the fatherly art of breaking baby's wind," I said, "but that's not it, is it?"

She colored a bit. "All this trouble he's having with Gennifer, well…I'm nervous around him." Never a great one for eating sweets, she absently spooned up some batter and sucked on it. Which was the sign she really was having a bit of a freaker. "What if I sort of forget myself, and put the moves on him? With you here, it'll help me keep my head on straight."

I was meant to be the level-headed one? We'd come full-circle, Justine and I. Now I was the supporter, instead of the supportee.

Justine was actually in a worse state than either of us had thought. Midway through the cheese mixing, she looked down at the bowl, aghast. "What in bloody hell was I thinking, to make cheesecake? It needs at least three hours to chill before you serve it!"

"I'll run down to the shop, pick up some biscuits or something," I suggested. Justine's slightly manic energy was wearing me out. Besides, if she and Ian were alone together, maybe he'd finally get a clue and see the right girl was in front of him—

"No! I can't offer him shop stuff," Justine said, her hair practically on end. "And I need you here—but he does like a sweet—"

"I'm going," I said firmly. "Go comb your hair, get out of that apron. And relax."

Strange, we really *had* exchanged roles. I escaped outside for the short walk to the corner shop. I was just steps away when my mobile chimed. An e-mail.

I dug in my bag frantically, thinking, *Rafe!* Were we still attuned? Could he have sensed I'd made up with all the people I'd done wrong, that I was worth another go?

No. But it was the next best thing: Alan Gallagher. At last, my invitation to join their holiday! Provence, here I come!

> Subject: Greetings from France
>
> Having a great holiday. We're all brown as nuts, swimming every day, and we're stuffing ourselves with the local bread and cheese. And here we've all kinds of chocolate at breakfast too. We've taken a couple of weekend trips as well—Marseille, then to St. Tropez to do a bit of celeb watching.

The beach, baguettes, and chocolate? Sure, I was up for that, after the way my life had imploded the last few weeks.

> With their granny in charge, the kids are thriving. She's got them outdoors for hours, so they sleep like tops. Geoff's got such a good appetite he even eats all his vegetables.

The "thriving" news took me aback. The kids *should* enjoy their granny, I told myself stoutly, though I'd have liked to hear that they missed me terribly, that the Gallagher household was in a horrible muddle without my nanny wisdom and organizational skills. But I shouldn't want their holiday ruined. Should I?

> We wanted to let you know that my mother's had such a grand time with the children she's offered to care for them full-time.

Unbelieving, I stared at the screen. A Dear John/Nanny letter?

We'll be awfully sorry to see you go, but we'll provide sever-
ance, of course, and a letter of reference, whatever you want.

"Whatever I want, my arse," I muttered, to ease the lump in my
throat. "I want to see the kids. And Provence."

I know we'd planned to have you fly over for a visit, but Sara
thinks seeing you would only confuse the children, especially
now that my mother's established a routine. But feel free to call
round when we get home.

Still hardly able to take it in, that I'd been sacked in an e-mail,
I slumped onto the bench in front of the shop. I'd always counted
on having the little Gallaghers in my life, to keep me going until I'd
have a little one of my own. What was left for me now? Going back
to Ballydara and helping Mam with her B&B? And if she moved on
to something else, then I really would have nothing. Eyes stinging,
I shoved my mobile back in my bag.

On top of having no Rafe, and no baby, now I'd no job. No
Provence. And no Ivy, Anna or Geoff.

The afternoon was gone by the time I finally heaved myself
off the bench, and slouched back to our flat, all my lovely Justine
supporter energy gone. "Justine?" I called as I opened the door. "I'm
sorry, I forgot the bisc—"

She appeared in the kitchen doorway, cheeks rosy, eyes alight.
"You will never, ever believe this!"

She looked so completely transformed, it was almost enough to
make me forget my own troubles. I'd have suspected her of having
it off with Ian, but in the kitchen? She wasn't mussed though. And
there was no sign of him. "Where's Ian? He didn't cancel?"

"No!" Grinning, she danced over to me and grabbed my arms.
"He was here, but Bridezilla Gennifer rang him twice, harassing
him something terrible, then he had to go—well, I told him to,
because I really didn't trust myself with him, but—"

"Love of God, will you just tell me what's going on?"

"I told you Gennifer's been all over Ian about his son, but that's not the half of it!" Justine clutched me tighter. "She rang again while he was here, and she had the unbelievably bloody *nerve* to say, Ian had to choose!"

"Between the pair of them?" I asked. "Never!"

She started jumping up and down, and since we were attached, I joined in. "Oh, yes!" Justine exclaimed. "'It's me or that baby' she told him, and guess what, guesswhat, guesswhatguesswhat?" Justine's voice rose another octave. "He picked the baby!"

Thirty-Nine

I stopped mid-jump. "Does he need a nanny?" I asked hopefully, detaching myself.

Justine only clapped her hands. "Ian's free! They split up!"

Ian had finally grown a real live spine. Now if he could only stop asking girls to marry him for a while. "That's super—fabulous news!"

Even Justine's freckles were sparkling. "Ian actually told Gennifer to stop ringing him—in a polite way, of course—because he would no longer take her calls. I could tell he was rather bummed about the breakup," she said, pirouetting back to the kitchen. "But then I took a page from your book. I pointed out now he has a little son to love him, which seemed to put him in better form."

"Fair play to you," I said, following her. "Just what he needed to hear."

"He had lots to sort out for the baby, so it seemed like a good idea for him to get right on it. Ian did give me a lovely hug goodbye, though." To show the depth of Justine's emotional state, she got the lukewarm cheesecake out of the fridge, cut us both a ginormous piece, and dug in right along with me. "Before he left, he said, 'if I ever mention proposing to anyone else, please stop me, will you?' Isn't that great?"

The cheesecake melted in my mouth. Chocolate really does make the world a better place. "But what if he wants to propose to *you*?" I asked.

Justine colored again. "I don't think I'm his sort, but if he ever decided I was, of course I'd have him. But it would have to be a decent interval, mind. I wouldn't want to be his rebound girl."

Like I'd probably been with Rafe. At least she and Ian had friendship. While I had treated Rafe so badly I'm sure if he saw me in the street he'd cut me dead.

To cheer myself up, I said, "If you're still on your work furlough, how about coming back to Ballydara with me in the morning?"

I knew as long as Ian was around Dublin there was hardly a chance, but no harm in asking.

"Actually, Bernie's been talking about heading back to County Galway."

"You've got to be having me on," I said. Bernie, to willingly revisit the scene of the crime?

"Ian thought it was a great idea, said a little Dublin goes a long way—he's ready for some peace and quiet."

Not that Ian had gotten much peace on his last visit to Ballydara, but our man probably wanted to lay low for a time, in case the G-girl and her family wanted to go after him. "Sure, the country air will be much better for the baby," I said.

"Maybe so. Anyway, he said he'd like to go to Ballydara, and you know Bernie."

I made a helicopter motion with my index finger. "Hovering as close as she can."

Justine laughed. "That's it. I'm still free, so all of us, me, Ian and Bernie, might turn up in a few days. You and your mam'll want to stand by, be ready to stock the larder and air the beds."

"And sort out a cot for the baby," I put in. Suddenly, things were looking a lot less bleak—if all went as Justine thought, we'd have a baby at Larkin House! And if the B&B got some real live customers, I'd have like, a job again. With Rory coming home in a few days, I'd sooner do a mystic walk over hot stones, than tell her I'd been sacked without having another situation lined up.

Most importantly, Ian coming with his little son would bring… whatchacallit? Closure. Because I knew seeing Jean-Michel would be as close to a baby of Rafe's as I would ever get.

I stared across the road at the "Hurley's Pub" sign, then sighed. I was back in Ballydara, and absolutely nothing had changed.

"Grainne, you're here to put in your mam's grocery order then?" asked Mrs. Murphy as I stepped up to the counter of her shop.

What order? "Actually I'm just getting my usual," I said. Still ensconced at Mam's a week after my visit to Dublin, without any update from Justine, I was starting to chafe a bit—like I was wearing sandpaper knickers.

Being unemployed was bad enough, but I still hadn't a jot of inspiration about the *Girl Talk* post Sara Gallagher would be expecting upon her return to work. Plus Rory would be home within days, full of news about Mary Alice's pregnancy. And without any of Justine's sweets for consolation, I had to depend on a Cadbury's Wispa to get me through the day.

Mrs. Murphy's face fell. "I'd just had it from Doreen, that your mam was expecting some paying customers at last."

"Oh!" I tossed down my euro. Was Justine finally returning to Ballydara? But wasn't it just like Mam, to tell Doreen before me. "Today?"

Mrs. Murphy wrinkled her brow. "Or was it tomorrow? Or next week? I've had such a raft of special orders this week I could've gotten it entirely mixed up." Her gaze moved behind me. "Bernard, not another packet of crisps, is it?"

"I need the energy," said Bernard Hurley, "what with all the new jobs coming my way. Grainne, tell your mam I haven't forgotten that leak in the kitchen taps she rang about."

"Sure, I'll let her know," I said, tearing open the Wispa. The last thing I wanted was to get pulled into today's latest. Ballydara had actually grown on me, but these days I wasn't quite up for the way the most idle topics of gossip were worthy of endless discussion.

Mrs. Murphy rang Bernard's crisps up on her ancient cash register. "God bless us, there's so much going on these days I can hardly keep track!"

Not for me, I thought, biting into my chocolate as I inched toward the door. I'd been seriously thinking of asking Pat Hurley to show me how to pull a pint so I could work for him. I'd even do it for free. What publican would turn down a teetotaling barmaid?

"Tell me about it," Bernard said, hitching up his tool belt. As he started droning on, I noticed a row of organic baby food that hadn't been there yesterday, with a price only a completely devoted new mammy would pay.

Bernard was saying something about brokering the sale for a caravan. "…Fanciest yoke I've ever seen, all silvery like a bloody flying saucer or something. I asked the fella why didn't he buy his caravan directly from the dealer, but he said he wanted to give me the commission…" *Blah blah blah.*

Peering at a sweet potato-brown-rice combo, I wondered if Aislin Carpenter, the yoga girl, had ordered the baby food, to stock her larder months ahead of time?

Bernard was still all over his caravan guy. "Sure I had to wonder if he had the full shilling." He chuckled, twirling his finger at his temple. "What with the thousands of euro of equipment, but he said he was making an investment in the community…" More *blah, blah, blah.* "After I'd got him all set up, I said, 'you've enough juice to power a marijuana-growing operation, but of course we'll have none of that in Ballydara—'" He and Mrs. Murphy laughed merrily. "Then he says, 'I like the nature experience myself, but my guest needs all the modern conveniences—hot water, microwave, and Internet—in case I need to Google anything.'" Bernard broke into laughter. "I thought, good man, but you'd better Google where your brains have gone."

I got two more bites of my Cadbury's down the hatch and escaped.

As usual, my chocolate bar gave me such a burst of energy I took off for my daily hike round the village. Not coincidentally, it was the same route Rafe and I had walked together, that day I'd thought I had him where I wanted him—then soon after, Rafe and I had had each other. One of the best days of my life, I thought wistfully.

Since Rafe and I split, my chocolate-fueled walk was the high point of a day that otherwise was mostly housework and chatting about the B&B with Mam. I was so bored I'd even welcome a proper row with Rory, but she and the kids weren't due home from Chicago for another three days. Even more restless than usual, I strode down the length of the Ballydara links, trying to push away the regrets and should-have-beens that had pelted my mind constantly for weeks.

I suddenly shivered. The clouds had thickened, with a bank of fog rolling in from the west. I zipped up my fleece and stepped up my pace. The mist was cool against my face as I rounded the woods, and hiked on toward the O'Donoghue place.

Happily, there was little wild-haired Ava O'Donoghue, playing on the rock-strewn lawn between her house and the gnarly deserted cottage over by the woods.

"Hey there Ava, what's that you're making?" She reminded me of myself at that age—she'd a feistiness about her that told you if you crossed her once too many, she'd plant her little fist in your gob.

"A new fairy house," she said, and carefully placed another stone on the cairn she was building. She'd quite a knack, by the looks of things.

"But haven't you got four or five houses already?" I asked her. "Almost a village."

"But Grainne, there's some new fairies coming out of the woods," Ava informed me. "And they need a place to stay."

"Why would the fairies come out of the woods?" I asked, smiling to myself. A daughter like Ava would sure keep you on your toes. "Isn't that where they live?"

"That man scared them away," said Ava.

"What man?"

"Him, in there." She waved her hand toward the woods.

I smiled at Ava. She'd some imagination, that one. Then I noticed the dilapidated "For Sale" sign at the edge of the forest was gone. The property had been purchased, then? Since it was so sizable, it had likely been bought by some folk from abroad—Germans, I decided—the only people with real money these days. Probably so loaded they wouldn't have wanted to stay at Mam's B&B, but had sprung for premium lodgings at Harmony House.

"We'll have to find the man then, and sort him out," I told Ava, stifling laughter. "It won't do, to scare the fairies."

She nodded vigorously, then turned her attention back to her stone pile.

I looked at the woods again—a shame it had sold. The buyers would probably bulldoze the place, then Ballydara would lose that bit of wildness. Maybe they'd already had surveyors in there—had the faint path leading into the forest become more of a trail?

Walking on past Mrs. Moore's cottage toward the village in the thickening mist, I wondered if the buyer was the same person Bernard Hurley had been burbling on about. I'd just passed Hurley's pub when I realized, *Ava's a bright little thing.* What if the man in the woods was real? A stranger—some tinker or even a disreputable sort?

Love of God, should I ring the Guards? Weighing which was closer for phoning, Hurley's or home, I looked up the road and saw a shiny hire car in front Mam's house, and all thoughts of Germans, tinkers, or strange men in the woods fled my mind. At last, Justine and our guests! And a baby to boot!

I ran the rest of the way to Mam's, burst through the front door, breathless, to find Justine and Ian in the entryway with Mam. "I thought you'd never come," I said, and fell on Justine with a bear hug. "And Ian—grand to have you back."

"Ian booked a room!" said Mam, all smiles. "Our very first real customer!"

I looked round, saw no vast pile of designer luggage, nor did I feel the queenly vibe in the air. "Bernie didn't come along?"

"She was too busy organizing things for the baby," Ian said. Justine chimed in, "She's planning a proper nursery, kitted out with the latest baby fashions."

Feeling right jolly without Granny She-Wolf around, I imagined the incongruously deluxe nursery in Ian's modest student digs, and snorted with laughter. "Nothing less would do for the scion of the Byrne family, now would it?" Then it dawned on me there were no baby yokes about. "But where is Himself?" I asked Ian.

Ian laughed. "Rafe?"

I stopped mid-chortle. I didn't even want to *joke* about running into Rafe. "No, your baby—I can't wait to meet him." Even if Jean-Michel was Rafe's half-nephew by blood, would he have his uncle's electric blue eyes? Or ever-so-slightly hooked nose? I felt deflated all of a sudden. If only I'd had the sense to accept Rafe's marriage proposal, the baby would've been *my* nephew too...

"Well," said Ian. "I'm taking a little break from being a full-time dad today."

You're already burned out on fatherhood, this early in the game?

Mam said, "Grainne, shall you put on the kettle? I'm sure our visitors would like some tea."

"In a minute," I said. "Ian, you left Jean-Michel with Bernie?"

"No, but don't worry," said Justine. "Ian's found a lovely minder." They exchanged a grin as Mam said, "I'll boil the kettle, I don't mind," and fluttered off to the kitchen.

Mam's willingness to embrace the domestic arts was lost on me. "But will I see the baby?"

"That's up to you," Justine said mysteriously. "And how you feel about...the nature cure." At that, she and Ian burst into laughter. "And the great outdoors," Ian added, guffawing.

Bloody hell—what was this pair of madzers talking about? "Do you mind just telling me what you're going on about?" I scowled at Justine. "Is there something I—"

"You're meant to sort it out yourself," she said, unfazed by my black look. She bent to pick up her holdall.

Ian beat her to it, lifting her bag and his own case. "That's what he said anyway—"

"Ian!" Justine broke in. "No more hints."

"He who?" I demanded. "And hints about what—"

"The rest is up to you," Justine said. As she started up the stairs, she exchanged another secret smile with Ian. "Mind the fog out there—the visibility looks something terrible."

What in the holy hell was going on here? Rubbing my forehead, I'd no clue what to do next. Then I looked at the misty fog out Mam's front window, then it burst upon me:

Rafe was close by. Maybe even right here in Ballydara...

Then a second brainwave rolled in: And I was meant to find him.

All I had to do was follow the example of Scarlett Fecking O'Hara! What had she done, at the end of *Gone With the Wind*, when her back was to the wall? After she realized she loved Rhett?

She'd gone after him, that's what. Not waited until he came round.

But...I'd never chased a fellow. And I wasn't going to start now...was I?

You're damn right I was.

I banged open Mam's front door and bolted outside. Racing down the road toward Hurley's, I told myself that I was the madzer now. I still didn't know where Rafe was. And if I did find him, what if he thought I was after him to pressure him into baby-making sex again? If he'd thought me a heartless cow before, now he'd think I was a slut.

Reaching Hurley's pub, I slowed down, and saw Bernard standing near the door. Without a word, he saluted me with his cap, then chuckled. I looked about wildly, then suddenly, I knew:

Jaysus, did I need to be hit over the head? Of course Rafe was the buyer of the forest property, the investor who liked nature, the nutter who bought the fancy space caravan! I shot toward the O'Donoghue place, seeing the last bit of *Gone With the Wind* in my mind's eye. I would be Scarlett, running through the fog to find Rhett—Rafe, in my case—and tell the man I wanted how I felt. And if I actually got up the nerve to say the "L" word to Rafe, and he said *Frankly my dear I don't give a damn*, I'd be fearless.

I'd say, "Too bad, I still love you." Just like Rafe had.

Despite my lovely, brazen, Scarlett-ish plan, one last doubt hit me as I sprinted past Mrs. Moore's cottage, then approached the O'Donoghue's, barely discernable through the mist. What if Rafe took one look at me, and kicked me off the property? Like he'd booted me out of his life back at the Harmony Hotel?

I was panting as I reached the edge of the woods—mint placing and pudding-testing at Mam's hadn't been the best track-and-field training. But I pushed on in the dimming light, following the path I'd seen earlier, into the forest.

Rafe had loved me once—in fact, right up until a few weeks ago, hadn't he? Didn't I have a fighting chance, then, of him giving me another go?

Here among the tall oaks and beeches, the fog was caught in the treetops, so the visibility was better than out on the road. Still, mindful of the uneven path, I slowed down. I pushed past saplings, leaves catching in my hair, just in time to see a huge, half-rotten fallen tree across the path, both ends lost in brambles. Eyeing the log warily, I considered hurdling it, but settled for a less heroic crawling over, getting bits of rotten wood and lichen all over my already damp jeans and fleece.

As the woods opened up ahead, I barely made out a flash of metal. Someone really was here, then. My last speck of adrenaline gave out, and I was alone with my trembling legs and quaking heart.

I lurched toward the shiny metal, willing myself not to turn tail. I could do a Scarlett as well as the next girl, I told myself stoutly, and stepped into the clearing.

The first thing I saw was the silver space-age caravan, parked under a stately oak tree. I quickly took in the line of solar panels arranged neatly on the grass, at least a dozen of them, and a boxy sort of motor yoke with a container of petrol sitting next to it, and nearby, a satellite dish lying on its side.

Across the clearing stood a tall man with a shock of black hair, a blue bundle in one arm. In his free hand he held a dart, gesturing toward a dartboard attached to a tree not far away. He was talking to himself.

"Wherever you live, Ireland or Seattle," the man was saying, "given the weather, you'll probably want to learn an indoor sport." He hitched the bundle in his arm closer to his side. "See, you need good aim for both golf and darts, but darts are a lot like poker—a mental thing. You do a little bluffing, a little hustling, and wait for your opponent to show some weakness before you throw. Works every time."

"Hallo?" I called out, my voice quavering. I mean, this guy did seem a bit off his rocker.

The man leisurely turned toward me, and the bundle in his arm materialized into a baby about six months of age, wearing dungarees and a matching cap. "Well," said Rafe, and threw his dart at the board without looking at it. "What took you so long?"

Forty

As the full impact of Rafe's electric blue eyes hit me, for the first time in my misbegotten life, I was speechless. I finally choked out, "W-what did you say?"

"You heard me," Rafe said with a cheeky grin, smiling into my eyes. I could swear sparks zinged off the invisible arc between us.

"But...but..." I stepped toward him and the baby. "You...meant for me to come after you?"

Rafe shifted the baby into his other arm. "I left so many unsuccessful hints around the village I thought I'd have to draw a map and nail it to the front of Hurley's pub."

"You know what I mean! It was you who...who..."

If Rafe hadn't been holding Jean-Michel, I'd have shaken him until his white, American teeth rattled. So, he'd engineered this, buying the property, setting up camp, conning me into chasing him down? Had all my angsting over being dumped, swallowing my pride, been for nothing?

"You pissed me about?" I snarled. "Again?"

Jean-Michel suddenly lunged away from his uncle's grasp. Swallowing my ire—after all, there was a child present—I watched Rafe recover him neatly, as if he'd been handling babies all his life. "I've learned that means he wants down."

I could light into Rafe later. He set the baby on the ground, so I sat down too a few meters away. As Jean-Michel looked at me consideringly, I held my breath. The worst time for a little person to meet someone new was when he was already with new people, in a new environment. This could be like trying to make friends with an Alaskan husky when he's having his first decent meal since running the Iditarod. You just have to wait for a dog, or a baby, to be comfortable before coming to you.

I smiled at the baby. His eyes were blue—no surprise there. Time would tell if they'd stay blue-ish like his father's, or grow to be as brilliant as his uncle's. But his tiny, distinctive nose...definitely some Rafe potential there. "So, you're called Jean-Michel." He didn't burst into tears, which was a good sign. "I imagine you're feeling shy. Being in your new place and all, without your mammy—"

I broke off. I could've kicked myself for mentioning her. To think, his mammy had chosen graduate school over him! What if she came back for visits, and he felt so abandoned and angry he didn't want her? I blanched, thinking of a child hurting so badly he wouldn't want his mother.

Or *her* mother.

I began again. "Jean-Michel's a bit of a mouthful, though, don't you think? While you're in Ireland, why don't we call you 'Seannie?'"

Jean-Michel/Seannie gave me another thoughtful baby look, then suddenly he pushed off with one foot, and crept toward me. He planted both hands on one of my knees. "So." I breathed in his lovely baby smell. "We're mates already?" Seannie grinned at me. "I'll take that as a yes," I said, and carefully lifted him into my lap.

He snuggled against my breasts, making one of those melty, baby sighs. Now that I'd a baby in my arms again, I felt my head clear almost instantly, like when you spray nasal medication up your nose. I looked up at Rafe, finding him watching us. "What's going on anyway? You've a nerve, the way you lured me here. What's more, I find you minding the baby after you'd snubbed Ian, and said you wanted nothing to do with—"

I snapped my mouth shut. The way babies sense emotions, it wasn't right to let Seannie witness a confrontation. I took a deep breath, so he could feel a calming vibe instead. I hated to admit it, but why should I be upset? Rafe wanted me! I set Seannie on the ground and clambered to my feet, so I wouldn't have to crane my neck at Rafe, and lifted the baby back into my arms. Slinging him onto my hip, I said, "Seems like a lot has changed since I saw you last."

"I couldn't have planned Jean-Michel's mother giving custody to my brother," Rafe said, coming closer. "But the rest...It was kinda like Fate."

"It wasn't Fate that got you involved with Ian's baby, or you coming back to Ballydara—and setting up this yoke." I gestured round the site.

Rafe scrubbed his hands through his hair, dislodging a ladybug and a small white spider. "I suppose I should explain."

Was that my cue? I swayed back and forth with Seannie, waiting. In all those relationship scenes on telly, the other person says, "You don't have to explain anything," but damn, I really wanted to know. "Seems like a real 180-degree turn."

"Here's the thing," Rafe said earnestly. "Once I'd come out of my little cave or ivory tower or wherever the hell I'd been living my half-life and came to Ireland, for the first time in my life, I was free to do whatever I wanted. Or not do what I didn't. But after you and I—hell, after feeling so alive with you, I just couldn't bring myself to go backwards. Crawl back in the cave, turn my back on the other people in my life. So I went to Paris. I felt...well, duty-bound to see my nephew, but once I did, I realized this little guy would be all but losing his mother—and living with a bunch of strangers. And the past sort of rushed up at me."

I eased the baby into Rafe's arms. "Your...childhood."

Cradling Seannie against him, Rafe smoothed the baby's little head. "When I was a miserable kid in boarding school, the only kids I knew were lonely little bastards without mothers, just like me," he said. "Which only made me feel worse about my own mother."

"I can understand that," I said slowly.

Rafe cleared his throat. "So when Ian was left kind of high and dry as far as raising his son, I thought this is my chance, to give my nephew a different life than I had." Seannie snuggled against his uncle's neck. "Whatever happened, I figured Jean-Michel... Seannie...could use all the...friends he could get."

Isn't that just like a man. Saying "friends," when he meant love. But you could hardly blame him, since we all know what happened when he'd said "love" to me.

"So...since you went to some trouble to get me here, does that mean we're friends?"

"Uh..." Curving his hand round Seannie's little head, Rafe

hesitated so long, I wondered if I should check his pulse. "I'd like to be," he said finally.

Clearly, Rafe wasn't going to make this easy for me. Well, I wasn't going to let my insane, Scarlett-inspired triathlon be in vain. "Is that…all?"

A muscle leaped in his jaw. I shifted my gaze to the satellite dish, askew on the grass, feeling naked again in front of Rafe. Sure, baring yourself physically with the man you love, especially if it's unrequited, is nothing compared to baring your soul.

But really, what did I have to lose? "Remember, you said you were done with me," I said, looking back at Rafe. "That I should go find someone else." Revisiting my worse moment ever with Rafe was awful, but I had to get to the truth of us. So with my heart in my tonsils, I went on, "And when I asked you about one last shag for the road, you said, 'No thank you.'"

Rafe's previous hesitation was the blink of an eye compared to this one. But this was our make or break moment. I'd no business rushing it.

"You don't know how much I wanted to take you up on it," Rafe said finally. "Although I should probably tell you…" The pain in his face actually hurt me. "Asking me for a baby… you'd…touched a nerve."

I went utterly still. Of course I knew what he meant. That all his life, folk had found a use for him. Well, my using days—at least where Rafe was concerned—were over. A softness I'd never felt swelled in me. "I'm sure you'd like to be wanted for yourself."

Rafe flushed, but only shrugged in reply. "Once I'd left my safe little world, and got in the scrum of life, I wondered why I hadn't done it a long time ago." He touched the tip of Seannie's nose, a grin tugging at the corners of his mouth. "Succumbing to my mid-life crisis was so great I figured I was game for a phase two. But if you and I were going to try again, I…I wanted you to come to me." As Seannie began wriggling, Rafe set him down. "So I put myself squarely in your path, so in case you tried to avoid me, you'd trip over me first.

"Then yesterday, Justine forwarded me your message to Bernie. I could see you'd been through a lot—and that maybe, the chances of starting over with you were even better than I'd thought."

Bless Justine, I thought. Best friend ever.

Rafe suddenly clasped my shoulders. "But I want to tell you right away—I'm still getting used to Seannie. Oh, I know how to heat his bottles in the microwave, and give him a bath. But I'm nowhere near ready for...you know."

I made a wild guess. "One of your own?"

"Uh...yeah. And I can't say for sure if I ever will be. Can you be okay with that?"

Right now, I did want Rafe more than a baby, though I knew the moment might not last long. "I think so," I said. He began stroking his thumbs on either side of my neck. "That is to say, I'm prepared to be a lot more patient than I was before," I managed, despite the new electrical charge singing through me. "But before you...go any further," I said shakily, "I've a confession of my own."

"I'm all ears," Rafe said, brushing his finger against across the hollow of my throat.

"You kept asking me why I'd left Seattle...left you, five years ago. It was that..." This was way harder than I thought it would be. "I guess I...I didn't completely trust what we had...trust your feelings for me. When it was so clear your family had chosen Lindy for you, and would push hard to get her in the family, I left before you could break up with me."

"I think you know by now I wouldn't have done it. But look at all the idiot stuff I've done."

"Like what?"

"You know—letting my pride get in the way of not coming after you, then the ultimate, marrying someone on the rebound."

"But..." I swallowed. "But when you asked me to marry you, so soon after Lindy, I thought I was the rebound girl."

"You?" Rafe slowly zigzagged one finger down my breastbone. "No, you're *the* girl. Always were, always will be."

Joy filled me. I knew later, we'd talk about how he'd reconciled with Ian and me with Mam, if he was going to repeat his marriage proposal, where we were going to live—and how in the hell he'd ever talked Bernie into letting him take Seannie camping. But for now, as Rafe pulled me close, we'd more important things to not talk about...

Our eyes locked, we inched our faces toward each other like a film kiss, stopping just shy of lip-on-lip contact, our breaths mingling. As primed as I was for another Rhett Butler/Atlanta-burning sort of kiss, all I could do was wait, my heart stuck in my throat, my whole body tingling with wanting him. But since I'd Scarlett O'Hara'd myself all the way here, like I said, Rafe had to be the one to make the first *serious* move...I closed my eyes. *Kiss me, before I go as mad as you have...*

Seannie suddenly wailed. We broke apart, me prying my eyes open with great reluctance, and I saw the baby looking round as if he'd got lost. With a rueful look at me, Rafe jogged over to the baby and swooped him up in his arms. "It's all right, buddy. I'm here."

As Rafe loped back to my side, Seannie smiled beatifically, clutching his uncle's shirt. "Guess that came just in the nick of time," Rafe said, and touched my cheek. "We wouldn't want the baby to suffer any psychological damage, by witnessing...uh..."

"A lusty, horizontal reunion right here on the grass?" I asked. Rafe laughed, and I was so overjoyed at *not* having to experience Rhett's crushing "Frankly my dear..." line to Scarlett, I had my biggest epiphany ever: If Rafe decided he really didn't want kids, and never, *ever* would, I'd...I'd...

I'd think about that tomorrow.

And as he tossed Seannie in the air, then tucked him against his chest, it hit me—Rafe adored this baby—and I'd plenty of time to pretend to not try talking him into one for us. In the meantime, I'd surround myself with all the babies in my life—Seannie, Nate's baby Mae, Joe and Sinead's, and if I was really hard-pressed, my sister Mary Alice's.

And whatever happened, I think I finally had the inspiration for my next *Girl Talk* post...

THE GALLAGHER POST

Gai Lannigan's Girl Talk

Baby Hunger, Revisited

If there's one salient truth Baby Lusters (and you know who you are) cannot escape from, it's this: You can't count on a baby to fix everything that's wrong with your life.

For every Baby Luster Happily Ever After, there must be a gazillion Crashes-and-Burns. B.L. disasters include girls who wander into the dating-without-commitment wilderness, and get lost in the brambles of guys who are no more interested in kids than the color of your nail varnish. (If they really *are* keen on your nail varnish—well, that's another column.) Other B.L.'s think they've found the right guy, but the right *moment* for a baby never seems to come. Your man—who may even want to marry you—puts you off indefinitely. You're hoping that baby hunger is contagious, but before you know it, years have passed, your fertility has turned to crap, and menopause is just around the corner.

Baby Hunger hits critical mass when you're in the absolute perfect relationship. You're mad for each other, you just know he'll make a lovely father, and he's good to his mam. There's only one teensy problem: he's just not interested in a baby. And he's proven to be unexpectedly immune to all your blandishments to make him see differently. In that case, you're no better off than the girl who isn't seeing any guy at all. You're doomed to BLL (Baby Lusters Limbo), and your baby itch will be going unscratched for the fore-seeable future.

Many frustrated B.L.'s are reduced to a predictable set of strat-agems, like haunting baby shops, surreptitiously fondling infant wear, taking altogether unnecessary pregnancy tests, or the worst: occasionally pretending someone else's baby is yours.

However, there's one ray of hope for all of you out in Baby Luster

Land: It sounds like something your granny would say, but baby-making, just like finding your dream guy, will happen in its own good time, and not a moment before. You've probably heard about girls who try online dating for years, then stumble across a great bloke at the shop down the road. Well, the same principle applies to babies. Haven't we all heard stories of women, who after years of fertility treatments, give it up as hopeless, then get pregnant a month later. Or the boyfriend, after months of putting you off about starting a family, suddenly sees the light. The stars will shift into the baby-making alignment only if you're not really paying attention. Or not pushing so hard you bollux up the process.

So here's my advice. Live your bloody life. And if you haven't got a life, get one!

THE END

Acknowledgments

I'm grateful to the first readers of *Mother Love*, Lori Nelson-Clonts, Becky Burns and Patty Kelly, for their friendship, critical eyes, and insightful suggestions. Many thanks as well to Kate Weisel, for all her care and creativity in designing this book, and to Patricia Davis, for her meticulous editing and proofreading job.

I dedicate this book to my husband John—and to him goes my deepest appreciation for his artistic eye, terrific cover concept, and most of all, his love, support, and encouragement.

About the Author

Susan Colleen Browne is the creator of the Village of Ballydara series, set in the Irish countryside. She's also the author of a memoir, *Little Farm in the Foothills: A Boomer Couple's Search for the Slow Life*, a Washington State Library "Summer Reads" book selection. Susan is a community college creative writing instructor and lives with her husband John in the foothills of the Pacific Northwest.

When Susan isn't digging compost, weeding veggie beds, or wrangling hens, she's working on her next Village of Ballydara story!

Visit www.susancolleenbrowne.com
for more about the little village of Ballydara,
and other fun Irish stuff!

You'll also find recipes and tales from Susan's little farm at
www.littlefarminthefoothills.blogspot.com

Books by Susan Colleen Browne

The Village of Ballydara Series

It Only Takes Once, A Village of Ballydara Novel, Book 1
Mother Love, A Village of Ballydara Novel, Book 2
The Secret Well, a short story
The Christmas Visitor, a short story
    and the sequel of *The Secret Well*

Children's eBook
Morgan Carey and the Curse of the Corpse Bride,
    a lighthearted Halloween story for middle-grade readers

Memoir
Little Farm in the Foothills:
    A Boomer Couple's Search for the Slow Life

A Washington State Library "Summer Reads" book selection:

"The Browne's foray into slower living…
is an enjoyable read. Their delightful, yet very real,
experiences in making the big leap toward their dreams
make for a humorous and charming book."
—Washington State Librarian Jan Walsh

"A delightful account."
—*The Bellingham Herald*

Proof

Made in the USA
Charleston, SC
27 September 2013